"AWAKE AGAIN SO LATE, MISS HAWTHORNE?"

Whirling around, I saw Drake Curtis lounging on the sofa, a lock of hair falling over his forehead. In the wavering firelight, his face was shadowed, vaguely sinister. I could not read his expression. There was a decanter and an empty glass on the table beside him.

"I—I was just coming to get a book," I said, flustered. "I did not realize anyone was—that is, I'm sorry I disturbed you."

I turned to go, but he caught my arm in a light grip. Alarmed, I tried to shake him off. I saw his jaw clench hard as all his weight was put on his bad leg for a moment, and I cried remorsefully, "Oh, I'm sorry. I didn't mean to . . ."

He looked down at me then, and I was shocked at the fierceness of his expression. His eyes blazing, he grasped me by the arms, saying, "Don't look like that! Do you hear me? I'm sick of that look of pity on your face, in your eyes! I don't want your pity!"

"I'm sorry," I stammered brokenly, my eyes filling with tears.

"I'll show you I'm in no need of your pity, despite what you think me," he said roughly.

He crushed me to him, his mouth bearing down on mine with a bitter savagery . . .

GOTHICS A LA MOOR—FROM ZEBRA

ISLAND OF LOST RUBIES
by Patricia Werner   (2603, $3.95)
Heartbroken by her father's death and the loss of her great love, Eileen
returns to her island home to claim her inheritance. But eerie things begin
happening the minute she steps off the boat, and it isn't long before
Eileen realizes that there's no escape from *THE ISLAND OF LOST RU-
BIES.*

DARK CRIES OF GRAY OAKS
by Lee Karr   (2736, $3.95)
When orphaned Brianna Anderson was offered a job as companion to the
mentally ill seventeen-year-old girl, Cassie, she was grateful for the non-
troublesome employment. Soon she began to wonder why the girl's family
insisted that Cassie be given hydro-electrical therapy and increased doses
of laudanum. What was the shocking secret that Cassie held in her dark
tormented mind? And was she herself in danger?

CRYSTAL SHADOWS
by Michele Y. Thomas   (2819, $3.95)
When Teresa Hawthorne accepted a post as tutor to the wealthy Curtis
family, she didn't believe the scandal surrounding them would be any concern of hers. However, it soon began to seem as if someone was trying to
ruin the Curtises and Theresa was becoming the unwitting target of a
deadly conspiracy . . .

CASTLE OF CRUSHED SHAMROCKS
by Lee Carr   (2843, $3.95)
Penniless and alone, eighteen-year-old Aileen O'Conner traveled to the
coast of Ireland to be recognized as daughter and heir to Lord Edwin
Lynhurst. Upon her arrival, she was horrified to find her long lost father
had been murdered. And slowly, the extent of the danger dawned upon
her: her father's killer was still at large. And her name was next on the
list.

BRIDE OF HATFIELD CASTLE
by Beverly G. Warren   (2517, $3.95)
Left a widow on her wedding night and the sole inheritor of Hatfield's
fortune, Eden Lane was convinced that someone wanted her out of the
castle, preferably dead. Her failing health, the whispering voices of death,
and the phantoms who roamed the keep were driving her mad. And although she came to the castle as a bride, she needed to discover who was
trying to kill her, or leave as a corpse!

*Available wherever paperbacks are sold, or order direct from the
Publisher. Send cover price plus 50¢ per copy for mailing and
handling to Zebra Books, Dept. 2819, 475 Park Avenue South,
New York, N.Y. 10016. Residents of New York, New Jersey and
Pennsylvania must include sales tax. DO NOT SEND CASH.*

CRYSTAL SHADOWS

MICHELE Y. THOMAS

ZEBRA BOOKS
KENSINGTON PUBLISHING CORP.

ZEBRA BOOKS

are published by

Kensington Publishing Corp.
475 Park Avenue South
New York, NY 10016

First printing: November, 1989

Printed in the United States of America

For Sylvia,
who first suggested the White Mountains to me

Say, wilt thou go with me, sweet maid,
Say, maiden, wilt thou go with me
Through the valley-depths of shade,
Of night and dark obscurity;
Where the path has lost its way,
Where the sun forgets the day,
Where there's nor light nor life to see,
Sweet maiden, wilt thou go with me?

Where stones will turn to flooding streams,
Where plains will rise like ocean's waves,
Where life will fade like visioned dreams
And mountains darken into caves,
Say, maiden, wilt thou go with me . . . ?

John Clare
(1793–1864)

business," what Miss Winston described as... judge more harshly," said Elizabeth. "To be expelled, you'd have to do something far worse, such as cheat on a test, or run off on the class and take part in her mischievous little fit if..."

Chapter One

The Crystal Hills Hotel is closed now. We do not wish it otherwise; we are content. These are different times, this a different age than that of its heyday. And now it, like us, is content to rest, for it has served us well.

No longer do the carriages drawn by six horses sweep up the drive of the sprawling lawn. No longer do the scarlet geraniums flutter in their boxes against the long white-columned porch. The chandeliers in the first-floor rooms do not sparkle, for the elegantly clad, jewel-studded revelers have long since departed.

The hotel sits serenely on its ridge, heedless of its tarnished state, its paint lackluster and peeling, its many windows opaque and glazed. Yet the mountains in their natural grandeur do not eclipse it. From a distance it is still the pearl shimmering amid the dusky-blue landscape of the swollen hills. And in the violet light of a fading day it looks as pristine and resplendent as it did when I first journeyed to the White Mountains with Drake and Emeline.

There was a feeling of carefree splendor, of smooth, uncontrived luxury at the Crystal Hills, a feeling as foreign to my experience as were the great granite-sculpted summits which raised their grooved bulks to the sky. It was a feeling set down by the Curtis family and perpetuated by their many guests, those guests that comprised the upper crust of the Northeastern cities—the Back Bay Bostonians, the East Side New Yorkers, the Main Line Philadelphians.

The hotel seemed to me to be a world unto itself, as self-contained as an ocean liner, a glittering jewel separated from the rest of the world by the ages-old, cloud-wreathed highlands which enclosed it. Yet from the first I was aware that all was not what it appeared to be. Within those walls smoldered a tumult of emotions so intense, so frightening, that from the first I dreaded their inevitable combustion.

The Crystal Hills Hotel has altered with the passing of time, but the Notch remains the same, with only the advent of each season to alter it. The air is still redolent with spicy pine and fir; the waterfalls still spill down the narrow gorges; the alpine flowers still tremble in the summer breezes. At the timberline the *krumholz* still grows, trees stunted and gnarled by cold and exposure into mats mere inches high.

Few people invade Nightshade Notch now; it has come into its own again. It is as inaccessible as it was in the years before the great resort hotels sprang up to cater to those seeking a cool haven from the steaming cities, a tranquil refuge from a harried, hurried world. Some of those hotels have been lost to fires; others, like ours, sleep and dream of their former glories, their rooms ghostly and echoing.

And we are content that it be so. We have all we desire, alone in our shingled and gabled manor. Our children are grown with families of their own. Our grandchildren visit from time to time, to wade in the rushing river, to relish the astounding beauty of the turning leaves, to play their innocent games at the Site of Stones, once used for less-than-innocent purposes.

Perhaps they, or even their children, will someday return for good and wake the old hotel from its slumber and open its doors again. There is life in it yet, we are fond of saying. We like to think of such things.

In the years to come, the Stones will remain, secretive and unfathomable. Placed perhaps thousands of years ago in their mystifying precise arrangements, they will remain for very long after he and I are gone. But something of us will endure in this landscape, in the towering black-green spruces, in the silver torrents of water, in the craggy, exposed ridges. For we have made them our own.

It is with difficulty that I look back over the years to the days when Nightshade Notch was nothing more to me than an obscure place on an even more obscure map, a place I had no intentions of visiting. For it seems to me that my life truly began when I penetrated its remote world and began to experience emotions both unfamiliar and undeniable. Before that my life pales and blurs in a dim, shadowy prologue.

But in order to tell my story, I must begin at the beginning, as they say, and so I will endeavor to recall some of that which came before.

I had attended Miss Winslow's Academy for Young Ladies in Portsmouth as a day pupil; as such I was of significantly less importance in the eyes of the headmistress. My father was a doctor, a widower, who tended to the ills of the families of sailors and craftsmen who lived in the poorer sections of that small coastal city. He could not have afforded the fees charged by Miss Winslow; but his friend, a kindly old lawyer who looked after the school's interests, had prevailed upon Miss Winslow to take me in at reduced rates. Up until then I had gone to a public school.

Miss Winslow did as he asked, albeit grudgingly and not without rancor. I was taking a place in the classroom which otherwise would have been filled by a boarding girl bringing more money into the school. Miss Winslow told me this herself on my first day there. Naturally I never forgot it, nor was I allowed to.

My father was pleased to have me attend Miss Winslow's school. He had always thought that I had a good mind and, circumstances being what they were, I would have to depend upon it someday to support myself. The most logical course open to me was to be a teacher. And after four years at Miss Winslow's Academy I was qualified for that occupation.

But shortly following my graduation, my father became ill with a painful, lingering illness. I nursed him for two years. I could not have left him alone every day and gone out to work, and the small income his practice provided was gone. For a time we lived on what he had managed to save; later came the months I was forced to sell family possessions such as pieces of silver and furniture to pay the bills, buy the medicine, and put food in our mouths.

My father deplored the way he was dependent on me, the way he perceived I was shut away behind drawn blinds in close, hushed rooms. As for myself, I lived from one day to the next, not grudging the way my hours were spent, yet hoping for some kind of miracle to suddenly rectify our futures. I shied away from considering my future should he be gone, and when the end finally came I was as unprepared for it as I was for the terrifying ordeals which came later. I was content to daydream, to fantasize about living an untroubled and romantic existence, rather than face the truth. Thus when my father died, it was a terrible blow, and it jolted me out of my trancelike, cloistering state into the cold, appalling reality of a bleak February day.

Standing at the graveside, the sky above a dark, streaked gray, the wind raw and piercing, I realized that I would now have to fend for myself. I could no longer ignore my precarious future. It was not merely a vague, distant abstraction sure to be miraculously and irrevocably resolved by an unexpected inheritance or a determined suitor. Instead it was immediate and overwhelming. On my own I had to face it, to solve it.

First of all I could not remain in our house. We had merely leased it during my lifetime and I could not afford the rent. I would have to move to a boardinghouse.

It was unfortunate for me that the month was February. Teachers were hired in the summer before the school year began in September. Unless someone were to leave abruptly, vacating a position, I would be out of luck.

I was out of luck. An application made to the Board of Educators of the Portsmouth Public Schools was answered cordially but decidedly in the negative. Yet it was imperative that I find some sort of employment, perhaps as a clerk in one of the shops near Market Square.

But there again I was unlucky. For days I visited shop after shop, most of which did not require the services of another clerk. The two that did insisted that a man fill the position. At the last place I humiliated myself and embarrassed the shopkeeper by almost pleading with him to take me on. Surely,

I pointed out, I could sell shoes as well as a man. But he shook his head firmly.

My options were narrowing rapidly. I did not blame my father for not making some provision for me; rather I blamed myself for giving so little thought to the dilemma I was now facing. One week's rent in the rooming house had taken most of my money. There was nothing in the newspapers except jobs for laborers down at the docks. But an advertisement gave me an idea.

With renewed hope I went out again, this time to the textile factory. For a few moments in the burly foreman's office I believed my search was over. But when he made further inquiries and learned my father had been a physician, and that I had attended Miss Winslow's prestigious Academy, he refused my application. It had not occurred to me to dissemble—what did it matter what my background had been when I was willing to work at almost anything to survive? But he stated bluntly that I was not right for a seamstress. It did me no good to assure him otherwise; his mind was made up. I perceived that he suspected that I would not fit in with the other women and problems might arise. He did not take me seriously as a prospective employee, that much was certain. In despair I made as dignified an exit as possible, and once outside the brick warehouse, my frustration dissolved into tears.

Some nights later in the chilled attic room I lay in bed thinking of the one place I had not tried. I had been sure that it would prove hopeless and so I had never seriously considered it. But now I was at my wit's end with no more money and nowhere to turn. Tomorrow I would go to the Academy and ask Miss Winslow for a position as teacher or even secretary. At that point I was willing to work for bed and board only, as a teacher's assistant.

This was an avenue I had been reluctant to pursue, but circumstances now demanded it. I tried not to dwell on the coldness Miss Winslow had always shown me. I had been a good pupil, if a quiet, unimportant one, out of the sphere of the other students. But Miss Winslow was aware of my qualifications. She had resented taking me in as a pupil, but even she had to admit I had done well.

13

The following morning I dressed in a simple white cotton blouse and navy-blue wool skirt, twisting my heavy red curls into a topknot. I felt slightly sick to my stomach, but part of that was likely due to having had nothing to eat the previous night. I could afford only the noonday meal at the rooming house, and the landlady did not allow us to serve our own plates.

Miss Winslow's Academy for Young Ladies was in one of the town's large mansions, which had been built by a sea captain who had traded in the Orient in the early part of the century. His family had later fallen on hard times and been forced to sell the house. Miss Winslow had purchased it and moved her school, which for years she had run successfully in her home, there. Many of the things original to the house remained in the front hall and parlor. She had added gas lighting and installed water closets.

It was a fine brick dwelling in the Georgian style, with five dormer windows jutting from the third story, which was topped with a railing. A six-sided cupola with narrow Palladian windows was perched on the roof. As students we were forbidden to climb the stairs to the cupola; we were not allowed above the second floor where the boarding girls had their rooms.

But in my first months there I had been fascinated with that cupola; I longed to gaze out its windows over the town and the river beyond. In such a glassed-in tower I could be Rapunzel, held prisoner by a wicked sorceress until a handsome prince risked all to rescue me. Finally the temptation was more than I could bear. One day during the free hour we had for lunch, I stole up to the third floor where the staff lived, and then, convinced no one had seen or heard me, climbed the narrow, winding stairs to the cupola.

When I reached the top of the stairs, the view was all that I had anticipated. The gables and roofs of the tidy coastal town gleamed red-rust in the noonday sun; the wrinkled surface of the Piscataqua River was creeping below in the distance. I could see the sprouting clock tower of the North Church at Market Square and the graceful white pickets on the roof of the Athenaeum. In the cupola the sun was warm, the dust motes

14

drifting in the rays of light.

For several weeks I continued this midday vigil, delighted that no one had discovered my secret, delighted that I alone could relish the enchantment of this solarium. I was careful to make certain that Miss Winslow's lunch had been taken to her on a tray. Then I was sure to have one half hour's safe, undisturbed respite in the glass tower.

And then one day, of course, I was found out. It was bound to happen. There were guests visiting the school, a small group of parents of prospective students. I supposed her to be occupied with them for an hour or more; I assumed her tour would be limited to the first two floors. But one of the guests must have expressed an interest in seeing the view from the cupola.

I heard the door to the third-floor corridor creaking open; I heard footsteps on the stairs. I also heard Miss Winslow's voice.

"I do not permit our students to come up here; the stairs could be dangerous. In fact, the girls are not allowed above the second floor. I feel very strongly about rules and regulations. They must be adhered to most strictly. All the girls are aware of the rules I have set down for their benefit and, I am pleased to say, they take them most seriously. Willful, wayward behavior you will not find at my institution."

There was nowhere for me to go; there was nowhere to hide. I stood there, my back pressed to one of the windows, this time not feeling the warmth of the sun. My teeth bit into my lower lip. First appeared Miss Winslow's gray head, her gold-rimmed spectacles braced in front of her cumbersome mound of hair. Mesmerized, I watched them glint in the harsh, exposing light. Then she was pausing on the top step; she had seen me. Behind her at various levels were the visitors, murmuring, chuckling. Then silence, as though we were all caught out of time for an indefinite period of what was to me an unbearable suspense.

"Teresa Hawthorne, go downstairs immediately. I will speak with you later," was all she said. But her color had mounted and her opaque eyes, the shade of water, had reduced me to a quivering jelly.

Clumsily I moved down the stairs, the visitors moving aside, regarding me curiously. I also felt that one stabbing glare. I heard her voice, inviting them to share her dilemma.

"She is our one problem student, I'm afraid. Her father is a doctor in town—not a successful one—and I've tried to help out with the child. Do not let anyone accuse me of being uncharitable, if you please. But she is not like our other girls."

When the summons came I was almost relieved. She would expel me and the whole awful incident could be forgotten. But no. If she had indeed wanted to expel me, which I am certain she did, then she must have considered what her lawyer would have said. My father had told him of my good grades. And even Miss Winslow could not pretend that going up to the cupola was a serious infraction. Now if I had been shown up as a thief or a cheat, she could have expelled me with a clear conscience, but unfortunately I had not been so obliging. Yet I had made her look a fool in front of possible future patrons. And that she would never forgive.

She did not expel me. She told me I was an ungrateful, uncontrollable child. That I had no business being in her school, that I was nothing but a charity case who did not deserve charity. That I did not fit in with the rest of the students and that I never would. Hadn't I noticed how I was excluded from their talk, from their play? My wearing the school uniform would never make me one of them. But as for herself, she would magnanimously give me one more chance.

She did not raise her voice. Her spectacles did not shift against her gray head. "A pity you're such a plain child," she added. "And with hair that shade of red. I recommend that you apply yourself most diligently to your studies. I doubt that you will attract any man of means."

It all came back to me in a stinging rush as I stood before the house, gazing up at the roof. The cupola, once the symbol of all that was charming and pleasurable, was from then on associated with misery and humiliation. But all that was years ago. Six, in fact. Giving myself an inward shake, I decided I was not going to allow those memories to prevent me from asking Miss Winslow for a position.

Opening the gate of the white picket fence, I walked up the brick pathway to the front door. My knock was answered by a maid I did not recognize; she looked curiously at me.

"I would like to see Miss Winslow, please," I tried to say firmly.

"Do you have an appointment, miss?"

"No." I flushed. "Please tell Miss Winslow that Teresa Hawthorne would appreciate a few moments of her time."

The front hall was unusually spacious, the walls papered with French pastoral scenes, the handsome staircase ornamented with alternating plain, fluted, and spiral spindles in the balustrade. There was a grandfather clock against one wall with a moon on its face; it always struck the hour with deep resonant tones.

To the right was a paneled walnut door, heavily varnished, which led to Miss Winslow's private sanctum. The maid went through to her parlor and office beyond while I stood in the foyer, twisting my gloves in my hands. Then the maid came back, saying, "Miss Winslow will see you now, miss."

"Thank you." I nodded, entering the private suite. The connecting door to the office was open; I went quickly through the parlor, weaving a path around the clutter of tables, chairs, and whatnots, and then hesitated at the office door.

Miss Winslow's head was bent, the spectacles rigidly in place. I took a deep breath.

"Good morning, Miss Winslow."

There was a long pause. Then she said without looking up, "You choose a rather early hour for your calls, Teresa."

I bit my lip. "I—I knew the students would have breakfasted and would be in their first classes of the morning so I . . . thought this a good time," I said lamely.

"You may sit down," she said, and her eyes were like still puddles of water on an overcast day. "You have come to ask for employment."

"Why—yes," I began, startled. "My father . . . passed away two weeks ago and . . ."

"And you have no money," she stated flatly, folding her hands in front of her on her desk.

Flushing, I said, "That's right."

"I read of his death in the newspaper. I wondered briefly what would become of you. Everyone knew there was no

17

money, of course. And Mr. Lawrence, your benefactor, is gone as well." Mr. Lawrence had been the lawyer friend of my father. Miss Winslow spoke with some satisfaction.

"Miss Winslow, when I graduated from the Academy I was qualified to teach. I have come to ask you if you have a position open."

She raised her brows, yet her eyes did not widen, did not shift. "At this time of the year? Rather a foolish question, wouldn't you agree?"

"Perhaps. But I—"

"I suppose you tried the public schools already?" she continued, her thin lips curved.

I nodded.

"And other places as well, I suppose. This is most likely your last hope, isn't it? You are, in fact, desperate. Or you wouldn't have come to me."

My face was hot. "I thought perhaps you might need a—a secretary or an assistant, if not a teacher." I felt incredibly stupid as I spoke, knowing how futile was my errand.

"What skills do you have for such a position?" she inquired.

"Well, I—I could compose letters for you. . . ."

"Do you know how to use a typewriter?"

Naturally I did not. My father could not afford such an expenditure, nor had one been necessary. He had not made out exact bills for his patients; he had taken whatever they could afford. Often his payments were made in kind. I shook my head.

"Do you possess a knowledge of shorthand? No, you do not. I do not see what possible use you would be to me as a secretary if I needed one, which I do not. Just because you were taken in as a charity case years ago does not mean I will hire you as a charity case now. That is not the way of the world, Teresa, as you will learn."

I had already learned it. "I see, Miss Winslow, that I am wasting your time and my own." I got up, overcome with the sheer hopelessness of it all, but desperate that she should not see it.

"Just a minute, Teresa. Why don't you tell me exactly what it is you have been doing since you left school?"

18

"Looking after my father. He was ill a long time."

"So you are now looking for your first position? Well, I may have the very thing for you, keeping in mind the skills you have utilized since you graduated."

I sat down again, my heart giving a faint leap.

"There is a position here that I need to fill rather quickly," she continued. "The girl I hired last year to cook for the staff and students has just announced that she is getting married and will be leaving this week. Most inconsiderate of her." She pursed her lips distastefully. "Married indeed. I suspect a more nefarious reason prompted her decision. And she knows my standards for my employees are very high. I rather doubt the existence of a fiancé. But that does not concern us. Well, Teresa, that is the employment I can offer you." Again the slight curve of the narrow lips, the fixed, pool-like gaze.

"You wish me to—cook?"

"Precisely. You have been cooking for your father for years and so you must be admirably suited to the task by now."

"Naturally I can cook. But . . ." I bit my lip.

"Not the position for yourself you had in mind?" she asked mockingly.

"It just never occurred to me to—"

"Seek out that type of menial employment? Beggars can't be choosers, Teresa, to quote the cliché. I am offering you a position at my school, which I understood was the reason you have taken so much of my time this morning. If you feel such an occupation to be beneath you, then I have no more to say to you. Good day."

Even as she spoke and made to busy herself with some letters on her desk, I was aware that she assumed I would accept her offer. She knew I had exhausted every possibility I could think of before coming to the Academy. Her cool, casual demeanor did not fool me. I realized that she wanted me to take the job, that my doing so would gratify her. The old but potent grudge she bore me would be assuaged.

"How many students are here now, Miss Winslow?"

"Twelve. And two teachers. Not a large group. Surely you can manage that?"

"Yes, I can manage that," I answered deliberately. "When

19

do I start?"

"Tomorrow at seven sharp. You can help Abby prepare breakfast, learn about the running of the kitchen and how to order from the butcher, greengrocer, and milkman. Tomorrow is her last day, so after that you are on your own."

"Very well. I will be here tomorrow at seven."

Our eyes met; she acknowledged herself the victor. In truth I scarcely cared—at least now I would have a place to live, enough to eat and a little money. I did not have to stay at the school forever, but for the next few months it would suffice.

"One more thing, Teresa. From now on you are not to use the front door. The servants use the door at the rear side of the house. The front door is only for guests, the students, and their families."

Naturally she was not going to overlook any opportunity to humiliate me. A lump in my throat, I looked down at the darning on the thumb of my wool glove.

"I expect the meals to be served promptly at eight, at one, and at six o'clock. You will follow the meal plans I provide each week. And I don't permit my women servants to be out late at night. You will be in your room by ten o'clock. And I shall expect you to enforce the rules and regulations I have set down for the students. Surely you remember what those entail." For an instant a glint darted in the depths of her opaque eyes. Then it was gone and they were still, murky. "Aside from that, you will speak politely to the students and accord them the proper respect."

From student to cook, I thought glumly as I walked back to the boardinghouse in the frigid wind. It was ironic that the factory foreman had refused to hire me because I had once attended a finishing school. A school where I would now be employed as a cook. I gave a rather hysterical giggle. Surely the job of factory worker was higher on the totem pole of occupations than that of cook. The pay was certainly better. But at least I had employment of a sort; I was no longer desperate. Preparing meals for twelve young ladies was not the end of the world.

Hopefully I would not have to see Miss Winslow very often. And she need have no qualms that I might entertain gentlemen

20

callers or be walking about the town at late hours. There wasn't the least likelihood of my doing either of those things.

The next morning I rose at sunrise, dressing in a pale blue blouse and gray skirt. Shivering in the cold room, I brushed on some face powder to subdue the slight sprinkling of freckles across my nose and cheeks before braiding my hair in one long braid, pinning on my hat, and buttoning up my worn coat. When I reached the school I went around to the side of the house to the kitchen door just opposite the carriage house. I hurried inside, grateful to be out of the bitter wind. The kitchen was warm and smelt wonderfully of coffee. I felt weak with hunger.

A young woman stood before the black cast-iron stove, stirring something in a large pot. " 'Bout time you've come," she said without turning around. "It's going on ten past the hour now. And I got a late start this morning. You can start by filling the pitchers with milk and maple syrup."

"All right," I said, taking off my coat and hat. I saw an apron hanging on a peg on the pantry door and put it on.

She was regarding me doubtfully, her rather sharp features wrinkling. "You're the new cook? The old witch didn't let on it be somebody like you. Havin' a good joke on both of us, I guess."

"I think she is."

"Don't I know it! Well, the tables're set; you always do that the night before. The oatmeal's setting up now. When you've filled the pitchers and put them on the tables you can have a quick cup of coffee before we make the toast. By the way, I'm Abby."

Less than an hour later I was backing through the swinging door that led to the dining room with a heavy tray laden with bowls of oatmeal. There were four small tables in the room, three occupied by students and the fourth by two teachers I remembered from my days here. Miss Winslow did not take her meals with the students and staff.

"Good morning, Miss Davis, Miss Forest," I said, coloring slightly.

"Teresa?" said Miss Forest, frowning. "What are you doing here?"

21

"I'm taking Abby's place," I said, trying to speak casually.

"Oh, dear," said Miss Davis, her pink and white face registering concern. "This is most unusual, most . . ." She broke off, reddening, and began to hastily eat her oatmeal.

"Teresa, it is not your place to converse with the staff members. The young ladies' oatmeal will be getting cold. Continue your duties at once," ordered Miss Winslow, who had entered the dining room from the front parlor.

With hands that trembled slightly, I served the bowls of hot cereal to the girls. They all wore white blouses, the collars piped in navy, with navy ties and navy blue skirts. Each head of hair was tidily tied back with a navy satin bow.

"Girls, may I have your attention please?" said Miss Winslow briskly. "This is Abby's last day with us. Teresa will be taking over as cook. You may eat your breakfast after asking God's blessing. Teresa, you may bring me my breakfast when Abby has it ready."

"Yes, Miss Winslow," I said, returning to the kitchen.

"Didn't she love that, putting you down in front of the rest of them! Are you sure you want this job, Teresa? It ain't hard—but it might not be as easy on you as it is on me. There's a lot of cleaning and scrubbing, and standing on your feet all day."

"I'll manage," I said. "But I understand you are to be married. May I wish you every happiness?"

Abby's face softened a trifle and a faint blush crept into her cheeks. "Thank you, Teresa. And now I've got to fry up the old witch's bacon and eggs or she'll have something else to say to you."

"Why don't you let me do that since I'm to take it to her?"

"All right, and then we'll cook ourselves a big breakfast. I'm famished."

So was I. Bridget, the maid, and Sam, the groom and handyman, ate with us at the pine table after the dining room was empty. Unabashed, I ate two enormous helpings of scrambled eggs, bacon, and toast. Later Abby explained some of my duties.

"You'll have to set the tables before the meals, and then do the cleaning up yourself. Breakfast tables are always set up the

22

night before, like I said. Every Monday Miss Winslow'll give you the menus for the week. It's pretty much the same things week after week, although she sometimes uses French names for stews and such. If she does that, just fix the same meal you did the week before. She ain't much a one for variety."

"What about ordering the groceries?"

"After you've got the menus, you make up a list. Again, it's pretty much the same stuff week after week. Then you call the butcher and the greengrocer with the order. Do you know how to use a telephone? There's one in the pantry."

"What about the milkman?"

"Oh, he knows what to leave every morning. If you want something extra one day, or less of something, just leave him a note in the milk box."

Lunch was beef and vegetable soup, and so the two of us got to peeling and chopping the vegetables after Abby put the meaty bone in a pot of water. I decided I liked the kitchen with its varnished brick floor, its gleaming array of saucepans and skillets hanging on hooks. Despite Miss Winslow's belittling attitude, working here might not be as bad as I had expected. The work was time-consuming and tiring, but certainly not beyond my capabilities. And after I grew accustomed to the tasks and the routine I hoped Miss Winslow would not be able to find fault with my work.

"Make certain that when you serve her plate there's plenty of meat on it. Plenty of everything, for that matter. And she always takes apple butter with her morning toast. And cream but no sugar in her coffee. And every night before you serve dinner she takes a glass of that sweet brown sherry—can't stand the smell of it myself." And so on.

For dinner we fixed roasted capon with a sausage and mushroom stuffing, and there was red cabbage cooked with apples. After we had served the teachers and students, and I had taken Miss Winslow's tray to her, we four employees ate our dinner. When we had finished, Abby made a pot of tea, and Sam took his cup over to the rocking chair by the fire along with the newspaper.

"Bridget reads the tea leaves, you know," said Abby expectantly.

Startled, I looked up. "She does what?"

"Reads the tea leaves. It's a way of tellin' the future, ain't it, Bridget?"

Bridget nodded solemnly. "I could do it again tonight," she offered.

"Oh, not mine again," said Abby. "I already know my future. Gettin' married tomorrow and a baby comin' in the summer. Bridget told me that there'd be a surprise coming in the summer, didn't you? She's a wonder; her old grannie taught her to do it back in Ireland. Do Teresa's leaves, Bridget. See what they say. Let's hear what's in store for her."

"Oh, no, really I . . ."

She waved away my protests, reaching for my empty cup. "Here, Bridget. Give Teresa here a good readin'."

Bridget took the cup and held it with both hands, gazing down at the deposit of dark, wet leaves. Ever so slightly she tilted the cup from side to side, an expression of deep concentration on her face.

"Really, this is foolish. I wish you wouldn't," I protested feebly, conscious of a faint misgiving.

"Shhhh," said Abby. "She's got to have quiet."

There was a prickling at the back of my neck; my throat felt suddenly dry. I did not want her to do this. Not that I believed in it for a moment, foretelling the future. But it seemed wrong, it struck a jarring note which vaguely alarmed me. It was as though one were offering a challenge to Providence: Well, what have you got in store for me? Come on, give it your best. No, I did not want Bridget to do this.

But she was beginning. "I see you, Teresa. It's dark and you're bent over, crouching in the darkness. You're hiding from someone." Her voice had altered, lowered to almost a whisper. Her eyes stared unblinkingly into the dregs of the cup. A chill washed over me. But now I was powerless to stop her; I was caught in the grip of her hushed words. "You're in a sort of cave. And you're frightened. Terribly frightened. Someone is out there, someone is calling your name. . . ."

The kitchen clock was ticktocking; the gas jets made their soft whooshing sound as they filled each glowing globe with light. The fire sputtered in the hearth while Sam dozed, snoring gently.

"Wait, do you hear that?" asked Bridget suddenly.

"Hear what? What is it?" demanded Abby.

"Water—rushing, rushing. It's below where she's standing now."

My fingers grasped the edge of the table. I was scarcely breathing, my body taut as a wire, my eyes wide with dread as I stared at her face.

"Get back, Teresa," came Bridget's voice again, hoarse, anxious. "Why don't you get back? There's danger—evil. Can't you feel it?" In horror I realized that she was no longer with us in the kitchen; in her mind she too stood over the rushing water.

"Oh, no," she wailed. "You're trapped. Caught—caught in a trap!" She gave a tremendous shudder, her eyes closing, and let the teacup fall. It knocked against the table, where it spun once before landing on its side, the leaves marking a glossy trail to its rim.

Chapter Two

"God, Bridget!" cried Abby. "What kind of a fortune was that? Caves and rushing water—I never heard such foolery!" But her face was pale and her voice tremulous, the words lacking conviction.

"I only tell what I see," said Bridget a little sullenly. "What else did I say?"

"Don't you know? Now don't go creepy on us. It was all a lot of nonsense anyway. It don't mean nothing. Just a game, you know, Teresa. I've always said it's just a silly game."

Yet you believed Bridget before, I thought. I felt rather dazed now that the sharp fear had subsided. It had not been Bridget's obscure words and images—for what had they meant?—but her manner which had alarmed me. She had seemed to retreat from the warm, cozy kitchen and enter a different place, a place of mystery and dread—and danger. Shivering, I moved closer to the fire.

Abby gathered up the tea things and carried them to the large enameled sink. "I'll do those," I said, forcing myself out of my bemused state to the work at hand. "It's time you left. I can do the rest."

"Time enough for that tomorrow when you'll be on your own," she said rather gruffly. "But this is my last day and I'm puttin' in a full day's work."

Bridget shook Sam lightly on the shoulder so he could see to the horses for the night, and then went upstairs to collect any mending the girls needed done. Abby and I set the tables for

26

breakfast the next morning. She had regained her cheerfulness, and it was with difficulty that I tried to recall precisely what Bridget had said. Yet I could not altogether dismiss the peculiar eerie feeling which lingered furtively.

"Good-bye, Abby," I said when it was time for her to leave. "I'm certain you'll be very happy. And look after yourself—and the baby."

She wrapped her long scarf around her head and neck. "You'll make out all right here, Teresa. Don't take anything that old witch says to heart. If I was you, though, I'd look for another place after a while. Something better ought to turn up for you before long." She hesitated and then added, the gruff tone back in her voice, "And don't pay no mind to Bridget either. She makes that stuff up most of the time."

I smiled. "I won't, Abby. Good-bye and good luck."

"Good luck to you, miss."

She was gone. The kitchen was very quiet except for the ticking of the clock on the wall. My duties were over for the day and I could go to my room. The servants all slept at the back of the house in the kitchen wing. My room had a pine bureau with four small drawers, a narrow bed, and a small white table, the paint chipped in places. I pulled down the window shades and got ready for bed.

The days moved rapidly into a routine. I made a few errors in the cooking, which Miss Winslow was quick to point out: My gravies were thinner than she liked; my chowder had too many clams and not enough potatoes; she did not care for the liberal use of herbs I used in my roasts. Rather than calling me to her office, she chastened me in the dining room before the students and teachers. I tried not to let her see how this mortified me. I hoped Abby had been right, that these petty humiliations would cease once the novelty of my being hired as cook wore off. I knew the meals I was preparing were more than adequate; the girls and teachers ate hungrily, and even Miss Winslow's tray was always empty when I came to collect it.

One afternoon I was walking down the drive to fetch the newspaper where the boy always left it when I met one of the younger students, a girl of about fourteen, coming the other way from the street. She was tall for her age, with dark brown hair cut into bangs at the front. Behind wire-rimmed spectacles, her eyes were a smoky blue, fringed with long, thick lashes. As I smiled and started to speak to her, those eyes widened, her face freezing.

"Emeline Curtis!" came an icy voice behind us. "Where have you been?" Miss Winslow was moving purposefully toward us. She was dressed to go out in a black coat with overcape and a black broad-brimmed hat with feathers. In spite of myself I felt a surge of the fear she used to instill in me. Or perhaps I was putting myself in the girl's place, sensing her dismay.

"Well, Emeline? I am waiting for an answer. Have you or have you not been off school property? I warned you the last time that you would be severely punished if you did so again. The rest of the students will be instructed to not speak with you for one week this time rather than just two days. And it's not pleasant to be ignored day after day, is it?" Miss Winslow stood beside us, a black tower of rigid supremacy.

Yet the child said nothing. Her face took on a mutinous look which did not altogether eclipse her anxiety.

"She—she was just going to the end of the drive to pick up the evening newspaper for me, Miss Winslow," I said breathlessly, "but the boy doesn't seem to have dropped it off yet. She was just telling me so."

Miss Winslow turned her glazed, colorless eyes on me. "You have no business asking any of the students to perform tasks for you, Teresa. That is not the reason they are in school here," she said witheringly.

In relief and surprise that she had believed me, I tried to look sufficiently crestfallen and said, "I'm sorry, Miss Winslow."

"Return to your room, Emeline, and remain there until dinner time. You know very well that that is where you are supposed to be at this time of day, not wandering around the grounds doing the servants' work. And you know the rule about not reading newspapers."

Emeline cast one fleeting glance at me and then hurried into the house. Miss Winslow said nothing further to me, but climbed into the carriage Sam had waiting. After he had assisted her inside, he looked sideways at me and winked.

That evening I was setting the tables for breakfast when the door from the front parlor opened and Emeline came in. "I came to thank you," she said. "You knew I'd been off the grounds, didn't you?"

"I suppose it was wrong of me to lie to Miss Winslow about the newspaper," I said without a trace of remorse. "Where had you been?"

"I stole out to buy some candy. I do once in a while. She caught me the last time and no one was allowed to speak to me for two days. The first day I didn't mind it, but the day after it bothered me a great deal. And for a whole week—I'd feel like a leper or something equally horrible, if I didn't go crazy first. That's why I'm so grateful to you for covering up for me the way you did. Sometimes I feel that I just must go out, that if I have to stay inside another hour I'll die."

"I suppose Miss Winslow feels you should be chaperoned when you leave the school."

"Oh, I only went to the store two blocks away," she said with impatient scorn. "And she never lets us go out, except to church on Sundays. Everything's so dreary here and we live like prisoners. I hate it."

"How long have you been here?"

"Since last May. It seems like forever, though. Before that I used to have lessons at home, but then my mother suddenly decided that I should go to school. And to have to spend last summer here as well! They said Charlotte was getting too old to have to look after me and my governess had left. Someone told my mother about Miss Winslow's Academy and they packed me off in a terrible hurry, just at the start of the season," she cried indignantly. "And it was sweltering here. *And* Miss Winslow made us do lessons all summer." She brightened. "But only two more months and I can go home again. And this time I'm never coming back."

"I understand how you feel, I think. I was a student here myself, though not a boarder."

"You were? Then at least you could go home at night."

"That's true, but do you know that I always wanted to be able to eat in the dining room with the rest of the students?"

29

She grinned. "I guess people always want the opposite of what they have. But why are you working as a cook here, if you were a student?" she asked, frankly curious.

"Because I needed a job and couldn't find anything else at the time."

"That's too bad. But I do think you're a very good cook, much better than Abby was. All the girls think so."

"Thank you. Now you had better go upstairs. I don't normally think as quickly as I did earlier, so I doubt if I could come up with a reason why you're here in the dining room at bedtime! Not one that would satisfy Miss Winslow a second time."

"All right. Your name is Teresa, isn't it? I like you; I'll come and talk to you again."

And she did, usually in the evenings before bedtime when the rest of the pupils were gathered in one or more of the bedrooms. Emeline confessed to me that she didn't much like the other girls, whom she considered very silly. This was stated in solemn, lofty tones, but I was painfully reminded of how I had not fit in as a student here, and wondered whether she was as unconcerned as she sounded.

She told me about her home in the White Mountains where her family owned a large resort hotel.

"Do you live at the hotel?"

"No, we have a house nearby. My grandfather built it after he built the hotel. The Crystal Hills it's called. Have you ever heard of it? It's quite famous, really. He and my grandmother were the first ones to erect such a grand hotel in the White Mountains. There are others now, of course, but I think ours is the best. And Nightshade Notch is the most beautiful location."

"Nightshade Notch? That's a rather . . . odd name."

"That's its original name. The first settlers called it that a hundred years ago. They mistook the black nightshade for the deadly kind—belladona, which grows in Europe. And one of the maids told me once that parts of the Notch seem always to be in the shade, no matter how bright the day, and that's why *she* thought they had called it that. My grandfather wanted to change the name when he purchased the land for the hotel. He was afraid it might be bad for business. But my grandmother wouldn't allow him to. She said it had a certain charm, a ring to it. And she was right. She was always right. People flocked to the Crystal Hills and still do."

"She's gone now?"

"Yes, she died when I was eight. I remember her, though; she played with me often, and even liked to have me with her while she worked in her office. I had to play very quietly so as not to disturb her, and she always said how different I was from my father and my uncle, who would never sit still when they were that age. But I liked to be with her." Surreptitiously she reached under her blouse and drew out a locket she was wearing. "We're not supposed to wear jewelry, you know, but I always wear this, even under my nightgown. Grandmother gave it to me the last Christmas."

She flicked it open and held it close for me to see. On each side was a miniature portrait, one of a striking older woman, the other of a young child I had no trouble recognizing as the girl before me.

"What a beautiful thing, Emeline," I said. "Thank you for showing it to me." I sensed that it was something she very rarely shared and that it meant a great deal to her.

"Charlotte says I ought not to wear it in case Miss Winslow sees and takes it away for safekeeping, but I wrote her back that I'm very careful not to let anyone see it."

"Who is Charlotte?"

"Oh, she was my grandmother's friend. She came to live with her and was a sort of a secretary. After Grandmother died, she looked after me."

"Your father runs the hotel now?"

"Yes, with my Uncle Drake, Papa's younger brother. But since last summer Drake's been in the war in Cuba, and then in the hospital, so Papa's done it alone. Charlotte wrote me that Drake came back just before Christmas. I wrote Mamma, asking her if I might come home for Christmas, but she answered that I knew how difficult it was to travel through the Notch in wintertime and it would be better if I just stayed at school until the summer. Actually, she just didn't want to make the trip to come fetch me, and Miss Winslow would never

31

allow me to travel across New Hampshire alone 'into the wilds,' as she says. Mamma sent lots of presents, though, and Sam put up a tree. And Abby gave me some of the Christmas punch when Miss Winslow wasn't looking."

I felt sorry for her. With me she was a likeable, talkative child; with the other students I noticed she was subdued, at times even slightly arrogant. I knew she was very lonely but was too proud to show it, hiding her true feelings under a nonchalant aloofness. So when she visited me from time to time I did not discourage her, no matter how disapproving Miss Winslow would have been had she known.

Spring comes late to New England but when it comes, it is glorious. It is not so much a gradual change, the way fall approaches. April is often cold and damp with lingering spots of freezing rain, even snow. But then suddenly it is May and bursting with warmth, fragrance, and color. Giant bushes of heady-scented lilacs bloomed about the school; the cherry trees with their narrow, gnarled trunks unfurled their spindly branches laden with pink, white, or coral blossoms.

The end of the term was nearing, and Emeline would come into the kitchen in the evenings with questions about her lessons. The end-of-term examinations naturally preceded the long-anticipated summer holidays. I had gotten into the habit of helping her with her schoolwork, and enjoyed doing so.

She was in better spirits then because in a matter of weeks she would be returning to her home at Nightshade Notch. "And no matter what my mother says, I'm not coming back here. Though I hate to leave you, Teresa," she added a little gruffly, frowning into her notebook.

As usual her talk was of the Crystal Hills Hotel. "It's such an exciting place to be in the summer. The guests coming up the drive in carriages from the railway station, strolling the grounds in their elegant clothes, sitting in the white wicker chairs on the long porches. We have tennis matches, and picnics on the back lawn, and balls and concerts at night. And there are always excursions to places of geological interest, such as the gorges and waterfalls. And hayrides up and down the winding roads."

"It sounds wonderful, Emeline."

"In the basement of the hotel are shops, and the ladies can have their hair arranged and the gentlemen can go for a shave if they haven't brought their own valets. We have to provide these types of services, you see," she said with an air of earnest importance I found rather comical, "because there are no real villages in the Notch—just houses and barns. That's one thing my mother has never liked about it. There's nothing there, except scenery. So the resort hotels must be self-sufficient and supply everything the guests should require."

"You sound like a hotel owner yourself," I teased her. "Have you heard exactly when you're going home?"

"No, my mother hates to write letters. Charlotte writes me, but she hasn't said either."

The pupils took their examinations the last week in May; shortly afterward they were free to return to their families. Some were going abroad to Europe; a few looked forward to a summer spent on Cape Cod or at Newport. Emeline naturally confided to me that none of those places had anything on the White Mountains.

She now joined in conversations in the dining room; she had lost some of her pretended remoteness and was less of an outsider. Many times I would hear her voice raised excitedly as she told her classmates about her family's hotel in Nightshade Notch.

Two of the girls were to remain at school during the summer holidays. They were orphaned sisters, Elizabeth and Mary Jamison, who were under the guardianship of an elderly Philadelphia gentleman. He had written to Miss Winslow to request that they spend their summer in Portsmouth; undoubtedly he made it worth her while to consent.

"How awful. Just like I did last year!" was Emeline's appalled reaction. "I don't know how they can bear it, though they don't seem to mind so much. Mary said they really haven't got a real home so it doesn't make that much difference. But I know what summers here are like, and I have a wonderful home!"

Every day Emeline would rush into the dining room at lunchtime when Bridget handed out the mail. The week of exams came and still she did not hear from her mother.

Watching her eagerness swiftly turn to disappointment every time she learned the letter still had not come, I found myself becoming increasingly impatient and annoyed with the girl's mother. And mixed in with my annoyance was a steadily building distress that the outcome would not prove to be what Emeline had expected.

Finally a telegram came for her, delivered by the boy at the telegraph office. Bridget took it up to Emeline's room while she was in class, and we both waited nervously to learn what it said.

We did not have long to wait. Less than an hour later Emeline flew down the back stairs into the kitchen, her face flushed and stormy, her mouth trembling. My worse fears were realized; nothing else could have accounted for that look of outrage, of betrayal.

"My mother s-says I'm n-not to come home!" she cried in a terrible anguish. "She says I m-must stay here at s-school!" And she burst into fierce sobs.

Gathering her in my arms, I exchanged helpless glances with Bridget. "Oh, Emeline, I know how you must feel. I'm so very sorry. But your mother must have a good reason for her decision." I was aware how foolish my words sounded, and even if she had had a good reason, why point it out to the child now? Her mother had not even taken the time to explain in a letter; she had informed her daughter in the briefest possible terms. I felt a surge of rage inside me directed toward the unknown, but already disliked, Mrs. Curtis.

"She doesn't," said the voice muffled in my shoulder. "She just doesn't want to be b-bothered with me. She never did. And it's easier with me at school so she's making me st-stay here!"

Words of comfort were useless. I did not even try to stem her flow of tears, to assure her we might have pleasant times together that summer. She was inconsolable, and rightly. What on earth did Miss Winslow's Academy for Young Ladies have in comparison to a grand resort hotel? I felt useless in the face of such wretchedness. And then, in the midst of it all, Bridget hissed, "Oh, Lord. It's *her*."

Her could only mean one person. The door from the dining room swung open. Miss Winslow's countenance was stiff with distaste and disapproval.

"Stop that disgraceful noise at once, Emeline Curtis. Even in the parlor I could hear the commotion you are causing. You are acting like someone on a stage. I will not have such displays of frenzy in my school. Let the child go, Teresa. You are only encouraging her."

"Emeline has just learned that her mother wishes her to remain at school for the summer. She had been looking forward to going home," I said deliberately.

"Is that all? Good heavens, young lady. I thought it was something quite terrible the way you were carrying on."

Emeline shot her one darkly furious look.

"Yes, I myself had a letter from your mother today. She thinks the school would be a better place for you to spend your holidays than a . . . a hotel where she is kept busy. I must say that I agree with her."

"That hotel is Emeline's home, Miss Winslow," I said quietly.

A sniff told us what Miss Winslow thought of that. "Emeline, go to your room until you have recovered sufficient calm. Such melodrama is quite unbecoming. We must meet our disappointments and frustrations with fortitude."

Emeline turned to go, squaring her shoulders. That little movement went straight to my heart and for once I cared nothing about Miss Winslow's hostility. She reprimanded me for catering to the girl's mood rather than curbing it, for not having the presence of mind to restrain her emotional display. Such behavior was not to be condoned, much less indulged. And why had the child come into the kitchen at all?

Her reproaches washed over me; I scarcely heard them. I was deeply distressed about Emeline's predicament and was beginning to wonder how it would affect me. I had hoped to look for a different position this summer, a teaching position if possible. But now I did not feel as though I could leave Emeline. She was devastated; she now had three months of misery to look forward to before the fall term began all over again. If I left the Academy while she was in her present state, she might view that as another betrayal, and view me as another person who had let her down. Yet I was disheartened at the contemplation of an indefinite future at the Academy. I could not take responsibility for the girl's moods and actions. That would do neither of us any good. But neither did I feel as though I could leave in the weeks ahead, not until she became adjusted to the life there. I had done so, I reminded myself. And I too had not been happy as a student. But I had become reconciled to school routine. Of course, I had only been a day student, which I had to admit was very different. I had been able to leave the rigid, stifling atmosphere every evening and return to my home. I decided then that I could not leave Emeline just yet. The summer would be the most difficult period for her. I would do what I could to help her adjust, and then look about for another job. She knew that I did not want to spend my life cooking at the Academy. I comforted myself with the thought that I was young, only twenty, and had plenty of time ahead to pursue a different course. A few more months at Miss Winslow's would not make any difference.

The days grew hot, with occasional cooler respites in between. Miss Winslow was determined that the three remaining pupils not waste their time. Idle hands made the Devil's work, after all, and so she herself conducted Bible classes in the mornings, followed by embroidery and needle-point instruction. Emeline was miserable.

"I just can't help thinking about what's happening at home," she would say, her bottom lip quivering. "The Alpine azaleas and Lapland rosebays will be blooming just now. Did I tell you that some of the same flowers which grow high in the Alps grow in the White Mountains as well? Perhaps today a party of guests will be taken to see the Old Man of the Mountain, or the Flume. And tonight after dinner, dancing. Did I tell you we have our own orchestra?"

Poor Emeline; she wore a blighted look in those days. And Miss Winslow only made matters worse by ordering her not to sulk, to hold her head up and straighten her shoulders. The Lord had made her tall and nothing was worse than seeing a tall girl stoop, Miss Winslow said. I, on the other hand, could think of many things which were worse.

July came and the sultry, hazy weather set in. It was uncomfortably hot in the kitchen, especially in the late afternoons and evenings. Miss Winslow was not a believer in altering menus to suit the seasons; she ordered the same heavy roasts and stews that she had in the winter months. Cooking, something I had always enjoyed, became a pastime I loathed, and the black iron stove, in the winter so comforting, a monstrous inferno.

In the evenings Emeline, Mary, and Elizabeth sat on the back lawn, listlessly occupied with stitchery or a book, waiting for a fresh breeze to ruffle their hair. At that time of day the house was sweltering, having baked in the afternoon sun. Bridget and I would sit on the door stoop, fanning ourselves, until night fell.

One day I hit on the notion of asking Miss Winslow whether I might take the girls on a picnic. They needed some sort of holiday, yet I knew she would refuse instantly if I suggested taking them out of Portsmouth, into the country. But there was a pleasant park with floral gardens near the water only blocks away. I hoped she would have no qualms about our going there.

The next day I prepared her favorite lunch of lobster salad and took it to her. When I returned to get the tray I noted that she had eaten the very substantial portion I had served her. She was yawning behind her hand; the large meal on a hot day had made her sleepy. I only hoped it had put her in a conciliatory mood.

I made my request simply and directly; she would have seen through any pretensions of cajolery. To my surprise she considered the suggestion. "Just to the park for a few hours? You would take full responsibility? Well, perhaps no harm would come of it. Sam could drive you in the carriage and keep an eye on all of you. It would not be seemly for you to go unescorted. What day were you thinking of?"

I could hardly believe my ears. Even though I had considered it a perfectly natural and sensible request, I had not dared to assume that she would consent to it. The reason came to light with her next words.

"I have an appointment in Boston on Thursday. Therefore I will be unable to give the young ladies their morning lessons. Perhaps an outing, strictly supervised, would be just the thing for that day. But remember, Teresa, you will be held accountable for the well-being and behavior of the girls."

Elated, I went back to the kitchen. That evening outside I told the girls. I was pleased to see that Emeline responded with a touch of her old enthusiasm.

"A picnic? And she said we could? What shall we have to eat?"

"What would you like to have? You three can plan the menu."

"Chicken salad. We always have chicken salad for picnics at the hotel. Please don't put any hard-boiled eggs in it, though. I don't like it that way. And do let's have strawberries, with their green tops still on. We can dip them in confectioner's sugar."

"May we have potato salad too?" asked Elizabeth shyly. "And pink lemonade?"

"And green olives and radishes," said her sister.

"No radishes for me," said Emeline.

"I'll bake a cake, if you'd like," I offered, smiling.

"Oh, yes, we must have a cake. And put a few drops of red food coloring in the frosting to make it pink. I do so love pink frosting."

My only concern now was that Miss Winslow might change her mind. Or that the weather might not cooperate and the picnic would have to be called off. And it was not realistic to suppose that Miss Winslow would automatically agree to another date.

But Thursday dawned pearl-blue, with a break in the oppressive humidity. I was up early preparing our picnic lunch, and by eleven o'clock we were assembled outside waiting for Sam to bring the carriage. That day the girls wore cool summer dresses rather than their uniforms. Emeline was in white organdy with a pale blue sash; Mary and Elizabeth were in matching dotted Swiss frocks of yellow and pink. All three wore straw hats and white gloves.

Emeline's pallor was gone; her cheeks were flushed and her eyes sparkled. We rode through the streets lined with Georgian and Federalist homes, many of which were topped with widow's walks. When we reached the park, the girls scrambled down from the carriage in an impetuous fashion, Miss Winslow's admonitions about ladylike behavior forgotten.

It was not a large park, but at that time of day it was not crowded. We were the only people except for two mothers with small children on the opposite side, a boy rolling a hoop down the center brick walkway, and an older lady on a bench reading under a frilled parasol.

Sam sat down on the grass against a tree and lit his pipe while the girls and I strolled down to the water. Bridget had come as well.

"Oh, look, ducks!" said Emeline. "We'll have to come down again and feed them crumbs after we've eaten."

Later they set out the croquet wickets we had brought and played a game before I unpacked the food, spread it out on the damask tablecloth, and called them to eat.

"You weren't holding the mallet right," I heard Emeline say. "You would hit the ball much harder if you held it like this."

Bridget was pouring the pink lemonade into glasses. "Come on, girls," I said. "Lunch is served."

"May we stay here all afternoon, Teresa?" asked Elizabeth. "I've brought my pad and I'd like to do some sketches."

"Not me. I want to watch the boats on the river," said Emeline. "And feed the ducks."

"I'm going to pick some flowers to press in my book," said Mary.

"How cool it is today, as though it knew we were planning a picnic. This lemonade is lovely, Teresa. Why does food always taste better out of doors? I haven't felt hungry like this in weeks," said Emeline. "To think we've actually left the school, even for a few hours—and not to go to church!"

Bridget laughed, and I said, "We'll have cake later in the afternoon. You girls amuse yourselves as you like, but don't wander off."

"These strawberries are so sweet—as sweet as the candy ones I use to slip away and buy," said Emeline.

"Are you still doing that, Emeline?" I asked. "You know how Miss Winslow feels about rules and regulations."

"Yes, she might expel you," said Mary.

"Oh, no, not for something like that. We just would be told not to speak to her again, like we weren't supposed to speak to

Eleanor Burleigh when Miss Winslow discovered she was reading after hours," said Elizabeth. "To be expelled you'd have to do something far worse, such as cheat on a test. Or run off to the store and take something without paying for it."

"I'd never do that!" said Emeline.

It was after five o'clock when we finally packed up and rode home. I was feeling pleased at the success of the day, delighted that Emeline had regained her spirits. I had no way of knowing then how that fateful day would end, or how the outcome of so innocent an outing would affect me.

That night I had an odd dream. I dreamt I was enclosed in a dark place with cold stone walls, rather like a cave only quite small. I could reach out and touch the rounded, creased surfaces; I could smell the dampness of earth. In my dream my body was rigid, my breath held because I was deathly afraid, afraid for my life. But the terror did not stem from the place I was in. I did not live in dread of the secluding stone chamber; I did not long to be outside. For whatever I dreaded was somewhere out there, and I was safe as long as I stayed silent and did not attract attention. The darkness enveloped me, soft and shielding as a velvet cloak. But still I held my breath, my ears strained for the slightest sound, my heart hammering in my breast. And then the blood ran thick and slow within me as I heard someone calling my name, an indistinct, muffled voice I could not identify. I heard footsteps in the fallen leaves, scraping the granite floor. I crouched against the wall, paralyzed with horror. And when a shadow fell across the entrance to my sanctum I knew that whoever it was that I so feared had found me. I was caught, caught in a trap. . . .

With a tremendous jolt I was awake and sitting up in bed, my nightgown damp, my breath coming in great heaves. Hastily I lit the kerosene lamp by my bed and leaned back against the pillow as the small, familiar room was revealed. There was a cool breeze wafting through the window; the shade shifted and rapped against the wooden frame. Still trembling, I pressed the sheet to my moist face. There was something about that dream . . . of course! I sighed in almost absurd relief. Bridget had described something similar when she had told my fortune that first night. I recalled the trepidation I had felt then, and realized that for some unknown reason the memory had lain buried in my mind for months and then surfaced tonight in my dream. And I had experienced it while asleep just the way I used to experience scenes from books I had read.

But I had no further time to ponder over this. From the open window came shouts and cries. "Teresa, come quickly! There's a fire—at the carriage house!" It was Emeline's voice. I pulled the shade slightly before releasing it and it shot up to the top of the window. Emeline stood in the darkness just outside my window; with difficulty I made out her stricken face, her eyes wide with shock.

"Teresa!" she cried. "Did you understand what I said? A fire! And it's all my fault!"

Bolting from the bed, I reached for my dressing gown and cried, "Wake Sam!" And then I was hurrying down the hall to the kitchen and out the door.

The stable doors were open, the fire spreading rapidly over the hay-strewn floor. I could hear the horses kicking in their stalls, their piercing whinnies filling the night air. Just inside the doors the buckets were kept, lined up against one wall. I grabbed two and rushed back to the kitchen to fill them with water. When I hurried out again, lugging the sloshing buckets, I saw Sam and Emeline at the old water pump, filling more pails.

I tossed the water I carried over the flames, closely followed by Sam. The smoke rose in a cloying, stinging mist bringing tears to my eyes and making me cough. When we ran back to the pump Bridget was there and the four of us formed a kind of assembly line. I pumped the water into pails while the others passed them along to be thrown on the riotous flames. My arms and shoulders began to ache savagely as I endlessly filled and refilled, the water splashing and soaking me.

When Sam shouted, "It's out!" at first I did not understand. I was still viciously pumping, the ache a hot welt of pain across my shoulders. But then Bridget repeated what he had said and I dropped the pail I had just filled. "Thank God. Are . . . are the horses . . . ?"

"They must be all right because they're still making that racket. Sam's gone in to soothe them."

41

"How in the world did it start?" I asked, reaching behind to rub my shoulder.

"That is what I would like to know," said a voice behind us. It was Miss Winslow. She carried a kerosene lantern which cast her face into deep shadows; it looked carved from stone. "And why did none of you rouse me when the fire started? I would have summoned the firemen. They are trained for such work, and by trying to put it out yourselves you caused a delay which could have proven disastrous."

"I thought I should get to the carriage house as soon as possible, Miss Winslow," I said shortly. "I did ask Emeline to wake Sam. And then Bridget must have heard us. When I saw the fire I thought we could put it out before it got out of control. If we had waited until the firemen arrived, then that might have proven disastrous."

"Don't you dare repeat my words back to me, Teresa Hawthorne. Just answer me this, how did it start? How did you discover it?"

"Why, Emeline shouted to me from the window," I said before I thought.

She turned her icy stare on Emeline. The girl wore a white nightgown which was now streaked with grime; she seemed to shrink into herself, her face a small white blur in the darkness.

"How did you know about the fire when your bedroom is on the opposite side of the house as is my own? What were you doing outside at this hour?"

Emeline was twisting a fold of her nightgown. "I—I had to go to the stables."

"To the stables? In the middle of the night? Would you care to give a reason for such a foolish action?"

"Well, I . . . I had to look for something. Something I lost today. I—I hoped it might be in the carriage." Her voice was scarcely above a whisper.

"And what were you looking for? What was so important that it prompted you to break several rules of the school?"

"It—it was my locket. I lost it somewhere today, maybe at the picnic. I didn't realize it until I was getting ready for bed. I was hoping it might have dropped onto the carriage floor on our way home. I had to go out and look for it."

"So, I learn you have broken yet another rule by wearing jewelry, something you know is strictly forbidden."

"It was a locket given to her by her grandmother, Miss Winslow," I put in.

"I was not aware that I had expressed a desire to converse with you, Teresa. I want to know what that locket has to do with the fire. Well, Emeline?" Her face was like a judge's, condemning, implacable.

"I went to the stables to search for the locket. But it wasn't in the carriage where I'd so hoped it might be. I—I had set down the kerosene lantern next to the carriage. When I climbed back down, I . . . my foot . . . knocked over the lantern," Emeline said miserably.

"So you admit that you started the fire. For the sake of a paltry piece of jewelry you had no business having in the first place. You started a fire that could have destroyed my school and burnt us to a crisp in our beds. Is that what you did, Emeline Curtis?"

"Y-yes, Miss Winslow," she whispered.

The headmistress turned to me. "I knew that picnic scheme was foolish from the very beginning, but I agreed to it against my better judgment. And now look where it has led! The stupid girl loses a necklace and nearly destroys the school because of it. And now I learn that you were aware that she wore this locket. Don't you recall my telling you, Teresa, that you are to enforce my rules? Emeline Curtis, in the year you have been here you have shown a pronounced disregard for regulations. You are totally unmanageable, headstrong, and wantonly impulsive. I will not have you remain in my school any longer. First thing in the morning I will send a telegram to your parents informing them that you are to be removed as soon as possible. It is time you became someone else's problem. In a word, Emeline, you are expelled."

"Oh, no, Miss Winslow," I protested. "Please reconsider. She was wrong to go out at night, perhaps wrong to wear the locket, but the fire was an accident."

"An accident. Exactly. And if I kept her on here what further accidents or catastrophes might I look forward to? I am relieved that I have discovered what she is capable of before something even more calamitous occurred. I refuse to take charge of so unprincipled and unthinking a child as you have shown yourself to be, Emeline Curtis."

"She did admit her part in it, Miss Winslow. Isn't that worth something? Must she be expelled?"

"How dare you question my decision, Teresa Hawthorne? If you're not careful you'll find yourself without a job. I'm not forgetting that indirectly you were the cause of this with your ridiculous notion of a picnic. Emeline, go to bed at once. And save your tears for your parents—perhaps they will be more responsive to them than I am. I wouldn't count on it, however. You have behaved very badly and are getting nothing more than what you deserve. And I'm certain your parents will agree."

Chapter Three

Emeline did not come down to breakfast the next morning. I had no intention of letting her go hungry from shame and remorse no matter what she had done the night before. After I had served Elizabeth and Mary, who had somehow managed to sleep through the excitement, I prepared a tray for Emeline and took it up to her.

She was fully dressed, lying flat on her bed, her arms folded across her stomach, her face pale and forlorn. "I can't eat anything, Teresa. I doubt if I'll ever be hungry again."

"I think perhaps you will be. But what is it, Emeline? Are you worried about what your parents will say?"

She sat up, her thin legs stretched out before her, her hair falling in plaits over her shoulders. "Oh, Teresa, I'm afraid they'll be so angry. I don't know—I've never done anything like this before. They're very seldom angry with me—but to be expelled! What a disgrace. My mother won't like that, not at all. I know I've been wanting to go home all along, but not like this. And Charlotte—to have to tell her I've lost Grandmother's locket! I just can't do it! That's far worse than being expelled. If at least I had found it and still started the fire—and still helped all of you put it out, of course—then maybe I wouldn't feel so awful."

"I'm sorry about your losing the locket. I wish you had come to me last night before going to the stables yourself."

"I didn't want to get you in trouble. I thought I could just take a quick look." Her voice trailed off despondently.

45

There were footsteps in the hall. We both looked up to see Miss Winslow coming into the room. "Teresa, go downstairs at once. You have no business being up here."

"I was just bringing Emeline some breakfast," I said.

"If the child wants to eat she must go down to the dining room like everyone else. I have sent the telegram to your mother, Emeline, informing her of your expulsion. I assume that she will arrive this evening or sometime tomorrow. Until she comes you are to remain in your room except at mealtimes."

"Yes, Miss Winslow," said Emeline, her face downcast.

I gave her what was meant to be a reassuring smile before going back to the kitchen. I was not surprised at her impulsive search of the carriage; I only wished that she had come to me so that I could have persuaded her to put it off until morning. To Emeline that locket was more than a sentimental token. I realized it was a symbol of all that she held dear, of the home she so desperately loved.

I hoped that her parents would not be hard on her. Had they any idea of how unhappy she had been at school? Despite the disgrace she was now in, despite her humiliation, she would soon be returning to Nightshade Notch. Once her present feelings of guilt and shame had dwindled, the excitement at the prospect of seeing her home would return. Perhaps all of this had happened for the best as there had been little damage of significance. Repairs would have to be made on the carriage house, and I was certain that Miss Winslow would hold Emeline's family accountable for the expense. It was an unfortunate situation, but not a tragic one.

As for myself, I realized how much I would miss her. She was an endearing child and had never once shown me any of the haughtiness that some of the other girls had. Despite the differences in our ages and circumstances, we were friends.

But on the other hand, I forced myself to think of the future. When Emeline was gone there would be nothing to keep me at the Academy; I might look for work elsewhere, better work, work for which I was qualified. When Emeline left I would inquire about teaching positions for the fall. Perhaps there were one or two openings. It might be that I would have to leave Portsmouth. I could write to the state education board for locations throughout New Hampshire where teachers were needed. Surely some of the smaller villages were in need of a teacher. If there was an opening and the board accepted my application, I could give Miss Winslow notice and begin a new life in a new setting. The prospect appealed greatly to me, but first I had to stand by Emeline. After she had gone, I could begin to make plans.

That Emeline dreaded coming face to face with one or both of her parents was easily comprehensible. Because I understood what had motivated her foolish, desperate search of the carriage which had taken us to the park, I reasoned that the least I could do for the child was to explain matters to her parents and attempt to justify her behavior. The fire had been a most unfortunate accident which could have had tragic results had she not summoned me instantly and then gone to rouse Sam. Her prompt action then deserved commendation, despite Miss Winslow's abrupt decision to expel her.

Naturally, the headmistress would conduct an interview with Mrs. Curtis on her arrival, outlining the child's disgrace and emphasizing any character flaws. Then, in her outrage, Miss Winslow would demand recompense. By that time Mrs. Curtis might be very angry with her daughter if she had not been before. I imagined her, tall, formidable, elegantly dressed, sweeping up the staircase to retrieve her truant daughter: "Emeline, I have never been more disappointed in anyone in my life. How dare you behave in such a fashion? To think that my own daughter would show so little thought, so little concern! We sent you to a fine school so you could be with girls your own age and this is how you behave, how you repay us. . . ."

No, I must speak to her if possible *before* Miss Winslow did. If I waited until after the interview it was likely that she would not be in a receptive mood; she would doubtless not care to hear her daughter's actions justified, or listen to any pleas on her behalf.

It was one of Bridget's duties to answer the front door and announce the callers; I told her I would listen myself for the doorbell for the next day or so, and I told her the reason. I only

47

hoped that Miss Winslow, secluded in her private suite, would not be aware of an arrival until I had the opportunity to speak with Emeline's parents. Once I had spoken my peace I would then conduct them to Miss Winslow's office. At that point I would have done all that I could.

Emeline came down to dinner that evening. She greeted Elizabeth and Mary with an air of studied unconcern; it was obvious that she was feeling her humiliation keenly but did not want to show it. Bridget and I sat in the kitchen until ten o'clock, but there was no sound of an arrival.

"It will be tomorrow after all," I said. "They must not have received the telegram until this afternoon or this evening. I suppose they'll take a morning train from the mountains and arrive by mid-afternoon." We turned down the gas jets, locked the doors, and went to our rooms.

The following day was Saturday, and it was one of my Saturday chores to clean the globes of the kerosene lamps which were lined up on a shelf in the kitchen to be used when the gas lighting failed. It was a hot, sticky morning. My gray gown, so carefully washed and starched, was already limp; my hair, curling riotously in the humidity, refused the restraint of the pins; my face felt flushed and moist. After lunch I would change my gown for another and subdue my hair in order to cultivate a more prepossessing appearance for Emeline's mother.

When the ringing of the front door bell sounded in the kitchen, I was in the middle of my work at the sink. I did not believe it could be Emeline's mother arriving so early, but I had asked Bridget to let me answer the door, and so I dried my wet hands on my apron and hurried through the dining room and the parlor to the front hall.

Unbolting the door, I opened it. To my surprise a tall, powerfully built man was standing on the portico. His thick black hair was brushed back uncompromisingly from a rather high brow; by contrast, his eyes were blue, and they surveyed me coldly. His face was set in grim lines, and there was a cleft in his square, determined jaw. It was evident that he was too young to be Emeline's father, and so I blurted out foolishly, "I—I think you must have made a mistake, sir. This is a school for young ladies."

His gaze raked over me, taking in every detail of my unprepossessing appearance, and I flushed scarlet under his derisive scrutiny. When he spoke his voice was dry. "It is one young lady in particular whom I have been ordered to retrieve. Be so good as to tell Miss Emeline Curtis I have come for her."

"You are Emeline's father?"

"That is one responsibility which has not yet come to me, thank God," he said bluntly. "Are you going to let me in, or must I stand outside while waiting for my niece?"

Biting my lip, I stepped aside for him to enter. This then must be Emeline's uncle who had been wounded in the war with Spain last summer. I saw that his tall, broad frame leaned to one side; he was using a cane.

"P-please come into the parlor," I stammered, looking away from him.

"Tell me," he said ironically, "is this your usual manner of welcoming visitors to this hallowed Academy, accusing them of having made a mistake in the address? A charming courtesy."

He had followed me into the parlor and I was closing the door behind us. "I beg your pardon," I said stiffly, flushing. "Usually I do not answer the door."

He raised his brows, a slight smile twisting his mouth. "It's no wonder."

"I mean that you took me by surprise. Would you care to sit down?"

"No, I shall stand," he said curtly. "Please summon my niece. I assume she is still here—or have you already thrown her out, bag and baggage?"

"Naturally she is still here," I said, nervously wiping my hands on my apron. "I—I want to explain what has occurred, Mr. Curtis. I felt Miss Winslow's decision to expel Emeline was too harsh. You see, she lost a locket two days ago and hoped it might be in the carriage we had ridden in that afternoon. She just couldn't bear to wait until the next morning to look for it. I quite understand that, but—"

"Then your understanding is a great deal better than mine," he said, cutting in. "Just what does all this have to do with her being sent home?"

"It—it was the fire, you see. She knocked over the lantern and . . ."

His black brows drew together. "Fire? You mean to tell me that Emeline started a fire?"

"Only by accident," I said earnestly. I was conscious that I was doing a very poor job of pleading Emeline's case. My carefully planned speech that I had prepared the day before had flown out of my head. And the way her uncle stood there scowling only made matters worse. Rather than presenting a clear picture of the whole business, I was babbling like an idiot.

I took a deep breath. "Won't you sit down, Mr. Curtis? I can explain everything. And I'm sure you would feel better if you sat down. Your leg—"

"You leave my leg out of this! The last thing I need is ministrations from a foolish young woman!"

I flinched at the bitter scorn in his voice, though I realized then that the set lines of his face were caused by the pain he must be suffering. "I just didn't want you to be too hard on Emeline, sir. She feels very contrite and ashamed of herself already, worried with what her family will say."

"Are you a teacher here?" he asked curtly.

"N-no, not exactly. But I—"

"Just in what capacity are you employed here?"

"As . . . as a cook," I said, coloring.

"A cook. And from such a lofty position you presume to tell me how to treat my niece. Do you think I'm going to beat her? I don't give a damn why she's been expelled. Just get her and we'll be off, or I *will* be tempted to beat someone."

It was then that Miss Winslow entered the room. We both looked over at the opened door, but before I could say anything, she said, "I was not aware, Teresa, that I had given you permission to entertain guests in the parlor. Just who is this?" Her tone was milder than it might have been, though, because, despite his boorish manner, the man was obviously a gentleman, well-dressed and quite handsome.

"Drake Curtis," he said shortly. "I've come for my niece."

"Of course. We have been expecting you, Mr. Curtis. But before you see Emeline there are one or two things I would like

50

to discuss with you concerning the child."

"Address them if you like in a letter to her parents," he said rudely. "As I have been telling this . . . young lady . . . I am not interested in the events which led up to this moment. I only want to do what was requested of me—take Emeline home. That was your express wish as you conveyed it in your telegram, was it not?"

Miss Winslow's lips tightened. Her colorless eyes darkened to a smoky gray. "There is the matter of repairing the carriage house. Emeline caused, through sheer carelessness and foolishness, a fire which could have destroyed the stables, two valuable horses, and the Academy itself. The cost of the repairs must be met by her family." With surprise I heard the usual note of authority lacking in her tone, despite her words. Miss Winslow found our male visitor rather intimidating as well, I thought, suppressing a smile.

Emeline's uncle's face lightened suddenly and his lips twisted in an ironic smile. "By all means, send me the bill," he said. I wondered vaguely what he found so amusing in the thought.

Miss Winslow inclined her head. "Tell Emeline her uncle is here, Teresa."

In relief I left the room. What an impossible man, I thought. I had been very tactless to mention his leg wound and he had not forgiven me for that. The fact that he had refused to sit down revealed his determination not to give in to the pain he was evidently feeling, and my calling attention to it had infuriated him. Yet he had not seemed to be angry with Emeline, just bad-tempered in general.

Knocking on her door, I called, "Your uncle is here, Emeline. He's ready to take you home."

"My uncle?" She was opening the door, wide-eyed. "How odd. I never expected that he might come. He's never had much to do with me—and I thought he was wounded."

"He is. He limps rather badly, I'm afraid. But if I were you I shouldn't refer to his leg at all. I'm afraid I was very tactless and irritated him. Come, I'll help you carry your bags."

"Sam took down the big one already. There are just these two little ones. I can manage both quite easily."

We made our way downstairs to the front hall. There was no sign of Miss Winslow; she must have retired because for once she had not come out as the victor in an encounter. At that point I felt almost charitable toward Emeline's uncle. He stood there waiting for us, slightly frowning.

"Hello, Uncle Drake," said Emeline faintly. "How—how are you? Where's Mamma and Papa?"

"They are away from the hotel at present. I received the telegram from your headmistress and so it was up to me to come for you. As it happens I had business in town anyway. Is this your bag?"

She nodded and then turned to me. "I'll miss you, Teresa. I won't forget you."

I hugged her tightly, saying, "I'll miss you too, Emeline. But you'll be much happier at home. And you can write to me; you can send me a postal card from your hotel."

"I will," she promised.

Drake Curtis opened the front door and then reached down for Emeline's heavy, bulky valise. He picked it up easily enough, but his jaw clenched as he made to carry it. His knuckles as they gripped the handle were white.

"Let me take that for you, sir," I said without considering his reaction, and wrested it from his grasp.

"I assure you that I am quite capable of carrying a light suitcase," he said, a tinge of color in his dark face. "I do not require any assistance from you."

Ignoring him, I conveyed the valise to the waiting hansom cab and helped Emeline into it. Her uncle was behind us; he hesitated a moment, and I realized that the step up into the carriage was going to be very painful for him. For a few moments he would be forced to put all his weight on his bad leg.

"Lean on me," I said matter-of-factly.

Briefly a fierce look of outrage came over his face before he submitted stonily to my request, gritting his teeth. He was large and muscular; I nearly stumbled while trying to support him but held my ground, my own shoulder aching from his weight. He let his breath out sharply but did not flinch before collapsing on the leather seat, his face pale. "Thank you," he ground out as though against his will.

"Good-bye, Emeline," I called.

When I went back into the house I used the front door unthinkingly. Miss Winslow was just coming out of her parlor but she did not appear to notice. "Perfectly dreadful man," she said. "Though I'm not at all surprised. Innkeepers, that's all the girl's relations are."

"He was wounded in Cuba, Miss Winslow," I said softly.

She went on as though I had not spoken. "Mind you, I did not realize. I did not recall her uncle's name when I admitted her to my Academy. I try to be so careful of scandal, even a whiff, and in that case there was more than just a whiff. The papers were full of it, though naturally I do not read the scandal sheets and do not recall any details. But Drake Curtis. I know that name. Now they may call him New Hampshire's Own Rough Rider, but a year ago it was something else entirely. So all of this is really for the best, despite the damage to the carriage house. But I must remember to be extra careful the next time I admit a student here."

I gaped at her, not having the slightest idea what she was talking about. She had been speaking as though to herself, almost rambling, and that was totally unlike her. What an effect Emeline's uncle had had, I thought wryly. And not just on me. He had certainly pierced Miss Winslow's rigid hauteur.

Then she came to herself. "Well, don't stand here in the hall. Go back to the kitchen, it's nearly time for lunch. And you may bring me a glass of sherry with my meal."

Sherry before lunch! She really *was* shaken, I thought, delighted.

Later that afternoon I was sitting at the kitchen table composing a letter to the Board of Education in Concord when there came a rapping at the door. It was a boy holding an envelope.

"For Miss Teresa Hawthorne," he said. "I was told to come around to the side door."

"Thank you, it's for me," I said, puzzled. The envelope was of heavy parchment with my name written in a bold black scrawl. I took the letter opener from the desk and, sliding it across the top of the envelope, pulled out the letter.

The handwriting inside was the same as on the envelope, and

totally unfamiliar to me. At the top of the paper was engraved "The Rockingham Hotel," Portsmouth's most luxurious hotel which catered to wealthy patrons and national and state dignitaries.

Miss Hawthorne:

I realize it is likely you have no wish to hear from me after the rudeness I showed you earlier today, but I ask that you do me one more kindness by reading this letter through. Emeline has told me something of your circumstances, and how you were unable to find employment other than in the capacity in which you are now engaged. I understand that you have the qualifications to be a teacher, also that you have helped Emeline with her studies from time to time. I believe I can speak for my brother and his wife in this. Would you consider returning to the White Mountains with Emeline and me as the girl's tutor? She is too old for a governess and does not wish to be sent to another school at this time. The ideal solution would be for someone familiar with the curriculum to give her lessons at her home. Naturally you would have ample free time, as she is used to looking after herself, and the salary would not be ungenerous. Emeline is anxious for you to agree but you must do as you think best. Whether or not you decide to accompany us tomorrow, we would be pleased if you would be our guest for dinner tonight at eight o'clock at the Rockingham Hotel.

Yours,
Drake Curtis

I set down the letter, shaking my head in wonder. It had taken me totally by surprise, and I felt faintly annoyed as well. It was an attempt at an apology, but there was a note in it of confidence that I would agree, rather than entreaty. Despite his acknowledgment of his former churlishness, it was apparent that he expected me to seize the offer he was making. Why else invite me to dinner? I would feel compelled to accept the position if I dined with the two of them. Tonight was not my night off; if I were not planning to accept his offer, then I could not leave my work this evening.

I felt I was being manipulated in some manner. He must be aware of the attraction such a post held for me, and unaccountably I resented him for it. Naturally I would jump at the chance to leave Miss Winslow's employ; I had already planned to do so if possible. My letter, half-written, lay on the table, mocking me. I had had high hopes while I was composing it. But they were only hopes.

This was real, immediate, a position already being presented to me. I had only to accept. I need not go through the painstaking process of applying to the state board; I need not work one day longer at the Academy. My first impulse, in wild, giddy relief, was to accept the offer, to regard it as a godsend. Yet something made me hesitate. It seemed too easy, the ideal solution, just as Drake Curtis had written.

Yet what alternative had I? To remain here as a drudge until something turned up at last? I could not hope to get a better offer than Mr. Curtis's (a fact of which he must be aware, I thought resentfully); a country schoolmarm was the best I could aspire to. Tutoring Emeline, on the other hand, would be most enjoyable. I realized that there was nothing I would like better. And if I went to Nightshade Notch I would see that she was not neglected. Her parents might not have time for her, but I would be her friend as I had been here. I need not see much of Drake Curtis, after all. He would doubtless be busy at the Crystal Hills most of the day and evening; we would rarely have to meet. I would not let my prejudice toward him influence my decision. He was surly and disagreeable but, I had to remind myself, he had lately been released from the hospital. And, I thought with a smile, he had certainly put Miss Winslow out of countenance. That alone should make me overlook his shortcomings.

I stood there clutching the letter in my hand, rubbing the parchment with the ball of my thumb. I realized that I would be a fool to eschew this post as Emeline's tutor. If I had handpicked a job for myself, it surely would not have been any better than this one being offered to me. And what if I could not find any work as a teacher and had to resign myself to yet another year spent in Miss Winslow's employ?

No, I could not do it. I was tired of her sharp criticisms, her petty cruelties. My father had always said that I had a good mind; he had expected it to see me through. To refuse Mr. Curtis's offer on the grounds that I did not like him would be ridiculous. And what did it matter what I felt about him when it was Emeline I was going to be tutoring?

First I had to inform Miss Winslow. Now that I had made my decision I felt only a dazed sort of elation. I was leaving this house today, not next month or the month after that. Today! After I had spoken with her I would prepare a cold supper, pack my things, and leave. My mind reeled from the unexpectedness of it all.

I went to Miss Winslow's office. She was sitting at her desk, an account ledger open before her. "Well, what is it?" The brisk, cold manner was back in place.

"I . . . I have come to resign, Miss Winslow," I said hurriedly, "I'm leaving tonight."

"Leaving? Is this some sort of joke, Teresa? What do you mean?"

"I've had a job offer, as a teacher," I said, the words coming out in a rush.

"Really. And where is this job, may I ask?"

"It's to be Emeline Curtis's tutor. I'm going with her and her uncle back to their home tomorrow." I tried to speak firmly but there was a betraying tremor in my voice.

"When in the world was this offer made?"

"Just now. I—I received a letter. From Emeline's uncle. She needs to continue her studies and I'm going to instruct her."

"Do you actually believe that she will listen to you in that new capacity after regarding you as one of my servants all this time?"

I stiffened. "She has always treated me with respect, Miss Winslow."

"So you're going just like that, at the drop of a hat. That man had an interesting effect on you, didn't he?"

Flushing, I said, "I don't know what you mean, Miss Winslow. I am fond of Emeline and it is a good position."

"So this is what becomes of the intimacy I've observed which has grown up between you. Doubtless you've been hoping for something like this all along, hoping her parents would take her from school and hire you to tutor her. Was the notion of the fire your idea as well? Or was that an improvisation of hers?"

I could not answer her, shocked that even she could suggest such a thing. Her eyes bore into mine, malevolence in their murky depths.

"Well, go on then, and good riddance. I hired you against my better judgment and I can see my misgivings were correct. You are ungrateful and irresponsible. But remember, Teresa, I warned you about that man. You haven't the slightest experience with men and he was involved in something quite unsavory in the past. I, for one, would not care to spend a moment in his company. Emeline can hardly be considered a chaperone, can she? And you're not bad-looking, despite that red hair. I would just make certain, if I were you, that he does not have something entirely different in mind for you other than being Emeline's tutor. He is still a man, after all, in spite of that limp. And persons of our sex have been known to respond most foolishly to wounded men, especially wounded heroes. And you are as naive and foolish as they come."

Coloring hotly, I turned to leave the office. But just as I was storming out, her voice followed me. "Don't think for an instant that you can come begging for your old job back. But if you are forced to leave this glorious new opportunity, I daresay you'll find something else. The world is full of kitchens."

Hurrying to my room, I began to haphazardly pack my things, trying to close my mind to the scorn in her voice, to her ugly insinuations. When I had calmed down somewhat, I went to find Bridget to tell her of my decision.

"I'll put out a cold supper—there won't be much washing up," I said. "But I'm sorry my leaving suddenly like this makes more work for you."

She shrugged. "There's only a few of us. And it's a good chance for you, Teresa. This was never a place for you."

After I had set the places and served slices of cold roast, I took a bath and dressed. Not one of my gowns was suitable for the splendor of the Rockingham Hotel, but I selected the best one I had. Before my father had been taken ill, he had tended to a seamstress whose frequent headaches made it difficult for her to work. And she had repaid him by sewing some gowns for me. The best was of ivory muslin, trimmed with double yokes of lace across the bodice and three flounces below the knee. The sleeves were generously puffed to the elbow and tied there in narrow satin ribbons. I had had scarce occasion to wear it, and hoped now it was presentable enough for dinner at a fashionable hotel. It was undeniably becoming, and should give me confidence.

It was another muggy evening, the roofs in the distance blurred and shimmering. Combing my hair, I pinned it loosely in a knot on top of my head and left shorter strands to curl about my face. I smoothed some powder over my cheeks and pinned my straw hat to the knot of hair. Pulling on a pair of crocheted lace gloves, I took my bag and let myself out the kitchen door.

The Rockingham Hotel was not far from the school. I had passed it many times but had never been inside. It was large and imposing with a brownstone facade, two massive bay windows, terra-cotta medallions depicting the four seasons, and two gables crowning the roof. In front of the building sat four cast-iron lions painted gold, their manes long and curly.

Taking a deep breath, I went up the stairs and through the front door held open for me. My stomach fluttered uncomfortably; I doubted whether I would be able to eat any dinner at all. Looking about me in some nervous confusion, I noticed that the walls of the vestibule were ornately paneled and varnished; the floor was laid out in diamonds of white and black marble.

Was I to meet Emeline and her uncle in the dining room or in a private suite? His letter had merely stated eight o'clock at the Rockingham and I saw with dismay that it was seven minutes past the hour.

"May I help you, miss?" said a man at my elbow, giving a slight bow.

"Yes. That is, I'm to meet Mr. Curtis and his niece for dinner. Drake Curtis."

"Ah, yes, Major Curtis. He told me to expect you. One of the boys will take your bag up to the room the major has reserved for you. If you will follow me, Miss Hawthorne."

He led me through a set of large plate-glassed doors to what was obviously the dining room. Scenes of wild game decorated the wall panels, and still lifes of fruit adorned the ceiling frescoes. There were green and gold curtains at the long windows, and a marble mantel at either end of the spacious room.

The room was crowded; every table looked to be occupied. As I scanned the faces of the guests and took note of their elaborate evening finery, I felt more out of place than ever.

"Your party is just ahead," the man was saying, and then Emeline was looking up happily. "Oh, Teresa, I did so hope you'd come!" she cried.

A chair was pulled out for me. Drake Curtis rose, leaning on his cane. "Good evening, Miss Hawthorne," he said quietly. "We'll have that champagne now," he added to the waiter.

"Very good, Major."

Regarding Drake Curtis while he conversed with the waiter, I decided he looked worse than he had that morning. The lines about his firm mouth were more pronounced; his dark face was a shade or two paler. He wore a well-cut dark evening suit and his heavy hair was neatly brushed, but his handsome appearance did not conceal the fact that he had overtaxed his leg and was feeling it even more than he had earlier. It was a shame that he had had to be the one to make the journey to Portsmouth when it would have been much easier for one or both of Emeline's parents to do so. I wondered where the two of them were and why Emeline's father had left his younger brother, who was still recovering from his injuries, to manage the hotel alone at its busiest season.

"Well, Teresa, don't keep me in suspense any longer!" said Emeline. "Are you coming with us tomorrow to the Notch?"

I smiled. "How can I refuse, Emeline?" I turned to her uncle. "I'd like to thank you, sir, for your generous offer."

He made an abrupt dismissing gesture. "It is I who am once again in your debt, Miss Hawthorne. And with you to take charge of Emeline's education, that is, at least, one less worry for me."

I thought that was a rather odd reply; surely Emeline's

education was a matter of concern for her parents. His curt manner was still intact, despite the words of appreciation. I did not know how to respond to him.

Fortunately Emeline was exclaiming, "I'm so glad, Teresa. We'll have such fun. I never thought that terrible night of the fire would end like this! To think I cried myself to sleep, and now everything's much better than it ever was!" Her face was flushed, her blue eyes sparkled. Gone was the woebegone schoolgirl in stiff white blouse and navy blue skirt. She wore a pink dress with a high ruffled collar and satin sash, white stockings, and white buttoned shoes.

A waiter was pouring champagne into my glass; Drake was drinking what looked like whiskey. He downed one glass and ordered another.

"Just wait until you see Nightshade Notch, and the Crystal Hills Hotel," Emeline said. "I'll show you everything. It's truly the most wonderful place, isn't it, Uncle Drake?"

"Read your menu, Emeline," said her uncle brusquely.

I picked up mine from the table and began to study it, glad to have something to do. There was a choice of Rhode Island turkey with cranberry sauce, boiled lobster, breaded lamb chops with tarragon, fried Maine smelts with lemon, broiled scrod with dill—the list went on.

I had hoped by now that my apprehension would have lessened and my appetite returned, but that was not the case. Emeline seemed oblivious to her uncle's grim mood; she was at that age when her emotions still centered on herself. She was overjoyed at the prospect of going home to the White Mountains the next day and that occupied her thoughts to the exclusion of all else. She had dreaded the meeting with one or more members of her family but the worst was now over, and Miss Winslow had not had an opportunity to denounce her to her parents.

On the other hand, I felt uneasy in her uncle's presence, and had the distinct impression that he would have rather been anywhere else than sitting there playing the host to the two of us. Nervously I swallowed a large sip of champagne.

"I'm going to have the turkey with Delmonico potatoes and garden peas," announced Emeline. "And Chantilly cream for dessert. I've scarcely eaten all summer."

"I'm certain that's no reflection on Miss Hawthorne's cooking," said Drake with a twist to his lips.

"No, of course not. Where are Mamma and Papa, Uncle Drake? I've been meaning to ask you all afternoon but I haven't seen you."

"I haven't the least idea," said her uncle shortly, his mouth tightening. "But that needn't concern you. Miss Hawthorne will keep you company, and Charlotte is looking forward to seeing you. I've telegraphed to her that you are coming, Miss Hawthorne, and she is to have a room prepared for you."

"I hope it's not too far from mine," said Emeline.

"As you will both be living in the same house, what does it matter?" snapped her uncle. She looked across at me, wincing at his tone.

"I'm looking forward to seeing the hotel," I said. "Emeline's told me so much about it."

"Be prepared for its being somewhat different from what she has told you. Be prepared for a change, Emeline."

"A change? How do you mean?"

"I mean that you may notice some differences in the hotel from the way it used to be, only that." He took a drink and set down his glass with a snap.

She turned a troubled face to his. "But . . . why?"

"I won't bother you with the dull details. But you may as well be prepared."

Our food was brought then. Emeline forgot her questions and applied herself to her dinner, but I found it difficult to eat. I had ordered the scrod because I had thought it would be light fare, not rich like the other entrées, but the flakes of fish felt dry in my mouth. I was beginning to wonder whether I had made the right decision after all to accompany Emeline and Drake to Nightshade Notch. Surely his manner did nothing to encourage me. The initial elation I had felt at the chance to leave Miss Winslow's employ had swiftly dwindled in the face of Drake Curtis's forbidding demeanor.

"About your parents, Emeline," he said. "They are supposed to be in Boston, but I was not able to locate them at their hotel. I assume they will return to the Notch before too long."

I bit back words of surprise. Boston was a brief train ride from Portsmouth. Why on earth hadn't the child's parents come to visit her? They had not seen her in over a year, and yet they had not bothered to spend a few hours with her while they were close by. But that is no concern of yours, I told myself severely. And that should show you how much Emeline needs you.

Emeline's dessert had just been served when Drake said, "If you ladies will excuse me, I'll say good night to you now. The train leaves at eleven o'clock tomorrow, so I expect you to be downstairs at ten-thirty."

"All right, Major Curtis," I said. "Good night."

He stood up, his knuckles whitening as he grasped the cane. Giving a slight bow, he turned. His limp was pronounced as he made his way across the room, and I noticed several ladies surveying him with unveiled interest—and pity. How he must hate that, I thought.

"His leg must be paining him a great deal," I said. "You musn't mind his short temper."

"I don't. He's never talked to me all that much. But he was never so awful as he acts now," said Emeline.

"He came all the way to get you," I reminded her. "He could have kept trying to contact your parents, or sent someone else. But he came himself. And it's been too much for him."

"I wonder what exactly is wrong with his leg, and if it will get better."

"I wouldn't ask him if I were you."

"No, I'll just ask Charlotte. I've missed her. It will be so good to get home, no matter what Drake is being so mysterious about. But I do wonder what's been happening there." There was a pucker in her brow.

"You'll find out soon enough. I expect your uncle is having a difficult time adjusting to being back home, that's all. Don't worry."

We left the dining room shortly after and went up to our rooms on the third floor. "Number Thirty-three, that's your room, Teresa. Drake's is just there and mine is down the hall."

"Thank you. Good night, Emeline, sleep well. We'll have

breakfast together, all right?"

My room was done in red brocade. The furniture was walnut, ornately carved and varnished to a sheen. I did not feel tired; indeed, in my disquieted state I did not know when I would be able to sleep. My bag had been brought up and my things unpacked; my nightgown and dressing gown lay across the bed. There was a collection of books propped up on one of the bureaus; I took one at random and then got dressed for bed. Then I sat down to read.

The sounds of the hotel grew dim; in the background I heard laughter and chatter as people went down the corridor to their rooms. Later there was nothing but silence. I read until very late, partly because the book, a collection of supposed real-life ghost stories, was so absorbing, and partly because I was still too overwrought to sleep. It had been such a strange day, full of so many unexpected events. I still found it hard to believe that I had left the Academy for good and tomorrow would be leaving Portsmouth. I tried to suppress the misgivings I was having.

Finally I knew that I must put down the book and try to get some sleep. I had climbed into bed and switched off the electric light at the bedside table when I heard a loud thud through the wall, as though something heavy had crashed to the floor. What on earth, I thought, at this hour of the night . . . Then it dawned on me that Drake Curtis's room was next to mine and the sound had come from his room.

Swiftly I slipped on my dressing gown, opened the door, and went out into the hallway. Now there was nothing but silence. I hesitated a moment before knocking softly at his door, and when I heard no response, twisted the knob, relieved that it was not locked, and went inside.

He was sitting on the floor in an awkward position, his face resting on one of his hands. He was bare to the waist but still wore his evening trousers. He looked up, scowling.

"What the devil do you want?"

"I—I heard a noise. I thought you must have fallen."

"Did you? What perception. Well, now that you've satisfied your curiosity, you can go back to bed."

"Can you manage, Major Curtis? I can help you get back into bed." I felt the color seeping into my face at the sight of his massive shoulders and chest. I looked down at my bare feet.

"How magnanimous of you," he snarled, "to offer again to help a poor cripple. Otherwise you'd never have come into my room dressed like that at this time of night. Well, I don't need your help, Miss Hawthorne. Leave me now."

"But—"

"I said, leave me!"

Chapter Four

The next morning Emeline knocked on my door at half past eight to rouse me; I had not slept so late since taking the job at Miss Winslow's Academy. But I had found it difficult to fall asleep, lying uneasy and restless for some time after Drake Curtis had ordered me from his room. It had occurred to me what a singular appearance I had presented—dressed only in my night attire, rushing into his room, preparing to assist him to get to his feet. He must have been shocked; upon reflection I had badly shocked myself. He had scorned and rebuffed my offer of aid and made me feel a fool; I would try not to make the same mistake again. He seemed a different person from the man who had written the letter to me yesterday. I supposed that now that the problem of Emeline's education was solved by my accepting the post as her tutor, he felt he did not have to treat me with any semblance of courtesy. It was almost as though I brought out the worst in him. The farther I stayed from him the better.

It had begun to rain in the night, a dismal, persistent sound which only contributed to my mood of disquiet. Emeline and I breakfasted together downstairs in the dining room; her uncle did not join us. "I knocked on his door," she said. "He said he was shaving and would eat in his room."

That was just as well, I thought, relieved.

"Did I tell you I went to the park yesterday afternoon?" she went on. "Drake was out for hours and so I walked there by myself."

"Whatever for?"

"Why, to look for the locket, of course," she responded a bit impatiently. "I didn't find it, though."

"I'm sorry, Emeline."

"Yes, I suppose someone saw it and stole it," she said somberly. "Oh, well, at least I'm going home today. And you're coming with me."

After we had finished we went back upstairs to pack. We were both dressed in traveling suits appropriate for the dusty, sooty train; mine was bottle-green, the fitted jacket buttoned to the throat with leg-o'-mutton sleeves, the skirt flaring gently. Emeline's was a red and beige tartan, and she wore a jaunty little cap to match.

I was rather childishly excited about traveling on a train. I had only done so on rare occasions with my father when we would go to Boston. I remembered the way the steel locomotive had snorted impatiently in the station; then, when it was fed its first burst of steam, it began to move slowly, its wheels spinning. As it gained momentum the rails would sink and then click back into place. I remembered the jangling of the car couplings, the trail of black smoke and steam spewing from the engine, and the steam whistle which blasted unwary eardrums and filled all who heard it with dreams of adventure in faraway places.

"It's a shame it's raining today," said Emeline. "It'll make a rather dreary train ride—especially since we won't be able to see much of the mountains at all. They're always covered in mist when it rains."

Drake Curtis was in the vestibule paying the reckoning. He did not look as though he had rested well, and in spite of my dislike for him, I was concerned. Again I wondered exactly what was wrong with his leg. The man who had shown me to the table last night was saying to him, "It has been an honor to have you stay at the Rockingham, Major Curtis. Please come again."

"Thank you," he said coolly. He turned away, his eyes flickering over me, moving to Emeline. "I've a cab waiting to convey us to the station. Are you both ready? We must leave now if we are to make our train. I've wasted enough time here already."

Emeline made a slight grimace at me, which I pretended not to see, and the three of us went outside. Gathering my full skirts in one hand, I climbed into the cab after Emeline, and had enough presence of mind to look out the streaked window at the glossy, puddled street while Drake got in. When he reached the railway station, he requested three tickets to Nightshade Notch.

"One-way or round-trip, sir?"

"One-way."

As he spoke I felt an inexplicable twinge of dread. One-way to Nightshade Notch, no return trip. The words conjured up an eerie dream-image of dark, smothering mountains that enclosed one, bore down on one. . . .

We took our seats in the first-class carriage, its walls paneled in mahogany, its seats upholstered in plush wine-red mohair. Raindrops spattered against the wide windows. Across from us Drake reached into the breast pocket of his gray coat for a box and took out a cigar. He clipped the end with the slender silver knife on the end of his watch chain and lit it, settling back into the seat, his bad leg stretched out stiffly before him. Others were sitting down as well, and within a short time the locomotive gave a vigorous belch and sounded its whistle. We began to inch forward unsteadily.

Gazing out the window through a veil of rain, I watched as the city of Portsmouth moved away, as the skyline of handsome, prosperous buildings became blurred and indistinct. Gone were the cobblestoned streets, the cultivated gardens, the gaslights. Now we were traversing saltwater marshes, bayberry-colored in the bleakness, the sky above a heavy, sodden mantle. In the distance, across the flats, the woods began, black and brooding.

Emeline was quiet beside me. I had expected her to be chattering away in anticipation of reaching her home that day, but I guessed her uncle's presence made her subdued. He made no effort to make conversation. I stole a glance at him; to my surprise he was regarding me with narrowed eyes, his brow knit. Our eyes met; hastily I looked away. The image of him the previous night in the half-light, his chest bare and matted with hair, his shoulders and arms molded into hard muscle, rose before me. I could feel the color seeping into my face and I became preoccupied with the sleeve of my jacket, brushing off an imaginary spot of dirt.

Later the landscape changed, became green and rolling. We passed farms where unperturbed cows grazed in the lush, wet grass. Under the whimsical weathervanes the barns were painted red or their shingles had weathered a pewter gray. We passed villages with white cottages and white churches, their squat steeples open to reveal bells. We saw horses and carts disappear into long, covered bridges over narrow, rippling rivers. It occurred to me that I had left all that I knew, all of life that was my experience—town life. We were moving rapidly away from bustling civilization toward what was little more than a wilderness despite the existence of several grand resort hotels.

Just then we rounded a curve and I could see the remainder of the train stretching out before me; above the cars the trail of black smoke and cinders looked ominous. And to my ears the wheels seemed to be chanting, "No going back, no going back, no going back . . ."

"I'm hungry," said Emeline some time later. "Let's go to the diner car and have lunch."

Diffidently I looked at her uncle, but he waved us away. "Go ahead, Miss Hawthorne. I dislike eating on trains."

I rather doubted this, suspecting that his refusal to join us had more to do with the fact that the lurching, unsteady progress through the cars to the diner would be severely taxing on his leg. I started to offer to request that a sandwich be brought to him there, but stopped myself. Hadn't I been shown several times, brutally even, that he did not appreciate solicitude? He did not wish to be reminded of his affliction, much less to have it remarked on by others. Even at the hotel, he had spurned the attempts of the doorman to assist him into the carriage. And now he was doubtless paying for his stubbornness.

Once in the dining car, sitting at a table covered with a white linen cloth and set with elegant luncheon service, Emeline regained her good spirits. "We're nearly halfway there now,

Teresa," she said. "I can hardly believe it! It's been so long since I was home. Why, Drake was still there then—he hadn't gone to Cuba yet. One evening my mother told me I was to leave for school the next day—just like that! I tried crying and pleading, but she wouldn't be moved. And early the next morning she took me on the train herself."

She sunk her cheek in her hand, musing. "Uncle Drake has always been different from Papa, who talks and laughs all the time, but now he's so bad-tempered. I feel as though anything I say may be the wrong thing, don't you? I wonder when Mamma and Papa will return from Boston. Mamma likes to get away from the Notch sometimes, and now that Uncle Drake's returned I suppose they have more time for traveling and such."

But not enough time to visit their daughter, to spend an afternoon with her, to even temporarily allay her loneliness. But that was all in the past now, those bleak months at Miss Winslow's, bleak for both of us. She was going home, and I was going with her, and we would keep one another company. How ridiculous those swift, unaccountable twinges of foreboding, of uncertainty, now seemed.

"You know, I've never seen you dressed as you are now and as you were last night," she went on, brightening. "You look so different out of those old gowns and aprons."

"And I must say that your suit is an improvement on your school uniform as well," I said, smiling.

"Drake said that Charlotte had ordered some of my things packed when they knew he was to fetch me. That reminds me. Do you know, Teresa, Drake didn't have one thing to say to me about being expelled? I thought when I saw him that he looked very angry—he looked so fierce—and I was afraid to go off with him in the carriage. But he never referred to it all. He seemed preoccupied with something else, and acted almost as though I weren't there. We drove to the Rockingham, where he ordered lunch for me in my room, and then he asked me some questions about you. I told him all about your father being so ill, and you not being able to find any work when he died except cooking at the school—I hope you don't mind—although you had graduated from there yourself and should

69

have been a teacher. I told him you had helped me with my lessons, and then he said something about how was I going to continue my education, and perhaps I should have a tutor. He was frowning and staring off into space, and I cried out, 'Teresa could be my tutor!' His expression didn't change, so I suppose the same thing had occurred to him. So it was easy to persuade him, although at the time I wasn't certain if I had. He didn't tell me he was going to write to you. He just left sort of abruptly and didn't come back for hours. That's when I went to the park. When he did return, he came to my room and said we'd be having dinner in the dining room and he'd invited you to join us. He also said then that he'd offered you the job as my tutor."

"Yes, he wrote me a very civil letter which I received just as I was in the process of inquiring about a teaching position. It didn't take me very long to decide to come with you today!"

We ate our lunch, which began with bowls of steaming creamy soup made from herbs, and continued with slices of roast beef, mashed potatoes, and bright-green asparagus. The tables were all full, but the first-class travelers were quiet, speaking in low voices punctuated by the clinking of flatware on crockery, the sudden hissing of a champagne cork. Glancing about, I thought they were oblivious to the scenery rushing past, to the fact that we were descending deeper into remote country, hurling past quaint hamlets to lonely settlements through somber, dense forests.

Wisps of mist swathed the trunks of trees as if to shield some secret that was theirs alone. The woods now engulfed us on both sides so that even the dismal gray light of day could barely filter through. And I found myself wishing as I gazed out the window at the forbidding wall of trees that we could move silently through this primeval landscape, that the monstrous black brute of a machine would not bellow our intrusion, brazenly announcing our presence with its shrill, clamoring whistle, with its shuddering, thundering engine, its whirling, chattering wheels. The brash locomotive did not falter in its course, and its occupants scarcely heeded the terrain sweeping past them.

In the elegance of the diner car, they were perfectly at home, at ease with themselves. Yet for all of us the ride would end; the train would stop; we would disembark in a very different world from the place we had begun our journey. No matter the glories of the hotels, outside their doors and windows would be the same untamed landscape, the secretive gloom of the forests, the massive, brooding mountains.

There went my imagination again. It was my worst enemy. Immersed in it I had sought to prevent my father from dying; I had awaited an easy solution to my destitution. The months spent at Miss Winslow's should have cured me of that. Indeed, I had thought I had grown more realistic, more practical. But there I was again, indulging in foolish fancies, allowing mood dominance over rational thought.

Giving myself an inward shake, I said, "We should go back to our seats now, Emeline, if you've finished."

"Oh, no, let's not," she said, her nose wrinkling. "I know. Let's go to the observation platform at the rear of the train. We'll be able to see better there—if everything's not obscured by fog. I can feel the train beginning to climb even now, can't you? Soon we'll be in the mountains."

In the observation platform we relaxed in the green velvet parlor chairs fringed in gold. There was a middle-aged couple there before us, the man blond, robust, mustached, his wife by comparison frail-looking, sallow. He sat smoking a pipe, reading a newspaper, while she fidgeted restlessly with her handbag, her shawl, and whatever else was available.

"This trip seems endless," she said in a petulant voice. "And the rain only makes it worse. I wonder if we shall actually reach the place today. The tracks may be washed out, or something equally dreadful."

"I don't think that very likely, my dear," he answered absently, not raising his head from his newspaper. "Just relax."

"There you go again, telling me to relax," she said angrily, her face reddening. "As if I can with that continuous clackety-clack sound and that terrible whistle! But you've no sympathy for my poor nerves, none at all!"

"Now, my dear, calm youself. We've only a couple more hours to go. And remember that I'm taking time off from the office to give you this trip. Your doctor advised it and so naturally I agreed. But we're very busy at the office just now, so don't accuse me of having no sympathy."

"Oh, you're always busy, always leaving me to that gloomy townhouse with no one to talk to but the servants. I hate New York—it's what made me ill in the first place. And lately, the dreadful heat and filth in the air—"

"Well, then, be glad that you are getting away from it for a while. The doctor said the fresh, cool mountain air was what you needed to restore you and then you'd be right as rain."

He went back to his newspaper, unperturbed, and she subsided into a sullen silence. Emeline and I exchanged pointed glances, relieved that their quarreling was apparently over for the present. Not that you could call it quarreling. The man never varied his pleasant tone. I noticed that he avoided looking directly at his wife and seemed detached. Not that I altogether blamed him. But was that the correct manner to assume to an ailing woman who evidently craved attention and felt neglected?

Feeling a little awkward to have witnessed their telling domestic interlude, I turned my attention to the window. The farm-studded green hills moved past us in a backward rush; sheenless lakes and ponds reflected the melancholy sky. There were no longer any villages now, no cottages clustered tidily around a cheerful green, no churches projecting their reassuring beacons toward the sky. In the hollows between the slopes, lone mean houses crouched gloomily, porches sagging, shutters askew.

In a while we were climbing again, the train moving slower now, its earlier blustering propulsion lacking. Urging itself upward, it went around a bend in the tracks. I was startled to see how high we suddenly were. Unexpectedly the ground had fallen away to one side revealing a sheer drop as we edged our way around a mountain precipice. In awe I looked down at the minaret peaks of the black-green spruces below us, and then across to the rugged crests with their exposed slabs of granite.

Below the timberline the slopes bristled with pine and fir trees. The near ridges huddled together, dipping low in the notches and then rising to the next sculpted summit. Low-hanging clouds enveloped the distant violet bluffs. And then the locomotive, gathering momentum, streamed downwards. We watched as the mountain we had just scaled rose majestically behind us. In our wake the streak of coal vapor lingered to mingle with the shrouding film of translucent cloud.

Once again the train had penetrated the forest, and on both sides of the tracks, graceful silvery birches threaded against the backdrop of pines, maples, and poplars. Vulnerable birch striplings hovered at the edge of the woods, their leaves a whispery green. We passed pockets of dead trees grouped together like skeletons, and tiny pines, their branches featherlike and wispy.

The man had risen to open the window, and suddenly the car was filled with the overwhelming scent of moist pine, delicious and refreshing in the stuffy platform. But his wife said querulously, "The rain is coming in on me. Close that at once or I shall take a chill."

"I'm sorry, my dear. We must avoid a chill at all costs," he replied rather ironically, and she flashed him a sharp look. After she had complained about the sweltering heat of New York City, it was surprising that she should shudder from the first burst of cooler air. He stood up again, drew in several deep breaths of the mountain air, and shut the window. His wife regarded him resentfully as though his obviously good health and stocky, robust build were distasteful to her, which perhaps they were. I thought them singularly ill-matched.

But the rain was coming down harder now, the pelts slashing at the windows and hammering on the roof. We crossed a trestle over a swollen stream studded with amber-hued stones, the water foaming briskly down a grade in its bed. Upstream was another covered bridge, its slats and roof painted barn-red. Coils of mist nestled eerily on the stream's surface, unmoving.

"Everything's so lovely," said Emeline rapturously, and I had to agree.

"Perhaps we should return to our carriage now. Your uncle may be wondering where we are, and it can't be much further, can it?"

"Oh, we've still a while to go," said Emeline, "but I suppose we should go back. We don't want to annoy Uncle Drake, after all."

We walked back the length of the train, taking special care with the car couplings, which were wet and slippery. But the smell of the pine trees was so intoxicating that we didn't mind the gusty moments between cars, though we had to hold onto our hats with one hand and clutch the metal handles with the other.

When we reached our compartment, I was surprised to see it was nearly empty. Most of the people had already disembarked at early stops in the mountains, it appeared.

Even Emeline was surprised. "Where did all the passengers go? I would have thought that a number of them would have been going to the Crystal Hills."

Approaching our seats from behind, I saw Drake Curtis's dark head slumped against the window. I gestured to Emeline to be quiet, and we sat down across from him.

He was asleep, and now I had the chance and the leisure to observe him. In repose the lines about his mouth were gone, leaving his face curiously vulnerable. He also looked younger, not that he was much above thirty anyway, but whatever hardships he had endured had left their mark. Possessed of a somber handsomeness when awake, now he seemed almost boyish, despite his hard, broad build, a lock of black hair falling over his forehead.

Emeline was yawning, and soon had fallen asleep herself. It was little wonder considering all the excitement she had encountered the past few days.

Turning my attention back to her uncle, I rested my cheek in my hand and continued to regard him. Gone was the coldness, the harshness, the bitterness. He looked a different person.

Suddenly he shifted abruptly in his seat and his blue eyes flashed open. I was astonished by their expression—frightened, even . . . haunted. He stared at me without recognition for a few moments, still with that almost wild look in his eyes, his brow knit, his frame tense. Then he seemed to come to himself, sighing heavily, his face relaxing as he realized his surroundings. All this happened in swift succession, but again I found myself concerned about him, and at the dark thoughts which apparently did not let up even while he slept.

"Are you all right, Mr. Curtis?" I asked, noticing his hands trembled slightly.

A tinge of color rose in his cheeks. His black brows drew together. "Of course I'm all right," he replied gruffly. He turned to look out the window, his jaw set firmly, the lines of strain once again about his mouth.

I also turned toward the window to gaze up at the sheer granite cliffs alongside the mountains. Above them was a strange outcropping of short, twisted trees that resembled not trees at all, but dense, flat mats rising only a foot above the ground.

"How strange," I murmured.

"That's the *krummholz* you see there above the timberline," said Drake. "It's German for 'crooked wood.' At the high elevations the spruce and balsam trees cannot grow in height because that growth is killed off by the wind and the cold. Only the lowest parts of the trees can survive the winter under the protective blanket of snow, and any growth they have is horizontal. Winters in the White Mountains are savage, Miss Hawthorne. The terrain resembles an Arctic zone." He smiled sardonically. "We Curtises are used to it, but few visitors come to the mountains then."

"If you are implying that I shall flee at the sight of the first snowflake, Mr. Curtis, then you are mistaken."

He shrugged. "The mountains are easily enjoyed in the summer and early fall," he said, "when the hotels are open. But it becomes a different world in the winter. Thick layers of rime ice coat the ground, the wind blows in a perpetual high-pitched roar, the slopes are like huge glaciers."

Gazing up at the towering inclines, I could imagine them snow-covered, so white they hurt the eyes, windswept and barren at the summits, the trees below the timberline stark, skeletal, crusted with ice.

"You offered me the position as Emeline's tutor," I said softly. "Are you now trying to frighten me away?"

"I'm merely warning you, Miss Hawthorne, what to expect. You look rather delicate to me and these mountains

. . . are not for the delicate."

I did not understand him, nor did I care to. He evidently considered me a frail, unreliable creature; I wondered why on earth he had hired me if he were already having second thoughts as to my suitability. I was determined to prove him wrong.

I had just made this brave resolve when suddenly the ground fell away again. The train was making its way around a steep precipice on the mountainside and I had the alarming sensation that we were leaning away from the incline toward the sheer drop below. The rain spattered at the window, the drops streaming downwards.

Hastily I looked away from the formidable sight, hoping Drake Curtis had not noticed my start of apprehension. He would feel justified in his opinion of me if I revealed my panic, and so I deliberately opened my bag and reached for a handkerchief, willing myself to be calm. We went around another sharp curve, the train wheels clacking, the car couplings grinding. And then the whistle gave its shrill blast as we began to move down the mountain at what seemed to me to be a furious pace. I gave a gasp and then bit my lip.

"We're quite safe, I assure you, Miss Hawthorne," said Drake, and I looked up to see him regarding me with a faint smile, his face softened.

Flushing, I forced myself to look out the window over the spikes of the treetops. Then we were once again submerged in the dark woods, and this time I felt a solace rather than a vague menace in their enclosure.

The train was decreasing in speed. The whistle sounded again briefly, the brakes grated, and we slowed to a crawl before eventually stopping altogether.

"What's happening?" I asked. "Is it another stop? There doesn't seem to be anything around here."

He shook his head, perplexed as well. The door to the car opened behind us and one of the brakemen came in, soaked to the skin. He hurried up the aisle but just as he was passing us, Drake stopped him.

"Why have we stopped?" he asked.

"Trestle up ahead's covered in water. Can't tell if it's still there or not. The flagman's checking to see if we can cross it."

"What if it proves uncrossable?"

"Then we'll have to back up some distance and take the other track." He shrugged, not particularly concerned.

"Back up—around those curves?" I asked faintly.

"This ain't always an easy run, miss," said the brakeman, and he continued his way to the front of the train.

I must not show my fear, I thought sharply. I must not give Drake Curtis further cause to despise me. At the time I did not question why I cared for his good opinion; I thought of nothing but keeping the creeping fear at bay.

After what seemed an interminable length of time, the whistle sounded again and the train gave an abrupt lurch forward. We were moving again, slowly, jerkily.

"This means the trestle is still intact," said Drake. "You no longer have anything to worry about."

"But—covered in water! How on earth can we ford through it?" I looked out to see a river rushing past us, the lower section of the train submerged in water; no longer was it possible to hear the sound of wheels against the rails. I felt quite faint.

"Easily, I assure you," he said, his lips quirked. "But if you are still frightened I will hold your hand. I promise not to take any further liberties, as we are in a public conveyance and my impressionable niece is sleeping across from me."

I colored hotly. If his words were meant to goad or embarrass me out of my consternation, they very nearly succeeded. Within a short time we had traversed the trestle and were once again on solid ground, the wheels now making their comforting din.

"Not much further to go now," he said, still with that look of amusement on his face.

"No, the train is nearly empty, is it not? I suppose the other passengers got off shortly after lunch."

"Two summers ago we were turning people away," he said. "And now at the height of the season there are no guests en route to the hotel. How quickly word spreads." He spoke dryly, ironically even, yet I sensed a quiet despair behind his cursory manner.

"I daresay many people did not like to travel through such a storm," I said awkwardly, wondering at his last cryptic words. Again that vague feeling of unease rose within me.

Although it was only mid-afternoon, the cheerless sky made it seem later. In the dusky violet light the mountains merged with the clouds in an indistinct ghostly landscape. I had a queer fancy then that I was being inexorably drawn into this country, that my approach had been anticipated in some ages-old scheme, that I was no longer in control of my life, of my movements.

We were rounding other sharp curves in our ascent again, but this time there was no steep valley below; it was obscured in fog. There was an unearthly quality to this part of the train ride; it seemed as though we were scaling the clouds. On a clear day the views must be spectacular, if somewhat overwhelming.

Just then the steam whistle gave another shriek and we were enveloped in blackness. A soft cry escaped my lips before I realized that we were merely in a tunnel. And I felt a large hand take my own in its cool, hard grip, giving it a slight squeeze.

"We'll soon be out of this," came a low, reassuring voice in the darkness, and my momentary agitation subsided. When we did emerge from the tunnel I removed my hand from his, not knowing where to look.

"At least you've got some color back in your face now," he observed, amused. "You were looking very pale before."

"I . . . I think we should wake Emeline now," I said feebly, "if we are nearly there."

"By all means," he agreed, his eyebrow cocked, and I turned to her in relief.

When the conductor called out, "Nightshade Notch," I thought how appropriate its name was. Standing on the platform with Drake and Emeline, I saw the mountains surging on both sides, astonishing in their size and grandeur. From the train one did not have the same impression of their timelessness. Swathed in mist, the Notch was a deep, wide crevice between the towering purple-black ridges.

"I'm home," breathed Emeline. "I'm truly home."

"How cool it is," I marveled. The damp air, balsam-scented,

blew about us.

The train had not yet pulled away from the stop. Someone else was disembarking, and I realized it was the blond man and his wife. He was assisting her down the steps.

"Are you bound for the Crystal Hills Hotel?" Drake called out.

"That is our destination. Do you know it, sir? I believe the brochure stated a carriage was sent to meet every train."

"The carriage is over there," answered Drake. "We are going very near there ourselves. The driver will return for your bags and trunks."

"I hope it is not an open carriage," said the woman. "The rain is ruining my bonnet."

Drake said nothing, moving ahead of us to the carriage (which was indeed closed). His limp was not so nearly pronounced, though he moved rather stiffly; the forced immobility on the train must have done him some good.

The elderly driver took off his hat and said, "Welcome home, Mr. Drake."

"Thank you, Jim."

"What about me, Jim?" asked Emeline.

"You too, little lady," he said, grinning. "Though you ain't so little any more."

"No, I'm fourteen now, and five-feet-five-and-a-half inches tall," she stated before climbing into the carriage. I got in beside her.

The stocky man supported his wife as she stepped in, taking a place beside her, across from us. Then Drake climbed in with a little difficulty, and I moved closer to Emeline to make room for him.

"I am Horatio Aldridge," said the man, "and this is Mrs. Aldridge."

"How do you do?" said Drake to Mrs. Aldridge, who acknowledged his greeting with a slight incline of her head. "May I present my niece, Miss Emeline Curtis, and her tutor, Miss Teresa Hawthorne. And I am Drake Curtis."

"The hotel belongs to you, sir?"

"To me and to my elder brother," said Drake in unmistakably dry tones.

79

"I'm pleased to make your acquaintance, sir. Your hotel was recommended to us by friends who passed a most pleasant stay there some years ago. And the brochure was impressive as well."

"I hope you and Mrs. Aldridge will find it to your liking," replied Drake.

"The name certainly did nothing to recommend itself to me," said Mrs. Aldridge. "Nightshade Notch. How terribly dreary it sounds."

"There's a legend that an Indian girl poisoned her lover when she discovered he'd been untrue to her," said Drake deliberately. "She is said to have ground the leaves of the jimsonweed which grows at the foot of the mountains, and put them in his food."

"Really, Mr. Curtis, what a tale to relate," she said coldly. "I wonder you do not change the name." She wrapped her shawl more tightly about her.

"Nonsense. Most picturesque," declared her husband, rubbing his hands together. "That's why one comes to a place like this, after all. Touch of local color. Nothing like this to be found in New York."

Beside me Drake stiffened. "You come from New York?"

"We do, sir. I am a publisher there. But taking a much-needed vacation, eh, my dear?" He chuckled. "Mrs. Aldridge is always complaining that I don't take her anywhere."

"And you wouldn't have if Dr. Bright hadn't insisted," his wife snapped, her mouth tightening.

"I hope the hotel meets with your approval then," said Drake, sounding as though this were a near impossibility, which undoubtedly it was.

Emeline had been gazing out the window, not that she could see much in the deepening twilight. But then she cried, "There it is!" She turned to me. "See, we're going up the drive now, Teresa. If it were daylight you could see everything clearly."

Looking past her through the window splattered with raindrops, I saw we were approaching a very large edifice, four or five stories in height with long, low wings reaching out on either side. It shimmered white in the drenched, smoky dusk, and tiny lights glimmered from within.

80

"It looks just the same from here, Uncle Drake," said Emeline.

"That's a welcome sight indeed," said Mr. Horatio Aldridge, and then we had stopped under the domed entrance.

A man in a butler's suit came out to open the carriage door. "Good evening, sir, madam, miss."

"This is Mr. and Mrs. Aldridge," said Drake. "See to them, will you?"

"Yes, Mr. Curtis. We have been expecting the lady and gentleman. The rain caused a delay, of course. If you'll just step down, Mrs. Aldridge, I'll escort you inside."

"We'll meet again, sir," said Mr. Aldridge to Drake. "Good evening, ladies," he said, smiling at Emeline and me. Then the three of us were alone once again.

Emeline looked puzzled. "Where's Burrows? He's always received the guests for as long as I can remember. Is he ill?"

Drake tapped the roof with his cane and the horses moved forward again. "He's gone," he said shortly.

"You mean—he has left for good?" asked Emeline. "Why? I can't imagine the hotel without him."

"He has gone to work at the Crawford House in Crawford Notch," said Drake. "But I am hopeful that he may come back to work for us."

I sensed Emeline's puzzled dismay, but something in her uncle's voice kept her from pursuing the subject. She did ask, though, hesitatingly, "Are . . . are any of the other employees gone as well?"

"A number of them, I'm afraid. The head chef had been replaced by an incompetent fool. Getting rid of him was one of the first things I did on my return. The food he was preparing was . . . well, it left much to be desired. I hired another in Boston, an Italian man. Your mother protested at first, but even she has to admit now how greatly the quality of the meals has improved in the last month. Just because the former idiot had a French name—undoubtedly a pretense anyway—your mother and father assumed he could cook."

The carriage was stopping again, but by then the night had fully descended and I could make out nothing through the window. The driver opened the door and Emeline jumped

81

down. "Charlotte!" I heard her call, running up the steps.

"Here we are finally, Miss Hawthorne," said Drake. "I trust the journey was not too taxing on you today."

Remembering the ride through the tunnel, I blushed in the darkness. "No, not at all," I tried to say firmly. "But I am relieved it's at an end. Thank you, Mr. Curtis, for offering me the job here."

"You have nothing to thank me for," he answered bluntly. "Doubtless quite the reverse, as you're bound to find out for yourself."

Naturally I was at a loss for words; I hurriedly got out of the carriage.

I could get little impression of the house except that it looked substantial and seemed to be constructed of stone and shingles. The front door was standing open, and so I went up the stone steps. Behind me I heard Drake swear softly as he stepped down from the carriage.

A woman came to the entrance just then, saying, "Welcome, Miss Hawthorne. What a dreadful long journey you've had. And in such weather! You must be so tired. I've told Emeline dinner will be served shortly. I am Charlotte Conway."

"How do you do, Miss Conway?" She took my hand in hers. She was fine-boned and looked to be in her late sixties. The expression on her sweet face was kind and welcoming.

"Call me Charlotte, my dear. The rest of the family do. And may I call you Teresa? Such a lovely name—it quite suits you. It's a shame you had to arrive at the Notch on a night such as this—you must think it very gloomy here. Emeline, take Teresa to her room. Good evening, Drake. How are you feeling?"

"I'll be all the better after a large brandy," he said, but his voice was mild.

"There's a fire in the library as it's so damp and cool. Dinner will be ready within the hour."

We were all standing in the front hall, which reminded me of a baronial hall one finds in old manor houses and castles in England. Near to the high ceiling hung heads of deer and even bears; below them the walls were paneled. The floor was flagged stone, covered in places by Oriental rugs.

"You are looking at Drake's father's collection," observed

Charlotte. "He was a great hunter, and when he opened the Crystal Hills thirty years ago, he used to take out hunting parties. Emeline's father does so still from time to time."

A gallery ran along the upper walls. I followed Emeline up the broad staircase which led to the gallery. I heard Charlotte ask, "Well, what did the bankers say?" but Emeline was already turning off the landing to go down a long hallway.

"Your room is down here," said Emeline. "My parents and I live on the opposite corridor off the gallery, but Charlotte and Drake have their rooms along here as well. Though she said Drake has been using one of the downstairs rooms because of his leg."

She paused outside one of the doors and opened it. I walked into a pleasant room furnished with honeyed oak pieces. There was an Eastlake bed against one wall, its headboard tall and whimsically carved. There was an old-fashioned marble-top table, the cabriole legs decorated with bunches of grapes, leaves, and flowers. Two arched mullioned windows framed the black night.

"This is one of our guest rooms, but we never have guests. My father used to say there were enough of them at the hotel. Do you like it?"

"Very much, Emeline. Charlotte is most gracious."

"I'll come and get you for dinner. Charlotte said we just have time for a bath."

"All right."

To my surprise I found an enameled cast-iron tub in the water closet, fitted with pipes which ran along the wall. I had not expected to find both hot and cold running water so far from a town of any size, but I had underestimated the conditions the Curtis family lived in. There were gaslights on the walls encased in frosted globes.

The water was wonderfully soothing to my cramped limbs, and the white towels ample and fluffy. Clad in a clean camisole and pair of pantalettes, I unpacked the rest of my things, hanging my gowns in the large wardrobe. I put on a lavender cotton gown with ruffled yoke, long sleeves, and a high frilled collar, and redid my hair, taking it out of the heavy braid and pinning it up.

Emeline came soon after; she wore a white batiste blouse, its short sleeves delicately embroidered, with a plum-colored skirt. A black velvet ribbon was tied in her hair. We went downstairs to the dining room, which was just off the front hall. A maid was pouring wine into cut-crystal glasses.

"How pretty you both look," said Charlotte, smiling. "It will be nice for Drake and me to have some company. We've missed you, Emeline. And now that Miss Hawthorne—Teresa—has come as well, we will be quite jolly."

Casting a glance at Drake brooding at the head of the table, I thought he looked anything but jolly. Charlotte gestured for me to sit at Drake's right while Emeline pulled out a chair across from me.

"Have you heard from Papa and Mamma?" asked Emeline.

Charlotte exchanged quick looks with Drake. "Not lately, I'm afraid. We did have the address of their hotel in Boston, but they seem to have left there for the time being. I did write to them yesterday, explaining that you were coming home and Drake had gone to fetch you."

Emeline flushed. "Oh, Charlotte, I'm so sorry about being expelled. The whole thing was an awful accident. I . . . I started a fire in the carriage house next to the school while I was looking for . . . something." Her voice had dropped.

"A fire? Emeline! Was anyone hurt?"

"No, that was the only good part of it. The horses were all right too, just scared to death. As I was. But Miss Winslow was so furious with me that she expelled me on the spot."

"Well, Emeline, I can't say I'm at all sorry that you've come back, and so as long as there was no terrible damage we don't need to go into this again. Although your parents will likely want all the details. But don't worry. Now Teresa, may I offer you some of this duckling? It's prepared a special way, with raspberry liqueur."

Throughout the meal she and Emeline kept up a flow of pleasant conversation while Drake sat silently at the head of the table.

"Charlotte, I almost forgot," said Emeline at one point. "Burrows is gone, did you know?"

Charlotte looked swiftly across at Drake before turning to

Emeline. "Yes, dear, I did know," she said softly.

"But why? I can't believe he left us! He was so attached to the hotel, to Grandmother and Grandfather. And Uncle Drake says there are other changes too. I don't understand—why have things changed?"

"I'm afraid we haven't quite as many guests coming to stay lately," said Charlotte. "But your uncle is working very hard to fix that. Now finish your dinner, dear, before it gets cold. And don't worry your uncle with questions tonight."

Drake had changed his travel suit for an evening suit of black, the starched white collar setting off his dark, handsome face. He seemed to be miles away, a grim look to his face. I found it difficult to reconcile this forbidding man with the one who had teasingly held my hand in the railcar.

"Please tell someone to ready my old room," he said abruptly. "I'm moving back upstairs tonight."

Charlotte looked concerned. "Do you think you should, Drake? Climbing those stairs—your leg—"

"Forget my leg," he said, cutting in. "It's well enough."

Charlotte looked as though she would have liked to say more, but tactfully refrained from doing so. "Very well, Drake. You know best."

By the time dinner was over, Emeline and I were yawning frequently. Charlotte waved us up to bed while Drake stayed at the table with his after-dinner port. We said good night and I thanked her for the delicious dinner.

That night in my room I listened to the rain slashing at the Gothic windows, the wind whistling around the house. Just as I was on the verge of falling asleep, there came the sound of someone moving down the hall, slow footsteps punctuated by rhythmic taps. I realized it was Major Drake Curtis, veteran of the war with Spain, limping down the corridor, assisted by his cane now that there was no one to watch. A door creaked opened and shut, and then there was only the rain-brittle silence.

Chapter Five

Standing at the arched window the following morning, I peered through the leaded panes at a breathtaking sight. Over the pinnacles of the perfectly symmetrical fir trees, the Crystal Hills Hotel glimmered frosty-white against the blue-green backdrop of the lofty highlands. It was large and rambling with a cherry-red roof, a number of towers and turrets, and a wide, encircling veranda. With the rows and rows of small windows it looked to have a great many rooms. Above the swelling hills the sky was a brilliant blue, cloudless. As I opened the casement window, a fresh gust of pine-scented air poured into the room, pleasantly cool.

Reluctantly moving away from the idyllic view, I began to get ready for the day, taking my clothes from the wardrobe. I put on a pale blue blouse with a sailor collar and a navy blue skirt, laced up my black boots, and arranged my hair in one long braid down my back. I did not know what time it was, and had no wish to make a poor impression by arriving late at breakfast. As it happened, Charlotte was down before me, drinking her second cup of coffee, but Emeline did not come to the dining room until I had nearly finished eating. The dishes of food were set on the sideboard along with silver pots of coffee and tea, cream and sugar.

"I want to go over to the hotel after breakfast," she said. "You'll come with me, won't you, Teresa? I want to show you everything."

"Of course I'll come. But then I think we should decide

upon a routine for your studies."

"Why don't the two of you have a holiday for the time being?" suggested Charlotte. "After all, neither of you have had much of a summer from the sound of it. There's plenty of time for you to work, after all."

"Oh, let's!" Emeline exclaimed. "Miss Winslow made us continue some of our lessons all these last weeks when everyone else was having fun. Teresa needs some fun as well. What I'd really like to do soon is go on an excursion." She frowned. "We do still have them, don't we?"

"Oh, yes, your uncle reinstated the day trips earlier in the season. He has insisted that he is well enough to conduct them himself, and you know how stubborn he is. Although I think he overtaxes his leg at times. But he has been so determined to not give into . . . and he is desperately trying to build back some of the business we have lost."

"But why have we lost it at all?" persisted Emeline.

Charlotte hesitated. "Well, there are other hotels, you know," she said vaguely, turning up the palm of her hand. "And the competition between them is fierce."

"But the Crystal Hills was always one of the most popular!"

"Yes, Emeline, but times change," replied Charlotte, and this time there was a trace of annoyance in her voice. "Since you first went to school the hotel has not been attracting enough visitors to cover our expenses. With Drake away in Cuba and then in the hospital . . . last fall some of the staff left—we could not keep all of them on at the time—and when we opened again in April only a few of them returned. I never mentioned any of this in my letters to you because we hoped it a temporary thing. And I'm certain that's all it is even now. Our reservations were up a little this month from the last, and August does not look too bad. And Drake is hoping that the fall will be our best season this year. More and more people are coming to watch the leaves change, you know. It's becoming quite fashionable. And Drake has some other ideas about improving the hotel—putting in electricity, for one."

"What's wrong with his leg, exactly?" asked Emeline.

Charlotte sighed. "It was injured severely on the battlefield. A bullet fractured the bone and it was not set properly when

87

finally it was tended to. Then he was in the hospital for five months afterwards. But his condition has improved greatly since he came home in December. He is very determined, you know. Certain days it plagues him more than others, and there are days when he assures me he scarcely notices it. And those days are becoming more frequent, I am relieved to say. I was very concerned at one time."

"I hate to think the hotel is doing poorly," said Emeline single-mindedly.

"I'm confident we will come about again," said Charlotte. "Your grandparents devoted their lives to making the Crystal Hills Hotel one of the finest ones in the Northeast, and Drake is made of the same stuff."

"He shouldn't have gone off to war," said Emeline severely. "Why in the world did he volunteer anyway? It sounds to me as though all this is his fault for leaving."

"You mustn't talk that way, Emeline," Charlotte said sharply. "Your uncle did what he thought he had to do, and it is not appropriate for you to question the actions of adults. There are . . . circumstances of which you know nothing."

"I was just wondering what Grandmother would say," said Emeline in sullen tones. "She would be so disappointed if she knew the hotel was no longer the same."

"Your grandmother was not one to waste time in idle disappointment. She would have been doing everything in her power to improve matters, just as Drake is." She turned to me. "You must have Emeline bring you to my room soon, Teresa. I have a collection of scrapbooks filled with old photographs of the hotel, its guests, and, of course, Emeline's grandparents, Madeline and Theodore Curtis."

"I should like to see them very much," I told her.

"Madeline was my closest friend. We worked together. I did her correspondence and other duties she did not have time for because the managing of the hotel kept her so busy. There's a marvelous portrait of her hanging in the hotel lobby. Emeline will show you, if you're going there. Theodore commissioned John Singer Sargent to paint it."

"Are you ready, Teresa? We could go over now," Emeline said eagerly.

And so, a short while later, the two of us were walking through the stretch of woods which separated the house from the hotel. Spiky spruce needles carpeted the forest floor amid splashes of bright green moss, tree roots, and gray stones. The woods thinned out ahead with only clusters of slender birches and lichen-mottled erratic boulders to mar the sweeping expanse of grassy lawn.

We rounded the side of the hotel. Above the doors and windows were moldings of garlands and wreaths; creeping green vines clung to the stone foundation. Window boxes filled with red geraniums hung from the porch, and a line of white wicker chairs and occasional tables were positioned to take in the stunning view of the surrounding mountains. But most sat empty, forlorn.

"I'll show you my favorite area of the porch," said Emeline, and I followed her down the long porch and around to a circular veranda on the opposite side of the hotel from the house.

"We're under the East Rotunda here," she said. More wicker chairs were set up there between white Chinese planters; the wooden floor was a glossy gray. The red blossoms stirred in the breeze, gay splashes of color against the white columns.

"It's beautiful, Emeline," I said. "The mountains are just as you described them."

The view was even more impressive from the rear porch of the hotel. It took my breath away. The green bank sloped sharply downward to another copse of birch trees on the back lawn. There were several gazebos with red pagoda roofs and Chinese latticework connected by walkways of flagged stone; just beyond was a small arched stone bridge over a placid brook. But it was the mountains in the distance which commanded the attention. Beyond the flat tree-tufted acres spreading far back from the hotel's cultivated lawns and gardens, they rose, starkly and steeply.

"That's Mt. Washington," said Emeline, "the highest one of all. Many of them are named for Presidents—they call them the Presidential Range."

The lower slopes were thick with sugar maples, beeches,

aspens, and silver birches. Gradually the domed tops of the deciduous trees gave way to a solid stand of steeplelike evergreens. Higher up, the crowding columns became shorter and more gnarled until only the blue-hued *krumholz*, the "crooked wood," survived. Far above the timberline, ledges of sculpted granite scaled to the summits, bare and windswept.

"Sometimes in the summer you can still see snow up there," said Emeline, "when you can see the top at all. Often it's covered by clouds."

"Is that a railway going straight up Mt. Washington?" I asked, amazed.

She nodded. "The cog railway. It goes all the way to the top. Sometimes parties of guests go up—it takes a long time because the train moves so slowly. When the weather is fine you can see as far as New York, Vermont, and even the Atlantic Ocean."

"It must be an incredibly steep grade," I said.

"Yes, it is. A lot of people don't like it," she said. "Let's go inside."

Above the great door leading to the lobby was a fan-shaped mullioned window, and once inside I saw rectangular stained-glass windows set high in the walls. The lobby was elaborately papered in a coral and blue William Morris print lightened by a row of support columns painted white. Groups of chairs upholstered in the colors of the wallpaper were placed about the spacious room. Glass chandeliers hung from the ceiling. But in odd contrast to the splendor the room wore a forsaken air. It was not a bustling place, humming with voices; few of the chairs were occupied, few men paced, few women glided about on the plush blue carpet. I saw Emeline taking in the vacant sofas, the untouched periodicals, a look of baffled dismay on her face.

"Why don't you show me your grandmother's portrait?" I asked her. "The one by Sargent. Did he stay here at the hotel?"

She nodded, smiling, but her face still held traces of her perplexed and disheartened feelings. She led me over to the staircase, and we stood at the bottom looking up to the landing where a large oil painting was secured to the wall. This then was Madeline Curtis, chatelaine of the Crystal Hills Hotel. The picture showed an arresting woman of middle age, her black gown cut daringly low to reveal her magnificent bust and shoulders. She had keen blue eyes and arched brows so like Drake's and a great deal of decision in her face. From the portrait I gleaned an impression of the commanding presence she must have had; she looked both regal and fascinating.

"I remember her very well, you know, although Charlotte doesn't see how I'm able to since I was still a little girl when she died. But she would take me walking with her about the grounds. I had to run fast to keep up with her, but I didn't mind. She seemed very tall, nearly as tall as Papa and Drake, and she was always beautifully dressed even on our treks through the woods. And she would speak to people we passed, recalling their names. I once asked her how on earth she remembered the names of the guests, and could always place the names with the right faces. She said it was like a game she played, testing herself. It kept her mind quick and vigorous. Her hair wasn't black any longer but I didn't think of her as old."

"She must have been quite remarkable."

"She was. Everyone adored her. She was like a queen," Emeline said gravely, "and the hotel was her castle. Grandfather built it, but Charlotte always says it was Grandmother who made it the success it was. Would you like to see the dining room? One evening we can eat there rather than at the house, perhaps after my parents return. It's fun to have two places to choose from, isn't it? We can find out what our cook's going to serve and see if we'd rather eat at the hotel for dinner."

I smiled at her, glad she seemed to be regaining her spirits. In contrast to the lobby, the dining room was light and airy, with French doors framing the view of Mt. Washington. The walls were painted a delicate peach with white trim, and there the Grecian columns which accented the room were slender.

Emeline was frowning again. "Not many of the tables are set," she observed in rueful tones.

"Perhaps the staff hasn't finished setting up for lunch," I pointed out, but we both knew there was an empty comfort in my words.

91

I tried again. "Why don't you show me the ballroom?"

Retracing our steps under the archway to the lobby, we strolled through a pair of French doors which led to the east wing. Emeline opened a set of doors on the right, and we stood on the threshold of a beautiful, stately room. Sunbeams slanted through the leaded panes scattering diamonds on the parquet floor. The walls were painted a light blue; cherubs frolicked in the clouds on the ceiling frescoes surrounding a pair of classical languishing lovers.

"I'm not allowed to attend the balls, you know," Emeline said, "or I didn't use to be. But once in a while I would slip in without Mamma noticing. Father never minded, but Charlotte would find my room empty and guess I was here. She would come to fetch me, but for a time I would watch the dancers. And then when we got back to the house, I made Charlotte waltz with me. The music was always so lovely. The windows would be open and the music would drift to the house. I wonder when the next ball will be. Perhaps I'll be allowed to attend it if you are with me."

She showed me the other first-floor rooms as well—the library, the billiards room, and several private parlors, one reserved for ladies only. Later we wandered down to the lower level. There were the services provided by the hotel—shops, a post office, a telegraph office. We walked the length of the brick-sided corridor, peeking into the rooms for gentlemen—smoking parlors, game rooms set up for chess, checkers, backgammon, and cards, and a cavernlike pub. We spied a few elderly gentlemen smoking pipes or drinking a morning sherry, but the rooms were, for the most part, unoccupied.

"Well, I suppose I've showed you everything, except for the kitchen and employees' wing. And the guests' bedrooms, of course, but we can't very well peer into those. I guess we could look in the rooms not occupied but . . ."

"But we can't be certain which those are. We don't want to disturb anyone, especially Mrs. Aldridge. We'd never hear the end of it!" We had also succeeded in avoiding Emeline's uncle, and I hoped we might leave the hotel without coming across him. Though naturally I did not say this. "Shall we go back to the house?"

"No, not yet. I've saved the best for last," she said.

"And what is that?"

"Oh, I can't tell you. It wouldn't be any fun if I told you. You must see for yourself. Come on, we can go out this way— there's a back porch on this level just under the main one."

We went outside, turning down the lower porch of the east wing to the side lawn. Emeline kept looking over her shoulder at me, a gleam in her eyes, barely suppressed excitement on her face.

"Where are you taking me?" I asked as we entered a dense stretch of woods. The air was fragrant; long coppery needles cushioned the path. Miniature delicate pine trees resembled feathery ferns. We passed a speckled granite boulder, creased and pocked with age, over which spanned an octopuslike tree trunk, the tough exposed roots like grasping arms.

"I'll bet you've never seen anything like I'm going to show you," said Emeline rather smugly.

"You look like the cat that ate the canary," I said in mild irritation. "What is all this mystery?"

"We're almost there now."

The path led us up the slope of a hill. When we reached the top, the woods halted abruptly to reveal a large clearing. Emerging from the trees, we stood gazing on a peculiar sight.

"What on earth is this?" I asked, and my voice sounded faint, breathless.

"My grandmother and I used to walk here and she would play hide-and-seek with me. It was the best place ever for hide-and-seek. The Site of Stones, we've always called it."

Across the clearing sprawled a complex of low stone walls, large stone chambers, tall monoliths, and huge triangular slabs, all formed of gray granite. Something stirred within me, and then was still.

"Come, I'll show you about."

I was oddly reluctant to go any nearer, but there was really nothing to occasion such disquiet. Golden sunlight poured into the clearing; in the grass crickets chirped, locusts hummed. It was a peaceful place, I told myself. There was nothing in the least sinister about it.

We walked about, the heels of our boots scraping on the

stony surface. There were massive, primitively fashioned tables beside the beehivelike chambers which burrowed into the hill. At four points outside the complex, tall pointed stones had been placed in a curiously precise manner.

"Who built this place?" I asked haltingly.

"The Indians are said to have held ceremonies here, before the coming of the early settlers," said Emeline. "The local people who moved into the Notch thought that this was where the Indians had services to mourn their dead, and perhaps even buried their leaders here. There's a superstition about the place. Charlotte told me my grandfather was warned not to build the hotel too close to the Site of Stones, to select another piece of property. People said there was a curse on the area."

"What sort of a curse?" I asked slowly, my attention caught and held by a gigantic triangular slab lying flat, its rim grooved all the way around.

"Oh, that bad luck will eventually come to anyone who tries to live nearby," said Emeline airily. "Of course that's nonsense. My family's lived here for nearly thirty years and we've never been bothered in the least by a curse. Come on, I'll show you something."

She led me over to the grooved triangular slab of granite, saying, "Now stay right here," grinning again mysteriously. I watched her move down some steps and around a bend out of sight.

I was finding this secretive amusement of hers more irritating than endearing at that point, suppressing as I was an increasing desire to leave this place. Glancing about, I saw several smaller stone chambers which resembled primitive dwellings or storage structures. In each the dark opening yawned, black as coal and vaguely menacing. "Let's go, Emeline," I called out.

"Go? You must not go! Oh, no, not yet," came a hollow voice just at my feet.

I gasped, looking down at the slab of granite. It had sounded as though the grooved table itself had been speaking. There came a breathy giggle, also seemingly from the piece of stone, and I said sharply, "Emeline, where are you?"

I heard a shuffling and then her shoes clicking on the stone

94

steps. "Here I am," she said, coming into view again. "What did you think of the Oracle?"

"Is that what you call it?" I was conscious of a relief out of proportion with the event. "It did sound as though the table itself were speaking," I admitted shakily.

"There's a niche just under the table where one can crawl into, and speak through the speaking tube. It carries one's voice to the table above. My grandmother and I used to play here. She'd sit there and I'd talk to her and she'd pretend to be frightened."

"What an odd place this is," I said. "You were right—I've never seen anything like it before."

She nodded. "I've always loved to play here. I used to run away from my governess and come here. Charlotte always worried that I'd get hurt somehow—you know, fall and sprain my ankle or even break a leg, or hit my head. Adults always think something like that will happen."

"Some of the structures are probably precarious," I said. "After all, the stones are just placed together to form walls and chambers; they could easily be dislodged."

She rolled her eyes as though she had not expected me to sound like Charlotte. "I used to pretend I was an Indian wife cooking supper for her warrior husband. He'd be hunting or fighting somewhere and I'd be waiting for him at home. The day after a hard rain was always good because the ground would still be muddy and I'd pretend the mud was gravy for the venison."

I did not think I could have played here as a child so innocently and gleefully as Emeline had done. It evoked a strange, inexplicable feeling of unease in me, of apprehension. But I was at a loss to understand it. Pine trees loomed outside the stone walls, like lofty sentinels guarding a secretive place. They, like the site itself, had stood for many years.

Emeline was happily humming, kicking at the debris of leaves and stones, peering into the chambers. I wanted to insist we go, but this was one of her old haunts, after all, and I felt selfish in tearing her away from it. So I became occupied with pinning my hat more securely to my head, and then retying the sailor knot on the collar of my blouse.

But gradually my breathing and heartbeat quickened; my face grew flushed and moist. I became conscious of other sounds besides the noises Emeline was making, and then those sounds grew in intensity until Emeline's voice was drowned out and I heard nothing but a rumbling which in a state of rising panic I identified as chanting, many voices chanting the same indistinguishable words. Gone was the buzzing of the insects, gone was the flurry of the wind in the leaves. Emeline was looking at me; I watched in horror as her mouth moved but her words did not reach me; I could hear nothing of what she said.

Whirling about, I searched for the source of the chanting sounds, but there was no one else about. We were alone there in the sun-dappled clearing, alone with the Stones. My whole body trembled; I felt consumed with terror, convinced that a horrible evil was emanating from the site, an evil I had to escape. The chanting made an overwhelming din in my ears; desperately I clapped my hands over my ears.

I had to get away. I tried to call out to Emeline, but I could not hear my own voice, and so I had no idea whether she heard me or not. Jerkily, stiffly I took a few steps, feeling as I did that something pulled me back, drew me, held me. And then I flung myself forward, wildly lunging into the woods, down the mossy path, away from that dreadful clutching sensation which had threatened to propel me back to the center of the clearing, to the enormous grooved table. I had realized in a heart-stopping flash that it was the table, the rimmed triangular slab, which lured me, and the ghastly, rumbling, eager chanting also issued from around its boundaries.

Fleeing through the woods down the hillside I felt branches snag at my skirts; I felt twigs snap in my face; I felt the soft leather of my boots scuff against rocks and roots. But I cared nothing for any of this. Only one thing motivated me—to put as much distance between myself and that place, that roar, as I could. And gradually I realized that the sounds had died away. I slowed my pace, taking great gasping breaths, and suddenly my fear was gone as though it had never been. It had been completely snuffed, like a candle going out.

Confused, because my body still reacted to the effects of the terror, I stopped in my tracks and looked back up the hill. I could see nothing of the Stones, but Emeline was hurrying down after me, my hat in her hand.

"What's wrong, Teresa?" she asked as she reached me. "I thought you were going to faint or something back there, and then you were off running down the hill. Are you ill?"

Dazed, I shook my head, not knowing how to respond to her.

"Are you all right?" Her eyes were wide, her face troubled. "What is wrong?"

"It was just . . . I felt . . . did you hear anything . . . up there?"

"No. No one ever comes up there, you know. It's a lonely place."

"It is . . . lonely," I said shakily. "I can't imagine why I thought I heard . . . voices."

"I don't see how you could have, unless you're like Joan of Arc," she said, smiling. "You're not going a little crazy, are you?"

I forced myself to smile. "I hope not."

She took my arm solicitously. "You're just overtired from the last few days, that's all. Come on, we'll go back to the house."

She was right. I was overtired and strained from the journey, from the rapid changes which had taken place in the last few days. Overtired and suggestible. Had I not had foolish fancies on the train ride yesterday, that the mountains were drawing me in, never to release me, and ridiculous things like that? My wild imagination again. I had kept it tightly reined at the Academy, but since I had left, it had been breaking its boundaries as I had broken the bonds I had with Portsmouth.

I had a sudden reassuring glimpse of the hotel shimmering like a white jewel against the spruce-blue mountains, and then we were out of the crowding columns of the woods and again on the grassy lawn near the East Rotunda.

We walked across the lawn to the drive, our footsteps crunching on the gravel. As we passed the front porch, I glanced up to see Drake Curtis standing there, watching us. He wore a wheat-colored suit which contrasted with his dark coloring.

"Where have you been, Emeline? Miss Hawthorne looks exhausted. She doesn't have to be shown everything in one morning, you know."

"I know," she agreed sheepishly. "I've tired her out. We looked all about the hotel, and then I took her up to the Site of Stones."

To my surprise his face darkened and his black brows drew together. "Why on earth did you go there?" he asked roughly. "Surely Miss Hawthorne is not interested in that pile of rubble, and you are too old to play there!"

"Oh, but she was, Uncle Drake. That is, until she got all pale and frightened-looking, and took off down the hill."

I frowned at her, annoyed that she had so exposed me, while Drake's intent gaze was leveled at me, his eyes narrowing. I did not understand his expression.

"Stay away from that place, both of you!" he said savagely while we stood gaping at him.

"But why?" asked Emeline before I could gesture that she say no more.

"Because I told you to," he said, his voice curt with barely suppressed rage and something else I could not identify. Then he turned abruptly and reentered the hotel, leaning on his cane.

"Well, what's the matter with him? I don't have to do what he says—he's not my father."

"I daresay he is afraid you might hurt yourself, as Charlotte is," I said without conviction.

"Oh, pooh—he's just feeling bad-tempered, I expect, because of his leg wound. The less we see of him the better."

But he had greeted us pleasantly enough, I thought. It was not until after Emeline had mentioned the Stones that that dark, grim look had come over his face and his manner had swiftly altered.

We ate lunch with Charlotte, and I was feeling quite myself again. When she suggested we come to her room later in the afternoon to see her collection of scrapbooks, I was happy to agree.

"Madeline's room was that one, just across from mine," she said when Emeline and I knocked at her door. "And

Theodore's was further down. Would you like to see her room?"

I said I would, and so Emeline opened the door to her grandmother's old room. The first thing I noticed were the enormous mullioned windows extending most of the length of the wall. There was a cushioned window seat below them. Through the panes, the sun spilled across the Oriental rug, striking the cut-glass lamps and sending tiny rainbows to quiver on the opposite wall. The view from those windows was breathtaking. I was not surprised to see that it was of the hotel, but this view was subtly different from my own. Here the Crystal Hills was not glimpsed amidst the pinnacles of the fir trees; instead it was unobscured, glowing in the afternoon sun.

"As you can tell, this room has the best view of the hotel," said Charlotte. "When Theodore built the house, she chose this room just to the side of the woods so she could see the place clearly. She said she wanted it to be the first thing she saw in the morning."

"When the hotel was first constructed, Grandmother and Grandfather lived there," said Emeline.

"At the hotel?" I asked.

"Yes, with Aaron and Drake, who were boys," said Charlotte. "But after several years they decided to build their own house. Theodore wanted more privacy, although Madeline probably would have been just as happy to continue living at the Crystal Hills. They had their own wing, of course. I came shortly after the house was completed." She turned to Emeline. "By then your father had been sent away to school, but Drake still had a governess, the daughter of one of your grandfather's business acquaintances."

"And you came here to live," I said to Charlotte.

"Yes. The hotel was beginning to become famous by then, and that was due to a great part to your grandmother, Emeline. She spent many hours contriving various entertainments for the guests that the other hotels did not offer at the time. It was she who hired the hotel's own orchestra and chorus, and she who planned the lavish picnics and elaborate balls which became quickly associated with the name Crystal Hills. She even organized the men into teams to play games against male

99

guests at other hotels. She devised activities for children as well, such as treasure hunts and costume parties. She had the rooms installed with hot running water, proper bathrooms, any new improvements she could think of."

"Did Grandfather object to her ideas ever?" asked Emeline.

Charlotte shook her head. "Some men would have resented or deplored their wives taking such a role in their business venture, but your grandfather realized the hotel was as successful as it was because of your grandmother. She even did the hiring of the employees—she and I together. He gave her a free hand running the hotel and he dealt with the financial side of things. And then they would consult one another on many matters."

"Mamma has never been like that, has she? I mean, she always let Uncle Drake and Papa do everything."

"No, your mother has rarely become involved in the managing of the hotel. Your grandmother was unique."

"Perhaps Mamma feels she can't do things half as well as Grandmother did, so she just doesn't try," said Emeline thoughtfully. "But I want to help Papa and Uncle Drake when I'm older. I want to learn all about running a grand hotel."

"Your grandmother would be very proud to hear you say that," said Charlotte with a smile.

"May we look at the earliest pictures—when Grandmother and Grandfather were young?" asked Emeline. "I love to see her old-fashioned gowns with the bustles in the back."

We went out of Madeline's light-spattered room and into Charlotte's. As her room was on the back of the house, there was no view of the hotel. The wall of woods rose outside her window, casting long, deepening shadows across the room. There was a sitting area in front of the tiled fireplace, and she motioned us to sit down while she reached into a glass-fronted bookcase for some leather-bound albums.

"I've been collecting things for these scrapbooks for years," said Charlotte. "Now let's see, Emeline, you asked for the first ones first."

"It's the brown book, Charlotte," said Emeline.

"Yes, I have it just here." She sat down beside me on the velvet love seat and opened the book across her lap. "Here's a very early photograph of the hotel, just before it opened."

The hotel looked the same but the landscape was different; there were no copses of birch trees or bushes or creeping vines to soften the stark newness of the building.

"And here are Emeline's grandparents." I looked with interest at the tall man in the Panama hat whose face was in shadows, and a younger version of the woman I recognized from the portrait at the hotel; she stood nearly as tall as he.

Charlotte turned the pages while Emeline and I peered over her shoulder at the memorabilia she had so painstakingly collected, sorted, and arranged in the scrapbook. There were programs to various entertainments held at the Crystal Hills and a few from other hotels; there were playfully worded invitations to picnics, and dance cards with a man's name for every dance. There were photographs of lawn parties, of croquet and tennis games, of groups of guests lined up on the porch. Emeline's grandfather was photographed with a hunting party and the deer they had brought back.

We looked through each album while Charlotte reminisced about this or that event. There were a few pictures of Drake and her father as boys which Emeline found highly amusing. In one Drake stood sturdily beside a pretty, delicate-looking young woman—his governess, I presumed. There were some of Charlotte herself with Madeline Curtis, Charlotte appearing stiff and ill at ease before the camera while Madeline, by contrast, wore the air of confidence I assumed was habitual to her.

"I never liked to have my photograph taken," admitted Charlotte, "but Madeline sometimes insisted. See how well she looks—she loved the limelight—whereas I always longed to slip out of the photographer's range.

"One year Madeline directed a play. Well, a tableau, really. They used to be quite popular. It was one of those things with a classical theme—very little dialogue and a lot of posing in different costumes to strike a mood."

"Let's see the album of Papa's and Mamma's wedding," said Emeline.

Charlotte selected another album, this one of claret-colored leather, and opened it. "The wedding was held at the hotel, naturally," said Charlotte. "Although your mother's mother had expected that it would be held in Boston. But Madeline prevailed as she always did. They closed the hotel for a week so the wedding guests could all be accommodated. There were garlands entwined about all the columns and the orchestra sat on the back porch serenading the wedding party on the lawn. Later we moved inside to the ballroom; the dancing went on for hours, until close to dawn. That morning your parents caught the train to New York for their honeymoon."

We studied the photograph of the wedding party. There were Emeline's grandparents; there was Drake looking very young, standing a bit to one side. I was conscious of a slight pang noticing how casually upright he stood, his hand in his pocket. With interest I looked at Emeline's parents. Her father, a number of years older than Drake, was tall as well, but I could see little of what he looked like because his laughing face was turned toward his bride. She wore a wreath of flowers in her hair, and a lace gown with a very long train; she looked beautiful.

"My mother was a guest here, Teresa," said Emeline. "She came with her friend's family to stay one summer and met my father. Isn't that romantic?"

"And they were married the following summer," said Charlotte. "Drake was just seventeen—he was in college. Sadly, Theodore was taken ill some months after with a very bad case of pneumonia; he died from it. Madeline continued to manage the hotel with Drake's help—and your father's, of course."

"And I was born three years later," said Emeline, giggling at her baby picture. Her proud grandmother, now all in black, was holding her. There were also photographs of Emeline at different ages, her hair forced into curls, tied with bows. "How silly I look. I remember I hated that dress, but Mamma made me wear it."

"This was the last picture taken of your grandmother," said Charlotte.

She and Emeline were standing side by side in one of the gazebos on the back lawn. Madeline's hand was resting on the little girl's shoulder. She still wore the black of a widow; her face was more lined, but she stood erect.

"I'd really like to have that picture, Charlotte," said Emeline. "May I please? I'll take good care of it."

"Yes, of course you may, child." She lifted the photograph from the album and handed it to Emeline. I wondered whether Emeline had confessed to Charlotte that she had lost her grandmother's locket. "What did you think of the grounds, Teresa? I assume Emeline showed you all her favorite haunts."

A curious choice of words, I thought, considering the way I had fled wildly away from the Site of Stones. As if they were indeed haunted. "The Notch is very beautiful," I said.

"Oh, you haven't seen the half of it yet," said Emeline. "There's the footbridge, the Crystal Cascade—that's a waterfall—the Basin, the Flume. . . ."

"Geological wonders, all of them," said Charlotte. "There will likely be a party going out to one of them later in the week. I'll ask Drake, and then you and Emeline may accompany them if you wish."

"I took her to see the Stones," said Emeline.

"Now they are something entirely different—man-made, not geological."

"By whom?" I asked.

"That's a mystery, although the general consensus is that they were fashioned by a tribe of Indians many years ago."

"Emeline was telling me some believed there was a—a sort of curse attached to them," I said, trying to keep my voice light.

"Oh, you know how superstitious people can be," said Charlotte. "When the first settlers came to the Notch, discovering that there was a pass through the mountains, and some intrepid souls were willing to brave the severe winters and build homesteads here, one family in particular decided to use some of the stones to build their home. The story goes that during that winter, three of the five members of the family died—by natural causes what with the terrible winters and inadequate shelter, I'm certain—but that spring the father and his only remaining child moved away. Later another young couple took up residence near the site and improved the house the first family had begun. And later they were found frozen to death despite their huge supply of firewood just outside. It's likely they both took ill and died of a fever or something. But gradually the story was put about that the place in the clearing—the Site of Stones—was unlucky, for others were settling into the Notch without undue tragedies and hardships. Or maybe there were just as many hardships in other locations in the Notch, but natural causes were immediately linked to the tragedies. At the Site, it was easy to place a different interpretation on events."

"Exactly what kind of interpretation?" I asked, conscious of a growing fascination and impulse to know all I could about the place.

"Well, someone suggested that long ago Indians had built the area as a ceremonial headquarters, or perhaps a burial ground, and that their spirits—which somehow still lingered there—were angered at the settlers' trespass. People stopped setting up homesteads near there, and the place was left to itself again."

"They even warned Grandfather not to build the hotel too close to the Stones, didn't they, Charlotte?"

Charlotte nodded. "And that was thirty years ago—about seventy years following the first settlements. But the local people had clung to their aversion of the place, handing down the stories to the next generation, with warnings to steer clear of the Stones. Naturally Theodore and Madeline, being sensible people, paid no heed to these warnings and beliefs. They had found what they considered to be the ideal location for their hotel, and the mere fact that several hundred yards away there was this strange grouping of granite walls, huge standing stones, and chambers and tables did not affect their decision to begin to build."

"And evidently there was nothing to the superstition, to the curse, after all," I said, giving a rather forced laugh.

"Of course not," said Charlotte decisively. "The hotel was a success from the first, and continued so through all of Madeline's lifetime and for years afterward. It's only been lately that certain things . . . but that's neither here nor there. One can't always have good fortune, after all. And of course things are bound to get better again." But a degree of agitated uncertainty had crept into her voice, which I was quick to notice, although her words were reassuring and matter-of-fact. And there was a shade of anxiety on her white wrinkled face for a brief moment, but she quickly changed the subject, smiling as she did so.

The three of us ate dinner alone that night as Drake had told Charlotte he would take his dinner at the hotel.

"He's working much too hard," said Charlotte, shaking her head. "He probably won't eat at all—there are so many accounts to settle and things to supervise. He's driving himself very hard these days and he's still not well, not fully recovered."

"Why has Papa left then, if there is so much to do?" asked Emeline, a pucker in her brow.

Charlotte hesitated, looking uncomfortable. "Your mother wanted to get away for a short time, I daresay. And Drake had no real objection to their leaving. In fact, I think he prefers to carry on alone," she said lightly. "Now, Teresa, you must tell me more about your life in Portsmouth. I know that you were employed at Emeline's school."

And so I talked a little about myself, but my mind was elsewhere, hastening on another level. I was wondering at the relationship between the two brothers, Drake and Aaron. It did seem thoughtless, to say the least, for Emeline's father to leave the hotel at the height of the summer season when his brother was recovering from a war injury. But perhaps Drake had urged him to go away, insisting he could carry on alone. I already knew how obstinate Drake was, and how he eschewed any deference to his injury.

And there was not an inordinate amount of guests staying at the hotel. I had noticed that for myself. Yet it was still puzzling. And because he had been unable to locate Emeline's parents at their hotel, he himself had been forced to make the trip to Portsmouth to bring her back from school. Charlotte could not have gone; the trip would have been too much for her, and Drake had had business in Portsmouth. I recalled the forbidding, hard look to his face, his short temper, and wondered at the nature of that business. Charlotte had asked him something about the bankers. That night in the

Rockingham dining room in Portsmouth he had not looked pleased with the outcome of whatever business he had conducted that afternoon. At the time I had assumed his leg to blame for his gruffness, his churlishness, but now I questioned whether he might, after all, have had additional worries to plague him aside from the obvious physical one.

Emeline seemed quite happy to be back at the Notch, and not overly eager to be reunited with her parents. Perhaps she felt apprehensive about their reactions to her being expelled, but I was beginning to deduce it was more likely that she did not feel overly affectionate toward them. Relations with her parents could not have been particularly close, as they had shown by going to Massachusetts on holiday and neglecting to contact their daughter by even so much as a telephone call or a wire.

After dinner we sat in the drawing room. The plum and hunting-green wallpaper was another William Morris print, the overstuffed furniture was arranged with tapestry pillows, and there was a magnificent oil painting of the Notch at sunset above the stone fireplace.

Charlotte occupied herself with some knitting, explaining it helped her arthritic fingers, and Emeline and I played several card games. Later Charlotte suggested Emeline go to bed, and yawning, she agreed. "You're not quite used to the altitude yet. When you come directly from the seacoast to the mountains, it takes some days for your body to adjust to the change."

"I guess I'll go upstairs too," I said.

"If you care to read, there are many books in the library. Help yourself," said Charlotte. "I'm ready for bed as well."

We went upstairs to our rooms. I opened the casement window and breathed in deeply the pine-laden night breeze. It was a clear night, tiny stars pricking the velvety blackness. The wind ruffled the boughs of the trees. I could see a number of lights on at the hotel, but not nearly as many as there were rooms.

Feeling rather keyed-up, I was reluctant to undress and go to bed. Perhaps I was merely overtired, or perhaps I was reacting to the vaguely disturbing undercurrents I was perceiving more and more. I stood by the window a while and then decided to take a bath, hoping it would relax me.

But one half hour later I was still not ready for sleep. Some of my wakefulness was undoubtedly due to the sort of day I had had. At Miss Winslow's Academy I had always fallen into bed and been asleep rapidly because I had worked so hard all day. But now that sort of physical labor was significantly lacking. Not that I was wishing otherwise, but I was not yet used to being on holiday.

Charlotte had suggested I take a book from the library; I realized I should have done so before coming upstairs. But I could just as easily go down to the library and find something to read now. The house was silent; Charlotte and Emeline were doubtless asleep by now, and Charlotte had predicted that Drake would remain at the hotel until very late, perhaps even passing the night there as he did from time to time.

Slipping my dressing gown over my nightgown, I opened the door of my room gingerly and stood listening. Not a sound. The gaslight still glowed faintly along the gallery so I could see my way as I went down the stairs, my slippers silent on the polished wooden steps. I had not been inside the library before, but I knew which room it was. The front hall was in semi-darkness; my shadow loomed before me on the wall and the closed library door.

Turning the brass knob, I pushed open the door. I could barely make out rows of bookshelves on three of the walls, and on the fourth a pair of leaded windows with padded seat beneath. The only light in the room was from the dying fire. I should have brought a candle, I realized, to be able to read the titles of the books before selecting one.

Moving across the room, I was trying to adjust my sight to the gloom when a voice startled me.

"Awake again so late, Miss Hawthorne?"

Whirling around, I saw Drake Curtis lounging on the sofa, a lock of hair falling over his forehead. In the wavering firelight, his face was shadowed, vaguely sinister. I could not read his expression. There was a decanter and an empty glass on the table beside him.

"I—I was just coming to get a book," I said, flustered. "I did not realize anyone was—that is, I'm sorry I disturbed you."

107

"And if you had known I was here, wouldn't you still have come down?" he asked ironically. "After all, you came to my room at the Rockingham the other night."

"I thought you must have fallen and hurt yourself," I said, flushing. I did not understand his mood; it seemed almost playful, but tinged with bitterness.

He rose, leaning on his cane. Then he let it drop. He was coming toward me; I hardly knew where to look. I wanted to leave the room, but he was saying, "I suppose a proper young lady like you is aware of the danger in being alone with a man not once, but twice in her night attire—and in a darkened room? Or is it that you believe I present no threat to such an action on your part? Because I am the way I am?" His voice was still light, still faintly amused, but his eyes had narrowed.

"I . . . I don't understand you, Mr. Curtis." I was standing with my back to the bookshelves, my hands clenched at my sides. "I think I should return to my room. Good night, sir." Now I did not care whether I offended him or not; I only wanted to get away. He was frightening me, although I wasn't certain why.

I turned to go, but he caught my arm in a light grip. Alarmed, I tried to shake him off, pushing at his chest, and he stumbled slightly backwards, releasing me. I saw his jaw clench hard and his face wince as all his weight was put on his bad leg for a moment, and I cried remorsefully, "Oh, I'm so sorry. I didn't mean to . . ."

He looked down at me then, and I was shocked at the fierceness of his expression. His eyes blazing, he grasped me by the arms, saying, "Don't look like that! Do you hear me? I'm sick of that look of pity on your face, in your eyes! I don't want your pity!" He began to furiously shake me.

His fingers were like pincers in my arms; his face with its wild expression terrified me. "I'm . . . I'm s-sorry," I stammered brokenly, my eyes filling with tears.

"I'll show you I'm in no need of your pity, despite what you think me," he said roughly.

He crushed me to his broad chest, his mouth bearing down on mine with a bitter savagery. It was not the first kiss I had imagined someday to receive; it was an attack. His mouth forced mine to open, his tongue probing, invading. Then his lips were on my neck and his hands in my hair, pulling at the pins so that it tumbled down over my shoulders.

I was too horrified to struggle this time, and stood stiff and mute in his arms, the tears continuing to slide down my cheeks.

Groaning, he said, "Even your tears are sweet," and his voice was hoarse, his breathing ragged. Then his lips were claiming mine again, and this time the nature of his kiss was different, no longer punishing, but caressing, his tongue softly exploring, gently sweeping. With faint wonder I felt him begin to tremble.

I yielded to his embrace, no longer immobile, my senses responding, pulsing, clamoring in his onslaught. His hands left my curls and gripped my shoulders before moving down my back and around to the front of my dressing gown, groping for the buttons.

"Tessa," he whispered, "Tessa." I felt a strange steeliness pressing into me as his fingers covered one of my breasts, clasping it. His lips were on my neck, his tongue stroking my flushed skin, which felt hot as fire.

He began to fumble with the ribbons of my nightgown, and then his warm, rough touch was on my bare flesh, searing it. Instantly I came to myself, acutely shocked at the way I had allowed him to take such intimacies without even a mild protest, and tore myself from his arms, vaguely hearing through the drumming in my ears the sound of my nightgown tearing. This time I did not look to see if my sudden movement had caused him again to lose his balance. Clasping the folds of my dressing gown together, I whisked myself from the room, my senses still feverishly pounding.

Chapter Six

I did not want to leave my room the next morning. My mind cringed at the mere thought of coming face to face with Drake Curtis. How on earth could I speak to him with equanimity, how was I to act with any semblance of natural poise, with the memory of what had occurred between us last night scorching my mind? But I must not give Emeline and Charlotte the occasion to speculate on the manner I assumed with him, and then wonder at its cause. Charlotte, were she to learn of the dreadful episode, would undoubtedly be shocked, and I could not help fearing that she would hold me partially accountable as I had been wandering about the first floor of the house clad in my night attire. Naturally I would never have done so had I suspected that Drake had returned to the house. But now it was imperative that I school myself to act as though nothing untoward had occurred between Emeline's uncle and myself, as though Drake Curtis had never taken me in his rough, urgent embrace and demanded a response from me that I was painfully aware I could scarcely control. . . .

As for Drake himself, it was not difficult to understand what had prompted his actions. Pity of any sort was galling to him; he had taken abrupt, drastic measures to demonstrate to me, and perhaps to himself as well, that he was as much a man as he had ever been, despite his leg wound. His fierce embrace had not been motivated by any tender feelings; I was certain that I was not the sort of woman to arouse those particular feelings in him. He had been angry at me the way he seemed to be angry

110

with life, and suddenly he had seen a way to strike out, to hurt, to punish. While the nature of his caresses had subtly altered, I did not fool myself into believing it was because he had realized that I myself held a great attraction for him. I was a woman; I was in his arms. I was convenient. And I had dared to show concern for him. He had been desperate to prove his manhood, his invincibility, that was all.

It was my own response to him which confused and frightened me. At first I had struggled, trying to escape his ravaging mouth, but gradually I had become drugged with the feel and taste of him. And I had ceased to struggle. My face hot, I squirmed inwardly at the memory. It was undeniable that a treacherous part of me had not only succumbed to his fiery kisses and bold, searching fingers, but had longed for them to continue their onslaught. The only relief I could muster from the shocking incident was that somehow I had regained control, struck with the sudden realization of where we were headed, and had managed to break free of his masterful grasp.

I was not ignorant of physical love. My father had been a doctor, after all, and what he had not told me I had learned from several more worldly students at Miss Winslow's Academy. Yet the information that had been passed in hushed, giggling conversations bore no resemblance to the passion Drake Curtis and I had shared. Years ago I had listened to those secret, smug confidences and could not have imagined myself in any similar circumstances. But in Drake's arms last night my body had experienced a range of sensations which cast an entirely new significance on the mere biological facts I had been privy to for some time. He had not been mistaken about my quickened breathing, about the throbbing of my pulses, about my mouth, which had opened effortlessly beneath his, and so he had assumed that I was as eager as he for the culmination. For some moments he must have forgotten whom he held in his arms, not Emeline's prim, tongue-tied tutor, but someone completely different, beautiful, enticing, someone who would have had no difficulty in bringing the situation to its clamoring conclusion. It was both shameful and bewildering to me that my resistance had dissolved, that I had come very close to yielding my innocence to him, an innocence that once given, would be impossible to reclaim.

Yet I could not remain in my room, feigning illness or a headache. To do so would invite attention which might make matters worse. I had to face Drake Curtis; I had to act as normally as possible so as to not arouse notice. I knew that intoxicated people often had only the haziest recollections of an event afterwards. Perhaps Drake himself remembered little or nothing about it. Yet he had not seemed drunk; he had certainly been in full possession of his faculties and abilities. He may not have been drunk at all, just angry and looking for a way to vent his anger. And I had obligingly provided the opportunity.

I took a small consolation in the rain that was falling steadily outside. Emeline and I could stay inside today; Drake would be at the Crystal Hills, and there would be little chance that we would meet.

In fact, that is just what happened. Emeline, calmer that day, agreed easily to my suggestion that we have a quiet day beside the fire and leave the tour-guiding to a day of improved weather. The two of us sat in the sitting room with a book, talking occasionally, listening to the tranquil sound of the soft rain. Charlotte's arthritis was giving her trouble and so she stayed in bed. Emeline and I ate lunch and dinner alone as Drake did not return from the hotel. I could be nothing but relieved in this; I supposed that he was as eager to avoid me as I was to avoid him. It was apparent that he regretted his rash behavior, and unaccountably some of my nervousness shifted to a rather restless sort of depression as I lay in bed that night. Somehow I could find little comfort in the thought that he was as dismayed as I by what had passed between us, and might be asking himself what on earth had possessed him to take me in his arms at all.

The next day the rain continued to fall and, after another day spent indoors, Emeline was not the only one who longed to stretch her legs in the fresh air. Fortunately, by late afternoon it had stopped raining. The bulky masses of gray began to slit and divide, revealing splashes of blue sky underneath which swelled until streams of sunlight shot across the purple-black mountain crests.

"It should be a fine day tomorrow," noted Emeline with satisfaction, standing at the mullioned window. "We can go out again."

"I'll ask Drake if he will be taking a party of guests on an excursion," said Charlotte, who had come down to take tea with us. "It's likely some of them are feeling as restless as you. An excursion would be just the thing."

My stomach knotted at her suggestion of spending the following day in Drake's company, but I chided myself for my jitters. I would not be alone with him; I could easily hang back with some of the other guests and stay in the background.

A little while later we went upstairs to dress for dinner, and I put on the ivory muslin gown I had worn at the Rockingham. After pinning up my red curls and dusting powder over my cheeks, I was conscious of a strange fluttering feeling inside me, and I could not altogether dismiss the hope that Drake would join us for dinner, despite the natural agitation evoked by such a thought.

But common sense asserted itself with scorn. I was Emeline's tutor, nothing more, and I had better keep reminding myself of that. I had no business thinking about her uncle one way or the other. Rather than avoiding me in the past two days, it was far more likely that he was too busy at the hotel to waste even a thought on me. If I were wise, I would no longer spare any for him. I had come to Nightshade Notch to look after Emeline. To allow my imagination free rein, to muse, whether wistfully or apprehensively, on her uncle's behavior, could only lead to discontent and unhappiness. Either way my life here would swiftly become uncomfortable, perhaps even unbearable.

With this resolve in mind I accompanied Emeline downstairs, but I could not keep the color from seeping into my face as we entered the dining room and saw Drake there before us. He was gazing abstractedly down into his glass of sherry, but then he looked up and our eyes met. For a moment our gazes were locked and something flickered in his blue eyes—a light, an impulse—but then he was turning away, downing his glass of wine, and I was biting my lip, scorning myself for discerning something that was not there.

Charlotte had come in as well; we took our seats and helped ourselves from the dishes the maids held. My hands trembled slightly; my face still felt warm, but I kept my attention on my food and made no attempt to join in the conversation.

"Uncle Drake, when will the next excursion be?" asked Emeline. "Teresa and I are just aching to go out!"

"Tomorrow," he answered shortly. "I put up a notice about it earlier this evening, when it began to clear."

"Oh, good! Where are we going?"

"I thought we'd take carriages to the Cascade, have a picnic at Loon Lake, and then go on to the Basin."

"That sounds perfect. Teresa and I have been so bored today!"

I flushed at her words while he said, "Bored? I would have thought that's the last thing you would be, Emeline, after all your eagerness in wanting to return to the Notch. And what about your studies? I thought you and Miss Hawthorne had work to do."

"I told Emeline and Teresa to take a holiday just now," said Charlotte. "They haven't had time this summer to do so. Unless you have any objection . . ."

"I? Why should I? It's no concern of mine."

There was an uncomfortable silence. Charlotte looked across at Drake, an expression of concern on her face, before saying tentatively, "What time should they be at the hotel tomorrow?"

"At half past ten."

"I wonder how many guests will come, how many carriages we'll need," said Emeline. "I wonder if that Mr. Aldridge will bring his cranky wife."

"I rather doubt it," said Drake. "Ever since their arrival she has remained in her room. He has asked that her meals be taken up to her room, although he himself has occasionally eaten in the dining room. We dined together last night. I gather Mrs. Aldridge is still recovering from the arduous journey from New York."

"I hope she doesn't come tomorrow," said Emeline. "She'll only try to spoil everything with her complaints."

"Emeline," reproved Charlotte.

"Aldridge is a pleasant fellow and an avid outdoorsman, so he says."

"From New York?" asked Charlotte mildly, but with a note in her voice I could not identify. I watched her glance at Drake uneasily before turning to Emeline. And I recalled the way he had tensed beside me in the carriage when Mr. Aldridge had stated they lived in New York.

What was it about the mention of New York which prompted those subtle reactions? Drake looked up from his plate and noticed my uncertain expression. His mouth tightened; his black brows drew together and he returned my gaze with a hard, almost defiant one of his own. But there was more in it as well. With a slight shock I recognized shades of remorse, even despair. And then he was turning his head with an impatient shrug, reaching for the decanter of wine, while I was left wondering whether I had again imagined those nuances of expression.

Drake excused himself rather abruptly after dessert, saying he had work to do at the hotel. Retrieving his cane, which was propped against one wall, he left the room. Charlotte sighed, shaking her head.

"I hope Uncle Drake's in a better mood tomorrow," said Emeline. "And how can he lead an excursion with his leg that way?"

"Your uncle is aware of his capabilities, Emeline. He won't be leading an expedition up Mt. Washington, after all. Please do not let him see that you doubt him in the slightest. Don't stare at his leg or plague him with questions tomorrow. He hasn't taken out a party since before"—she paused, frowning —"before he left for Cuba. Your father has been leading them. But tomorrow will be good for him, and the two of you will enjoy yourselves."

The next morning I put on my green-and-white striped cambric gown with its ruffled shawl collar. It was one of my favorite gowns, and the green accentuated the color of my eyes. I attached a strip of green ribbon about the brim of my straw hat, slipped on a pair of white gloves, and was ready.

I was excited about the plans for the day, and eager to explore the Notch. The worst was over where Drake was concerned; I had managed to be in the same room with him without causing notice. Now I would do well to forget the entire episode as he had likely forgotten it. It had been a momentary impulse by a bitter man in a darkened room, a way to lash out at the blows fate had dealt him. Yet I could not help questioning the precise nature of those blows; I did not believe now that the wound in his leg accounted solely for the grim, troubled man he was.

Emeline and I made our way through the slight stretch of woods to the side lawn of the hotel. The dew sparkled on the grass; the breeze smelt of rain-drenched pine. On its ridge the Crystal Hills shimmered white in the morning sunlight, its red roof gleaming against the rich blue sky.

There were two open carriages under the front rotunda, and a small group of people were assembled on the porch. Emeline and I walked up the graveled drive to the steps, exchanging tentative smiles with a few of the guests. There was a young couple I assumed were honeymooners; the man's arm was clasped possessively about the young woman's waist, and she held a parasol trimmed in eyelet lace in one hand. A tall, very thin young man with a black mustache stood reading a book, a pince-nez set on the bridge of his nose. An old woman with a fierce hawklike nose and a sharp gaze was sitting in one of the wicker chairs; she wore a purple bonnet as wide as a tea tray.

Just then a matron sailed impressively through the doors of the hotel, followed by two fair young ladies who were so alike in features and size that they must be twins. They were elegantly, if somewhat overly dressed for a picnic and a drive in the country, in gowns of pink and blue respectively, the bodices and short sleeves lavishly embroidered. Their parasols matched their gowns, and their bonnets were adorned with flowing ribbons and silk flowers. Simultaneously they glanced at the lanky young man buried in his book, and then their haughty gazes washed briefly over Emeline and myself in a way that made me feel that my gown was countrified and my own hat woefully plain.

"Well, by my watch, it's half past ten," stated their mother, glancing down at the watch pinned to her massive bosom. "I wonder what can be keeping Major Curtis. I gather we are the excursion party."

A young woman came hurrying down the long porch from the East Rotunda, clutching her hat to her head. Her light brown hair was escaping its pins, and her face was gently flushed. "I am so glad I am not too late," she said breathlessly, clasping her hands together. "I was out walking behind the hotel, in the meadow. Bird-watching, you know. I believe I actually saw a golden-crowned kinglet, although it moved so quickly I could not be precisely certain. Such a lovely day, isn't it? I did not realize it was nearly 10:30."

The twins looked across at her before exchanging pointed glances; their mother turned to the young woman as though to speak, thought the better of it, and rigidly inclined her head.

"There he is, Mother. There's Major Curtis," said the pink twin.

"Poor brave man," declared her mother, watching as Drake rode up the drive on a black horse. "Nobly acting as though he hasn't a wounded leg at all. How the heroes of our country are made to suffer!" Her voice had become soulful.

The old woman stood up from the wicker chair, gave an indelicate snort, and said brusquely, "Nonsense. He's one of the fortunate ones. He's alive, after all, and he has the use of his limbs."

The mother of the twins bridled. "Really, Mrs. Hamilton. I ask you to remember that my daughters are innocent girls." She turned to the twins. "Well, go ahead, get in the carriage. You know neither of you can bear to sit backwards."

"I don't mind sitting backwards," said the bird-watching woman brightly, and climbed in.

Drake reined in his horse. Today he wore a cream-colored waistcoat and trousers with a brown jacket and glossy brown boots. He looked very much the virile outdoorsman; the twins were simpering, surveying him with unconcealed interest and admiration.

"Good morning," he said coolly. "If you will all make yourselves comfortable in the carriages, we can be on our way. First we will drive through the Notch to the Crystal Cascade waterfall. Then we'll ride on to Loon Lake, where I've instructed that a picnic lunch be set up for us. After that we

117

will go on to the Basin, a very unusual geological formation."

One of the menservants came out to help the ladies into the carriages, and Emeline exchanged a few words with both drivers. It ended up that Emeline and I got in across from the honeymooners, beside the tall, thin man and his book, while the second carriage was occupied by Mrs. Randall and her two daughters, Mrs. Hamilton, and the bird-watching young woman whose name was Miss Birche. Drake remained on horseback, patiently waiting for the party to become settled. The twins changed places twice before deciding they were comfortable.

Just as we were ready to leave, Horatio Aldridge came out of the door and called robustly, "Am I too late?"

"Not at all," Drake assured him. "I believe there is room in the first carriage."

"Good," he said heartily, and swung himself up to squeeze in next to the honeymooning couple. He lifted his Panama hat. "Ah, Miss Curtis, Miss Hawthorne. A pleasure to see you both. Wonderful day, isn't it? I was out riding at dawn—the sun rising from over the mountain was quite a sight, I can assure you." He wore a camel-colored riding suit, brown boots, and carried a gold-tipped walking stick.

"How is Mrs. Aldridge feeling today?" asked Emeline politely.

A shadow passed over his face before he replied, "Better, I think. She has been exhausted from the trip, she tells me, and unfortunately did not feel strong enough to join the excursion."

"Perhaps Mrs. Aldridge will feel well enough to go on the next one," said Drake before giving a signal to both drivers. We began to move down the drive of the sweeping lawn.

Aldridge introduced himself in a warm, cordial manner to the other occupants of our carriage. The couple, Mr. and Mrs. Prentice Cooper, were indeed on their honeymoon. The tall, thin man set his book on his lap before telling us he was Nathaniel Sloane. Glancing down at the book he found so absorbing, I saw it was entitled *The Geologist's Guide to the White Mountains*.

"Are you a geologist, sir?" asked Mr. Aldridge, who had also noticed the book.

Adjusting his pince-nez, Mr. Sloane replied, "An amateur one only. My family is in the textile business in Massachusetts, but every summer I take the opportunity to visit places of geological interest."

"Where have you visited?" I asked him.

"Last summer I spent several weeks on Mt. Desert Island off the coast of Maine. Quite a remarkable place, geologically speaking. It's the only place on the Eastern Coast where the mountains rise from the shore's edge. The boulders which litter the shore are debris left from the glaciers. The summer before, I went to Nantucket to see the natural boglands and heaths. Nantucket is the only location in North America where Scotch heather grows naturally, although initially the seeds had to be brought from the British Isles. You see, I'm also interested in botany. I understand, Major Curtis," he said to Drake, who rode beside us, "that you have some most unusual species of alpine flowers in these parts."

"I wouldn't know, Mr. Sloane," said Drake.

"Well, sir, it says here that it's the combination of high winds, moisture, cold air, and cloudy skies of the higher elevations which cause the alpine flowers to thrive."

Mrs. Cooper and I smiled politely, and he was encouraged to continue. "Mountain avens is supposedly common here, but elsewhere grows only in Nova Scotia, hundreds of miles north. Scientists believe the alpine plants moved southward ahead of the ice sheet. After the ice melted and retreated, so did the plants, but some species of arctic flowers remained on the highest elevations in New England. The dwarf cinquefoil is a tiny yellow flower which grows on Mt. Washington and no-where else in the world. And there are also patches of Lapland rosebay."

"You don't say," said Mr. Aldridge. Emeline was regarding Mr. Sloane with a glazed expression; Mrs. Cooper was pressing the tip of her parasol into her white boot; her husband was staring off into space.

"You are quite an expert, Mr. Sloane," said Drake.

We were riding down a rather bumpy dirt road, but I did not mind in the least being jostled. The mountains of the Notch rose steeply on both sides of us, the slender silvery birches glinting amid the maples, aspens, and beeches. Further up, the slopes darkened as the lush deciduous trees gave way to solid stands of evergreens. Tilting my head, I gazed up above the distinct timberline where the gnarled, scruffy *krumholz* reigned beside coarsely chipped patches of granite and vibrant splashes of wine-red mountain cranberry.

Mr. Sloane began to talk about the glaciers scouring the mountain summits and carving out the notches; he was very interested in glaciers.

"How do you like Nightshade Notch, Miss Hawthorne?" Mr. Aldridge asked me when Mr. Sloane had paused for breath. "I assume you are new to it as well?"

I nodded. "I like it very much."

"Yes, I'm tempted to stay here forever," he said, tapping his stick on the carriage floor. "I will hate leaving here in September; I much prefer this wilderness to a crowded city. However, I can't allow my business to run unsupervised through the year. That reminds me—Major Curtis?"

"Yes, sir?" said Drake, turning his head.

"I've been meaning to ask you—is it possible that we have met before? My wife seems to think you look familiar, and your name was familiar to her as well. Do you ever visit New York, sir? Perhaps we have met at a party, or at the house of a mutual acquaintance?"

Drake's square jaw clenched, tightening his face. "No, sir. The last time I was in New York I was in no condition to attend parties."

"After the war, of course," said Mr. Aldridge soberly. "No, I meant before that, some time ago. Mrs. Aldridge is convinced that you are known to her, but she cannot place how."

This time there was a trace of annoyance in Drake's voice. "Perhaps Mrs. Aldridge is confusing me with someone else," he said before riding ahead to speak to our carriage driver.

We passed a swamp where birch trees tottered out over the water, mirror images of their splayed awkward poses reflected on the still surface. The air was fragrant with balsam and the damp earthy smell of the woods.

"We're coming to a covered bridge," Emeline said. "It

crosses the river a ways down from the Flume."

"The Flume?" repeated Mr. Aldridge.

"A dramatic natural gorge, sir, with rock walls rising to ninety feet in height," said Mr. Sloane. "Quite an astounding sight, I must say. I was there several days ago."

"You can walk there from the hotel," said Emeline to me. "And there's a footbridge which goes across it at the most narrow point."

"The Flume can be a dangerous place," said Drake. "There are stone ledges for walking along one side, but they can be slippery. And that swinging footpath is a poor excuse for a bridge."

Emeline rolled her eyes at her uncle's warning. We turned off the road just then. Ahead was the covered bridge, its roof constructed of weathered shingles, its sides of weathered frames. The horses' hooves and carriage wheels made a din on the floor which reverberated on the walls. Below, chutes of water spilled between puckered granite boulders before rushing into a dark emerald pool further down the riverbed.

Then we were clattering off the bridge and drawing deeper into the woods. The dirt road became even more rutted, and we swayed from one side of the carriage to the other.

"We're nearly there now," said Emeline. "There it is up there. The Crystal Cascade."

We all turned in the direction she pointed, peering through the towering pines and spruces. From a great height a fine film streamed down in a silver-white sheer curtain over amber steps.

"'The Crystal Cascade at two hundred feet high is the highest in the state, banked by sentinels of white pines and croppings of feathery woodfern,'" read Mr. Sloane.

The carriage stopped; Drake got down from his horse, fastening the reins to a tree. "This is as far as the carriages can go, so we'll have to walk from here," he announced. "The path is easily defined and not at all hazardous for the ladies."

"Oh, Major! Major Curtis!" warbled the mother of the twins in the carriage behind ours.

He turned around. "Yes, Mrs. Randall?"

"Would you be so kind to keep an eye on Rosamunde and

Eleanor? I don't believe I'll get out of the carriage this time. I can see perfectly well from here, but naturally they are eager to pay full homage to your beautiful waterfall."

"I'd be pleased to take charge of them. I'm going to the falls," said Mrs. Hamilton, her sharp gaze filled with mockery. The twins regarded her in horrified dismay.

"Certainly, Mrs. Randall," said Drake in an expressionless voice. He walked to the second carriage, his bad leg slightly dragging. The twins looked greatly relieved and smiled prettily.

Emeline and Mrs. Cooper had already climbed from the carriage, and Mr. Aldridge was waiting to hand me down. I climbed out and began to follow Emeline up the path. Mr. Sloane's head was once again buried in his book; behind me I heard him stumble.

The sound of the falls grew as we approached, a gurgling, hissing sound. Above the falls the forest was swathed in a gossamer spray, the leaves of the trees and bushes a green wavering blur. The scent of pine and fir was heady, and the fronds of ferns glistened with wet. At the foot of the Cascade the silver torrents mingled with a dense, frosted vapor before spilling into the pool and churning about the smooth amber stones. Dark green leaves swirled on the surface of the water before hastening downstream.

"How lovely," cried Miss Birche, clasping her hands together. Her hair was even more untidy but she was totally oblivious to this petty concern, lost in admiration of the Cascade. "And how steep it is."

"Magnificent," agreed Mr. Aldridge.

"The highest in the state at two hundred feet," said Mr. Sloane.

"Hmmmph. Have you ever seen Niagara?" asked the fierce-looking Mrs. Hamilton, pointing her beaked nose at Mr. Sloane.

Mr. Sloane's mouth thinned to a narrow line. "No, madam, I have not."

"No more have I," she replied, "and what's more, I've no wish to."

"I wish I had brought my sketchbook," said Miss Birche vaguely. "I am always forgetting it, I'm afraid. Or else I bring it

122

and then leave it somewhere. I have had such a number of sketchbooks." Her tone was mournful.

Mr. Sloane cast her a disapproving glance before reaching into his pocket for a pair of binoculars. These he leveled at the Cascade for a few moments before offering them to Mrs. Hamilton.

She waved them away. "Why anyone should wish to see at close range what is perfectly adequate at a distance I have never understood. Besides, the things always waver and refuse to focus, giving one a headache."

"I'd like to look through them," said Emeline.

"Haven't seen you two before," said the old lady to me. "Are you staying at the hotel?"

"No, we live here," answered Emeline before I could. "Major Curtis is my uncle, and this is Miss Hawthorne, my friend and tutor."

"How do you do?" I said.

"I am Mrs. Thaddeus Hamilton. Your uncle seems to have his hands full," she said sardonically.

Glancing back down the path, I saw that Rosamunde, or perhaps it was Eleanor, was sitting down, shaking out her boot, her skirts pulled up slightly to reveal her lace-trimmed petticoat and black stockings. Drake was an unappreciative audience, however, broodingly gazing into the trees.

"Oh, come *on,* Rosamunde," said the blue twin. "Surely you've gotten that rock out by now. Major Curtis and I are going to join the others." Twirling her parasol, she smiled coyly up at Drake while the pink twin glared at her sister's back before slipping on her boot and following them. Eleanor, with Drake in tow, was advancing to the mossy ledge where the rest of us had gathered.

"Oh, Major, such a beautiful sight," intoned the blue twin. "Such a commanding view. How kind of you to share it with us. It's the perfect secret place, wouldn't you say so?"

Emeline nudged me with her elbow.

"Hardly secret, Miss Randall," said Drake dryly. "Not with parties of tourists from every hotel in the White Mountains coming to gaze or sketch."

"Yes," said Miss Birche, "I was just saying I wish I had

123

brought my sketchbook."

"Tourists," said Eleanor distastefully, "what a bore they are."

"I didn't realize that you and your mother and sister were permanent residents here, Miss Randall," said Mrs. Hamilton.

Emeline made a slight snigger, but the blue twin seemed unperturbed, saying soulfully, "No, but I would like to be. It's only by living in a place that one can grasp its essence."

"Oh—oh—is it?" cried Miss Birche. "Yes, I do believe there's a black-backed three-toed woodpecker!" She pointed to a bird which clung to the trunk of a nearby spruce tree. "I understand they are rare in forests on mountain slopes. Only the males have the yellow caps, you know. What good fortune that we have spotted one!"

"Thrilling," said the pink twin.

Drake smiled down at the excited Miss Birche. "Are you interested in birds, Miss Birche? We have a guidebook at the hotel on the various ones which can be seen in the Notch. I'll see that you get a copy when we return."

Miss Birche's pink face became pinker and she said, slightly flustered, "Oh, thank you, Major Curtis. I should very much enjoy that. If it's not too much trouble, that is. I don't want to be a nuisance."

"No trouble at all, Miss Birche," said Drake.

"I should like to have a copy as well, Major Curtis," said Rosamunde. "I am also interested in birds."

"Are you, Miss Randall?" asked Drake with a slight smile.

Suddenly, through the woods came a harsh scream. Startled, I glanced about; Eleanor and Rosamunde gave identical little cries.

"Goodness! What in heaven's name was that?" asked the pink twin faintly, grasping Drake's arm. "Is the Cascade haunted?"

He looked down at her, his brows raised ironically. "Not that I know of, Miss Randall. That was a barred owl. It's quite common in these parts, as I'm sure you and Miss Birche are aware."

"Oh, of course, a barred owl," said Rosamunde with a nervous laugh, and Eleanor said in malicious tones, "You

124

should have realized that at once, Rosamunde, being interested in birds the way you are."

Emeline laughed outright at that, the pink twin looking daggers at her. Then Drake suggested we go back to the carriages as we still had a distance to travel to reach Loon Lake.

"Yes, let's go," said Emeline. "I'm already starving." Both twins eyed her with distaste.

Our small group wandered back to the two carriages while Drake swung himself into the saddle of his black horse. He winced as he did so, his face hardening, and I felt a sudden burst of anger at the twins for clutching his arms and leaning on him the way they had.

"What stupid girls," said Emeline in an undertone to me. "As if Uncle Drake would take any notice of either of them!"

Traversing the covered bridge, we turned down the original road. The Notch began to be more narrow as we drove ahead, the bluffs soaring on both sides, cutting off the sun. It was cool in the shadows of the black-green spruces; above our heads the craggy, exposed granite littered the higher slopes.

"'A notch is an ancient river valley that was cut by a swift erosive stream,'" read Mr. Sloane. "One can clearly see how, during the Ice Age, the glaciers moved through the valleys and over the mountain crests, widening the notches and sculpting the summits. Amazing, when one thinks of it."

"It's a good deal darker here," observed Mrs. Cooper. "No wonder this place is called Nightshade Notch."

"Not precisely, madam," said Mr. Sloane. "The black nightshade, or *Solanum Americanum*, grows in rocky woods and thickets about here, and is fairly harmless. But the *Datura stramonium* can be extremely poisonous, causing delirium or worse."

"I don't understand, Mr. Sloane. Are you saying that this Notch was named for that thing?" Mrs. Cooper looked disconcerted.

Mr. Sloane nodded, adjusting his pince-nez. "You may know it by its more common name, the jimsonweed, Mrs. Cooper. It grows in fields. The flowers are white and shaped like trumpets; the leaves are hairy and pointed at the tip."

Mrs. Cooper looked pointedly at her husband. "I do hope it's

125

not bad luck."

A while later the Notch opened up again; the sun glowed overhead, warming the air. Before long we were stopping beside a small glittering lake surrounded by sheer sand-colored cliffs on one side and bristly dark-green highlands on the other.

"If you will all look up there on the face of that cliff, you can see the Old Man of the Mountain," said Drake, gesturing.

We saw a peculiar outcropping of granite which resembled a human profile, a face as cold and intractable as a judge's, staring over the rugged landscape. The brow was heavy, the chin square and ponderous.

"'Twelve hundred feet above Loon Lake is perched a great stone face, a product of postglacial weathering from frost,'" read Mr. Sloane. He looked up from his book, shielding his eyes from the sun. "Not remarkable in size, certainly, but an interesting sight all the same."

"It's often covered in clouds and impossible to see," said Drake.

"I understand that to some of the Indians it was the local god," said Mr. Aldridge.

"He looks rather fierce, doesn't he?" said one of the twins.

"Resembles Mr. Thaddeus Hamilton," observed Mrs. Hamilton. "He looked just like that when I bought a bonnet he didn't like. When he died I went out and bought a great number of bonnets."

"Lunch is served, ladies and gentlemen," said Drake.

Two small tables had been set up on the narrow sandy beach and covered with plates and bowls, silverware and crystal glasses. Two men in starched black and white uniforms stood by, waiting to serve us.

"How delightful everything looks, Major," said the mother of the twins.

"I hope you enjoy it, ma'am," said Drake. "But there is no reason for you to address me by rank. The war in Cuba has been over nearly a year."

She went on as though he had not spoken. "You must tell us of some of your battle experiences, Major. One of the famous and brave Rough Riders in our very midst! I know that Rosamunde and Eleanor would dearly love to hear your

126

account of the charge up San Juan Hill. Did you ride beside Colonel Roosevelt?"

"It was Kettle Hill, Mrs. Randall. And like the other Riders, I did my fighting on foot." There was a flat tone in his quiet voice.

"The state newspapers have dubbed you 'New Hampshire's Own Rough Rider,' you know," she said, tapping her fan on his sleeve.

"Excuse me, ma'am, but the newspapers print a lot of rubbish," he said, his face hardening.

"But surely you are too modest," went on the relentless lady. "To so nobly volunteer to free the desperate, oppressed Cubans—and in so dreadful a climate. And then to obtain such a glorious victory! I declare I am overcome at the mere contemplation of such manly courage."

"Courage had nothing to do with it," said Drake curtly. "Nor was the victory what I would call glorious with nearly fifteen hundred men killed or wounded in a day." He moved away to speak to one of the drivers.

"Isn't that just like a man?" sighed Mrs. Randall. "Hiding his light under a bushel, avoiding the attention he so richly deserves! Perhaps he'll talk to you on another occasion, girls, when there aren't so many around." She cast a deliberate glance at Mrs. Hamilton, Miss Birche, and me. "You must ask him another time. Men do love to talk about themselves and you must draw them out." Having contradicted herself thoroughly, she sat down on one of the ground-squares and motioned for the twins to do the same.

"By all means, ask him another time," said Mrs. Hamilton wickedly. "He'll appreciate that."

There were plates of finger sandwiches with fillings of salmon or shrimp, cucumber or turkey. Raspberries and blueberries had been tossed with sugar, and there were tarts and an angel food cake. To drink there was limeade, and beer for the men. I watched the current rippling the lapis water, and gazed up at the granite face of the Old Man of the Mountain. Across the lake the birch trees clustered at the water's edge, leaning weirdly out over the water.

Drake was standing beside one of the carriages, a glass of

beer in his hand. He looked forbidding, his face dark and tense. Mrs. Randall's persistent remarks had resulted in his change of mood. Was it just a normal reluctance to talk about the war, or was there a more serious reason behind his reticence?

"Two loons," cried Miss Birche beside me, pointing. "With your binoculars you could see them quite easily, Mr. Sloane."

"Be my guest, Miss Birche," he said, handing them to her.

"I love their call," said Emeline, and then it came, a drawn-out melancholy warbling which sounded across the lake.

Mr. Aldridge had gone over to where Drake stood and engaged him in conversation. Mrs. Randall looked across at them in exasperation; the twins were sulking. Miss Birche, Emeline, and I finished our lunch and then strolled along the placid shore.

A while later we were again traveling through the Notch, watching the ravens dart and wheel along the cliff faces, listening to the clip-clop of the horses, breathing in the spicy pine-scented air. Drake's cordial manner as host was again intact as he rode beside us, drawing our attention to various points of interest.

Eventually we stopped and disembarked, following a path springy with copper pine needles and tufts of bright green moss. A ferocious rushing sound came to us, and then we were out of the dense woods and standing on top of a short waterfall overlooking a giant bowl-shaped pool. Its streaked amber walls were smooth as marble, sculpted by the deluge of water plummeting down its sides. Inside the Basin the jade-green water spun in a never-ceasing frenzy.

"Another unusual geological formation for you, Mr. Sloane," said Drake. "A giant glacial hole carved smooth by ice and water."

"Is it very deep?" asked Mr. Cooper.

"Thirty feet wide, fifteen feet deep at its center," said Mr. Sloane, his book open.

"Not particularly deep, but definitely not for swimming," said Mr. Aldridge pleasantly.

"I wish the twins would go swimming in it," whispered Emeline to me. "And I'd like to toss in Mr. Sloane's book as well."

Gazing mesmerized at the madly churning water in the huge cavity, I was struck by the fascinating contrast of the timeless, weatherbeaten wilderness of the region with the recent man-made luxury imposed on it by the hotels and their guests. It sounded a jarring note to me then, one that would echo again and again in the coming weeks as I began to wonder what strange secrets those ages-old mountains possessed, and what bizarre happenings they had beheld.

along ... ... He had mellowed somewhat, or perhaps he

Chapter Seven

It was about a week later when Emeline's parents returned. Every day I had anticipated their arrival with a vague apprehension, all the while becoming used to the household comprising Charlotte, Emeline, and myself, with Drake making the odd uncomfortable appearance now and then. He spent most of his time at the Crystal Hills and we saw little of him except at dinner, an arrangement which suited me. Not that I thought about him any less just because I did not often meet him face to face.

I was enjoying my time spent with Emeline and Charlotte; I felt at ease with the two of them. The landscape was magnificent and the house very grand, but in a comfortable way rather than one I found intimidating. It resembled more a huge hunting lodge, I supposed, than a mansion, and thus was highly appropriate to its setting as a splendid mansion would not have been. But I dreaded Emeline's parents returning and, yes, intruding on our pleasant little world. With the return of the Curtises I feared the atmosphere would change; what I could not predict was the way it would change and how I would be left feeling a rather helpless, uneasy onlooker, greeting each new day with misgiving.

Emeline and I had gone on another outing, this one a nature hike through the forest for more intrepid souls than the picnic outing. Drake did not lead it himself, and I could not help noticing the absences of the Misses Randall. Miss Birche, however, was an enthusiastic participant, and Mr. Sloane, who had exchanged his book on geology for one on botany, went along as well. He had mellowed somewhat, or perhaps he wasn't as sure of his subject, because he was only heard to correct the guide's identification of a wildflower two or three times.

One afternoon I was in the sitting room reading. After lunch Charlotte had retired to her room to rest, and Emeline had gone out on one of her frequent rambles.

Through the opened casement windows I heard the sounds of an arrival—carriage wheels scraping on the graveled drive, the snorting of horses. Puzzled at first, I swiftly realized who the arrivals must be. Standing up uncertainly, I wondered whether I had enough time to go to my room before they entered. But it was more likely that they would see me scurrying up the stairs, and that would be worse than staying to confront them with some semblance of poise. They would be taken aback at the sight of me, a stranger, in their house. And I feared their reaction to the news that their daughter had been expelled from school and had brought home a tutor. For once I hoped that Drake might come in at that moment, or Charlotte come downstairs, but neither of these reprieves was granted me.

Voices could be heard in the hall, a woman's rather petulant, a man's hearty. "Well, where is everyone?" she asked impatiently. "Be careful with that hatbox; don't knock it against the banister."

"Drake's at the hotel, Nora. You know how he can scarcely leave the place," the man replied.

"Well, where is Charlotte? Someone might have been waiting to greet us."

"We didn't send a telegram telling them we'd be back today. I need a drink," he said, his footsteps striding across the flagged stone floor.

"A drink? Don't you think you've had enough already, Aaron?"

The man paused on the threshold of the sitting room. "Well, what do we have here?"

He did not resemble Drake. He was tall but bulky, his hair a lighter brown, his face heavy. He wore a striped blue suit with a white waistcoat that was too tight for him. His eyes moved over me in a way that made me feel hot and uncomfortable.

Before I could answer, Mrs. Curtis had come up behind him. "What is it?" she asked. He entered the room, stepping aside so that she could do so as well.

Emeline's mother was a beautiful woman. Her hair was a honeyed brown, highlighted with streaks of gold. She had lovely creamy skin and slightly exotic, long-lidded eyes. Her traveling suit was of plum taffeta and her lavender straw bonnet was adorned with cabbage roses. Immediately I was conscious that my hair was too vibrant a red, that my blouse and skirt were unstylish.

Her eyebrows were raised. "Well, who might you be?" she asked coolly.

"Teresa Hawthorne, Mrs. Curtis. How—how do you do?"

"Well, that's good enough for me," said her husband, walking over to me. "How do you do, Miss Hawthorne?"

I did not want to give him my hand but, as he was extending his, I had no choice. His smile was warm; his moist hand gripped mine too tightly. He smelt of spirits.

"Don't be ridiculous, Aaron," said Mrs. Curtis. "Who are you, Miss Hawthorne, and what are you doing in our house? Surely you are not a guest at the hotel." Her eyes swept over me derisively.

"No, I'm not, Mrs. Curtis. I—I am Emeline's tutor."

"Emeline's tutor? What nonsense is this? Where did you come from?"

"I knew Emeline at school, ma'am. I was . . . employed there. When she left, I accompanied her here."

"You mean to tell me that Emeline is home, that she has left school? And you took it upon yourself to come with her? Well, you can just pack your bags today, my girl. I know nothing about you, except that you are apparently quite conniving. Why did Emeline leave school?"

I flushed scarlet, biting my lip. Evidently they had not received Drake's telegram about her expulsion from Miss Winslow's Academy. I wished that he were here to deal with them.

"I'm sorry to have to tell you this, Mrs. Curtis, but Emeline was asked to leave the Academy."

Her brows drew together in a frown. "Asked to leave? Do you mean to tell me that she was expelled?"

"What on earth for?" asked Mr. Curtis.

"What did the tiresome child do? Really, Aaron, I wish we had stayed in Rockport. The child here on top of everything else, and our house full of strangers. Well, Miss Hawthorne, I hope you are prepared to explain."

I was going to have to go through it all over again. "Of course, Mrs. Curtis. Although Emeline may prefer to be the one to tell you herself."

"I am asking you to tell me," she snapped.

"Well, there was an accident at the school. A lantern was knocked over in the carriage house and it started a fire. The whole thing was an accident, but I'm afraid that Miss Winslow held Emeline responsible. Emeline felt very badly about it, but Miss Winslow was impervious to her feelings. She expelled her."

"When did all this happen? And why weren't we informed?"

"About two weeks ago, Mrs. Curtis. I understand that Major Curtis sent a telegram to your hotel in Boston, but did not receive an answer."

"Oh, Mrs. Curtis tired of the hotel," said her husband. "So we went up to the house in Rockport."

"Miss Hawthorne does not require an explanation of our movements, Aaron," said his wife icily. "I want to know by what means Emeline returned home and whose idea it was to hire a tutor for her."

"When Major Curtis could not locate you, he went to Portsmouth himself to fetch her. It was he who offered me the post." In dismay I waited for the next question, for I knew what it would be.

"Why you? How did Major Curtis find you?" she asked.

"Now, Nora, she was a teacher at Emeline's school. Where do you think he found her?" He chuckled.

"I haven't the vaguest notion." Mrs. Curtis was tapping her foot on the floor, two bright spots of color in her cheeks. "So Major Curtis hired you. Drake hires a tutor for Emeline—a ridiculous expense, when he has been rebuking us for every

133

penny spent. Of all the overhanded—! How dared he do this without consulting me? Has he forgotten I am the child's mother?"

If only the earth would swallow me up.

"I'm sure Miss Hawthorne is a good teacher, Nora." Aaron Curtis's voice was wheedling. "Aren't you, my dear?"

I gaped at him, hardly knowing how to answer. Heaven help me when they learned that I had not been employed at the Academy as a teacher, but as a cook.

"What has that to do with anything? I'm tempted to go across to the hotel right now and— But that can wait. Where is Emeline, Miss Hawthorne? I want to talk to her."

"I'm not certain where she is, Mrs. Curtis. I haven't seen her since lunch."

"You haven't seen her? Falling short in your duties already, aren't you?" she asked, tightlipped.

"Now, Nora, Miss Hawthorne is Emeline's tutor, not her nursemaid," said her husband, giving a rather forced laugh.

"Exactly. Why aren't you tutoring her right now? Instead of conducting lessons, which is what Major Curtis is paying her to do, she is here in our sitting room, acting like a lady of leisure. And she has no notion of the child's whereabouts."

"Emeline is fond of taking walks. I do not accompany her on every outing; she would not wish me to."

"Of course not," said Aaron Curtis heartily. "The girl's been cooped up in that dull school for so long. Stands to reason she wants to be outside. She was always like that before, Nora."

His wife threw him a withering look.

"Miss Conway suggested that we postpone lessons for a short while to give Emeline a real vacation," I said. "Although there were only three students left at the school this summer, Miss Winslow insisted they continue their studies. The rest of the students went away for the duration of the summer."

"True enough. We did leave her there rather than sending for her to come home. You thought it best, my dear," said Aaron.

"I still think it best, but that's neither here nor there, is it?"

snapped his wife. "As Drake has highhandedly arranged everything."

"Let's not be hasty, Nora," said Aaron, who was pouring himself a drink from the tantalus on the side table. "These may turn out to be the best arrangements, at least for the time being. You've complained more than once that the school fees were too high. Having Miss Hawthorne here is less of an expenditure."

"Oh, don't be a fool, Aaron!" she said furiously, and went from the room.

"You mustn't mind Mrs. Curtis, Miss Hawthorne. It was the journey, you know, and then hearing that Emeline has been sent home. She'll calm down." He gulped his whiskey.

With relief I heard Charlotte's voice in the hall; she was speaking soothingly to Emeline's mother.

"You realize he hired that girl to teach my daughter; he'd no right to do so without consulting me!" Leonora Curtis's voice was raised indignantly. "Just bringing her to our house like that—!"

"And the right thing it was to do, Leonora," said Charlotte. "Miss Hawthorne is just what Emeline needs. And the child needs to be home. I'm convinced it all happened for the best. Now I suggest that you go up to your room and have a good long rest. Emeline will come up to you when she returns."

"Have one of the girls bring up a pot of tea," said Leonora, and I heard her going up the stairs.

Charlotte entered the sitting room, giving me a warm, reassuring smile, before saying, "Well, Aaron, welcome home. We have been looking to see you for some time now. I assumed that when you received Drake's telegram—"

"We never saw the thing, Charlotte. Leonora wanted to leave the hotel in Boston. She said the heat was too much for her, and most of her friends were going to the North Shore, so we went up to Rockport as well. I would have come home sooner, but you know Leonora. There was just no moving her."

Charlotte regarded him skeptically, but she merely said, "Drake has had his hands full at the Crystal Hills."

"Oh? How are things going on over there?" Aaron asked casually, pouring himself another drink.

"Drake can tell you himself." Her voice was short. "I assume you'll be going over this afternoon."

"Well, you know, Charlotte, I'm feeling all in from the long train ride. I thought I'd wait until tomorrow. Without many guests surely he can handle things."

Charlotte regarded him with scarcely concealed disdain. "He may want to talk with you, Aaron."

"Oh?" Aaron's voice had taken on an uneasy note. "How is he—er—feeling these days?"

"His leg is still bothering him, if that is what you mean. On top of everything, Aaron, he shouldn't have had to fetch Emeline home from school."

Aaron's puffy face reddened, and he took another gulp of whiskey. "I told you that Leonora wanted to leave the hotel," he blustered. "How were we to know the girl would cause such a rumpus?"

"I suppose it didn't occur to you to leave a forwarding address." She turned to me. "Would you look about for Emeline, Teresa, and tell her that her parents have returned? Though she may be gone for the afternoon."

"Of course, Charlotte," I said, relieved to be able to leave the house. I went upstairs to my room, got my straw hat, and went outside.

I headed through the trees to the Crystal Hills, going up the steps of the long white-columned porch. Mrs. Hamilton was dozing in one of the wicker chairs, and she opened her eyes as I passed.

"Have you seen Emeline—Miss Curtis?" I asked her, but she shook her head and closed her eyes.

Emeline was not under the East Rotunda, but two familiar voices came to me from round the corner on the back porch.

"I was certain that I had seen him somewhere before, my dear Mrs. Randall," Mrs. Aldridge was saying triumphantly. "And just last night it came to me. I remembered while I was lying there trying to fall asleep, though how I was able to do any such thing with Mr. Aldridge snoring so loudly—! Really, men have so little consideration."

136

"My husband snored as well," said Mrs. Randall. "Many nights I lay awake listening to those repulsive sounds. I do feel for you, Mrs. Aldridge. But you were saying . . ."

"Oh, yes. Well, this morning at breakfast I told Horatio that I'd remembered where I'd seen Major Curtis before. I was so delighted that it had finally come to me. I do hate it when a thought or memory eludes one . . . so provoking."

"It is provoking," agreed Mrs. Randall solemnly.

"Mr. Aldridge did not seem interested. He was more interested in the fact that the maid had brought orange marmalade rather than blackberry jam. But I said, 'Horatio, what does it matter? When you hear this, you'll be sorry we ever came to this place. And orange marmalade won't have anything to do with it!'"

"Goodness! I hope—I hope it's not something unpleasant about the major?"

"Unpleasant! I'm afraid that's putting it rather mildly, Mrs. Randall. Indeed, I hardly know where to begin. But I feel it is my duty to tell you because you have two impressionable daughters. Such charming girls, Mrs. Randall. So prettily behaved."

"Why, thank you, I'm sure, Mrs. Aldridge. But what exactly is the nature of this . . . unpleasantness? I confess you have me quite absorbed—and alarmed."

"As you may well be, Mrs. Randall. The whole business is quite dreadful really, most distressing."

I shouldn't be listening to any of this, I thought, pressing my back to the wall. I won't listen.

"It's about Major Curtis, you see. I couldn't help noticing that your twins . . . well, he is handsome, although too sinister-looking for my taste. Those dark types always are."

"Are you implying, my dear Mrs. Aldridge, that the major has been involved in some scandal?"

"That's precisely what I'm saying, Mrs. Randall. I was lying in bed, as I said, trying to place the memory. His face was so familiar—I have a great memory for faces, much better than most people's, although I have difficulty with names. When it came to me, I knew instantly that that's what it was, because I recalled that it happened at a hotel in New Hampshire. Not that

137

I had paid much attention to the locale at the time. My husband had suggested that I had seen the major at some social function in New York, and I was inclined to agree with him. But try as I might, I could not recall the occasion. And then it occurred to me that I may have seen his picture in the newspaper."

"And that's when you remembered?" asked the mother of the pink and blue twins breathlessly.

"Indeed it was. It struck me like a thunderbolt. Well, naturally, I couldn't get to sleep for a long while after that. I could not wait until the morning when I could tell Mr. Aldridge. And then, wouldn't you know it, he said it didn't matter!" Her voice rose, outraged. "'Doesn't matter!' I said. 'Well, perhaps you don't mind subjecting your wife to a man of his sort, but I shall warn Mrs. Randall. She has two daughters to worry about, you know.' And he said—that I ought to keep my mouth shut!"

"It was very considerate of you to think of us, Mrs. Aldridge. But what exactly did the major do?"

Mrs. Aldridge gave a snort. "Nothing at all, if you ask my husband. Men all stick together. All he could say was that he was sorry he had badgered the poor fellow—poor fellow indeed—about meeting him before. But there was a woman, you see. I knew of her although we had never met. Everyone in New York knew of the Grant Schylers—one of your oldest Dutch families, you know. *Married,* though that did not prevent her or the major—though he wasn't a major then— from conducting a disgraceful *liaison.*"

"She was a guest at the hotel?"

"Yes, married to a man years older. It was all in the papers last May, a year ago—I wonder you don't recall any of it. The New York *World* and *Journal* were full of it. But they are that sort, aren't they?"

"What happened?" It sounded as though Mrs. Randall was beginning to lose her patience, as indeed was I.

"Well, she was . . ." To my frustrated dismay Mrs. Aldridge lowered her voice. Scarcely breathing, I strained to catch her words, but a man's voice startled me from several yards away.

"Good afternoon, Miss Hawthorne." I gave a start, and looked up.

"Oh, hello, Mr. Aldridge," I said, stepping away from the wall and over to where he stood. It was so difficult to smile pleasantly at him when I was so frustrated and disappointed at missing out on what Mrs. Aldridge had to relate about Drake. Serves me right, I thought glumly.

"Have you by any chance seen my wife?" He tapped the whip in his hand against his leg; he was dressed for riding.

Flushing, I stammered, "Your—your wife? I—I believe she is on the back porch with Mrs. Randall."

"Then I won't disturb them. I'm just off—they're bringing a horse round for me now. Very fine stables they have here. I understand that Major Curtis is a bruising rider himself, though he'd have to be to have qualified for the Rough Riders. Well, there's the chestnut now. Good day to you, Miss Hawthorne."

"And to you, sir."

He strode down the steps and across the lawn to where a man stood holding a horse. Despising myself, but unable to resist, I swiftly slipped back to my former post against the wall and stopped breathlessly to listen.

"Was anyone arrested?" asked Mrs. Randall. "Not—not the major?"

"No one at all—on lack of evidence," declared Mrs. Aldridge disgustedly. "The local authorities must be fools—if they have local authorities in this wilderness, which I doubt."

"Shocking! Quite shocking!" cried Mrs. Randall.

"I knew you'd think so," came Mrs. Aldridge's voice, satisfied. "Horatio says it's none of our business, that it's all in the past, and if the police were satisfied, then we ought to be as well. Then he had the audacity to ask me if I was certain I had the right man. Me, with my memory for faces! It was all over the newspapers, as I've said, especially the New York ones as Mrs. Schyler was a prominent socialite. But it makes no never-mind to Horatio. He's having a marvelous time playing cowboys or something. He won't consider changing hotels; he claims it's more restful without so many people about."

"Well, I'm sorry for you, my dear, but I do see what has to be done. I must cancel our reservations immediately. We will change hotels tomorrow. I daresay the girls and I will be safe here one more night, though I shan't get a wink of sleep. Now I had better go up to our rooms and start the maid packing. And I must tell Major Curtis that we are leaving. To think of the narrow escape my twins have had! It's a well-known fact the Army will accept almost anyone in times of war. But a Rough Rider! An officer! Well! And the New Hampshire papers have made him a hero since!"

"It looks as though the Almighty has punished him, Mrs. Randall, if that's any comfort to you," said Mrs. Aldridge wisely.

"You mean his leg. I daresay." But she sounded uncertain.

"And you have no doubt wondered at the Crystal Hills not being full, or even close to it?"

"Do you mean that . . . ?"

"Precisely. It seems many people have not forgotten that scandal."

There was the sound of a chair scraping against the floor. "Good day, Mrs. Aldridge. I am in your debt."

The geraniums were waving in their white planters, flutterings of crimson against the glossy gray floor of the East Rotunda. But I could not feel the breeze on my face. What had happened here over a year ago to hurt the hotel's business and drive Drake to enlist in the war? For the two events must somehow be linked. Miss Winslow had warned me that there was a nasty scandal attached to his name, and Mrs. Aldridge had spoken of a woman, a socialite from New York with whom he evidently had been involved. But I had missed the crux of the story. The knowledge that I was guilty of blatant eavesdropping added to my exasperation.

Emeline—I must find Emeline, I thought. I had forgotten the errand on which I had come. "Have you seen Miss Curtis?" I asked the doorman.

"I did, a while ago, miss. She went downstairs, I believe."

"Thank you." Crossing the lobby, I went down the wide staircase just under the portrait of Madeline Curtis. But Emeline was not anywhere on the ground floor. It was then that I thought abruptly of the Site of Stones. She was fond of the place; it held special memories for her associated with her

140

grandmother. It was likely that she was there.

Shuddering, I recalled the terror which had overwhelmed me there, the way I had felt compelled to move toward the enormous grooved slab, the ghastly inhuman sounds I had heard. At the thought of going there again, a sick feeling rose in my stomach and my heartbeat quickened. Slowly I went up the stairs, my hand moist as it clutched the banister.

But this was absurd. The place was nothing more than an arrangement of rocks in a clearing in the woods. What was there to occasion such fear and dread in me? But the fear and dread were there, all the same.

Absorbed as I was, I did not notice Drake Curtis and Mrs. Randall until I was practically on top of them. He stood behind the circular front desk in an ivory-colored jacket and waistcoat. She stood before him, fidgeting with the rope of pearls about her neck.

"And so, Major Curtis, we must take the morning train from Nightshade Notch tomorrow. I know I had reserved our rooms for another three weeks, but I will have to cancel that."

"I'm sorry you are leaving sooner than you'd planned, Mrs. Randall," said Drake civilly. "I will make reservations for the three of you on the morning train to Concord."

"Well, no, that won't be necessary, Major Curtis," said Mrs. Randall uneasily, her face flushing. "That is, we're not going directly back to Concord. We're—we've been asked to join some friends at one of the other hotels. I received a letter this morning. You understand how it is." She gave a nervous titter.

"Quite, ma'am," said Drake. I saw that he did indeed understand. He knew that there was no letter, no party of friends.

Mrs. Randall said, "Well, good day to you, Major Curtis," and hurried past me, doubtless thankful to have the awkward task behind her and to have survived her encounter with so scandalous a person. I could imagine her describing the incident to her friends at another hotel, bonneted heads together, fingers grasping teacups, faces filled with delighted shock. "What quick thinking, my dear!" "Yes, I wouldn't have cared to have crossed him, I can tell you. There was something in his face, in his eyes, which caused me disquiet from the first." "Well, they say a lady can always tell a man from a gentleman." "I understand from a friend of mine, a Mrs. Aldridge, who was conversant with all the sordid details, that they carried on quite shamelessly under the husband's very nose." "If that's the sort of behavior which goes on at the Crystal Hills Hotel, I shall be careful never to go there. Full of heathens, I expect, my love. What a lucky thing you left when you did!" "And to think my daughters and I went on a drive and a picnic with him—why, we were practically alone with him all that day, in the middle of nowhere! I tremble to think what might have happened!" "How frightful for you." More nodding, tongue-clicking, and twittering.

I realized then that Drake was regarding me intently, his black brows drawn together. "Well, what is it, Miss Hawthorne?"

"Why, n-nothing. I mean, that is, have you seen Emeline?"

"I have not," he replied curtly. "I thought that was your responsibility." He was making a notation in the large black-bound register.

"Charlotte asked me to look for her. Her parents have returned."

He looked up at that, his face grim. "They have, have they? Something told me this wasn't going to be a favorable day."

"I—I overheard Mrs. Randall cancelling her reservation," I said awkwardly.

He shrugged. "Three more or less make little difference, Miss Hawthorne. Here's something you might be interested in." He gestured to a paper lying on the desk.

"What is it?"

"From your former employer. A bill for the damage to the school carriage house. A rather substantial bill." His smile was twisted. "I told her to send it to me. I did not, however, tell her that I would pay it. She'll have to wait. And now you tell me my brother and sister-in-law have arrived. I wonder what further joys this day holds." Abruptly he turned away, going into the office.

I went out the back door and down the steps to the sloping lawn. The Coopers were seated in one of the gazebos. Waving to them, I walked the length of the hotel to the path in the woods which led to the Site of Stones.

Hesitating, I called out, "Emeline! Emeline!" But there was no answer except for a sudden raucous cry from a wheeling raven overhead.

Go up that path and find her, I told myself sternly. Every step I took I had to force; my heart was hammering unpleasantly as I moved up the slope of the hill, passing the massive tree trunk, its thick roots gripping the boulder like octopus arms.

"Miss Hawthorne!" called a female voice behind me, and I turned in sudden relief to see Miss Birche coming up behind me. Her rather untidy appearance was endearing, her cheerful face comforting. "Are you going to have a look at the Site of Stones?"

"Well, I'm looking for my charge, Emeline, you know. I thought she might be up there."

"Do you mind if I come along? Mr. Sloane was talking about the place last night at dinner and I am most eager to see it."

"It is—unusual. By all means, come with me. It's just at the top of this hill." The sick feeling in the pit of my stomach had lessened in intensity. I gave a little laugh. "I must admit that I'm delighted you came along, Miss Birche. I find the Stones rather—spooky, I'm afraid."

"Are you saying that they might be haunted?" she asked, putting a hand to her throat. "How utterly delicious. Mr. Sloane did say that the place is rumored to be an Indian burial ground, or at least, a ceremonial ground."

We had reached the edge of the clearing. Before us the Stones loomed in the afternoon sun. "Emeline!" I called, but there was only the humming of the locusts. High up, the branches of the towering pines stirred in a breeze that did not reach us.

"It—it doesn't look as though she's here after all," I said nervously. That day I felt nothing more than a vague unease standing there, but I had no desire to linger.

"What a peculiar place this is. And you say you find it spooky. Perhaps you're a sensitive."

"I beg your pardon?"

"A sensitive. Someone who can sense certain emotions or

occurrences from the past in a locale. Most people can walk into an old house and feel nothing. Yet someone else may cross the same threshold, go quite pale, and refuse to take another step."

"That sounds as though I'm some sort of freak," I said shakily. "And besides, never before have I had a similar experience."

"Perhaps you've never been tested," she said. "But it was not my intention to upset you, Miss Hawthorne. But look at this place! Those grotesque cell-like chambers built into the hill—they look as though anything might crawl out of them! And that gigantic flat rock over there—it looks as though it might be some sort of ancient table. Funny, the way a gutter has been cut round the edge."

"Yes," I acknowledged. I wondered what she would say if I told her I had thought I heard voices coming from its perimeter.

"What a fascinating place. It's ideal for a murder, you know."

I caught my breath. "A—a murder?"

"Yes, don't you agree? An eerie setting, a timeless feeling to the place—it seems very far removed from any pretense of civilization. A place with its own rules. A place outside the world."

"I see what you mean," I said faintly. "Well, I should continue looking for Emeline."

"I'll walk back with you."

When we reached the side lawn of the hotel, I spotted Emeline under the East Rotunda. "Where have you been?" I asked her.

"In the kitchen, talking to the new chef, just lately. Did you want me?"

"Your mother and father arrived earlier this afternoon. They were asking for you."

She paled a little at my words. "They have? They're at the house now? Oh—do I look all right?"

She was wearing a pink and gray plaid dress, white stockings, and gray high-buttoned boots. I smiled at her reassuringly. "You look very pretty. Your hair ribbon needs fixing, though." While I did that, she wiped her spectacles with her handkerchief.

"You'll come with me, won't you, Teresa?"

"Of course I will. Emeline, your parents did not realize that you were home, and your mother was rather put out by my presence," I said ruefully. "I'm afraid she is not happy that your uncle hired me."

"Well, only Uncle Drake can let you go. He's certainly too busy to make other arrangements now. And my mother grumbles a lot, but she rarely does anything. Don't worry."

In the sitting room, Charlotte said, "I'm glad you've come back, Emeline. Your mother is resting upstairs, but she'd like to see you. Don't look like that—she's had a chance to calm down. I've also assured her how indispensable Miss Hawthorne has been. Go up to her now."

Emeline left the room and Charlotte said, "I must go speak to the cook about dinner. I suppose Drake will be here as well." She looked worried at the prospect. "I wonder if he knows that Aaron and Leonora are back."

"Yes, he does," I said. "I told him."

Rather apprehensively, that evening I dressed for dinner in a white linen blouse with cut-lace work on the sleeves and at the neckline, and a dark green skirt. Then I combed through my curls before twisting them into a loose topknot, and hoped that I looked the part of a dutiful governess.

Once again in the living room, I studied the oil painting of the Notch while waiting for the others. One side of the sky was serenely blue, but an ominous purple cloud was encroaching from the opposite side, heralded by swirls of mist crowning Mt. Washington. Massive boulders jutted out from the hillside, and the black-green spruces towered above the masses of topaz and orange trees like church steeples. In the foreground was a pool of water, dulled to a murky gray by the thundercloud, and encircled by dead tree trunks in weird contortions.

"Thomas Cole painted that over fifty years ago, long before the hotels were built and people began to vacation here."

"It looks much the same, though," I said, turning to see Drake behind me in a black evening suit, the starched points of his white collar contrasting with his dark good looks.

"Well, have you met Emeline's parents?"

"Yes, I was here when they arrived. They were—surprised to find me here, to say the least. I don't think Mrs. Curtis approved."

He shrugged. "Her feelings do not interest me, nor should they trouble you. Leonora should be grateful you are here, though naturally that's too much to ask of her. Would you care for a glass of sherry?"

"Yes, thank you."

He moved over to the sideboard. I noticed he was not using his cane, but his limp was noticeable. He poured out a glass for me and one for himself.

"Good evening," said Charlotte, coming into the room with Emeline. "I suppose you haven't yet seen Aaron, Drake. I suggested that he go over to the hotel, but . . . Are you going to bring up—?"

"I have no desire to spoil your dinner, Charlotte, or my own," he said.

"Was your mother angry?" I asked Emeline.

She pushed back her spectacles. "Not very. She kept saying how tall I'd grown, frowning and peering into her mirror."

Aaron Curtis strolled in then. "Evening, all," he said breezily.

"Hello, Papa," said Emeline.

"Well, there's my girl," he said heartily, and dropped her a kiss on her brow. "And Miss Hawthorne, I see. How do you do?"

"Hello, Aaron," said Drake, his back to the sideboard, his hand in his trouser pocket.

"Drake! Well, you're looking fit, I must say." His eyes met his brother's for an instant before falling.

Drake said nothing, surveying his brother coolly.

"Well, how's business?" asked Aaron jovially.

"It could be better." Drake's voice was crisp. "Where is your wife?"

"Oh, Nora's nearly ready. You know how it is. She bought quite a—I mean, a few new things in Boston, and couldn't decide what to wear tonight."

"At a family dinner what does it matter?" said Drake, his

146

mouth a narrow line.

"Perhaps I should tell the cook to put back dinner a quarter of an hour," said Charlotte, glancing uneasily from brother to brother.

"No, no need. Here she comes," said Aaron in relief, looking out the door toward the staircase.

If I had thought Leonora Curtis beautiful in her travel-worn suit, she was stunning in a low-cut evening gown of teal blue with the barest of sleeves, her hair elaborately arranged and studded with pearls.

"Good evening, everyone. I'll have a glass of sherry, Aaron. Hello, Drake. You're looking better. I suppose we must thank you for retrieving Emeline from that school. I'm going to write that headmistress a letter tomorrow informing her that I will never recommend her precious school to anyone."

"I would not do that if I were you, Leonora," said Drake.

"Why not?" she asked. "If you've no family pride—and heaven knows that's very likely true—that doesn't mean that I—"

"We owe that school a large sum of money, Leonora, and unless you are willing to enclose a check in your letter expressing your outrage, you would be wise to let the matter lie," Drake said, cutting in swiftly.

She glared at him for a moment, then took the glass of wine her husband held out to her.

"Shall we go in to dinner?" suggested Charlotte.

We took our places in the dining room, Drake and Aaron at opposite ends of the table, Leonora on her husband's right across from Emeline, and myself on Drake's right across from Charlotte.

Leonora Curtis had not once looked at me or acknowledged her daughter. But after we had sat down, she said, "Emeline, I told you this afternoon to take off those ridiculous spectacles. I had hoped that after a year at school you would not need them anymore. How can you expect your eyesight to improve if you wear them constantly like a pair of crutches?"

Emeline flushed, slipping off her spectacles and setting them down on the white tablecloth.

"Only you would see a comparison between a pair of

spectacles and a pair of crutches, Leonora," said Drake. "The child cannot see well without them, and not wearing them will only serve to make her eyesight worse."

"When I want advice from you, I shall ask for it, Drake," said Leonora. "You've interfered enough over Emeline." She looked pointedly at me.

Drake frowned. "If you are referring to my hiring Miss Hawthorne, it was the wisest thing to do in the circumstances. To put it bluntly, Leonora, we cannot afford to send Emeline to another school, especially as you and Aaron chose to take that ill-advised vacation."

"I might have known you'd throw that in our faces. It wasn't as though you needed Aaron at the hotel. With so few guests it's hardly a job to oversee things," she said spitefully.

Drake's eyes narrowed but he said nothing. Dinner was roast lamb garnished with mint, potatoes, and garden peas, but I had little appetite. In this strange atmosphere my stomach felt tied up in knots; I pushed my food about on my plate with my fork.

Across from me Emeline's eyes, vulnerable without the spectacles, wore a rather glazed expression, as though she had withdrawn into herself and was not affected by the tension.

"Sorry you had to make the trip to the coast, Drake," Aaron was saying. "It must have been hard on your—er—"

"Nonsense. It seems to have been just the thing for him, Aaron," said Leonora. "He's not even using his cane tonight, have you noticed? Don't you remember that nice doctor we met at the Cabots' home? He told you that Drake's leg would improve with exercise, when you asked him about it. After all, the worst is behind him now, I said, and the doctor agreed."

Drake shot her a furious look, his square jaw clenching, but she gazed limpidly back at him.

"Actually, business is picking up, isn't it, Drake?" said Charlotte. "He's received a number of bookings for August, far more than for July."

"We lost three today," said Drake shortly.

"Oh, well, what's three?" said Aaron, giving a careless laugh.

"Nothing in itself, but it may have repercussions. We can only hope that we don't receive cancellations for the upcoming weeks, and we desperately need the business. The Glen Echo, I understand, is full to capacity."

"Oh, let's not talk about all of this. It's so dreary," complained Leonora.

"What do you mean by repercussions, Drake?" asked Charlotte, concerned.

"Let's just say that I hope that a certain matron and others like her do not have a large sphere of influence," Drake said. "And it must be understood, Leonora, that both your and Aaron's reckless spending is over for the time being. I agreed reluctantly to funding your vacation for partly selfish reasons. But I hope you've gotten it all out of your systems, because from now on there is going to be a change. We are in serious financial difficulties, as you can't help but be aware of, and I can no longer afford to support your habits."

"Habits!" Leonora went off in a peal of laughter. "That's rich! You're a fine one to talk of habits, I must say."

"Leonora!" said Charlotte.

Drake's face whitened, a muscle working in his cheek.

"And what of Miss Hawthorne here?" continued Leonora. "If we're so short of money, am I to believe that you've persuaded her to tutor Emeline for free?" Her voice was malicious.

"Naturally you would count your personal expenses more important than your daughter's education, Leonora," Drake said in icy tones. "Nonetheless I'm warning you, things will have to be very different from now on."

Chapter Eight

"I've decided that we should begin our studies today, Emeline," I said to her at breakfast the following morning. "Now that your parents have returned I ought to begin earning my keep. I owe that to your uncle, and to you."

"I suppose so," she acknowledged reluctantly. "Mother isn't exactly pleased that . . . although once she knows you better I'm sure she'll feel differently."

"No doubt," I said, having every doubt. "But let's not give her any more reason to dislike the situation." I was still smarting over the way Drake and Leonora had debated the wisdom of hiring me to tutor Emeline over dinner the previous night; it had been humiliating to me to do so in front of the others. Plainly Leonora wanted to send me packing, not because of any personal animosity toward me, but merely because Drake had taken it upon himself to make such a decision and act upon it.

"And one more thing, Emeline. Perhaps it would be best . . ." I paused, biting my lip.

"I know what you're going to say, Teresa," said the girl earnestly, her large blue eyes concerned behind the spectacles. "I won't mention that you were the cook at Miss Winslow's. Not that there is anything wrong with that, of course, but since Mamma has assumed that you were a teacher . . ."

"Your parents might consider that a great deal wrong. Naturally, if they make pointed inquiries into my background, I will not dissemble. I'm not asking you to lie, you understand."

"Don't worry, Teresa. My mother won't make inquiries. She'll have other things to occupy her. I never realized, though, how much she disliked Uncle Drake."

"Yes, well . . . I suggest that we have lessons in the mornings, and then a break after luncheon. Then we'll work for another hour or so in the mid-afternoons."

"All right. But I'd like to devote extra time to mathematics, Teresa, rather than history or something. Because that's the subject I'll use the most in the future when I'm old enough to help run the hotel. I'll need to be very efficient in mathematics, you know, for accounts and things."

"Well, I'll teach you as much as I can, but that's not as much as you'll need to know in order to run a hotel or any large business. But later I'm certain your father and uncle will begin to teach you what you need to know to work at the Crystal Hills. When we've finished breakfast, we can get our books and begin. This blackberry jam is delicious, by the way. Won't you have any?"

She wrinkled her nose. "No, I don't like it. Charlotte and I don't like the seeds in our teeth."

"Where is she this morning?"

"Having breakfast in bed, I expect. She doesn't always feel well enough to come down, you know." And the tension at dinner last night had not helped her any, I thought.

Charlotte had said that we could use the library for our studies; in a short while the two of us were seated at the long table, our heads bent over the books. And while we worked I tried to suppress the memory of the last time I had been in this room, when the flickering firelight had cast a shadow looming large on the wall, a shadow of a man who had dragged me into his arms, crushing my mouth under his, while I trembled in my nightdress. I might have dreamed such an embrace, such a night, so remote had he been ever since, if not for the torn place on my nightdress which I had been obliged to sew. . . .

At lunch it was the three of us, Charlotte explaining that Aaron and Leonora were at the hotel. "You know your parents enjoy being with the guests," she said.

"And Mamma has new gowns. Of course she wants to show

151

them off," said Emeline. "I think I'll go up to the attic after lunch."

"To the attic?" I asked in surprise. "Why?"

"Oh, I haven't been there since coming home. I used to like to poke about, find things of my grandmother and of the hotel. Before I went away to school, I played up there a lot, didn't I, Charlotte? Though of course I'm too old for playing now."

I suppressed a smile. "I'd like to see this attic of yours, if you don't mind." As the two of us were going upstairs, I asked her, "Emeline, when your mother decided to send you to Miss Winslow's over a year ago, did it seem rather sudden?"

"I'll say it was sudden. One evening my mother came into my room and said that she and my father had decided that the hotel was not the right place for me at my age and that I should go to school. My mother said that she was taking me to Portsmouth the next morning."

"So it was a complete surprise to you?"

"It sure was. I cried all that night, hoping she'd change her mind by the morning. But in the morning, even Charlotte was saying what a good thing it would be for me and what a nice city Portsmouth was."

"What about your uncle?"

She frowned. "Uncle Drake? He wasn't there at breakfast. Papa and Mamma never get up that early, but they were both in the dining room that day. I didn't see Uncle Drake before we left. My mother wouldn't let me go to the hotel to say good-bye to anyone. I was angry about that, but she kept saying that if I didn't like it at Miss Winslow's Academy, then I could come home, that it was only a temporary arrangement and I would enjoy meeting other girls my own age. I said I could meet plenty of them among the guests, but she said that wasn't the same thing. She said that if I kept on arguing, then I would stay at school even longer, so I stopped." Her face took on a mutinous look. "She didn't keep her word. They knew I didn't like it there, yet they never sent for me to come home."

"Well, Emeline, you're home now," I said soothingly.

I was fairly convinced by now that the scandal alluded to by Miss Winslow and recounted with relish by Mrs. Aldridge, involving Drake and the married New York socialite, had coincided with the sudden dispatching of Emeline to school. Her family had determined to send her away from Nightshade Notch for a time because something had happened. Something from which they feared might have serious repercussions. Something about Drake . . .

We went upstairs and down one corridor before climbing up a narrow staircase to the attic. At the top Emeline opened a door into an enormous room illuminated by the small deep-set windows in the row of gables along the roof. The musty room was filled with an overwhelming jumble of things no longer deemed useful or fashionable—pieces of furniture, crates, trunks, boxes, various knickknacks, lamps, and other household furnishings amassed over a period of years.

"Let's find the trunks that have Grandmother's old gowns in them. I love to look at them," said my charge. She began to make her way through the maze of clutter. "They're not where they used to be," she called. "Someone's moved things about since I left. They must be here somewhere, though. We never throw anything away."

That much was obvious, I thought, grinning. While she wandered about, I moved off in another direction. I stumbled upon an old set of dining room furniture, the dust thick on the chairs, the table piled with boxes of old dishes. Bandboxes, discolored and dirty, were stacked against an old wardrobe, and I found a series of old maps of the mountains in the Presidential Range. There was also one of the Notch itself, yellowed and torn. On it I found the locations of the Flume, the Crystal Cascade, the Basin, and Loon Lake, although there was no mention of the hotel. There was some hunting equipment propped up against one wall—rifles, packs, and even a black and battered camp stove.

"Here they are!" called Emeline from halfway across the room, and I followed the direction of her voice past some nursery furniture and a well-worn rocking horse.

"This is it," she said, delighted. "This old steamer trunk has some of Grandmother's clothes in it." She had lifted the lid and leaned it back against a rolltop desk, and was now putting aside the layers of tissue paper. "These were some of the things she had when first coming to the White Mountains thirty years ago. She always had beautiful clothes. Look at this one." She held up a gown of blue-gray taffeta with pink silk roses scalloping the frilled skirt and bustle. "I like these gowns better than the ones today, I think. This one would have looked lovely on you, Teresa, with your red hair and green eyes." It was an emerald ball gown, the sleeves trimmed elaborately with lace. "I do like the ball gowns best. I hope we can have a ball soon at the hotel, and that Mamma will permit me to stay up for a while. Let's see what else we can find. I know there are trunks filled with old bonnets and things. I used to try them on and pretend to be Grandmother. I would hide up here from my governess when I didn't want to have lessons."

"Well, now I'll know where to find you."

"Silly! That was years ago, and I don't mind lessons with you."

While she shoved boxes this way and that, I wandered among the thirty years' worth of accumulation. There were bolts of fabric which had never been used, stacks of fashion periodicals, boxes of linens and laces, now yellowed and stained. We stayed up in the attic poking around for a while longer until I reminded Emeline that it was nearly time for afternoon lessons.

"Oh, all right," she said. "But I haven't found Grand-mother's wedding dress yet."

"You can look another time."

We were nearly to the door when Emeline stopped, saying, "I wonder what's in here. I don't remember this trunk being here before. Let's see what's inside."

"If this is your way of postponing English Poetry, I can assure you it won't work."

"No, that's not it. I'm coming right away. But first I want to look inside. It's definitely not Grandmother's or Grand-father's."

"Perhaps it belongs to one of your parents—or even one of the servants, Emeline."

"There's a padlock, but it's not locked." She crouched down, her fingers on the lid.

I had a sudden misgiving. "Wait, Emeline. We don't know whose it is. Perhaps you shouldn't—"

But she was already opening the trunk and peering inside. She lifted something out. "It's just a suit."

"It's a uniform," I said, looking at the dusty-brown fatigues.

"Look, there's something pinned to the jacket—a medal." It was an ornate medal attached to a blue ribbon with small white stars on the ribbon. "There's a wool blanket too, and a canteen and some other stuff. Do you think they belong to Drake?"

"I think they must."

"I know he went to New York and joined the Army soon after I went to school. Charlotte wrote and told me so. But I didn't think about it much. I mean, it didn't seem real to me. It's funny to imagine him going to Cuba, and fighting, and getting wounded and all that, while I was stuck at Miss Winslow's and every day seemed the same there. It looks like no one has touched these things since he came back, that they just brought the trunk up here and haven't thought about it since. Look, here's a knife and—"

"Emeline, put everything back." My voice was sharper than I'd intended. "This is not one of your grandmother's trunks from many years ago; it's your uncle's and none of our business. Put back the uniform and let's go downstairs."

Kneeling down myself, I began to fold the set of fatigues she had discarded. I took them gingerly, half-expecting to see blood or torn spots, but they were clean and had been neatly pressed. They had not been through a battle; he must have worn these while in the hospital in New York, or when traveling home last winter. The insignia of a major were on them, along with the curious-looking medal.

"Look at this, Teresa," said Emeline, who had ignored me and was still rummaging through her uncle's things. "It's a document—oh, it's only a paper to say he was let out."

"It's a medical discharge paper," I said, taking it from her. I read, ". . . in view of the injuries you sustained in combat, and the attendant medical dependence, we regret that you are no longer physically qualified for continued service. Accordingly, you are hereby honorably discharged from service in the Department of the Army. You are authorized to wear the uniform of your grade with all military decorations prescribed in transit to your home of record. Done this 17th day of December 1898."

Suddenly I felt guilty and furtive, reading Drake's papers, examining his clothes. I had told Emeline that things were none of her business; they were even less of mine. The less I thought about Major Drake Curtis, the better.

"Put these things away exactly as you found them," I told her severely. "And I wouldn't mention this to anyone."

"I don't know what's so secretive about an old uniform and stuff," she grumbled.

"Well, your uncle has made it clear that he doesn't like to be asked about the war or his part in it, so we can't ever bring it up."

"Do you mean I can't ask him what that medal means, and what he did to get it?"

"No, you cannot. If Major Curtis wanted it talked about, he would mention it himself. I think it's better you never go in this trunk again."

"Oh, very well. It's not all that interesting anyway."

Later when our lessons were over for the day, and it was still much too early to dress for dinner, I felt in need of some fresh air. The afternoon had grown overcast and there was a damp chill in the air, so I tossed a shawl over my shoulders and went outside. It looked as though a storm were approaching, gray masses of clouds blotting out the mountain crests and advancing down the slopes. The wind had come up, and above my head the ravens dove and circled, ominous black splashes against the pale sky, their harsh cries mingling with the reedy sound of the rising wind.

I entered the stretch of woods which separated the house from the hotel, and had only gone a few yards where I heard the sounds of male voices. Peering up the twisting path through the trees, I saw Drake and Aaron coming in my direction. Having no wish to see either of them, I did the first thing which came into my head; I ducked behind a large lichen-spotted boulder to the side of the path and waited for them to pass. They were coming closer; I realized what a fool I would look like if I were seen crouching there, but it was too late to hurry back to the house now.

"I expected you to come to the office today, Aaron," Drake was saying coldly.

"Oh, well, I was doing my bit, Drake. Visiting with the guests, making them feel at home—you know that's as important as all the dull business. You know what a muddled head pouring over those accounts gives me."

"It's something else entirely that gives you a muddled head, Aaron, and you do plenty of it while 'visiting.' But that's your affair. I hoped you'd come to me man to man for a frank talk. That was apparently too much to hope for."

Aaron gave a nervous laugh. "A frank talk? About what? I know you run the hotel much better than I. I don't dispute that. I've given the reins over to you again. What more do you want?"

"An explanation, dear brother. You know exactly what I'm referring to."

"Honestly I don't, old boy." Aaron's voice was blustery. "You're being rather mysterious. And I feel like a drink. I'm going on to the house."

Drake's voice was flinty. "You're not going anywhere, Aaron, not yet. I hoped you'd be man enough to come to me, but it's clear I have to be the one to bring it up. I know about the mortgage, Aaron."

To my dismay they had both stopped and were standing very nearby.

"Oh, that. Well—"

"Did you think I wouldn't find out? When I was in Portsmouth, I paid a visit to Choake and Sumner, to apply for a loan. A loan to tide us over, to make improvements, to draw in more business. Imagine, if you will, my chagrin when I'm told the amount I proposed to borrow was out of the question due to the mortgage we—we—had taken out in January on your trip to the coast."

"Now, Drake, it's not what you think. A little mortgage. We'll pay it off," said Aaron in wheedling tones.

"Twenty-five thousand dollars? A little mortgage! My God, Aaron, what did you need twenty-five thousand dollars for?

157

Why the hell did you do it? To forge my name—"

"That's a rather strong word, Drake," put in Aaron. "After all—"

"Forgive me," Drake said, cutting in in biting, sarcastic tones. "Why did you *sign* my name to a document you knew I would never agree to while I was here . . . but that's why, isn't it? Because you knew I couldn't go with you, you knew you could get away with it while I was damned helpless!"

"I couldn't trouble you with it then, Drake. But if I had, you'd have agreed that I'd no choice but to borrow against the Crystal Hills. Even Mother would have agreed."

"Don't bring her into this, you stupid clod! Just tell me what the money was for. It certainly wasn't to hire new employees after you'd let half of them go—those that didn't quit, that is."

"Well . . ."

"What was it for, damn it! There was plenty of money in the bank when I left in May. You went through all of that—you embezzled hotel funds—and then also took out a twenty-five-thousand-dollar mortgage! *Where did the money go?*"

"All right," said Aaron, his voice suddenly ugly. "I owed some money. I owed some money, all right? And it had to be paid. That's the honorable thing, after all, to pay one's personal debts."

"Personal. Yet you embezzled hotel funds, went through those, and when they gave out, you sold a large interest in the hotel, after I'd returned and yet without telling me. You had agreed to begin making payments in May of this year, at the start of the summer season. Yet when I visited Choake and Sumner, it was July and they had not yet received one monthly payment. Did you think they would forget, Aaron? When did you plan to tell me? Or were you just going to act as if the mortgage didn't exist?"

"I was going to get round to it, Drake, really I was. But you haven't been well. I thought it best to wait."

"Spare me your consideration. It's sickening. Instead of telling me, you went off on a vacation we could not afford, running away again."

"Oh, shut up, Drake! If we're to talk of running away, you'll come off far worse. You're so damned self-righteous, but you weren't that way last spring, were you? Not when you were carrying on with Alice Schyler. Whose fault is it that business fell off in the first place, I'd like to know? And if you're so concerned about the mortgage payments, then sell some of the land! Just remember, you were the one to leave the hotel, to run out, to—"

There was a hard smacking sound followed by a heavy thud. My heart hammering, I saw Drake stalk off down the path toward the house. On the other side of the boulder I could hear Aaron getting to his feet, his breathing slow and heavy. "You'll pay for that, little brother," he mumbled before moving unsteadily in the other direction, back toward the hotel.

For a while I stayed there, motionless, afraid either of them might return and realize I had overheard their ugly argument. The wind was getting stronger. I hugged my shawl about me. I was being inextricably drawn into the tensions at Nightshade Notch, and I felt powerless in preventing it.

So Aaron had forged Drake's name to a legal document, a mortgage on the Crystal Hills Hotel. And Drake had known nothing of it until the day he had come to take Emeline from school. She had said that he had been gone the entire afternoon while she had searched in the park for her necklace; I recalled the way he had looked that evening in the hotel dining room— pale, grim, forbidding. At the time I had put his manner down to his wounded leg and the pain it must have been causing him, but it was now clear that there had been more to it than that. He had suffered a shock that afternoon in the offices of Choake and Sumner; he had learned that while he lay helpless in the hospital, Aaron had embezzled funds from the hotel, and later had signed his name to a document which bound them to make monthly payments on a business his family owned. It was no wonder he had savagely struck his brother; he had doubtless wanted to wring his neck. Aaron had not only never informed Drake of their financial obligation, but had taken his wife on an expensive vacation the hotel could little support.

I was forming a clear picture of Aaron Curtis's character. Poor Emeline, I thought, to have such parents. She loved the hotel and looked forward to helping to run it the way her grandmother had. There seemed to be more than a slim chance that her dream would never be fulfilled, that the Curtises would lose the Crystal Hills.

Now I understood Charlotte's attitude toward Aaron; now I understood Drake's curt remarks to Emeline while in Portsmouth. But I still did not understand what lay at the root of all this strife, the scandal which had occurred, with effects that were being felt more than a year later. Aaron had accused Drake of running away when he had enlisted. He must have been running from something quite dreadful. . . .

The wind had changed from a whine to a roar; the light was fading rapidly. Overhead the mounds of clouds were a charcoal gray; the ravens had fled, screeching their last defiance, powerless against the stalking storm.

I made my way back to the house, conscious of a distant rumble of thunder. As I came round to the front of the house, I saw Drake ride off furiously down the drive, gravel spraying, a black scowl on his face.

Charlotte, Emeline, and I dined alone. Leonora and Aaron were at the hotel; Drake did not come. I told Charlotte that I had seen him ride away.

"But there's a storm outside!" cried Emeline. "Isn't it dangerous to be riding during a thunderstorm?"

"Your uncle can be reckless at times," said Charlotte.

Rain slashed at the Gothic windows like tiny, flailing hammers. Flashes of lightning, brilliantly menacing, lit the earth and sky in brief, eerie glows. The thunder mounted, booming across the mountainous ridges.

Charlotte retired early that evening, and Emeline and I went to her room to play checkers. She had a large pleasant room filled with white wicker furniture, the walls papered in pink and white stripes. On her desk was displayed the photograph Charlotte had given her of herself and Madeline Curtis.

The storm raged outside, but the maid had lit a crackling fire and so we sat cozily at our game. It was after nine o'clock when I said good night and went out into the corridor. Emeline's parents had not yet returned; they probably would not do so until the storm let up.

At the end of the long hallway, I heard a door close; Drake was coming toward me. In the glow of the gaslights I could see his clothes were drenched, his thick black locks plastered to his head and over his brow. One leg, encased in a mud-spattered boot, dragged along the carpet behind the other.

"Just one moment, Miss Hawthorne," he said as I paused to open the door to my room.

My pulses leaped; I stood gazing at the varnishing on the door.

"I wanted to apologize for my sister-in-law's behavior the other evening. It was not you she was annoyed with, but me."

I glanced up. "Does she want to dismiss me?"

"I have no idea of her wishes. But she cannot do it, Miss Hawthorne. I hired you and it is I who am paying your salary. On the other hand, you may well feel that you wish to leave here." His face was inscrutable.

"Leave?"

"You must admit that this house is not always a pleasant place in which to live. I told you that you might regret coming to the Notch."

"I don't wish to be the cause of any friction between you and Emeline's parents," I said slowly.

"Friction!" He gave a brief, hard laugh. "I assure you that your presence here is the very least cause of our friction. We manage quite well enough on our own."

I did not know what to say. "Well, good night," I murmured after an awkward pause.

"Teresa," he began, and looking up, I saw with surprise that there was a strange, urgent appeal in his eyes, an appeal which at the same time perplexed and unnerved me. "Teresa, I . . ." He broke off, his face tightening. "Good night, Miss Hawthorne," he said, his voice cool and distant, before turning on his heel and limping down the corridor.

And I was left to battle with the harsh realization that I had wanted nothing less than to be taken once again into his fierce, passionate embrace. But I did not delude myself into thinking that I had anything to offer a man like Drake Curtis. Falling in love with him would lead to nothing but humiliation and anguish for me.

The next morning the sun shone again, glistening on the wet leaves of the trees and hedges. When I opened the casement window, the familiar heady scents of moist pine and fir rushed in. While I dressed in my lavender cotton gown and braided my hair in one thick plait, I managed to dispel most of the previous night's dejection. Perhaps what I thought I felt for Drake was nothing more than empathy and gratitude. Gratitude, because he had provided me with an opportunity to leave Miss Winslow's employ. Because he had brought me to this rugged, wildly beautiful land which both fascinated and stimulated me. And with his other problems, it was not difficult to have sympathy for him, to put myself in his position. It did not mean I was falling in love. But none of these comfortingly rational thoughts explained why in the hallway last night I had longed to throw myself into his arms. . . .

The days continued in the same routine Emeline and I had begun. We saw little of Aaron and Leonora, who passed most of their time at the Crystal Hills. Aaron was taking out excursion parties, leaving Drake with the actual managing of the hotel's affairs. A party had lately arrived from Boston, several of them being Leonora's friends, and she was occupied with them. When we did see Drake, he was preoccupied and remote.

One evening when Emeline was in bed with a head cold, I went down to dinner and saw with surprise that the table was set for five. Leonora's friends must have left; either that or she had run out of new gowns to wear, I thought uncharitably.

"I asked if we could all make the attempt to dine together tonight," Charlotte explained. "This family needs badly to be reminded that it is a family."

"Perhaps I should eat upstairs with Emeline," I said uncomfortably.

"Certainly not, Teresa. I need you to help balance out some of the others," she added, smiling.

"Well, and how is our Miss Hawthorne tonight?" asked Aaron jovially, coming into the room.

"Fine, sir."

"Good, good. Haven't seen enough of you lately. Aren't making Emeline work too hard, I hope. Don't want to ruin those pretty eyes of yours, do you?"

"I wouldn't concern myself with Miss Hawthorne's eyes, Aaron," said Leonora coldly. She wore a pale green and mauve chiffon gown. Her long white neck was unadorned, but there was a bracelet of emeralds on one wrist. "It is Emeline who wears the spectacles, after all. Where's Drake? Or are we to be spared his cheerful company tonight?"

"He'll be along shortly," said Charlotte.

"Nora's annoyed with Drake because she asked him to hire a social coordinator," said Aaron, grinning. His own animosity toward his brother seemed to have faded.

"Yes, and he refused, just as I expected he would," she declared, her mouth a narrow line.

"If you expected that I would, why did you bother to ask?" said Drake, joining us.

"I believe they are ready to serve dinner," put in Charlotte hastily. "Shall we sit down?"

"I understand that the Glen Echo has one," said Leonora sullenly.

"When we are once again bringing in the business that Glen Echo does, I will consider it," said Drake evenly.

"You realize that I am in a most humiliating position," she went on. "The Evanses and the Harrises are often comparing our hotel to the one they stayed in last summer—not favorably, I might add."

"Then the Evanses and the Harrises ought to cancel their reservations and remove themselves to another hotel," said Drake.

"You really mean that, don't you?" Leonora's eyes glinted angrily. "If it weren't for me, we wouldn't even have their business, just remember that."

"I do remember it, every time Mrs. Harris complains to me about the food being too flavorful. Just what is too flavorful? I asked her today. Or when Mrs. Evans complains that she can never locate her husband because he is enjoying himself too much."

"At least next month's reservations are an improvement on those of this and last," Charlotte said stoutly. "We will weather this, and by next year I feel certain that the Crystal Hills will once again be the most popular hotel in the White Mountains."

Leonora cast her a look of contemptuous disbelief; Drake

163

said nothing. Yet he did not seem to be in bad spirits.

"Well, we may be able to make that claim before next summer," announced Aaron heartily.

"What are you talking about?" snapped his wife. "That would take nothing less than a miracle."

He patted his breast pocket. "I just may have one. Right here."

"What do you mean, Aaron?" asked Charlotte.

"I mean that we may not have to wait until next summer before business is up again and we are turning people away the way we once did." He leaned back in his chair, looking very pleased with himself.

Drake's eyes were speculative as he regarded his brother.

Charlotte said, a trace of irritation in her voice, "Well, Aaron, you have our full attention. Just what is this miracle in your pocket?"

He smiled and set down his glass of wine. "All right, I'll tell you. But remember, it was my doing. I don't get nearly enough credit around here." He glanced around pointedly at all of us. Reaching into his breast pocket, he drew out an envelope. "I have here a letter from Ernest Willoughby. Does that name ring a bell, Leonora?"

She frowned, considering. "No, I can't say that it does."

"He was the archaeologist we met at the house party in Rockport," said Aaron.

"Oh, the little man who digs in the dirt all day. I wondered how on earth he managed to get invited to that party. What a bore he was. How on earth could he help the hotel, Aaron?"

I glanced at Drake. His eyes had narrowed; he sat very still.

"It's very simple, Nora. And we don't have to do a thing, that's the beauty of it. He can make a momentous discovery on our land, a discovery that will bring in business, drawing people to the Crystal Hills. I tell you, we'll be turning 'em away."

"What on earth is there to discover around here?" asked Leonora scornfully. "You're talking nonsense, Aaron." Charlotte looked baffled as well.

"Have you forgotten, all of you, the Site of Stones?" he

asked triumphantly.

There was a palpable silence. Charlotte glanced swiftly down at Drake, putting a hand to her throat.

"That pile of rubble?" Leonora laughed. "You have lost your mind, Aaron."

Aaron flushed. "That pile of rubble, dear wife, may just be the remains of a very old civilization."

"Yes, the Indians. But I've never heard that by unearthing tomahawks and arrowheads one was making a great discovery."

"But that's just it, Nora. Mr. Willoughby will not be searching for arrowheads or tomahawks. He believes . . . well, I don't know exactly what he believes. But I've given him permission to come here and excavate—or whatever they call it—at the Site of Stones."

"You've what?" Drake had risen to his feet.

"Now Drake, old boy, calm down. It'll be good for business, like I said."

"Good for business!" He was very pale.

"Yes. In a month or so, people will hear of his excavations and will come to see for themselves what all the fuss is about. We'll give people a better reason to come than to just watch the leaves change colors."

"Aaron, have you thought about what you are doing?" asked Charlotte. "Have you thought about what Mr. Willoughby's presence there may stir up? Just as we are trying to—"

"Of course he didn't think," said Leonora, her lips twisted. "He rarely does. It's not enough that Mr. Sloane is boring everyone to tears with his array of useless knowledge. Now we'll have another one just like him, and dirt everywhere, I expect."

An expression of ludicrous dismay came over Aaron's face.

"How did Mr. Willoughby know about the Site of Stones?" asked Drake, his voice soft but deadly. "We've never advertised its existence."

"Why, I'm not sure," began Aaron uneasily. "Could have heard or read about it someplace, I guess."

"Read about it," repeated Drake. "Could he possibly have read about it last May, a year ago? *In the newspapers?*"

"I—I daresay he did. He said it—fascinated him at the time,

got him to wondering. What, I don't know. The Stones, I mean. Wondering about the Stones." He shifted in his chair, his face red. "Now look here, Drake, this is something totally different. No one will connect those two events. No one will remember—"

"They'll remember just as soon as the papers get wind of his investigations," Drake shouted, a muscle working in his cheek. "And then we won't have to be turning people away. They'll leave of their own accord—because the whole damn sordid thing will have begun again! You think this may bring in business, Aaron? I think it may finish us once and for all!"

"Well, whose fault is that if it does?" cried Leonora. "Who the hell started all the problems to begin with? Who left Aaron and me to deal with the departing guests, the reporters, the canceled reservations? I ask you, Drake, who was the cause of all that 'damn sordid thing'?"

Drake glared furiously at her, his face hard as granite, as white as marble. Then he flung down his napkin and stormed from the room.

Chapter Nine

"Leonora," began Charlotte sternly, "I asked most particularly that we all make an attempt to have a pleasant meal together this evening. If you cannot say something civil, then why must you say anything at all?"

Leonora shrugged. "Nothing irritates me more than Drake's holier-than-thou attitude, as though he is the only one to care anything about the hotel. I only spoke the truth when I said all our troubles can be laid at his door. It seemed to me he needed reminding of that."

"If you truly believe that, then you are even more delusionary than I realized. But I have no wish to argue with you. But you, Aaron, how on earth could you agree to that man coming here? Have you no foresight as to the damage he can cause, even inadvertently? I assume your agreement is in writing? Yes, I thought so. Then Drake cannot very well gainsay him."

"Oh, Drake's just looking at it from the very worst angle as he does everything now," said Aaron carelessly, pouring himself another glass of wine. "I should have known he'd take it like that. Instead I presumed you'd all be pleased."

"More fool you," said Leonora smoothly.

Aaron's eyes narrowed. "I don't care what any of you think. This fellow Willoughby's investigations will improve business, I tell you. Someday you'll all be grateful to me. Even Drake."

"Oh, shut up, Aaron," snapped his wife. "Improving business. That's all anyone ever talks about. I'm sick of the whole idea. If you want my opinion, I think the Crystal Hills is doomed. It's a pity Drake hasn't the means to buy you out, Aaron, before things get much worse. I, for one have no wish to watch everything we have collapse about our ears."

She rose from her seat, her contemptuous glance resting on my face. "I daresay that in coming here, you have got more than you bargained for, Miss Hawthorne. If you take my advice, my dear, you'll leave very soon. There is undoubtedly too much melodrama here for a simple schoolmarm."

Perhaps it was her condescending tone of voice which caused me to say what I did. Perhaps it was her disdainful expression. But before I could think, I said coldly, "You are laboring under a slight misapprehension, Mrs. Curtis. I was never a schoolmarm."

Her perfectly arched brows drew together. "Never a schoolmarm?" she repeated, startled. "Then—"

"Oh, I was employed at Miss Winslow's Academy for Young Ladies, Mrs. Curtis. But not as a teacher, although I was trained to be one. I was the cook. So, you see, I am not the only one to whom Major Curtis has not explained the full state of affairs."

Leonora's face took on a look of astonished fury; then, swiftly her expression changed to one of amusement—still, however, with bright, angry eyes. "The cook! Oh, that's rich! Isn't it just like Drake to spite me like that? The cook!"

"I don't believe Major Curtis intended any spite," I said a trifle uncertainly. Had part of his motivation in hiring me been to get back at his brother and sister-in-law for their irresponsibility in leaving the hotel? Had the fact that I had never worked as a teacher appealed to some perverse sense of humor?

"You are scarcely in a position to judge, Miss Hawthorne," said Leonora scornfully. "You know nothing about what Drake is capable of. I daresay if you did, you would never have come here in the first place."

"That's enough, Leonora," said Charlotte with meaning. "Enough has been said on every conceivable subject, I believe. I can see how mistaken I was to suggest a family dinner tonight."

"I tried to warn you how it might be, Charlotte, but you always know best, don't you? Charlotte the peacemaker. Charlotte the self-proclaimed preserver of the Curtis family. You've been playing that role for as long as I can remember."

Charlotte's eyes flickered once as she gazed up at Leonora. Leonora's face was mocking, her lips curved in a derisive smile. I looked from one to the other, not understanding them. Charlotte's gaze did not waver; there seemed to be something passing between the two women that Aaron and I were not privy to.

Then Leonora was looking over her shoulder at her husband and the moment was over. "I'm going back to the hotel, Aaron. Drake has hired an orchestra to play tonight and I feel like dancing. Are you coming?"

He pushed back his chair. "Yes, my love. Perhaps a waltz with you would be just the thing."

"You mean a waltz with Amy Evans," said Leonora cynically. "And she barely eighteen."

"Well, you must admit she's the best-looking of the lot," said Aaron jovially, his good humor restored. "Damn sight improvement on that Miss Birche!" He laughed and followed his wife from the room.

Charlotte's head dropped on her hand. "Please forgive all of us, Teresa. At least Emeline was not a witness to this disastrous evening. We mustn't upset the child with these abusive scenes."

"I believe she senses a great deal anyway," I said softly. After hesitating a moment, I went on. "Have—have relations between Major Curtis and Mrs. Curtis always been as they are now?"

"They were never fond of one another, but things have rapidly deteriorated between them in the past few months. It does not help that Aaron and Leonora squandered huge sums of money—hotel money—while Drake was away." She sighed. "I know that common courtesy prevents you from asking further details concerning certain matters alluded to tonight. So I will tell you what I can. One of the guests—a very wealthy young woman—was found dead a year ago last May at the Site of Stones. And that kind of notoriety can be close to

169

fatal for a place of business such as the Crystal Hills."

"I see." In actuality, of course, I saw no more now than I had earlier. All I had learned was the location of the tragedy.

"And now I'm afraid I must ask you to excuse me," said Charlotte. "I feel a headache coming on and so I shall go to bed."

"May I help you up the stairs, Charlotte?" I asked with concern as she rose unsteadily from the table.

"I confess I would be grateful for some support. I'm sorry to be such a nuisance."

When we reached her room, she turned to me with a faint smile. "I know I haven't any right to ask you this, my dear," she said gently, "but I hope you won't let Leonora's words influence you. I hope you will stay a while, for Emeline's sake."

"I have no intention of leaving at the present," I assured her. "I too feel that Emeline needs—care and attention. I am relieved that you do not think any less of me for being the cook at the Academy. You see, I had tried to get a position there as teacher, but the only job open was one of cook, and I so desperately needed work at that time—"

"You have no need to explain to me, Teresa. I place full reliance in Drake's judgment, and since he hired you, and since I have gotten to know you myself, I know you are the ideal person to tutor Emeline. And what is more important, the two of you are friends. When I heard that Emeline was returning home—well, I confess I was worried. You have seen how much attention her parents give her. But since you have come to look after her, I feel as though a burden has been lifted from my shoulders." She laughed a little. "How melodramatic! I fear tonight has depressed me. As if Emeline could be a burden! I only meant . . ."

"I know exactly what you meant, Charlotte."

"Madeline always wanted the best for Emeline. Leonora was far from being the ideal mother, even when Emeline was a little girl. And Madeline was fully aware of Aaron's shortcomings as well. Many times she would say to me, 'Thank heaven for Drake. He'll take care of things. He'll preserve the Crystal Hills for the next generation—he, and then Emeline.' She had high hopes for Emeline." She smiled, but there was a pucker in her brow.

"You are worried that perhaps the family will lose the Crystal Hills Hotel," I said.

"Well, this is a troubled place, my dear, don't deceive yourself into thinking otherwise. And I'm very much afraid that there is worse to come. I feel it brewing . . . in my bones, as they say. I'm saying this to prepare you, not to frighten you. If only Aaron had not granted that archaeologist permission to excavate at the Site of Stones. Any publicity he incurs may bring back the appalling scandal. But Aaron has always been rash and imprudent." She shook her head. "As if Drake hasn't enough to worry him. And especially now that more guests are arriving every day or so."

After I said good night to her, I went to my room. It was clear that Drake's involvement with Alice Schyler, the married socialite from New York, had directly resulted in her death. But just how had the woman died? I wondered uneasily. Mrs. Aldridge had referred to an investigation, and from various people I had learned that newspaper reporters had flocked to the hotel. Charlotte had omitted telling me the cause of her death—perhaps because I would be compelled to ask further questions she might not wish to answer. Maybe she feared that if I was privy to more details, I might not want to remain in Nightshade Notch, despite my brave words. And she wanted the best for Emeline.

Had the young woman taken her own life? Had she been murdered? I recalled that Mrs. Aldridge had stated that no arrests had been made. Naturally a suicide or murder of a young woman of birth, wealth, and social position would be sensational news, news which at the very least could severely harm a posh hotel's reputation.

And then, sometime shortly afterward, Drake had escaped. Escaped—now why had that word come to mind? He had departed the scene of the tragedy and ensuing scandal, and had traveled to New York to sign up with the First Volunteer Cavalry, better known as the Rough Riders. To what extent had he been involved in the unfortunate woman's death?

I opened the casement window and leaned out. The full

moon shone high overhead, a gilded disc against the velvet darkness. By its light I could see wisps of clouds drifting eerily across the sky. The mountains were indiscernible, cloaked by the night, but I knew they were there, formidable, brooding. I had the impression of something ominous out there, something which simmered and seethed, something we were helpless to extinguish. Like Charlotte, I could sense it, and like her, I knew to be afraid.

The following day Emeline's fever was gone, but I suggested that she remain indoors and we would not resume lessons until the morrow. Her mother brought in a few of her fashion periodicals before going off to the hotel, and so we thumbed through those for a while. To cheer Emeline up, because she wanted badly to get out of bed and get dressed, I arranged her hair in several grown-up styles, and we giggled over the results. I took lunch with her in her room, but suggested afterwards that she rest quietly for a while.

"More rest!" she grumbled. "I feel much better!"

"I think it advisable for you to remain in bed one day longer," I said. "Try to take a nap."

I left her room, deciding that while she rested alone I would take a long walk. Outside the sky was a mottled white, and a closeness, a heaviness hung in the cool air. No wind stirred the heavy boughs of the spruces or swayed the wraithlike silver birches. I decided that I would explore the far woods behind the hotel, and set out across the meadow which was littered with erratic boulders and clusters of birch trees. In the distance were Mt. Washington and its neighbors, enormous bulks of undulating forest land, highlighted by pale outcroppings of granite and divided at the timberline by the black *krumholz.*

As I drew close to the solemn woods, I turned back to look at the hotel. It gleamed with an unreal quality amidst the shaded Notch, its white walls and cherry-red roof looking slightly bizarre, out of place. From there it did not exude its usual air of welcome. Rather it was secretive and remote, the very tiny windows lined up like rows of wary eyes, suspiciously scanning the wilderness. It was as though it knew it did not belong in that landscape, and feared what lurked outside its walls.

172

When I reached the edge of the woods, I began to search for a path cutting through the close columns of trees. I found one further down, and turned once again to gaze back at the Crystal Hills, my mind lured by its image. But the hotel was not visible from where I stood. It had been swallowed up by a wall of dark, prickly evergreens. Nothing could be seen but the lofty blue-green highlands, surging in the distance. There was no sign of the opulence of the Crystal Hills, the grandness that man had contrived and erected. So had this land looked thousands of years ago, and would likely look thousands of years in the future, after we had come and gone. There was a powerful force, an energy to this domain which could never be ignored. For the present it tolerated the presence of the Crystal Hills, of the frail human creatures who inhabited it, but there was a timeless mystery to Nightshade Notch that we would never be able to subdue, much less eliminate. Now it was not the hotel which seemed secretive, but the rugged landscape which surrounded and dominated it. The towering mountains, the stark crags, the shadowed pockets of gloom, they possessed secrets at which we could only guess. They had watched the twisting of events, events I now felt compelled at all costs to unravel. And gravely, they watched still.

I entered the woods where the rough brown trunks merged into darkness up ahead. The green gloom of their laden branches blotted out a good deal of the milky light. Further into the forest the path began to climb; stones littering the way made walking difficult. The stones were worn so smooth that I suspected that in spring this was not a path at all, but a streambed carrying overflow down the slope from a water source higher up. Miniature pines and spruce trees, achingly vulnerable, sprouted from the forest floor. I became conscious of a faint whooshing sound which gradually grew into a roar. The scent of pine was strong in the close, still air.

The noise was intensifying; I began to hurry up the hill to locate its source. Then the trees thinned; the path opened onto a rocky ridge dotted with shrubs and ferns. And I was standing above it—a dramatic natural gorge. Steep granite walls rose very high on either side of the chasm with many jagged ledges and crevices. Reddish-brown rock blended into the dark gray granite. Headlong rushed the water below. The force and sound of the Flume, for that was what it was, was tremendous; I could feel the vibration as I stood on the ridge. The air was damp with rising mist.

Just in front of me was a narrow footbridge fashioned of ropes and wooden frames, and secured by two great trunks of trees on either side of the gorge. It swung slightly, but I put one cautious foot on it and was reassured to find it sturdy. If I cared to walk along the Flume itself, I had to cross to the other side, where there was a flat, wide ledge running alongside the steep walls of the cliff. On my side there was no such ledge which went the length of the twisting gorge. I gripped the rope railings and crossed the footbridge as quickly as I was able, careful to look ahead rather than down at the thundering water. When I was across, I began to walk up the side of the Flume.

At some points the ledge became very narrow; the cliff loomed high, jutting out over the path. But most of the time the way was easy enough, the surface wide and smooth, and I could see my way ahead. A luxurious growth of flowers, ferns, and mosses grew on the uppermost ledges of the chasm, the ferns spilling downwards in feathery cascades, the young, delicate pines trembling.

Pausing, I gazed down the torturous length of the Flume. I had a strange sensation of freedom, of release. From this height the view was spectacular, a cavernous opening of the earth gouged out by a constant, violent surge. Peaks of rock jutted from the swirling, plummeting water.

After a time I decided I had better start the trek back along the stone walkway; I should return to the house and see how Emeline was doing. I began to follow again the contorted line of the Flume, and I was not able to see much ahead in some places. At one point the path got very narrow as a cliff surged out from the bank. Not able to see round it, I cautiously stepped along the precipice, my fingers gripping the jagged stone wall beside me. Again I was careful not to look to the other side or down into the Flume depths, but instead looked down at the steps my feet were taking. The noise made by the thundering cascade was deafening.

As I was rounding the cliff, I felt myself bump against something which threw me off balance. Stumbling, I saw with horror the gorge rising up to meet me. A sharp scream escaped my lips as I tottered on the precipice, certain I would fall into those brutal torrents. But two strong arms gripped and steadied me, pulling me roughly away from the edge and onto the wide ledge ahead.

My heart was in my throat; I was gasping for breath as my eyes met those of Drake Curtis, his no less wild, no less terrified. Then abruptly he released me and I stepped back from the precipice until I felt the sharp, rough cliff pressing into my back.

Some of the color was returning to his face. He raked his fingers through his black hair. "This is not a place to explore on your own, Miss Hawthorne," he said, his lips compressed.

"I see that now," I said faintly. "I didn't realize that particular spot was so dangerous as it is."

"What are you doing so far from the house?" His voice was rough.

"Emeline is resting; she hasn't been well the past day or so. I—I wanted to get away, to get some fresh air. I didn't realize that this path led to the Flume."

"Isn't that a coincidence?" he asked, his lip curling. "I too wanted to get away." He had shed his coat, and his shirt sleeves were rolled up. Dark hairs bristled along his forearms. "Shall we get away together?" He took a step or two closer to me.

I felt the color staining my face. "I did not mean that I wanted to get away for good, just for a little while."

"So you too find the atmosphere at the house rather . . . oppressive. I did wrong to bring you here." He was frowning.

"No. Emeline needs me. At least, she needs someone just now. Perhaps later she'll decide she wishes to go to another school."

He was standing very close to me now. I leaned into the cliff wall, my heartbeat quickening. Rather urgently I looked to one side and then the other.

"Do you think Emeline is the only one who needs someone just now?" he asked, his voice a caress.

A pulse was beating wildly in my throat; I felt almost choked.

"I didn't bring you here just for Emeline's sake, Tessa." And then he was straining against me, his hard, broad torso and muscular legs pinning me to the pocked cliff wall. He bent his head, his breath warm and sweet, his lips hovering for a moment before they descended on mine. I felt the rough surface of rock at my back as his mouth hungrily devoured mine, his tongue parting my lips insistently.

For the second time, I sensed an urgent desperation in his embrace, in the way his hands gripped my shoulders, in the way his mouth claimed mine. That desperation was not only for a physical gratification, but for something else as well. Something I could not identify, for which he yearned and sought.

My lips felt bruised, but I took a delicious pleasure from the rough pressure of his mouth, from his body bearing into mine. The water thundered below; the noise was all around us, enveloping us in its fury. All the tenseness left my frame; I was suddenly limp. Rather than feeling trapped, I was conscious again of the same feeling of freedom I had experienced earlier as I gazed down at the gushing Flume.

My hands left my sides and moved up to his face, my fingers caressing the hard lines of his cheeks before threading through his thick dark hair. His mouth left mine and he breathed sharply, raggedly in my neck. I felt his fingers in my hair, pulling out the pins until the red curls tumbled down my back and over my shoulders.

"Like molten copper," he said, his voice hoarse, his words slurred. He bent to kiss the pulse at my throat. I was trembling and had to once again grip his shoulders so that I would not lose my balance.

With the fingers of one hand, he was unbuttoning my blouse. When I started to feebly protest, his mouth descended again on mine. I could taste the heat which coursed through his body as I was certain he could taste that which shuddered through my own frame. Achingly we hungered for a release, our lips and tongues seeking, uniting, consuming each other in a passionate frenzy. The thunder in his heart echoed the sound

176

of the Flume below us.

My blouse was open to reveal my camisole; the air was cool and damp on my flushed skin. His hands cupped each of my breasts while he traced the line of my collarbone with his tongue. I gave a sudden shiver, trembling uncontrollably in his arms and sensing an answering trembling in his own taut, hard build. From deep within me came a desperate yearning, a potent straining sensation which I had felt once before in his embrace. As before I felt an almost painful, steely pressure butting into me even as the rocky surface of the cliff pressed into me from behind. Suddenly I no longer felt free; I was being stifled, crushed. The fear took away the thrilling sensations, the wonder, the heart-stopping joy.

Pushing against his broad chest, I began to move my face from side to side, away from his roving mouth. And then, to my surprise and relief, I was released. I stared at him apprehensively, as he took several swift, hard breaths. His gaze seemed unfocused, his expression uncertain, almost dazed. But then he was raking back his hair from his brow in the same familiar gesture, the cleft in his square chin tightening. And his blue eyes frowned into mine.

"You better run along," he said crisply, "or I might feel inclined to inflict my presence on you even further."

"You weren't—inflicting—anything on me. It's just that I mustn't . . . we mustn't. . . ." I bit my lip.

"I know," he said, sighing heavily. "I'm in no position to—but sometimes I can't help myself." He smiled wryly. "I'm sorry about your hair. I don't know where the pins have got to. Down the Flume, I expect."

"It doesn't matter." I began to self-consciously braid my hair. "Did—did you ride here?"

"No, I walked."

"You walked? But—"

"If you're referring to my limp, I've been instructed to walk as much as possible. One of the doctors in the New York hospital—the only one who wasn't a fool—was clear about that." His mouth tightened. "That, among other things."

"I was surprised to see you here, that's all. It's rather precarious."

"As you found out for yourself in more ways than one." He sounded amused, but there was an underlying bitterness in his voice. Then he frowned. "Don't waste your time worrying about me. I can manage."

"I think you are a danger to yourself," I said gravely.

"And to you as well?"

"Perhaps."

His blue eyes were cold and clear. "Well, then, my advice to you is to run. To get as far away from Nightshade Notch—and from me—as you can. Because you're right in your estimation of me. Not only am I a danger to myself, but to others as well. As I've proven in the past. As I might have proven to you only a short time ago. And then there would have been the devil to pay."

I felt the hot color seep into my face. "I should be going back," I said.

"Yes, go on."

"Well, good-bye, then," I said faintly.

He did not answer. Walking down the stony slope to the footbridge, I crossed it gingerly. From there I could not see him. There were only the torrents of water rushing pell-mell through the gouged-out chasm.

When I reached the house, I found Emeline still tucked in bed, though I was concerned that she looked and felt slightly feverish. "It's a good thing that you did not go out this afternoon," I said, pouring her a glass of water. "What have you been doing?"

"Oh, I took a nap," she said. "What about you?"

Flushing a little, I said, "I went for a walk. Did you need me?"

She shook her head. "Charlotte looked in on me just after you left. She was going to rest as well. The house seemed very quiet. Will you take supper in here with me tonight?"

"Of course I will, if you'd like me to. And then we'll read some more of *Jane Eyre*. Oh, by the way, Emeline, last night I told your mother I hadn't been a teacher at Miss Winslow's."

Her eyes widened. "You told her you were the cook? What happened?"

"Nothing dreadful. So you no longer have anything to conceal."

"She didn't insist that you leave today?"

"She may have wanted to dismiss me, but your uncle has made it clear that only he can let me go. So let's not worry about it any longer."

It was about an hour later when we heard Leonora's voice through the door. She was shouting at someone.

"Goodness, whatever can be the matter with Mamma?" Emeline asked nervously. "I hope—I hope she's not in a state."

"I'm sure it's nothing you need to worry about," I said.

Aaron's voice was answering hers in placating tones, and there was also the sound of a woman sniffling and weeping. This was too much for Emeline, who got out of bed and had opened the door to the corridor before I could stop her. We stood there listening.

"I never touched it," the maid was wailing. "I never touched it, ma'am, I swear to you."

"But I saw it there on the dressing table this morning, and now it is gone," Leonora cried furiously. "And you were the one to go in my room and clean it."

"I saw it there, Mrs. Curtis. It was there on the little mirrored tray. And that's where it was when I finished tidying up and left."

Charlotte had come out into the hall as well. "Whatever is going on, Leonora? Stop crying, Amy, I'm sure we can straighten everything out. Did you break something belonging to Mrs. Curtis?"

"My emerald bracelet is missing, Charlotte," said Leonora. Emeline and I exchanged horrified glances. "I wore it last night and then, at noon when I left the house, it was still on my dressing table. Now it is gone. And I've looked everywhere for it."

"I've told you not to leave things lying about, Nora," said Aaron.

"Shut up, Aaron. I thought—until now—that everyone in this house was trustworthy," she said.

"And so they are," Charlotte said soothingly. "Amy would never take anything which didn't belong to her, nor would any of the other servants. Why, they've all been with us for years! You may go, Amy. You must have put it somewhere and forgotten it, Leonora."

"No, because Amy herself saw it on the dressing table when she did the room early this afternoon," cried Leonora. "So it had to have been taken in the past couple of hours. That's why I thought she had done it, but if she is to be believed, then someone else must have entered my room, poked about, and stolen it." There was a pause before she cried, "And there is only one person who could have done it!"

"Now, Nora, let's not be hasty. What are you—"

"She can't think I took it," whispered Emeline, cringing. "But I think she's coming in here!"

Leonora came into view. She was wearing a pink ruffled tea gown, tied at the waist. Her eyes flashed angrily; I felt slightly alarmed.

"Well, miss, I thought you were ill," she said irritably to her daughter. "Get back into bed."

"Yes, Mamma," mumbled Emeline.

Leonora's wrathful gaze fell on me. "If it isn't our dear Miss Hawthorne, looking so innocent and beguiling."

"Leonora, you can't think that Teresa has anything to do with your bracelet's disappearance," said Charlotte, aghast. "Come back with me. I'll help you to search."

"Oh, I am going to search, but not in my room. I've done enough of that. I am going to search Miss Hawthorne's room!"

"Miss Hawthorne, you can see what a state my wife is in," said Aaron uneasily after I had gasped. "She has lost a piece of jewelry, a bracelet."

"The emerald bracelet I wore last night at dinner. Don't say you don't recall it, Miss Hawthorne. I saw you looking at it."

"I do recall it, Mrs. Curtis," I said coldly. "But I did not take it from your room."

"Of course she didn't," said Charlotte earnestly. "Enough of this, Leonora. You don't know what you're saying."

"Teresa would never steal anything, Mamma! She just wouldn't!"

"Be quiet, Emeline. I haven't asked your opinion. And naturally you would protect her, just the way you never mentioned that she had been employed at your precious school as a cook! If Miss Hawthorne is blameless, then she should have no objection to my searching her room."

"You have no right to demand such a thing," said Charlotte, outraged.

"It's all right, Charlotte," I said. "If Mrs. Curtis wishes to look through my things, she may do so. She will not find anything, and then at least Emeline can have her dinner in peace."

Leonora glared at me. "You are always the perfect governess, aren't you? But I would not be surprised if you had a thing or two to hide. After all, we just discovered last night that you had been passing yourself off as a teacher. You're scarcely a fit companion for my daughter!"

"That's enough, Leonora," said Charlotte. "Teresa has agreed to your looking through her room. You are not to speak to her like that."

"I can't wait to show her up in front of all of you. I tell you, she has you all deceived! When I find the bracelet you'll see for yourself."

"You stay here, Emeline," I said. "I'll be back in a few minutes."

"I'm so sorry about this," said Charlotte in an undertone to me. We followed Leonora down the hall, her high-heeled slippers clicking along the carpet.

"I'll stay out here," said Aaron. "Don't worry, Miss Hawthorne," he added in a low voice.

"I am not in the least worried, Mr. Curtis," I said.

I was as coldly furious as Leonora Curtis was hotly so. I hated the thought of her looking through my personal belongings, subjecting me to so humiliating an ordeal. But I knew that there would be no peace until she had convinced herself that I had not taken the bracelet.

Charlotte and I followed Leonora into my room. She was already pulling open the drawers of the dresser, rummaging through my undergarments, unfolding my shawls and lace collars. I stood there trembling with rage while she shook out my gloves. From the dresser she went to the wardrobe and proceeded to reach for my hatbox, lifting the lid and feeling inside the brim of my bonnet.

"Really, Leonora, this is disgraceful," objected Charlotte.

181

Ignoring her, Leonora went over to my neatly made bed and shook out the pillow, throwing aside the bedclothes. Finding nothing, she was nonetheless determined. She went back to the wardrobe and began to turn out all the pockets of my gowns.

"You're making a dreadful mess, Leonora! Hasn't this gone far enough? You can see that Teresa doesn't have it! For heaven's sake, stop!"

Leonora had reached my bottle-green traveling costume that I had not worn since the train ride, and she was slipping her fingers into the skirt pocket.

"Leonora—" began Charlotte again, but she was cut off by a cry of triumph.

"I told you—I told you she had it!" She was holding up the emerald bracelet; she looked like a vengeful fury, but there was also glee in her expression.

"That—that's impossible," I said faintly. "I didn't put it there."

Charlotte looked from Leonora to me.

"I don't have any idea how that got in my pocket," I said. "I swear to you both that I am telling the truth!"

"You swear? And you think that we will take the word of a thief? You had better start packing your trunk, Miss Butter-Won't-Melt-in-Your-Mouth Hawthorne. Because you've been found out. And you're going to be out of this house before you have a chance to take anything else. God only knows what else is missing!"

"How dare you, Mrs. Curtis!" I said heatedly. "I have never taken anything from anyone. I have no idea how that bracelet came to be in my possession, but I assure you that I did not take it from your room and hide it in the pocket of my skirt."

Aaron had entered; Leonora turned to him. "See—she did have it! You were all so protective of our little Miss Hawthorne—and she has been craftier than any of you! But not me. I saw her instantly for the little sneak she was."

"Be quiet, Leonora. Teresa, my dear, I must ask you this. Can you think of any way the bracelet got there?" asked Charlotte worriedly.

"As I did not put it there myself, only one way. It was

planted there by someone who wished to discredit me." My voice rose.

"Are you accusing me of taking my own bracelet and—and—hiding it in your clothes? I assure you, Miss Hawthorne, I have far better things to do with my time!" cried Leonora.

"What the devil is happening? I could hear the racket as soon as I walked in the door!" Drake stood on the threshold, a black scowl on his face, his hands on his hips.

"You may well ask, Drake," said Leonora spitefully. "It seems the girl you hired to tutor my daughter, the perfect Miss Hawthorne, is a thief!"

"What nonsense are you talking, Leonora?"

"Nonsense, is it? Just look at this!" She held up the bracelet. "I found this—my emerald bracelet—in one of her pockets! Now what do you have to say?"

Drake glanced from her angry face to my own. "Well, Leonora," he said coolly, "I'd say that you probably put it there yourself."

She let out a vicious cry and stormed at him while Charlotte and I looked on in horror. He put up his arms to ward her off, but not in time to stop her from scratching one cheek with her nails. Then he took her wrists and shook her. "For God's sake, calm down, Leonora! Get a hold on yourself!"

"Calm down!" she repeated fiercely. "You tell me to calm down! Naturally I'm the one in the wrong, not the little miss cook—or tutor—or whatever she is. I demand to know where she was this afternoon!"

"I took a walk, Mrs. Curtis. I left the house around one and got back an hour or so ago."

"I have only your word for that. Did anyone see you? Where did you go?"

"I walked to the Flume," I said, coloring. "Emeline was napping and I went out for some fresh air."

"I don't believe you! Haven't you deceived me from the first? I should never have agreed to—"

"She was with me, Leonora," said Drake deliberately.

"With you? And how did that happen? My eyes are open now! Did the two of you plan a rendezvous while Emeline was sick in bed? Is that the real reason you hired Miss Hawthorne,

Drake? After all, it couldn't have been for her teaching abilities, could it? I've seen that for the farce it is!"

"We met by accident," I said. "And then I came back and I've been with Emeline ever since."

"Yes, she has, Mamma," said the girl who had just come in.

"You could have taken the bracelet before you came to Emeline's room, just after you returned from the house," Leonora insisted.

"I suppose I could have, but I didn't," I said. "I don't know how that bracelet came to be in my wardrobe, but *I did not take it from your room, Mrs. Curtis.*"

"I demand that you turn her out, Drake. The evidence is here for all to see. Charlotte herself saw me remove the bracelet from Miss Hawthorne's skirt pocket. You can't possibly excuse that."

"I am not going to try to excuse it, Leonora," said Drake briefly. "I believe Miss Hawthorne to be innocent. And the matter is over."

"The matter is over!" she shouted. "So you're going to hold her hand through all this, are you? You and Charlotte and even Emeline—you're all against me in this! You'd all rather believe this curds-and-whey miss, this little tramp from the kitchen—! Aaron, you saw me take the bracelet—do something! I won't have her teaching my daughter!"

"Yes, perhaps I had better leave," I said frigidly.

"Now, Nora, since Miss Hawthorne says she didn't put it there, and she was out most of the afternoon, there does seem to be some doubt that she's guilty."

"Please, Teresa," said Charlotte.

"Oh, you can all go to hell! I wish I were far away from this place!" cried Leonora savagely before storming from the room.

Sitting down on the ravaged bed, I covered my face with my hands. I heard Charlotte tell Drake and Aaron to leave the room, and then I began to cry. I had no doubt that it was Leonora who had concealed the bracelet in my room in order to give Drake an undeniable reason to dismiss me. She had disliked me from the first, and when she had found out that I had never before taught school, she must have made up her mind then and there to get rid of me. She had accused

Drake of hiring a cook to spite her, and so she had decided to prove me untrustworthy to spite him. It was all clear to me; I had a dangerous enemy in Leonora Curtis.

But Drake had not risen to the bait. He had recognized the ruse for what it was, and had refused to dismiss me for a theft he was certain I did not commit. Still, I did not feel any less soiled, any less sickened. It was very fortunate for me that Drake and Charlotte had taken my word over the evidence of the bracelet found in the pocket of my suit.

Charlotte put her arm around my shoulder. "There, there, my dear, don't cry so. Come, let's put your room to rights."

I groped for my handkerchief and blew my nose. "You don't believe I took the bracelet, do you, Charlotte? I couldn't bear it if you also—"

"No, of course not, my child. Though I find it hard to believe that even Leonora would do such a dreadful thing. But I'm certain you didn't take it."

"Not in a million years would you steal, Teresa, we know that," said Emeline.

"You should be in bed, Emeline. You'll catch cold. I'll help Teresa straighten up in here and then she can come and eat dinner with you."

"Oh, I couldn't eat a bite," I said after she had left.

"I'm going to ask one of the maids to bring you a glass of sherry, Teresa, and then perhaps you'll feel a little better. I'm sorry you had to be subjected to Leonora's rage in such an outrageous and offensive manner."

"Perhaps I should go," I said. "I shouldn't stay here—not with her hating me the way she does. That can't be good for Emeline."

"I can imagine how mortifying the past half hour has been for you, my dear. It was very unpleasant for all of us. But I wish you would not make an impulsive decision. If you leave, then Leonora wins, don't you see? And the person who loses is Emeline. Despite Leonora's behavior, or because of it, she badly needs you."

"If you're certain of that," I said, "I suppose I should stay for at least a while longer. Thank you for believing in me, Charlotte."

"I'm very grateful, my dear. Of course I believe in you. Now let's straighten up this room, shall we?"

Some days later Emeline requested that we go to the Crystal Hills for dinner rather than dining at the house. I was reluctant because I hadn't seen Leonora Curtis since the bracelet affair, but I realized that I could not continue avoiding her. Charlotte declined to join us, to my disappointment, saying she preferred a tray in her own room. I longed to say the same thing, but agreed to Emeline's request. After all, I was her companion.

At dusk we left the house and strolled through the thin stretch of woods. The sunset glowed mauve, fringed with apricot; the woods were filled with smoky lavender light. Through the trees glinted the lights of the hotel, beckoning in the fading twilight.

"When I'm grown up," said Emeline, "I'm going to take all my meals at the hotel. All except breakfast. That's what my grandmother did most of the time even though she employed a cook at the house. She wanted to assure herself of the quality of the meals being served. Charlotte says my grandmother always said she wouldn't expect her guests to eat a meal she wouldn't have eaten herself. She kept the chef and staff on their toes that way."

"She sounds a most formidable employer."

"Oh, everyone loved her," Emeline assured me hastily. "It's just that she set high standards for the Crystal Hills."

"And you plan to be just like her." I smiled. "Have you ever considered that some day you may leave here?"

"Leave?"

"Well, if you were married, you would probably move to your husband's home."

"Oh, no. I don't think I want to be married. I only want to run the hotel."

"Well, I daresay your husband could move here and join the family business. But remember, Emeline, your uncle may marry himself some day, and then he and his wife would be running the hotel." Even as I spoke I felt a potent stab of jealousy toward that unknown woman.

She frowned. "I don't think Uncle Drake wants to be married, Teresa. He's just not interested in that sort of thing."

186

"Of course he's taken you into his confidence," I said teasingly.

"Well, no, but years ago I used to wish he was married so that I had cousins to play with. Now I'm accustomed to being the only child. And someday Papa and Uncle Drake will teach me all about running a grand hotel."

"It must feel very secure to have your future worked out. But Emeline, things don't always go according to plan. Your uncle is having some financial difficulties, you know."

"Yes, I know. But he will set everything to rights," she said with confidence.

We had reached the steps of the hotel. A large man in black evening livery was holding the door open for us.

"Burrows, you're back!" cried Emeline joyfully.

His long, grave face creased into a grin. "Hello, Miss Emeline. So you remember your old friend Burrows."

"Of course I remember you! It hasn't been *that* long ago. I'm so glad to see you again."

"Well, it's good to be back at the old place now, working again for your uncle. Almost like old times, it is, when your grandmother was still alive."

"How's Mrs. Burrows?"

"Well, thank you, miss. Your uncle's given her her old position as head housekeeper, so we're both back to stay."

"That's wonderful." She introduced me, and then we entered the hotel.

The dining room was festively lit by the chandeliers, and I was surprised to see that all but a few of the tables were occupied by elegantly dressed ladies and gentlemen just taking their seats. The cloths covering the tables were of linen and Battenberg lace with an underdressing of peach, and each table was centered with a silver candelabra. There was a hubbub of conversation; I saw a few of the guests I knew but most of them were strange to me.

"There are Mamma and Papa," said Emeline. "I suppose we should sit with them."

"Oh, Emeline, you here?" said Leonora, waving her hand carelessly. She did not look at me.

"Good evening, Mamma. Good evening, Papa."

187

"Hello, Emmie. Good evening, Miss Hawthorne," said Aaron Curtis, his eyes warm on my face.

The table was set for six; Aaron pulled out the chair beside his for me. Like the other men in the room he wore black evening attire; there were square gold cufflinks on his cuffs.

"Emeline, this is Mr. Willoughby," he said, gesturing to the other man at the table who had risen at our approach. "Mr. Willoughby, my daughter, Miss Emeline Curtis. And this young lady is her tutor, Miss Hawthorne."

"Mr. Willoughby has come to dig up the Site of Stones," said Leonora.

"Not dig up, Mrs. Curtis. No, indeed," protested the man. He was short and plump with a broad, smiling face and a few wisps of hair stretching across the top of his shining, bare head.

"What does Mamma mean?" asked Emeline, a pucker in her brow. "What about the Stones?"

"Mr. Willoughby is an archaeologist, Emeline," announced her father impressively. "He's going to begin excavating at the Stones tomorrow."

"What does excavate mean?"

"To go over a selected area looking for clues to its former inhabitants," explained Mr. Willoughby. "Clues such as ruins, pottery shards, tools."

"I don't think you'll find anything like that at the Site of Stones," said Emeline. "The things that belonged to the settlers were taken long ago."

Mr. Willoughby took a sip of iced water, still smiling. "I'm not talking about finding artifacts on the surface, Miss Curtis. Not on the surface. I plan to conduct a dig into parallel layers, or strata, in the ground. In the ground, you see."

"You mean you are really going to dig holes around the Stones?" she asked.

Mr. Willoughby nodded energetically. "Your father has most generously granted me permission to pursue a certain theory I have regarding the Stones."

"It's just a place the Indians built," said Emeline.

"That is what I am here to determine. I don't believe it was constructed by the Woodland Indians at all, although I'm not denying they may have used it. I believe it to be far older than people realize. Yes, far older. You see, Miss Curtis, Miss Hawthorne, I first became aware that such a place existed in this country from a painting I saw years ago by Mr. Albert Bierstadt. He and Mr. Thomas Cole painted several landscapes of the White Mountains of which Mr. Cole's 'Crawford Notch' and Mr. Bierstadt's 'The Emerald Pool' are the most famous. But it was Mr. Bierstadt's portrayal of what he called 'The Stones at Nightshade Notch' which fascinated me. Fascinated me, I say."

"Is that so, Mr. Willoughby?" said Leonora, taking a bite of the salmon appetizer.

"Yes, indeed, Mrs. Curtis," said Mr. Willoughby earnestly. "If you are familiar with Mr. Bierstadt's style, you know that all his paintings have that mystical, primeval quality which gives the viewer the impression he's looking at the scene the way it was a very long time ago—a sort of eerie paradise. He painted the standing stones, slabs, and chambers at the site in a thinly veiled mist, and there was a feeling of great mystery, even menace. In fact, I thought at the time he had imagined them in the landscape. Late Neolithic structures of that sort haven't been seen on American soil. But then I read about the place—er, in the newspapers—and realized it actually existed on land belonging to the Crystal Hills Hotel. I became determined to make an expedition here and see it for myself."

"Well, Emeline, what do you think of that?" interjected Aaron heartily.

"Will you be working alone, Mr. Willoughby?" asked Leonora, who had listened to him with a noticeable lack of interest.

"Yes, Mrs. Curtis. Perhaps at a later date, if I come across something undeniable, I will get the backing I need and will therefore be able to hire a team of diggers. But for the present I am on my own. On my own."

"I suppose you know there is supposedly a curse on the site," said Leonora. "I've always kept away myself."

"Many ancient places are said to have curses attached to them," said Mr. Willoughby. "The tombs of the Pharaohs, for instance."

"And what do you think to find in that pile of glacial

rubble?" Drake was setting down his cane and pulling out a chair for himself.

"Not glacial rubble, Major Curtis, nothing of the sort, I can assure you."

"Do you hope to uncover an ancient Troy or Ninevah? I would say that you are on the wrong continent for any discoveries of that nature," Drake said sardonically.

Mr. Willoughby did not take offense. "So do my colleagues, Major Curtis. They've laughed at my theory. Laughed. But I'm determined to prove them wrong, to make a name for myself such as Schliemann has. I do not harbor any hopes that the remains of a great civilization of which we know nothing will be uncovered. But I do hope that my theory will be given the credence it deserves. Yes, the credence it deserves."

"And what exactly is that theory, Mr. Willoughby?" asked Drake.

"Well, sir, ever since I've known about the existence of the Site of Stones, that it was not a figment of Albert Bierstadt's wonderful imagination, I've wondered about one distinct possibility. I've wondered if the Stones were erected and arranged by an ancient seafaring people dating back to the early Bronze Age, about 2000 B.C. Perhaps the Phoenicians or another group from the Middle East. Perhaps the Ancient Britons, the same race of people who fashioned Stonehenge," he said impressively, looking at each of us in turn.

Aaron said, "You don't say," and gestured to the hovering waiter to refill his wineglass. Leonora raised her brows ironically, and Drake made some sort of derisive sound.

"You see," continued Mr. Willoughby, undaunted, "Indians have never been known to construct stone chambers and erect monoliths and tables as are found at the Site of Stones. But historians have always rejected the notion that any people crossed the Atlantic to North America until perhaps the Vikings in the Middle Ages—certainly not thousands of years ago at the very end of prehistoric time. But we know that there was long-distance trade in the early Bronze Age between Ireland, England, Denmark, Iberian Spain, and the civilized eastern Mediterranean cultures. Some of those cultures were highly advanced in mathematics and astronomy. How do we know that they did not possess the navigational skills to cross the ocean? How do we know that?"

"But why on earth would those people have traveled inland hundreds of miles, across hazardous mountains, to build this site? Why not build it along the coast somewhere?" asked Drake, frowning.

"I am not as concerned with the 'why' of it all, Major Curtis. Perhaps they were following the stars, perhaps they felt guided, or were fulfilling an even more ancient prophecy. It is likely that we will never know why. But it is my goal to prove that they did indeed sail the Atlantic and invade these mountains, and then construct a site of religious or astronomical significance. How long they stayed here—whether they returned to their homeland or died out—I have no idea. No idea at all."

"It's fortunate for you that you are not traveling with a team of assistants. That I would have to forbid, despite your agreement with my brother," said Drake in a hard voice. "I want this excavation of yours kept quiet. I don't want crowds gawking about the place, or newspaper hounds getting wind of it. If that happens, if your dig becomes some sort of sensationalistic story, I will see that it is stopped, theory or no theory. Do I make myself clear, Mr. Willoughby?"

"Very clear," said the archaeologist, meeting his gaze squarely. "I will agree not to contact the newspapers until I come across something startling and irrefutable. But if and when I do, you would not wish me to keep silent and deprive the world of an astounding discovery."

"I think the world might just survive without it," said Drake dryly. "Word of mouth with the guests we can't control, but I warn you, if this thing turns into a three-ring circus, you can forget about proving your theory. I for one, am more concerned with the future of the Crystal Hills Hotel than all this damn nonsense about an ancient past."

Chapter Ten

"Uncle Drake acted awful funny about the Stones last night," said Emeline the next morning while we sat at the long gleaming table in the library. "He wasn't exactly polite to Mr. Willoughby, was he?"

"I don't think he puts much faith in Mr. Willoughby's theory," I said. "And you must admit, it is rather fantastic. He admitted that his colleagues consider his ideas . . . un-orthodox."

Emeline nodded, her brow knit. "I didn't understand a lot of what he was talking about—all that stuff about the Bronze Age."

"That just refers to a time in prehistory when a particular culture began making and using metal implements rather than ones of stone. It was a major step in the development of man and society, and different cultures made that step at different times. I don't know much else, I'm afraid." I grinned. "It was scarcely on Miss Winslow's curriculum."

She grimaced. "Her boring curriculum! Teresa, could we go to the Stones this afternoon and watch Mr. Willoughby work? I want to see what he's doing. I've never seen an archaeologist at work before. It would be educational."

Smiling wryly, I said, "Very clever. Well, I suppose so." I tried to suppress a sudden sick feeling at the pit of my stomach at the notion of visiting the Site of Stones again.

"It's still odd the way Uncle Drake acted, don't you think?" she said musingly, her chin cupped in her hand. "I mean, why should he mind Mr. Willoughby's working at the Stones, as long as he doesn't do anything to mess up the place? You don't think it's because he believes in the curse, do you?"

"I hardly think so, Emeline."

"It's as if he doesn't want anyone going there. Do you remember the way he shouted at us that first day I took you around? It was almost as though he was frightened of something." She bent her head over her book.

It was obvious that Emeline knew nothing about the woman's death at the Site of Stones. Evidently the scandal had filled the newspapers, but Miss Winslow did not allow her young ladies' minds to be sullied by anything such as the sensationalistic press. And I, isolated in my limbo-world, tending to my sick father, had not made it a practice to read the newspapers either.

Did my first terrifying experience at the Site of Stones, when I had been overwhelmed by the sensations and sounds of some horrible malevolence in the atmosphere, have to do with the death of the woman? What was behind Drake's fury at Aaron granting the archaeologist permission to excavate? Was it just that he feared a possible resurgence of the scandal would hurt business at the hotel? Or was there something else, a more sinister reason behind his wanting the place left to itself? But I did not want to speculate on the notion that there might be something about that woman's death that had never come out, something that Mr. Willoughby might inadvertently discover at the Site of Stones. Something that might link Drake indisputably to her death.

I found myself hoping that Ernest Willoughby would conduct his excavation quietly, discreetly, and swiftly, and that he would uncover no startling evidence to attract public attention. Just now I cared little for the pursuit of science or of ancient history; my only desire was for peace and prosperity to come to the Crystal Hills. For Emeline's sake, I told myself.

That afternoon I reluctantly accompanied Emeline to the Site of Stones. As we passed the hotel, we saw a number of open carriages drawn up under the rotunda. Aaron Curtis was sitting astride a horse, talking to a few of the people who were climbing into the carriages. I noticed Mrs. Aldridge was one of the excursion party, as well as her husband. He took off his hat to us and she nodded.

"Mrs. Aldridge seems more cheerful these days," observed Emeline. "Have you noticed?"

"No, I can't say that I have. I haven't seen her lately."

"I wonder where Papa is taking them. I didn't know there was an excursion planned for today."

It occurred to me then that Drake might have requested his brother to lead an excursion in order to divert guests' attention from the hotel grounds on the day that Mr. Willoughby was to begin his dig. If that were the case, surely he could not fool himself into believing that the dig could be kept secret for long. It was likely that people would begin to flock to the place, curious about the archaeologist's work and perhaps curious about the alleged curse as well.

I was uneasy as I followed Emeline through the woods. Although the feeling of evil which had horrified me the first time I visited the Stones, had been absent when I had gone there a second time with Miss Birche, still I had been conscious of a vague but undeniable apprehension.

The sun's rays slanted between the towering pines, mellowing the strange stone formations. The chambers brooded sullenly like great beehives; the monoliths, creased and pocked with age, loomed up from the hard ground, their peaks jagged. The Stones looked to be a crude and rambling arrangement, but for the first time I was struck with the deliberate organization that had gone into the design. There had been a fixed purpose in the planning and erecting of these Stones, but a purpose which might always elude us.

Mr. Willoughby was sitting with his back against one of the stone walls, jotting something down in a notebook.

"Hello, Mr. Willoughby," called Emeline.

He glanced up, smiling. "Good afternoon, Miss Curtis, Miss Hawthorne. Have you come to see me work? I'm afraid there's very little for you to observe today."

"Haven't you begun to dig yet?" asked Emeline, glancing about.

"Oh, dear me, no. No, I will not begin to dig for a while yet. Not for a while yet. First I must make precise maps and carefully scaled drawings of the entire site. Only then will I select an area to excavate. That decision should not be made hastily. An excavator destroys evidence as he digs, so he must observe and record as he goes. Observe and record, I say."

Emeline frowned. "Destroy? What do you mean? You're not going to change or ruin the Stones, are you? We like them just as they are."

"No, Miss Curtis, I assure you that is not what I meant. But I have to dig a narrow trench at a high point to the undisturbed soil below in order to determine the stratigraphy of the site. In order, that is, to learn how many layers of occupation there are."

"I don't understand," she said.

"Well, any artifacts found in the soil just below the surface would be from the most recent time of occupation—say, a hundred years ago. Below that I hope to uncover Indian artifacts from hundreds of years before that."

"But I thought you wanted to prove it wasn't built by the Indians."

"Oh, I do, I most certainly do. But I must first establish a pattern of occupation. I will continue to dig deeper, hoping to come across something very old, very old indeed, and most definitely not of the Owasco or Woodland Indian cultures."

"Such as what?" I asked.

He squinted in the sunlight, scratching the top of his round head. "Shards of pottery, perhaps. Clay, if baked, lasts almost forever in most climates. Almost forever it lasts."

"But how could you be sure that anything you find was not made by the Indians themselves?" I asked him.

"Simply by comparing the shards to those which have been uncovered and identified by archeologists in other parts of the world, and by matching them to various cultures of already established dates."

"Excuse me, Mr. Willoughby," said Emeline. "I don't mean to be rude, but I don't understand what is so important about finding out exactly who built our site and when. Does it really matter now?"

Mr. Willoughby was not offended. He regarded her thoughtfully before answering. "It matters, Miss Curtis, because scholars are interested in discovering the achievements of prehistoric man. It has always been believed that no one from across the Atlantic invaded this continent before Christopher Columbus, although there are some who believe the Vikings discovered Newfoundland, Nova Scotia, and New England, and wrote about those places in their sagas. But those explorations were not in the distant past. No, not in the distant past. If an ancient culture did travel here from Europe or the Mediterranean, not hundreds, but thousands of years ago—thousands, I say—wouldn't you want to know? If that theory of mine can be proven, why, then we would have to totally reconstruct our history, our image of prehistoric man.

"Many archaeologists have scoffed at my theories, at my research. 'There is no worthwhile archaeology but that done in the Cradle of Civilization, the Middle East,' they claim. They call excavating in one's own country 'the poor man's substitute for classical antiquarian research.'" His voice rose angrily. "Well, it's true I haven't the financial backing to conduct a dig in the Middle East. But still I don't listen, no, I don't listen to them. I believe that other advanced cultures flourished simultaneously or before the Mediterranean cultures. They scoff at the burial mounds and stone monuments in pre-Roman Europe as well, deeming them not worth excavating. They mock the tales of the Ancient Britons and of their great temple of Stonehenge, calling them crude barbarians because they did not make written records, or work with iron or gold or copper. Well, they may not have done those things, but they may have possessed vast knowledge and secrets of their own. Yes, secrets." His eyes were filled with an almost unholy gleam. "Secrets of astronomy and mathematics more sophisticated than any we have today, more sophisticated than the Greeks or the Egyptians or the Assyrians! And they may have developed them *before* the other cultures. Before them, I say. I have studied very carefully William Stukeley's drawings and scales of Stonehenge, and I plan to execute drawings of a similar nature of this place. That in itself will take a good amount of time, a good amount of time. And I must prepare accurate maps before I begin to dig."

"So you won't be digging this week," said Emeline rather

lamely as though she had not expected such a long and involved reply to her question. It was apparent to me now that Mr. Willoughby's work was near to being an obsession with him, and that he desperately longed for recognition in the academic world.

"I'm afraid we're keeping you from working, Mr. Willoughby," I said.

"Not at all, Miss Hawthorne. I'm very pleased, very pleased indeed, to have your interest in my progress. It's just that at this stage there is little for you to observe. Once the maps and drawings are complete, even before I begin to dig, I will have to carefully go over the site for clues of any kind that may not have been buried. But those, if I find any, will most likely be artifacts left by the families who attempted to settle nearby one hundred years ago."

"How will you know where to start digging?" I asked. "Much of this site is on high ground."

"I will have to select several places almost at random, at random," he answered. "And I will have to note all changes in the color and consistency of the soil. The shape of the land can provide evidence in areas where there are mounds or ditches. Grass is richer and thicker if it is growing in the deep soil of a filled-in grave or ditch. But grass and weeds are sparse if they are growing in shallow ground over the ruins of stone foundations, which appears to be the case here."

"It sounds like a lot of work when you don't know whether you'll find anything important," said Emeline, her brow wrinkling.

"Ah, but therein lies the excitement, Miss Curtis. Therein lies the excitement. Each day of slow, painstaking drudgery heightened with the hope—just the hope, I say—that one may come across something of significance. It's what the archaeologist lives for. It's like a fascinating treasure hunt, with all sorts of possibilities for riches and fame and glory. All sorts of possibilities." He rubbed his hands together.

"We wish you the best of luck, Mr. Willoughby," I said in spite of my private feelings.

"Thank you, Miss Hawthorne. I will proceed slowly, slowly will I proceed at first. Apparently it has always been believed that this place was an Indian burial or ceremonial ground. If it is indeed the former, I will expect to uncover some graves. There is a distinct possibility that this Site of Stones was used by several cultures in perhaps different ways. But I am most interested in the one which designed it, the one I believe existed here four thousand years ago, yes, four thousand years ago."

"How far down will you have to dig?" asked Emeline.

"About six or seven feet, Miss Curtis. Probably not more than that. That is how deep the deposits are in British prehistoric sites. As I told your uncle, I don't expect to uncover nine different Troys or Mycenaean cities which existed at the same place at different times in history. But Schliemann's discoveries do inspire me. He loved Homer, you know, and set out to search for traces of those fabled cities which the academic world had dismissed as legends. He was accused of following an obsession, of chasing after fairy tales. But he did not listen, no, he did not. He persevered, just as I am doing. The only difference between us is that he was a man of wealth. He discovered a brilliant Bronze Age civilization that no one had suspected existed, one hundreds of years earlier than Agamemnon's city. Legends are often rooted in fact, you see. Just like the legend of the curse right here. Who is to know how far back that notion goes? Who is to know?"

"What do you mean?" I asked, conscious of a growing urge to leave the Site of Stones.

"Well, we know that several tragedies occurred to families who set up homesteads nearby. Those settlers were told by the Indians who remained in the area that this was a place of evil. The Indians themselves did not claim that it was a burial ground, from what I have gathered by talking to some of the local people myself. So the question is, where did the Indians get the idea that the Stones were evil? They may have invented it themselves, or it may have been passed down through generations of Indians for thousands of years from an unidentified source, a source lost in the distant past.

"There is a large doughnut-shaped stone in Cornwall, England, called 'Mên-an-Tol,' and for hundreds of years local mothers there have passed their sick children through the hole in the stone because it is said to have healing powers. Healing powers. But the stone is thousands of years old, and it was cut by man. No one knows who built the stone, or why. All that knowledge has been lost. There's just that legend attached to it, and a powerful legend it is. And that is why the God-fearing Methodist women still practice that pagan ritual, passing their sick babies through the opening in the stone."

"Gosh," said Emeline.

"And so it is with this place—the legend of the curse. Perhaps I will learn enough to be able to shed some light on why the Site of Stones has been shunned through the years, until your family, Miss Curtis, bought all the property hereabouts and built the hotel. If the Indians considered this place taboo as did the white settlers, then how did that notion come about—and by whom was it started? By whom, I say!"

"It is certainly fascinating to think about," I admitted reluctantly. "I must tell you that I feel . . . uncomfortable here myself."

He regarded me intently. "Do you, Miss Hawthorne? You may be merely responding to suggestion, because of what you have heard of the curse, or you may be a sensitive. That is, you might be picking up emotions in the atmosphere not felt by most people. I myself have not been conscious of anything out of the ordinary here," he said ruefully. "But I would like to talk to you sometime about your reactions."

"Well, perhaps," I mumbled, annoyed that I had brought it up, "although I daresay you'll think me very foolish. Come, Emeline, we must allow Mr. Willoughby to continue his work."

"Good day, ladies," he said, smiling, before reaching into his pocket for a flask. Waving at us, he took a large gulp of whatever liquid was inside.

"What was that all about?" asked Emeline as we walked away. "What did he say you might be? A sensitive? Sensitive to what?"

"Oh, things that may have happened here, feelings—it's a ludicrous idea. Forget it."

"You mean like ghosts or something? I think Uncle Drake may be right about Mr. Willoughby after all, if he believes in ghosts and the curse. I remember the first time I brought you here—you got all white and trembly and then you ran off down the hill."

"Yes, that day I was very frightened—it just came over me very fast. Perhaps someone was walking over my grave," I said lightly.

"Goodness. And now Mr. Willoughby wants to interview you, like an experiment," she said, wide-eyed.

"How delightfully you phrase things. Let's drop the subject, shall we? I've had enough of it today. Now would be the perfect time for you to recite 'Kubla Khan.' You did tell me this morning that you had learned it by heart."

Our days continued to be full, and when it was possible, we participated in the various entertainments offered at the hotel. One evening Emeline and I attended a delightful recital of songs by Gilbert and Sullivan performed by a group of musicians from Boston. And a day or so after that, we joined the guests in an alfresco luncheon behind the hotel. We helped ourselves to the elegantly prepared dishes such as shrimp mousse, honeydew with lime, and iced tea with mint leaves, and then took our plates to one of the tables covered in pale yellow damask scattered about the lawn. Some of the people drifted over to the gazebos with their pagoda-shaped red roofs, and to the stone bridge which curved gracefully over the placid brook. In the distance soared Mt. Washington, dusky-blue, titanic, the minarets of the spruce trees banding up the grade until, like giant birds' nests thatching the upper slopes, they became the crooked wood of the *krumholz*.

Emeline and I sat with the Aldridges and Mrs. Hamilton, Miss Birche and Mr. Sloane. Mrs. Aldridge, in a trailing gown of sea-foam green, was much improved in looks and spirits, and she did not complain except to say twice that the sun was in her eyes. As her husband had changed places with her after the first time, there was nothing more to be done the second time she expressed her grievance. But to do her justice, the sting was gone from her voice; she seemed to be speaking more from habit than from actual discomfort.

"That was a most enjoyable concert the other night," said Miss Birche cheerfully. Her hair was, as usual, untidily

that the last thing he would wish would be for public attention to once again be focused on the place."

"Oh, for God's sake, leave the poor man alone," said her husband. "He's a very decent sort, and he runs a damn fine hotel."

Mrs. Aldridge flushed. "I admit that the Crystal Hills is a lovely place," she said rather stiffly. "And I'm certain that's due in most part to the ministrations of Major Curtis. However, you can't totally ignore that—former business."

Mrs. Hamilton, who had been slicing a pear with a small knife, turned her sharp eyes and hawklike nose on Mrs. Aldridge. "If you are alluding to that brouhaha of a year ago, I should think you'd do your best to ignore it," she said shortly.

Emeline returned to the table just then and the conversation was steered in another direction. After luncheon was finished, Emeline expressed a desire to play croquet, and so another pleasant hour was passed. Even Mrs. Aldridge was observed to enjoy herself, caught up in the spirit of the game.

That evening I had been out for a walk, and was crossing the front hall of the house when I heard angry voices coming from the library. My hand on the banister, I paused.

"I'm asking you to explain this bill, Leonora." It was Drake's voice.

"It seems perfectly lucid to me," she answered.

"You know very well what I mean. I told you when you returned from Boston there was to be no more reckless spending!"

"And by what right do you hold the purse strings?" she asked furiously. "Aaron's the elder brother—or have you forgotten?"

"By the right that I'm the one determined to see the hotel doesn't go under. You and Aaron had your time to run things—and I came back to a worse mess than I could have imagined! Well, the reins are back in my hands now and that's where they're going to stay!"

"I wish to God we could desert this sinking ship!" she cried.

"You and Aaron can leave at any time, Leonora, with my blessing."

"Not on your life. Not unless you agree to sell some of the

land and give us our share."

"If I am ever forced to sell some of the land, Leonora, it would only, I repeat only, be to save the hotel from certain ruin—and only if there were no other possible means of doing so."

"Oh, I know that land is sacred to you Curtises. But it's Aaron's land as well, so he should have a say in how the money from it would be spent!"

"I would have agreed with you some time ago, but Aaron forfeited any say or right to family property when he forged my signature on a bank mortgage to pay his gambling debts, debts he accrued while using hotel funds to finance his games of chance. Or have you forgotten that, Leonora? Not that either of you have ever done much to benefit the hotel. You've just taken from it!"

She gave a low laugh. "What a hypocrite you are, Drake. As though you've always had the best interests of the hotel at heart. Have *you* forgotten that it was your conduct which placed the hotel in jeopardy, after years of similar conduct? You may feel remorseful and may have abandoned all of that, but I daresay you're not as altered as you'd like to appear. I wouldn't think that wound in your leg would prevent you from starting anew! Now, who with? I've noticed that more than a few of the ladies have their eyes on you. But perhaps a guest wouldn't be wise at this point, not with that little man going about his business at the scene of the crime. No, I daresay a guest would not be a wise choice."

"Shut up, Leonora," came Drake's voice, knife-edged.

"If not a guest, then who?" she continued in the same bantering tones. "One of the maids would be in very poor taste. Oh, of course, I have it! Our little governess! I should have thought of her instantly. Anyone can see that she's smitten with you, despite her downcast eyes and prim mouth. You could begin on her—just to assure yourself you haven't lost your touch, that you're still a man, despite your . . . recent vulnerabilities. Your bad leg isn't a hindrance, and I don't think Miss Hawthorne would mind."

"I said, shut up, you bitch! Or so help me, I'll—"

"You'll what? There's nothing you can do to me. But there's

a good deal *I* can do, you know. I could tell our Miss Hawthorne a thing or two, couldn't I? It would be a pity to disillusion her, but after all, in a way she's my responsibility, isn't she, as Emeline's tutor?''

"You wouldn't dare," he said. "That's no one's concern but my own! And I wish to God I could have kept it that way!''

"It would be her concern, wouldn't it, if she were in love with you? I wouldn't advise tempting me, Drake. And about that bill. You will have to pay it, you know. Since you've taken control of the family finances again, all the bills become your responsibility," she said coolly.

I could not listen any longer. A hand to my hot cheek, I went swiftly up the stairs before one or the other of them came out into the hall and saw me there. I was overcome with horror and shame that my feelings for Drake were so transparent that Leonora Curtis, of all people, had remarked on them. Was Charlotte aware of them as well, and Emeline? And the sharp-eyed Mrs. Hamilton? A fine example I was setting, falling in love with my charge's uncle. Until now I had not even admitted to myself that I was in love with him. But I was, of course. And for Leonora to have so smugly exposed my innermost feelings to Drake was more than I could bear. He might have guessed them as he held me in his arms at the Flume, but as I had denied the truth even to myself, I had not considered that he realized the depth of my emotions. Now there was no turning back.

Later in the week Emeline asked if we might again dine at the hotel. It was the very last thing I wished to do; up until then I had managed to avoid both Drake and Leonora Curtis. But Charlotte expressed her wish to join us, and I had no choice but to agree to the scheme. Perhaps Drake would be taking dinner in his office, and Leonora was certain not to notice me were she with a group of her fashionable friends.

To my confused dismay I saw Drake immediately upon entering the dining room. He was standing at one of the tables, conversing with Horatio Aldridge; he looked relaxed, his hand in the pocket of his black trousers. Mrs. Aldridge was seated across from Leonora, listening to her chatter, a rather frozen polite smile fixed on her face. Again the room was crowded, and there was an incessant buzz of conversation punctuated by the clinking of dishes and silverware. In one corner of the room, a chamber orchestra was playing Vivaldi; the waiters were hastening about, pouring champagne and iced water into glasses. I felt out of place in those glittering surroundings in my striped green and white cotton gown, but then, I reminded myself, I was not a guest, but merely an employee.

Emeline, Charlotte, and I sat down at the table with Emeline's parents, Drake, the Aldridges, and another lady and gentleman who had just come from Philadelphia. I was careful not to look at any of them, and kept my attention on the plate of watercress and Boston lettuce set before me.

Aaron Curtis was describing the excursion some of the guests had taken that afternoon up Mt. Washington on the cog railway. "I thought one or two of the ladies were going to swoon," he said, grinning. "I warned them it took nerves of steel to make that trip. Nearly straight up and down it is in some places, and the train moves very slowly. But we were fortunate that the day was clear. The view, when it's there, is amazing—you can see for hundreds of miles in each direction. I remember when they built that railway. Just as well build a railway to the moon, they said, as up Mt. Washington." He laughed heartily.

"I'm sure the view is all you claim it to be, Mr. Curtis," said Mrs. Aldridge. "But I choose to remain here, at this elevation."

"I found it most invigorating," said her husband to the gentleman from Philadelphia. "I recommend it to you, sir."

"And Mrs. Aldridge and I will be content to observe the train's progress from the hotel veranda," said the lady.

The waiter removed our salad plates and served the lamb chops and tiny new potatoes and carrots. Emeline was talking happily to Charlotte; she loved taking dinner in the hotel, where she felt smart and grown-up.

Then I heard the lady from Philadelphia say, "Major Curtis, I understand you were in the war in Cuba last summer. Won't you tell us of some of your experiences? I'm certain we shall all be fascinated."

Drake's mouth tightened. "They are not worth recounting, I assure you, ma'am."

"But you were a Rough Rider, were you not? I understood from one or two of the other ladies—"

"I was, ma'am. But that hardly—"

"But you were the heroes of the war! Everyone everywhere was forever talking about the daring and bravery of Colonel Roosevelt and his men!"

"I assure you I was no hero, Mrs. Langston. I merely followed orders like everyone else."

"I'm sure you are too modest, Major. You must have had many dealings with Colonel Roosevelt. Tell me, what was he like?"

Drake gave a twisted smile. "He was the most courageous and reckless of anyone—and he was with his men every minute of the charges."

"Won't you at least describe your charge up Kettle Hill?" she went on relentlessly. "It must have been so thrilling; the newspaper accounts certainly made it seem so. Mr. William Randolph Hearst of the New York *Journal* was there himself, and he wrote so eloquently of the charge Colonel Roosevelt led."

"Yes, he was there," said Drake, his face hardening. "I understand that Mr. Hearst is of the opinion that he brought about the war, and with the journalistic tactics he uses, I wouldn't be at all surprised if he were right."

There was an awkward silence.

"It's no use prodding my brother-in-law, Mrs. Langston," said Leonora. "He can be the most tight-lipped man imaginable. We've gotten very little about the war out of him. The truth is he spent far more time in the hospital than he did on the battlefield."

Drake shot her a dark, furious look while Mr. Aldridge said mildly, "Well, the war only lasted a matter of weeks, after all. Now, Major Curtis, you were going to tell me how I might ride up that mountain on horseback."

We were having dessert, a meringue with strawberries and whipped cream, when Burrows, the doorman, approached Drake at the table. His long face looked very worried.

"Yes, Burrows, what is it?" said Drake in a low voice.

"I beg your pardon, sir, but there's a . . . gentleman here to

207

see you. He—he doesn't have a reservation, but he has come for an indefinite stay, he says."

"Well, find him a room then," said Drake. "You know the ones which are unoccupied."

Burrows looked more pained than ever. "I offered to, sir, but he . . . well, sir, he insists on seeing you. I'm afraid that he insists on making the arrangements with you, sir. I—I told him that I wasn't certain whether I could locate you."

"Well, you knew I was in here, didn't you?" Drake said, rising. "Will all of you excuse me?" he added to the company, and then turned to Burrows again. "Who is he? Did he give you his name?"

"He did, sir, though it—it wasn't necessary."

"So you know him, do you? Do I? Well, speak up, man. Who is he?"

"It's—it's Mr. Schyler, from New York, sir," said the doorman quietly.

Rapidly the color drained from Drake's face leaving it an unhealthy frozen gray. His knuckles were white where he gripped the back of the chair. Leonora gave a startled gasp, and across from me Charlotte put a hand to her throat, her expression aghast. "Oh, my God," she whispered.

Drake made a slight jerky movement as if to leave the table, and his leg abruptly buckled under him. He stumbled against the table.

"Come, sir," said Burrows, steadying Drake with an arm about his shoulders.

"There you are, Curtis. Not very good policy to keep your guests standing about in the lobby." A man had approached the table while our attention was fixed on Drake. He looked to be in his late forties, his salt-and-pepper hair waving back from his face. He was very well dressed, and when he spoke, I saw that one of his teeth had been capped in gold.

"What are you doing here?" asked Drake rather hoarsely. Mechanically he straightened his jacket. His face was still pale.

"Why, I've come to enjoy some mountain air," said the older man smoothly.

"I believe all our rooms are taken," said Drake, his eyes narrowing.

"Surely we can find one for Mr. Schyler," said Leonora, rising from the table. "How nice to see you again, sir. Please excuse my brother-in-law. He has not been well."

"So I have heard, Mrs. Curtis. A war hero, I understand. May I say that you are looking as beautiful as ever? And the hotel appears to be in fine fettle. I confess I had heard rumors to the contrary."

"Burrows, I will take care of Mr. Schyler. You see that his baggage is taken upstairs. Come with me, sir," Leonora said, drawing her arm through his.

Charlotte rose quickly and went to Drake's side while the other guests at the table began talking at random.

"I won't have that man staying at my hotel," said Drake between clenched teeth. He made a move as if to follow Leonora and Mr. Schyler, but Charlotte put a hand on his arm.

"Don't do anything rash, Drake," she said softly. "It may only make matters worse. Wait, wait a while."

"What the hell does he want here?" he whispered furiously.

Charlotte shook her head, her face anxious.

Drake gave a short, ugly laugh. "First that fool of an archaeologist, and now this. I'm beginning to think there's some sort of damned conspiracy." And shaking off her restraining arm, he limped from the room.

It struck me then that the unexpected guest was none other than the husband of the young woman who had been Drake's mistress, the same young woman who had met her death at the Site of Stones.

Chapter Eleven

I watched Drake's retreat from the dining room with mingled fear, confusion, and distress. Emeline turned to Charlotte in bewilderment; the ladies at the table were exchanging glances, while the men tried to act as if they had noticed nothing.

Aaron laughed rather awkwardly, mumbling something about Drake's leg paining him, and then launched into a rambling discourse on all the sights in the area, looking to the Aldridges for confirmation. Before long the guests were once again chatting comfortably, and the tense, baffling moments had passed.

But the remains of the meringue dessert before me had run together like a pink sponge, and my coffee had grown cold. With relief I heard Charlotte excusing herself, and I nodded to Emeline that we would do the same. Taking Charlotte's arm, we passed through the dining room to the lobby. There was no sign of Drake or of Leonora, nor of Mr. Schyler himself.

The three of us went out the front door and down the porch steps into the crisp, pine-scented night air. Charlotte began to tremble; I put my arm about her shoulders to steady her as we walked.

It was Emeline who broke the brittle silence. "Who was that man, Charlotte?"

"He . . . he was a guest here once, my dear," she answered faintly.

"I thought he looked familiar. And he knew Mamma, didn't

he? But why did Uncle Drake tell him the hotel rooms were all taken when it wasn't true?"

"Grant Schyler and your uncle had a—a sort of falling-out some time ago, Emeline," said Charlotte.

"What happened?"

"Perhaps Charlotte doesn't care to talk about it now, Emeline," I said.

"No, it's all right. I suppose that now Grant Schyler has come, much of the past is going to come out anyway. And it will be better if I tell Emeline the tale than if she were to hear one of the employees discussing it. You see, Emeline, Mr. Schyler and his wife came here from New York over a year ago. You may recall his wife; she was a beautiful, fair-haired young woman, much younger than her husband. She—she fell in love with Drake. And, as in many such stories, there was a tragic ending. She—Alice was her name—she was found dead one evening."

"How did she die?" asked Emeline, awed.

"I'm very much afraid that she took her own life. It was all very tragic, as I've said. Most unfortunate for all concerned. There was an investigation into her death and everyone was questioned. Especially Drake and Mr. Schyler."

"When did this happen?"

"May, a year ago. Mrs. Schyler's body was found one evening, and the following morning your mother took you to school. I admit that I persuaded her to do so. I—I didn't think you ought to be here—we didn't know what would come of it all."

"So that's why I was sent away to school in such a hurry!"

"It seemed the best thing to do at the time, child. This was no place for you then; your grandmother would have agreed with me on that. Later there was an inquest and it was determined that Alice Schyler had committed suicide. But the damage to the hotel had been done. For weeks the story was in all the newspapers, only twisted and made even uglier than it was. I was half-afraid you might hear of it, after all. We received many cancellations. Except for those impelled by a vulgar curiosity, people did not care to stay at a hotel which had been featured in all the scandal sheets. People come to the Crystal Hills for rest and relaxation, for elegant and genteel entertainments. Suddenly our name was synonymous with—well, a most unsavory tale. And it seems it takes people a long time to forget an unpleasant past association. We've had a difficult time recovering from the lost business, as you've observed, my child."

"I understand that now. But why has Mr. Schyler come back?" asked Emeline. "Is he here to make things worse again—just when they've been getting better?"

"I don't know, Emeline," sighed Charlotte. "I won't conceal from either of you that seeing Grant Schyler gave me a nasty shock, just as it did to Drake. Perhaps it would have been better if Drake had denied him a room, as he began to . . . if only your mother had not—welcomed him in the manner she did. But it's done now—and I'm afraid that it looks as though we must put up with his presence for a while."

"My mother shouldn't have treated him like an honored guest, fussing over him the way she did," said Emeline critically. "If only we knew why he was here—I don't want anything further to happen to the hotel!"

"I don't believe that Mr. Schyler's purpose in coming is an innocent one. I would like to think that he has come to take in the scenery and the fresh air—but only a fool would delude himself into thinking that," said Charlotte ruefully.

"Certainly he would not do so at the site of his wife's violent death," I put in.

"He couldn't do anything to Uncle Drake—or the Crystal Hills, could he?" asked Emeline, worried.

We had reached the house and were standing at the foot of the staircase. Emeline looked quite concerned; her eyes were dark pools behind the spectacles.

Charlotte shook her head, her voice suddenly brisk. "I've said too much. I shouldn't be alarming you, Emeline. Your uncle can handle Mr. Schyler; we must put faith in him. And now it's time for bed, my dear. I'm going up as well. I don't want you to lie awake worrying about this. We've tried to keep things from you since your return, but perhaps that hasn't been wise. You're growing up, and one day before long you'll own a portion of the Crystal Hills. But just now you must trust in Drake to take care of these matters. He's very strong and

212

determined, you know. And shrewd. He won't be intimidated by Grant Schyler."

Emeline smiled in acknowledgment, but there was a crease in her brow.

"Shall I tuck you in?" I asked, half in jest, but she nodded and the three of us went upstairs.

I was concerned about Emeline's reaction to all she had learned that night, and so I stayed with her for a time. She sat in front of her wicker vanity while I brushed her hair until it gleamed in the wavering light of the frosted gas globes.

"Uncle Drake shouldn't have permitted that woman—that Mrs. Schyler—to fall in love with him," she said gravely. "It's all her fault."

"No, Emeline. Each of them is partly to blame, or perhaps it was just circumstances." I had fallen in love with her uncle against *my* will and better judgment. "I know it's very difficult for you to comprehend, but things in life are not often what they seem to be in childhood. People are not always right or wrong; things are not either black or white. And sometimes we feel powerless against events. But as Charlotte said, most situations such as the one your uncle and Mrs. Schyler found themselves in do not end happily. How can they, after all?"

"But they don't all end in someone dying," she pointed out. "And because of that the hotel lost business. Not that I'm not sorry for Mrs. Schyler. At least now I understand why people stopped coming to the Crystal Hills for a while."

"I want you to remember one thing when you start to worry about the hotel, Emeline. The Crystal Hills is doing much better than it was when we arrived in July. Think of the difference just a few weeks have made. And that's mainly due to your uncle's efforts, I'm sure. Charlotte is right; you must have faith in him."

She rested her chin on her hand. "Everyone talks about Uncle Drake as though it's all his responsibility. Doesn't my father help?"

"Well," I began awkwardly, "I suppose your uncle has the business head. But your father and mother help out in other ways—entertaining the guests, leading the excursions, things of that nature."

"I suppose that's only because Uncle Drake doesn't have time to do those things too. He can't very well be in several places at once, can he? And I've realized something else, Teresa. He must have gone to the war just after the police investigation was finished. He shouldn't have, though. It only made things worse."

"Emeline, you really mustn't judge. You can know nothing of the circumstances. Charlotte doesn't judge your uncle."

She looked sullen. "Well, he left the hotel just when it needed him the most. And my parents were the ones who stayed. Now I understand why my mother has blamed Uncle Drake for the way the hotel has lost business. No one would tell me anything before tonight."

"Well, they wanted to shield you from it all. It's not a pretty story—and there was no reason for you to know the details."

"Oh, Teresa, you're just like the rest of them! I'm not a child any longer!"

"Your mother took you to Miss Winslow's Academy so that you wouldn't be hurt and confused by what resulted. The police, the newspapers, everything. They were only concerned with what was best for you. That's why they sent you away."

"I suppose so," she said grudgingly.

"Now you ought to try and get some sleep. I know this has all been very exciting, but try to relax and forget about it. I'll see you in the morning."

"All right. Good night, Teresa."

"Good night." I turned down the flames in the globes as she climbed into bed.

The house was very quiet. Charlotte must already have gone to sleep as there were no sounds of movement from her room. The dim gaslights made eerie, amorphous shadows on the walls of the gallery.

Tonight the pieces of the puzzle had begun to fit together. Alice Schyler had taken her own life and the chain of events had begun, the same chain in which Grant Schyler's arrival had forged another link.

Why had Alice Schyler killed herself? Had her husband discovered her infidelity and sworn to take her back to New York, away from Drake? Had she killed herself because she could not face a life without him? Had she been so overcome with shame and remorse at her adulterous behavior that she had inflicted the most severe self-punishment? Had someone threatened to betray her to her husband? Had she begged her husband for a divorce and he had refused?

And how did Drake fit into her final act? Was he totally blameless? Had he played no part in her final, anguished decision? If he was innocent of all except conducting a liaison with a married woman, then why had he rushed off to join the First Volunteer Cavalry as soon as the case was closed and he was free to leave? Had he played a greater role in her death than had been suspected?

There had been an investigation. That meant the police had thoroughly questioned the principal players, but one, and also the guests and employees. They had doubtless studied Alice Schyler's death from all angles. Before they had ultimately resolved that it was a case of suicide, they must have considered whether she could have died by other means. A violent death could occur three ways—by accident, suicide—or murder.

But in a murder there are suspects. And the suspects in this case would obviously have been Drake and Grant Schyler. No one else would have had a motive. What would the husband's motive have been? That he had discovered that his wife had been unfaithful to him? That was certainly a strong motive. What of Drake? Had he a motive? Surely not. And after all, the inquest had determined that the unfortunate woman had ended her own life. Yet Drake had run away. . . .

And now Grant Schyler had returned. Like Charlotte, I did not for a moment believe that it was for an innocent reason. I had been wary of his expression of sardonic amusement as he observed Drake's reaction to his arrival, his gold tooth flashing in sudden smiles.

I could not go to my room, lovely and serene as it was. Slowly I walked down the stairs and under the animal heads hanging along the walls of the gallery. There was a fire burning brightly in the empty sitting room; I went in and sat down on the plum brocade sofa, reaching for one of the tapestry pillows and leaning both elbows on it.

Ever since I had come here I had been conscious of a sensation in the atmosphere—a smoldering, a brewing feeling. The tension had grown thicker as time passed; the pressure had seemed to build; the hatreds had begun to surface more frequently. We were all moving inexorably to an end which I trembled to contemplate. And I had never been more certain of that end as I was tonight when Grant Schyler had entered the room and I had seen Drake's face, gray, frozen, his eyes wild, almost dazed. Now it was all to come back to him, if it had ever left. If ever a man had an enemy, Drake had one now.

There was another piece to the puzzle I could not fit, something else which baffled me. Drake refused at all times to talk about the war. I understood that there were those who did not enjoy refighting old battles, replaying old scenes, telling the same tales over and over, but Drake was peculiarly reticent about his experiences. He would be almost discourteous when pressed; sometimes he was plainly rude. Was his grim silence the result of his being badly wounded? Or was there something else—something which had happened to him, something which contributed to make him the hard, bitter man he was today? Perhaps he badly regretted volunteering, not so much because of the wound to his leg, but because he had left the hotel to flounder under the careless handling of his brother. Perhaps he blamed himself as he wanted to blame Aaron, blamed himself for wasted, pain-wracked months spent in the hospital while the hotel continued to lose business, while Aaron gambled away thousands of dollars and then signed his name to a document binding them to make monthly payments on their own property. He must have cursed himself many times for leaving, for recklessly rushing off to Cuba. That must be why he avoided the subject the way he did. Not because he was concealing some sinister secret, some emotional battle scar . . .

I sat gazing into the flames for a time before there came a sound behind me. "Can't you sleep, Emeline?" I started to say, looking over my shoulder. But it was not Emeline who stood on the threshold of the room. It was Drake.

"Don't look like that," he said roughly. "You give such a start when we meet—as though you're afraid I'm going to . . ."

He swore impatiently, shrugging off his dinner jacket. I could not tell him that it was my own reaction to him that caused me apprehension—the abrupt clamoring of my pulses, the way my heart lurched and thudded in my breast—and not his behavior.

He sat down heavily on one of the chairs beside the fire, easing down his powerful build, his bad leg stiffly stretched out before him. "Why aren't you in bed?" he growled. "It's late."

"I'm not sleepy." I had noticed the disheveled state of his evening attire; he had pulled apart his starched white collar and it hung about his neck. "Where have you been?"

"Out riding. I may as well make good use of the horses while I still own them."

"Are things as bad as that? I thought—I hoped that with more guests and all—"

"So did I. The tide was beginning to turn. It doesn't do to be overly optimistic, it seems." He bent his dark head, raking his fingers through his hair. The firelight flickered over him, casting a large, forbidding shadow on the wall opposite.

"It's Mr. Schyler," I said flatly.

He looked up at that. "So you know about him, do you?" But this time there was no curtness in his voice, only a bleak, empty quality that was far worse. "When I saw him tonight, when I heard his name, I saw it all again. Not the hotel dining room—the waiters, the crystal, the guests. But her as she lay there in the pool of blood which had congealed, the stab wounds which had darkened, crusted over—"

"Don't, Drake." I shuddered. "Hush."

He ignored me. "Her blond hair was streaming over her shoulders, her face was a hideous white. And she lay on that slab of stone like some sort of horrible sacrifice."

"Oh, God—you mean that slab at the Site of Stones? That's where she—?"

"That's where they found her, just hours after we'd—after we'd been together. May 1st it was. She had begged me again to run away with her, to go to Europe where we could pretend to be married. But I told her no, just as I'd told her before. I had no intention of leaving the hotel, of leaving everything I'd worked for, not for her sake. Even if she had gotten a divorce from Schyler I would not have married her. She was just part

217

of the spring, as others had been part of other springs, other summers. She wanted attention; she was bored. Her husband paid her little heed. I thought that was all she wanted—a flirtation, a temporary liaison. That had always been the understanding. But then she changed; she wanted to escape her husband for good, and she decided I was the way she could do that.

"They wrapped her up and carried her away. Her blood was still on the stone. I couldn't stop thinking that it was like some horribly primitive ritual—a sacrifice. She had always said that the Site of Stones was like a sort of pagan temple, for fertility rites, she'd laugh. And I saw then the fantastic irony. She'd done it herself—a sacrifice to love, or whatever. She was the flamboyant type."

He leaned back in his chair. "Schyler and I were questioned endlessly. Detectives came from Concord to help out the local police. Many of the guests were questioned as well, Alice's friends especially. She had talked, you see. They knew about us, that she had wanted me to run away with her, that I'd refused. They told the police."

"She had told her friends that you would not go away with her?" I asked softly.

"Yes, that the hotel meant more to me." He gave a short, ugly laugh. "Of course the hotel meant more to me. I had never deceived her. That last afternoon I thought I had ended it. But she played the last hand. I didn't think she would. Oh, yes, she'd threatened to kill herself if I didn't take her away.

"They thought at first that it might be murder. The morning after, the journalists arrived by train. I remember being surprised that they'd gotten wind of it so soon. I wouldn't allow them inside the hotel, but they spoke to everyone who went out—anyone who would speak to them—and took photograph after photograph. They even talked to Alice's maid. They paid her for the story, you see. It was a good one, even as much as she knew, and what she didn't, they made up. The thing was written from every angle, day after day—'New York Socialite Brutally Murdered in White Mountains Hotel,' 'Beautiful Woman Found Slashed at Mysterious Site,' 'Hotel Owner Rids Himself of Unwanted Wealthy Mistress,' 'Rich New Yorker

Kills Unfaithful Wife,' 'Evil Curse Takes Woman's Life.' The stories, the headlines, grew more incredible every day. I threatened to have the reporters forcibly moved from the hotel grounds, but the authorities advised against it. They said the stories would become even more sordid if the reporters were kept entirely away, although I found that hard to believe."

He shifted in his chair, turning to look at the crackling flames, now low and curling over the blackened logs. His face was hard, the square jaw clenched.

"I was trying to run the hotel. As usual Aaron was doing as little as possible; he was even talking to reporters. Leonora had taken the child away. . . . I was interrogated again and again, the same questions over and over. 'What was the precise nature of your feelings for the victim, Mr. Curtis?' Again and again, when they knew precisely what we'd been up to. 'When did you last see her?' 'What happened on that occasion?' There was one detective, a tough, shrewd fellow. He was convinced that I'd done it. In his mind I'd had the opportunity because she had died close to the time I was with her; I'd had a motive—to rid myself of a situation which had become unpleasant. It was an ordinary kitchen knife that she'd used, from the hotel kitchen. She'd ordered a picnic for us that afternoon, and so the knife had been included in the basket of fruit. But the detective couldn't be sure; he couldn't find the irrefutable evidence he needed."

"Did he also suspect Grant Schyler?" I asked.

Drake nodded. "He claimed to have been out riding that afternoon. And he had certainly taken one of the horses, the stable boy reported. Again, there was no solid evidence to do more than implicate him. There was blood on Alice's hands, so it did look as though she had killed herself. Finally they presented all the evidence at the inquest and ruled death by suicide. The excitement then over," he added cynically, "the guests began leaving in droves. We couldn't get them to the trains fast enough for their liking. I looked about one morning and the place was practically deserted. There seemed no point to anything anymore."

"You realized then that you had loved her?"

"No, I never loved her. I never loved any of them. I was always in control, always sure of myself, always taking what I wanted, but never from those who were not willing to give it, who did not want to play the game. But Alice decided that was not enough. She wanted more. And I had no intention of giving her more, of playing by different rules, disrupting my existence. My life was the way I wanted it then. I used to tell myself it was better than what Aaron and Leonora had in their wedded bliss. Even if I had wanted to run away with her—which I did not—I knew I could never have left the hotel to Aaron and Leonora. Of course, that's eventually what happened, but before Alice died I'd no intentions of leaving. Aaron had no business sense; I knew he'd run the thing into the ground if left alone long enough. He's eight years older than I, yet when I was sixteen I was doing more than he had ever done. So I had no intention of abandoning all I had worked to build and maintain to go off with a woman I'd enjoyed a mild flirtation with. There was passion—but nothing else. 'You don't love anything but that hotel,' she used to say. And so she struck back in the most devastating way. She had to have calculated what her death and the arising scandal would do to the hotel, to me. But when I stood alone in the hotel lobby that morning after the inquest, I felt no anger or bitterness toward her. No remorse or guilt in myself. I felt—nothing. I no longer cared about the hotel, about anything. I wanted only to get away."

The red embers glowed in the hearth; underneath them lay the ashes, dust-white.

"And so you went away," I said.

"I left, yes," he said curtly. "It was ironic that only weeks before I'd told Alice that I'd never leave. She'd won; she'd got her way in the end. They were calling for volunteers to fight the Spaniards in Cuba. That seemed far enough away. I went to New York. Congress had declared war on Spain on April 25th—at the time the news meant nothing to me. Why should it? It couldn't touch us in Nightshade Notch. I didn't give a thought to all the poor fools who were enlisting. Then, less than a month later, I was in San Antonio, in training for the First Volunteer Cavalry. The only regiment ever bringing together cowboys from the West and society men from the

East, organized by the former Secretary of the Navy, Lieutenant Colonel Teddy Roosevelt, a mixture of both types himself. The newspapers gloomily reported that if we were sent to invade during the rainy season, late spring and early summer, one third of us would die—and not in battle. I didn't care. It was either go to Cuba or to the Yukon for gold—and Cuba was closer. I said that to a particularly unpleasant woman in the hospital, after she'd gone on and on about my 'heroic sacrifice.' It was worth it just to see the expression on her face." His eyes glinted, his lip curling.

"I'd qualified easily for the Rough Riders," he went on. "They cared not at all if you'd been suspected of murder, only that you could shoot and ride well. My father had brought me up to do both—to hunt and to live off the land. When I was young we'd go off for a week or more in the wilderness, far from the hotels. Aaron never came. 'You must know how to ride, how to shoot, how to live in the open. No matter what comes, you mustn't squeal,' Colonel Roosevelt told us. Easy enough, I thought. I was made an officer along with some of the athletes from Harvard, Princeton, and Yale. It was all rather amusing when I bothered to reflect on it. Crack polo players and yachtsmen training alongside ranchers and trappers and miners. I felt very detached from everything.

"We went to Tampa on a very long, overcrowded, uncomfortable train ride, but I felt little of the other men's irritation and discomfort. Later they told us we'd be doing our traveling on foot—the government couldn't come up with the horses we'd been promised, except for the colonels. The men were furious; it struck me as incredibly funny. Rough Riders with no horses. Tampa was sheer bedlam, the food rotting in train cars before it reached us, the water very poor; the confusion was fantastic, there was no direction, no system. Colonel Roosevelt and the other top officers were furiously waiting for the go-ahead from Congress for days while we sweltered in the heat. But even that affected me very little. I gave and followed orders when I had to, and slept much of the rest of the time. I remember wondering if I were always going to feel this remote, this uncaring for the rest of my life. Only weeks before I had been in the midst of a nightmare I could not

221

shake off, and then suddenly—nothing."

"And when you finally reached Cuba? When you began fighting—and were wounded? Did you still feel little and care little?" I asked him.

Into his eyes came the same expression I had noticed on the train—a helpless, hopeless look. When he spoke I had to strain to catch his words. "I had merely exchanged one nightmare for another."

I said nothing, waiting breathlessly for him to go on, but he did not. He shifted his stiff leg and winced. "And tonight Grant Schyler has returned. God alone knows the reason."

"Do you think he has revenge in mind?"

There was a long pause, then he sighed heavily. "He said he had heard rumors. He must be aware how poorly the hotel did last summer, how half the staff left in the fall when Aaron lowered their wages—as if that would solve matters! When I took off for the Army, there was plenty of money—enough to see the hotel through a severe slump. But Aaron used that money, he took hotel funds, to support his gambling. And then when he'd lost and lost and kept on losing, he mortgaged the hotel to pay his debts. When I arrived home in December after being discharged from the hospital, I thought I had had my fill of self-loathing, of guilt and remorse and shame. But no—for then I saw what I had done to the Crystal Hills."

"It wasn't you, Drake. You were not responsible for his—"

"I'd left him in charge, tossed him the reins and left him to cope. Just as Leonora said. I have only myself to blame for all of it. But even then I felt there was a good chance I could put it to rights I wasn't going to let the place go that easily, not without a long, hard fight. We opened in April as usual—and I suppose you've surmised the rest. I didn't learn about the mortgage until last month when I went to Portsmouth. That afternoon after I'd picked up Emeline, I went to our bankers to apply for a loan. And I sat there, stunned, while Mr. Choake withdrew the mortgage document and showed it to me. And there was my name, under Aaron's."

"What did you say?"

"Very little. I wrote him a draft for the amount of the first payment and told him he would receive the other two late payments very soon. I had no choice but to sell one of the horses. Again I was starting to feel we might pull through, when Aaron announced that he'd given Willoughby permission to excavate. We can't afford, you see, for the stories, the speculations to begin again."

"So far they haven't," I reminded him.

He nodded grimly. "So far. And every week more people have been arriving by train. They have been willing to give us a chance again, now that the hue and cry is back in the past. But they will depart just as quickly if the sordid details are resurrected. And now Schyler is here. There's a deliberate reason for his being here—and it can only be one which can do the hotel, and me, no good."

"And what if somehow business does fall off, what then?" I asked anxiously.

He sighed heavily. "I'll only have one choice then, I suppose, if things get that desperate. Aaron and I own a large amount of land, most of the Notch, in fact. I can agree to sell some of it. But I don't wish to do so unless there is no other way."

"Why not?"

"Because if the land is sold, it will likely be another hotel developer who is willing to buy it. This is not an area where the rich have chosen to build summer cottages. There is nothing here but the mountains, a few villages, and the hotels. And that is the way it should be. Even now there are enough hotels, and I don't say that out of a fear of competition. It's that I think the land should be preserved, and the idea of another hotel being built in Nightshade Notch I find extremely objectionable."

"Did Mr. Schyler know about you and Alice before she died?"

He frowned. "I don't know. He claimed he didn't, but then he didn't want to be saddled with a motive for murder. But in reality I don't see how he could have been totally unaware. She often told me she was used to amusing herself as she pleased; they did not get in each other's way."

"Do you think that he may have killed her himself, despite the authorities not finding evidence to support that?"

"I'll admit the notion passed through my mind a number of

times at first. But later I rejected it. Everything pointed to suicide. And even if he had killed her. Why on earth come back? I don't believe he's returned to the scene of the crime in some sick obsession. But he is here for a purpose."

"Perhaps there is no real reason," I said.

"Are you asking me to believe he's here as a tourist?" he snarled.

"Of course not. But perhaps he has come to make things uncomfortable for you—to torment you by his presence."

"To torment me?" He laughed without humor. "Like a ghost from the past? Making certain I've not forgotten, reminding me again and again? If that's the case, he's wasting his time. I need no reminders."

"Well, he knows how disturbed you were tonight when you saw him. If I were you, I should try to conceal my anger from now on."

"If you think I'm going to run, or shudder, every time I set eyes on him, you are much mistaken," he said roughly.

"It could be that if, after a time, he realizes his presence no longer affects you, he may eventually go away and leave you in peace."

"In peace," he repeated, his lip curling, his eyes narrowing.

Another thought had occurred to me. "Do you think that he suspects you of killing his wife, despite the inquest's decision?"

He raked his fingers through his black hair. "I don't know. I've been asking myself that this evening. Is he here in hopes that he can find evidence of my involvement in Alice's death? If he did, the case would be opened again. The inquest's ruling could be overturned. But what evidence can he honestly hope to find after over a year? The police themselves could find nothing at the time."

"There was nothing to find. You did not kill her. She committed suicide," I said deliberately.

Turning from contemplation of the dying fire, he looked across at me. "You believe that, do you? There's no reason why you should."

There was one very good reason, but I did not tell him so. I merely said, "You did not kill her, and so he can do you no

224

harm. You must act as though his presence here does not affect you one way or the other. I admit I was surprised when Leonora took him in hand the way she did."

"Oh, that's the one thing I find the least surprising. She did it just to spite me. Believe me, it was just what I would have expected of her."

At that point there came the sound of a door shutting and footsteps in the hall. It was Leonora and Aaron. I think we both stiffened, hoping they would go upstairs and not come into the sitting room. But we had not thought to turn down the gas lamps, and so it was apparent to anyone in the hall that the room in which we sat was occupied.

And then Leonora was saying, "Here he is, Aaron. And Miss Hawthorne too. How touching, sitting by firelight. Are we interrupting something?" Carelessly she tossed her wrap over the back of the sofa. "I'm not certain it's proper for the two of you to be sequestered here together at this time of night. I have Emeline to think of, you know."

"Do you? I wouldn't have thought so as a rule," Drake countered silkily.

Leonora's eyes narrowed. "Are you going to allow him to talk to me like that, Aaron?"

Aaron had come in after her, his gait unsteady. He was pouring himself a drink from the decanter. "Eh, m'dear? What's that?"

"Aaron knows you are fully capable of holding your own, Leonora."

"Him?" She spat out contemptuously. "He doesn't know a thing except the taste of good whiskey. You disgust me, the pair of you. Why I stay here—"

"The door is always open," Drake said.

"You'd like that, wouldn't you? But remember, if I go, so does Emeline. That wouldn't leave much for Miss Hawthorne to do, unless you give her a job in the kitchen. She could assist Magliori, or whatever his name is. I understand she's perfectly equipped for such a job."

"Whereas you're equipped for absolutely nothing, Leonora. You've never taken on the slightest responsibility."

"You mean I'm not like your sainted mother, I suppose.

Aaron never wanted me to be, did you, Aaron? He'd had enough of her pushing him and bullying him all his life. Just as your father did. Why else do you think your father carried on the way he did? Your mother paid him no attention except to tell him what to do about the hotel. She was always dismissing the maids, wasn't she? Even your governess, I understand. Are you going to carry on that tradition, Drake? With Miss Hawthorne, perhaps? She's an employee. And she has no husband. That's a variation on your style, isn't it?"

I colored hotly, feeling sick to my stomach.

"You really are the vilest bitch, Leonora," said Drake, his hands clenching.

"Sticks and stones, brother-in-law. Wasn't that a surprise when Grant Schyler walked in tonight? How did it feel, Drake, to come face to face with the husband again? I think he's got something up his sleeve. Somehow I doubt he's come to pay a social call." She yawned, "Oh, well, time will tell. I'm exhausted. Coming, Aaron?"

Aaron was slumped in a chair, his eyes shut. He stumbled to his feet, mumbling, "Bedtime, eh? Not sure I can make it up the stairs."

"Don't look to me for support. We'd both fall on our faces. Good night, all." She left the room and her husband lurched after her.

Drake swore under his breath, his face stormy.

"Don't pay her the slightest heed, Drake," I said, rising. "She will try any way she can to annoy you." I went over to him and touched his arm.

Impatiently he shook off my hand. "She's right about one thing. I can't involve you in any of this. I've been a fool tonight. You're so cool, so uncomplicated. Why on earth I choose to inflict my—past on you . . . it's the effect you have on me. But it's not an effect that I like."

Chapter Twelve

I had finally learned what I had wanted to know, the truth about Drake's involvement with Alice Schyler and the nature of her death at the Site of Stones. And I better understood what had happened afterwards—the investigation, the inquest, Drake's enlistment in the war with Spain, which had become a nightmare of another kind before he had returned home to face near financial ruin. I could now follow the progression of events, and was able to comprehend certain things which had puzzled me before.

Now the ugliness, the anguish, the strife which existed beneath the veneer of beauty, luxury, and comfort was at least partly explained. A casual observer would glance at the Crystal Hills and assume that neither its owners nor its guests had a care in the world. It seemed ideal, a haven from harsh reality, a place to delight in the splendid scenery, the elegance of the facilities. I would certainly have thought so; that was the image it presented to the world. Yet just as a veil can beautify and soften a plain woman's face under a romantic haze, so it was with the Crystal Hills. Beneath the coat of magnificence lurked volatile human tensions, passions that must be played out, hatreds that must be assuaged.

I was frightened. It was as though the plum-deep shadows of the Notch stretched across to darken the Crystal Hills, as though there crept from the scarred, brooding mountains a malevolence to blight the hotel and some of those associated with it. The undisturbed miles of dense black-green spruces, of jagged peaks and pockets of gloom which never saw the sun, the clearing of a hillside where a group of stones were arranged with careful precision and for some mysterious purpose— Nightshade Notch was an eerie realm, a land with an unearthly quality, a quality the Crystal Hills Hotel could not camouflage. The hotel had reigned unchallenged for more than thirty years. Perhaps now the time had come for the Notch to rebel.

Tonight I had learned that Madeline Curtis's marriage was not what it had appeared to be. Charlotte and Emeline had described them as an ideally suited couple, devoted to each other and to the task of building the Crystal Hills into a New England tradition and showplace. Now Leonora's acid comments had cast a new light over their lives. Evidently Madeline's preoccupation with the hotel had been too much for Theodore Curtis, driving him to seek companionship elsewhere. Or was it the other way round—that Madeline, unhappily married to a philanderer, channeled all of her love and energy into the running of the hotel? Either way it seemed that even years ago, when the hotel was brilliantly successful, things were not what they appeared to be.

And what of the scions of this union? What of Madeline's other legacy, her children? Aaron Curtis had grown up a weakling under his remarkable and domineering mother, eschewing responsibility, strength of character, and purpose. I doubted whether he had stayed faithful to Leonora or whether she, in fact, had remained faithful to him. They seemed two of a kind, motivated by selfishness, living for the moment.

Drake was not one to shirk hard work, and he had admirably carried on the tradition of Curtis hospitality and magnificent accommodations and entertainments at the Crystal Hills. But he had spent years drifting into aimless affairs with married women, taking his pleasure with no strings attached, no binds, never allowing his heart to become involved. Perhaps he was not capable of falling in love; perhaps he had no deep feelings to involve. Cool, arrogant, devastatingly handsome, sure of his place and purpose in the world—because he had never been challenged. He had always been in control, he had said, and he had been used to arranging his life the way he liked it. Until the day when Alice Schyler had killed herself, the day when the

228

ground beneath him had begun to give way.

He was now a very different man from that former self. Cold, withdrawn, bitter—a far cry from that rakish youth who made a game of pursuing women he didn't want and couldn't have except as momentary instruments of pleasure.

And this was the man I had fallen in love with, the man who had fascinated me from the first. I loved him no less for what he had been; I could not have loved him more for what he was now.

The next morning Emeline and I resumed our lessons. She was reading, "The Lady of Shalott," and, as always, the beauty of Tennyson's words arrested my full attention.

> Willows whiten, aspens quiver,
> Little breezes dusk and shiver
> Through the wave that runs for ever
> By the island in the river
>   Flowing down to Camelot.
> Four grey walls, and four grey towers,
> Overlook a space of flowers,
> And the silent isle embowers
>   The Lady of Shalott.
>
> There she weaves by night and day
> A magic web with colours gay.
> She has heard a whisper say,
> A curse is on her if she stay
>   To look down to Camelot.
> She knows not what the curse may be,
> And so she weaveth steadily,
> And little other care hath she,
>   The Lady of Shalott.

And it occurred to me then to ask myself, was I like that Lady who was warned away, but stayed, full knowing a curse would come upon her if she did so? Was I like that Lady, going about my work, delaying, when I should have been packing my things and fleeing from this shaded notch? Sir Lancelot had proven that Lady's downfall; was Drake to prove mine as well?

But I could help myself no more than she could.

"Let's go to the Site of Stones after lunch," said Emeline, breaking into my gloomy reverie. "Perhaps Mr. Willoughby has finally begun to dig."

I hesitated. "We don't want to disturb his work, Emeline."

"We won't. He liked having us there that other time."

"Well, I suppose so. Would you like it if he discovered something and made the hotel famous?"

"The hotel *is* famous," she said.

I smiled. "So it is. Now read me the next stanza and we'll talk about it."

Later in the day we set off for the Stones, crossing the hotel lawn and entering the far woods. Now that I had learned that the Stones, indeed that that repellent triangular slab, had been the scene of a grisly death, I was more reluctant than ever to visit the place. I was on my guard against that feeling of creeping malevolence, against the first faint sound of the horrible voices I had thought I heard the first visit there. But nothing came to me. At the top of the hill the breeze swayed the limbs of the tall pines; the crickets chirped in the tall grass. Clumps of yellow daisies made bright contrasts against the somber gray stones of the low wall. Across the clearing was Ernest Willoughby, down on his knees, his sleeves rolled up, bending over a narrow vertical trench dug in the soil before one of the beehive chambers.

"Hello, Mr. Willoughby," called Emeline as we approached. "We've come to watch for a bit. I hope you don't mind."

He took off his hat, smiling broadly. "Good afternoon, ladies. Certainly I don't mind. Although there is little to interest you, I'm afraid, little to interest you."

His round face was flushed in the afternoon sun. I caught a faint whiff of something mingling with the pungent scent of the pine trees and the sweetness of clover. Then I identified it as the smell of spirits. And the flask I had noticed before lay propped on the ground beside him.

"What are you doing today? Have you found anything yet?" asked Emeline.

"I'm doing a 'deep-sounding,' Miss Curtis. I'm endeavoring to ascertain how many layers of occupation there have been here. But I regret that I haven't found anything of an unexpected nature yet, as I have not dug far enough in the soil. I did find this spoon—from one of the early settlers, no doubt. Since they occupied this terrain most recently, I expect to find those kinds of artifacts. The trouble is that most materials decay in the soil after a certain number of years. Unless the soil is very dry, as it is in the Middle East. Naturally things are preserved there much longer. Much longer. And so discoveries made there are easier and more spectacular. But it is I who have the most difficult task."

"So now you don't think you'll find anything here?" asked Emeline.

"I did not say that, young lady. No indeed, I did not say that. It's just that I have a very difficult job ahead. Only stone and shell (and baked clay, as I mentioned before) are preserved for very long—they are the two hardest minerals. It's possible I'll come across some stone arrowheads, Indian artifacts. But they will not be what I am looking for, no. We know the Indians lived in these parts for hundreds of years."

"And if you find something that does not look to be made by Indians?" I asked.

"Then I will use a process called 'cross-dating,' Miss Hawthorne, wherein I compare any artifacts I may find to those of other cultures. The Indian artifacts will be considerably more primitive than any I hope to find from the earlier culture I am pursuing, the culture from across the Atlantic which, I believe, constructed this site. More primitive, yes, and not nearly so old. You see, the older culture will be the more advanced. North American Indians were still in their Stone Age when the English colonists first came, which meant they were not yet working with metal tools. Not yet with metal. What I'm looking for is an artifact, a tool, reflecting a Bronze Age culture which, by definition, couldn't possibly be Indian. A bronze ax will survive for thousands of years; the wooden shaft will perish, but the blade endures. Shards of pottery, as I've said, will last a very long time as well, a very long time. If I am fortunate enough to find some, it will be fairly simple to determine whether or not they could have been fashioned by the Indians."

231

"And so your theory will be proven?" asked Emeline, a pucker in her brow.

"If fate smiles on me, yes, Miss Curtis, if fate smiles on me. If I can come across some shards, or better yet, an ax blade, cross-date it with others to determine the culture and time-period, then my discovery will be an astounding one, whether or not I am able to fathom the significance of this Site of Stones. I'll put this place on the map, on the map. Your uncle should be very grateful to me if that day ever comes." He beamed, smiling, and wiped his perspiring face with his handkerchief. "Hot, dull work, though, just now. If you'll give me leave." He unscrewed the top of the flask and raised it to his lips, drinking deeply.

I wondered how he would be able to conduct a proper excavation if he consumed quantities of alcohol while working. I was beginning to realize why Mr. Willoughby might not be taken seriously in the academic world, and whether his reputation as a drinker, and thus unreliable, had preceded him there.

He put down the flask and took the small pickax in his hand again, scooping out dirt from the trench and examining it carefully with his fingers before tossing it aside.

"So far I've come across no evidence that this was an Indian burial site, as some have always believed. No evidence at all— no bones. No bodies." He chuckled.

"We don't wish to be here if you do," I said somewhat severely.

"Miss Hawthorne, you've promised to talk to me about your initial aversion to this place. Perhaps one evening soon."

I nodded uneasily, glancing at Emeline, but she did not appear to be listening. She was picking daisies and making a chain.

"Why don't you demonstrate to Mr. Willoughby the speaking tube over there, Emeline? Do you know about that, Mr. Willoughby?"

"All right," agreed the young girl. She walked away while Mr. Willoughby said, "What's that? Did you say a speaking tube?"

I motioned for him to follow me over to the huge slab—the

slab where, I remembered, Alice Schyler had lain dead. After one glance at it, I turned my head away and waited until Emeline's voice came to us.

> And at the closing of the day
> She loosed the chain, and down she lay;
> The broad stream bore her far away,
>   The Lady of Shalott.

Mr. Willoughby gave a sudden start, and even I was unnerved by the disembodied voice.

"What on earth—? This is most—most—it sounds as though her voice came directly from that stone! But how—what? Wait a minute, though. I recall when I was making the charts of the site. Down those steps there is a passage to a chamber about four feet in height. And there is a stone seat and shaft in the wall—I went down there myself!"

"And, if the shaft is spoken through, so Emeline tells me, the sound travels through to the open air, just beneath the slab," I explained.

"Uncanny. Most uncanny," he said, his eyes bright. "This is a great discovery, this speaking tube! Never have I heard of Indians building anything of that nature! This becomes more and more incredible. I must try it for myself. Thank you for your demonstration, Miss Curtis," he said as Emeline was scrambling up the steps.

"I really had no notion of such a thing," he went on excitedly, "no notion at all. It's like those oracles in the temples of Malta and Greece. And it brings new signficance to this slab of stone as well."

"What sort of significance?" asked Emeline, wrinkling her nose.

"Well, as to what its purpose may have been. Note the clearly defined gutter around the rim leading to the spout there."

Suddenly I felt hot and queasy; my mouth was dry. Why on earth had I brought the slab to his notice? Alice Schyler had lain there, her blond hair streaming about her, blood oozing from her gown and congealing in a dark pool beneath her.

233

"It's very likely a sacrificial stone, you see!" Mr. Willoughby went on. "How could I not have seen so before? And definitely not Indian! A sacrificial stone—the victim stretched out, held down, or perhaps drugged. Then down would come the knife to slash the victim's throat, or to slit open his belly."

"Ugh," said Emeline. "That's disgusting."

Mr. Willoughby went on, almost to himself. "The blood would run down the gutter to the spout, where it would likely have been collected for some purpose. It's fantastic—a pagan temple, just as I thought! I'll be famous! They'll have to listen to me now! None of those fools has ever suspected anything like this, but they can't deny it if they see it with their own eyes! I'll have them all here before long, and they'll be sorry they ever mocked Ernest Willoughby!" His eyes were burning feverishly as he regarded the slab with glee, his whole face working with excitement.

"Well, good day, Mr. Willoughby. We should be getting back now," I said, shuddering in revulsion. "Come along, Emeline."

She caught up with me on the opposite side of the clearing. "It couldn't have been what he says, could it? It was sickening, the way he was going on about it. You know, I think he was drunk."

"If he is not already, he will be soon," I said shortly. "And it won't do his reputation among his colleagues any good."

"He seems like a nice man, though, until he begins to talk about disgusting things. I suppose he will be famous now."

"Only if he discovers some evidence to support his theories," I said. "And he hasn't found any yet. So don't let his fanciful and gruesome notions give you nightmares. He's likely totally wrong about his conclusion."

I was not thinking then of sacrifices made thousands of years ago, but of an inert fair-haired beauty with a white face and a spreading stain of crimson. If Mr. Willoughby's grotesque notion of the sacrificial stone was made known in the newspapers, then the death of Alice Schyler would be recalled and relished. I only hoped that he would be discreet about his latest theory for the time being. Drake did not need any more to trouble him just now. But somehow I doubted Mr. Willoughby's ability to be reticent. When he was not under the influence of alcohol, he seemed both cautious and responsible. But this afternoon he had been swept away in a fervor of wild speculations and grandiose assumptions of achievements. If he were to begin imparting his thoughts concerning the so-called sacrificial stone, I dreaded to consider the outcome.

"Would you mind if we dined at the hotel tonight, Emeline?" I asked, frowning.

She was surprised. "Mind? Of course not. You know I love to—but I didn't think you cared to so often."

"I'd like to tonight."

After we had finished our afternoon lessons, I took a bath in the huge cast-iron tub. Dressing in the ivory muslin gown, I gathered a few front ringlets into a knot at the back of my head and left the rest down. I powdered my face and pinned on my cameo, wondering why I almost felt I was dressing for battle. In the looking-glass my eyes were large, apprehensive, and a smoky green.

Emeline knocked on my door. She wore a white cotton dress with pin-tucks down the bodice and a sash at the waist. There was a white satin ribbon in her dark hair.

"You look very pretty," I said.

"So do you, Teresa. But then you always do. I wish I would grow up faster!"

I smiled. "I used to feel the same way. Believe me, you'll be grown up soon enough. Is Charlotte going to the hotel as well?"

Emeline shook her head. "She's going to have a tray in her room tonight. I suppose that man arriving last night at dinner upset her. She hasn't been feeling well all day."

I had forgotten Grant Schyler.

The lawn was lush and dew-damp; the hem of my gown trailed in it. Against the frosted lavender sky the mountains were purple-black, ominous. I drew my shawl across my shoulders to ward off the deepening chill. Before long it would be fall.

We greeted Burrows and handed our wraps to a waiting maid in uniform. Perhaps my worries were for nothing; perhaps Mr.

Willoughby would not come to the dining room tonight. Grant Schyler sat at a table with Leonora and Aaron and several others; I could hear Leonora's rippling laughter.

"Look, Mamma's sitting with that man," whispered Emeline, frowning.

"Shhh," I said, for Drake had come up behind us.

"There you are, Drake," called Leonora coolly. "I've taken the liberty of placing Mr. Schyler here. Oh, Emeline, I didn't know you were coming over. This is my daughter, Mr. Schyler." She did not look pleased.

Emeline curtsyed, murmuring, "How do you do?"

Grant Schyler smiled at her, flashing his gold tooth. "Did you say your daughter, Mrs. Curtis? Surely you cannot be the mother of this young lady."

Emeline rolled her eyes at me while Leonora tapped his wrist with her ivory and lace fan. "You flatter me, sir," she said archly, her good humor restored.

We sat down at the table; I was quickly scanning the faces of the diners in the room for Mr. Willoughby's, but I did not see him. Perhaps he had fallen asleep from the effects of the alcohol, I thought hopefully.

Drake pulled out a chair, saying something to a couple sitting next to me. He looked totally at ease, despite Mr. Schyler's presence across the table. Indeed, the atmosphere seemed relaxed and genial. The waiters were pouring champagne and iced water; the orchestra was playing a soft, lilting waltz. I too began to relax.

The conversation at the table was general—the fair weather, the hometowns of the guests. It was all very ordinary and innocuous. We were eating our soup when Leonora made a startled exclamation, claiming the attention of everyone at the table.

"What on earth?" she asked, a bewildered expression on her face.

"What is it, Nora? What have you got there?" said Aaron heartily.

"How very odd. I didn't notice this before," she said, and picked up an object from the table, holding it so everyone could see. It was a hypodermic syringe.

"Ugh," said one of the women. "Where did that come from?"

"Must be someone's idea of a joke," said a man.

"Drake, you'll have to speak to the waiters about this. Of all things to leave on the table, I should think this is the unlikeliest," said Leonora.

"Perhaps it belongs to one of the guests—a doctor, perhaps?" said another woman.

Drake's face had darkened; he was regarding Leonora with an expression I couldn't identify—there was shock there and something else.

Aaron laughed abruptly, foolishly, looking from Leonora to Drake. "Damned unappetizing," he said. "Here, you," he added to one of the waiters.

"Yes, sir?"

"This was found on the table. Take it away."

Leonora held out the syringe to the waiter, who gazed at it in horrified fascination. "Well, take it," she snapped. "We've all seen enough of it."

The waiter took it gingerly, gave a small bow, and walked off.

"How strange," said the woman next to Drake. "Could someone have been taken ill in here just before dinner, and a doctor was sent for? But to leave something like that lying on a dining table! What do you make of it, Major Curtis? It's rather a mystery, is it not? Or is it a sort of practical joke?"

With an effort Drake turned to her. "Very likely, Mrs. Taylor." He picked up his soup spoon, his fingers trembling slightly. A muscle jerked in his cheek.

"So sorry to be late, ladies and gentlemen, many apologies. I was detained at the dig site." Mr. Willoughby was pulling out an empty chair next to mine. His voice was a trifle slurred, his round face pink, his evening attire a little untidy. Oh, no, I thought, what now?

"Is that so, Mr.—er—Willoughby," said Leonora. "How interesting."

He did not perceive the sarcasm. "Interesting is not the word for it, madam. Thrilling describes it, thrilling. With the help of your daughter and of Miss Hawthorne, I have made an amazing discovery."

Drake's black brows drew together as he glanced from Mr. Willoughby to me. I felt the color rising in my face.

"Oh? Have you engaged Emeline and Miss Hawthorne as assistants?" asked Aaron, chuckling.

"I showed him the speaking tube, Papa," said Emeline a trifle sulkily. "That's all."

"Oh, that foolish device," said Leonora with a dismissive gesture. "Really, Mr. Willoughby, I can't see what is so remarkable about that. And we all knew about it, so it's no discovery, is it?" She looked sideways at Grant Schyler while she spoke; he was buttering a roll and seemed not to be paying attention. Leonora smiled at the new guests, saying, "Do you know about the excursion to Loon Lake tomorrow? A vastly pretty sight. If it's a fine day you will be able to see the Old Man of the Mountain, a most formidable gentleman, I'm sure you'll agree."

Mr. Willoughby appeared very crestfallen at the way she had turned the subject from his excavation. But then he did not realize, as Leonora and some of the rest of us did, that the husband of the woman who had taken her own life on the sacrificial stone now sat across from him at the table. And so he could not be blamed for blundering on; he had consumed too much liquor to be able to sense when a subject was not welcome, or to recall what he had read in the newspapers over a year ago which had alerted him to the Site of Stones. He was concerned with a far more distant past than a recent one. He could not sense the building tension at the table, as I could: Drake glaring at him, sitting rigidly; Leonora flickering uneasy glances at Grant Schyler; Aaron punctuating boisterous talk with guffaws.

"I protest, Mrs. Curtis," he said stubbornly. "You did not allow me to finish. The discovery of the speaking tube has led me to another speculation, that of the precise use of the large triangular slab above it. I'm confident I know now what it is!"

"What is he talking about?" asked Mrs. Taylor, completely baffled.

"Mr. Willoughby is an archaeologist, Mrs. Taylor," said Drake, a grim note to his voice. "He is conducting an excavation off in the woods. He has some rather . . . fanciful notions."

"They may be fanciful, Major," said Mr. Willoughby belligerently, "but I'll stake my life they are true!"

It was now apparent to everyone he had been drinking. The elderly woman at the table raised her lorgnette and surveyed him disapprovingly. His rather high-pitched voice had broken through the conversation that Leonora had attempted to carry on with some of the others. All eyes were on him. Grant Schyler's face was inscrutable; his hands with the gold signet rings were poised, one holding a roll, the other a bread knife. Drake sat tensely, his gaze fixed on Ernest Willoughby's face. I dug my nails into my palms.

Mr. Willoughby puffed himself up, elated to be the center of attention. "You see, ladies and gentlemen, it's my contention that the Site of Stones was used for ceremonies—ancient pagan rituals that involved human sacrifices!"

"Well!" said Mrs. Taylor.

"Mr. Willoughby, this is not the place to—" Leonora began.

But he was past all pretenses at etiquette now. He picked up his wineglass. "Yes, human sacrifices," he said with relish. "Sacrifices made on the—"

He got no further. Just then my arm collided with his elbow, jolting his wineglass. The ruby red liquid spilled on the white tablecloth, splashing in a pool on his plate and splattering his white shirtfront.

"Oh, I'm dreadfully sorry, sir," I said forlornly. "Please forgive me. I don't know how I could have been so clumsy."

Mr. Willoughby stared stupidly down at his claret-dotted shirtfront before glancing at me. He seemed at a loss for words now that I'd broken his concentration. I dabbed ineffectually at the stains with my napkin.

"What a pity," said Leonora. "You'll have to change it at once, of course."

"Yes, indeed, I suppose I shall," said Mr. Willoughby, still a trifle dazed. "Excuse me, please, ladies and gentlemen." He rose, somewhat unsteady, and walked away.

"What an impossible man! Sacrifices!" said Mrs. Taylor, outraged. "And at the dinner table! Really, the people one comes across!"

"You did that on purpose," whispered Emeline to me, a delighted grin on her face.

"Shhh."

"He was drunk, of course," said the elderly woman with the lorgnette. "Most unsuitable. A man who cannot hold his liquor is no gentleman. My late husband, now. He could not hold his liquor either. And although his father and grandfather had been bankers, his great-grandfather was a blacksmith in England. My mother warned me. Blood will win out, she said. And she was right."

There did not seem to be anything to say to this. Uneasily I glanced over at Drake. To my surprise he was regarding me with amusement. "How careless of you, Miss Hawthorne," he said softly, his smile crooked.

"Well, at least we can eat our dinner in peace," declared Leonora. "Really, Aaron, why you agreed to let that man come here! That should be a lesson to you. Let's hope he finishes whatever he is doing and leaves soon."

"He had dirt under his fingernails," said Emeline.

"What do you have about here that would be of interest to an archaeologist?" asked Mr. Taylor.

"Oh, just a grouping of stones off in the woods," said Leonora airily. "Some Indian settlement or something. Now, have you heard about the concert scheduled for this week? And for those who've no wish to drive to Loon Lake, there will be a picnic and croquet party on the back lawn tomorrow afternoon."

"Mamma," asked Emeline suddenly, "when can we have a ball? There hasn't been one since I've come home."

Leonora raised her brows. "You are still too young to be thinking about balls, Emeline."

"No, the child's right," said Aaron. "We should have a ball. What do you say, Drake?"

"Oh, do you have balls here?" asked Mrs. Taylor. "How delightful!"

"Please, Uncle Drake, may we?"

"By all means," he answered smoothly. "If your mother would consent to see to the preparations."

"Why not? It might be amusing. Would you enjoy a ball, Mr. Schyler?" asked Leonora.

"If my name were on your dance card, my dear lady," he

replied, his gold tooth flashing in a smile.

"Well, then, we'll make it an end-of-the-summer ball, in two weeks' time. You will stay until then, won't you, Mr. Schyler?"

"My stay here is an indefinite one," said Grant Schyler.

"I'm enchanted to hear it," said Leonora.

"Well, that's settled then," said Drake, showing no perturbation at Mr. Schyler's words. "Now, if you will all excuse me . . ."

I nudged Emeline; we had both finished our dinner and I had no desire to remain at the table making small talk. We said good night and followed Drake out of the dining room and into the lobby.

"I have to speak to your uncle for a minute," I told her. "But I'll walk back with you to the house if you'll wait."

She nodded, yawning. "I'll sit by the fire."

Drake stood at the large curved desk, the reservation book open before him. "Well, if it isn't the clumsy Miss Hawthorne," he said. "Poor Willoughby—I doubt whether he has many dress shirts."

I put my hand to my mouth. "Oh, no, I didn't think of that. And I may have ruined that one. But I couldn't let him say what he was going to—about the stone slab."

"If I know Willoughby, he won't be able to keep silent for long," Drake said. "I suppose he's decided that the stone where Alice—died is some sort of table for sacrifices. After all, I thought the same thing myself when I saw . . ." His hand clenched into a ball, his face hardening. "You know what the newspapers will say if they get wind of his crazy ideas. 'Was Socialite Latest Victim of Ancient Sarificial Stone?' 'Was she forced to take her own life by some unseen evil force which demanded another sacrifice?' God only knows what rot they'll print."

"I know."

"It must not get into the papers," he said gratingly.

"How can you stop him from contacting them at some future date? If he really does make a discovery, if he finds some evidence to support these speculations . . ."

"He can't. He's got to be sent away before that happens. I

241

can't take the chance, not when so much is at stake. Not now, after what I learned today."

"What's different today—what have you learned?"

His eyes narrowed; he stared off abstractedly. "I received a letter from the Bank of Choake and Sumner in Portsmouth today. A letter stating that they no longer hold the mortgage on the Crystal Hills, that they've sold it."

"Sold their interest in the hotel? Why should they?"

He shrugged. "If they received a good enough offer for it, why shouldn't they? And I suppose they don't wish to wait on the payments as they did the first three months, thanks to Aaron's not having the nerve to tell me what he'd done. Naturally it would look very bad for them if they threatened to foreclose on one of New Hampshire's Heroes." His voice was sardonic. "The New Hampshire newspapers were very interested in my stint as a Rough Rider. That has made them overlook my former . . . aberration. At any rate, the bankers have sold the mortgage on the hotel to a company in New York, the Hudson Lending Company. A company that undoubtedly makes a practice of buying mortgages and then assuming the role of banker. A company that would not hesitate to foreclose on the hotel and sell everything at an auction if each payment is not made precisely on schedule. So you see, business must continue the way it is going. We cannot afford a reduction in reservations. Therefore Mr. Willoughby cannot be allowed to create a sensation, one that could revive last year's scandal—and last year's failing business."

"He won't leave, you know. He's too carried away."

Drake scowled. "The damn fool's obsessed. But that is irrelevant. I'm going to forbid him to excavate further."

I looked worriedly up at him. "But Drake, if you do that, if you send him packing, he may contact the newspapers anyway, out of spite and frustration. After all, he can cause a sensation whether he is there digging or not."

"No one would listen, if he has no evidence to prove his theories. They'll just write him off as a crackpot, which, I believe, is already his reputation anyway."

"Maybe. But the story might sound too good. Are you prepared to take that risk, especially if he makes it clear to them that you stopped his digging?"

He made an impatient sound. "Are you saying that I should allow him free rein? That I should just sit back and wait for the newspapers to get wind of his ridiculous speculations?" he asked roughly.

"Talk to him. Tell him that it's vital the public not be informed yet. It isn't as though he's found anything, after all. He's uncovered no evidence or proof that the site was built by his Bronze Age seafarers from across the Atlantic. Except for his contention that the Indians did not sacrifice people on triangular slabs. But there is still no proof at all—and he may never find any. Let him dig—just ask him not to make any announcements the way he nearly did at dinner tonight until he has some evidence. He'd be a fool to, anyway, and I don't think he's a fool."

"Just when he's drinking, which seems to be fairly regularly, according to the maid who does his room. But I'll speak to him."

I turned to go, gesturing to Emeline, when I heard him say behind me, "Thank you, Tessa. It seems I have reason to be grateful to you again."

Flushing, I shook my head, my eyes refusing to meet his. Then I walked away with Emeline.

The next morning I was on my way to the library when one of the housemaids handed me an envelope. "This came for you, miss, a little while ago."

"Thank you." Going into the library, I took the ivory letter opener from the desk and slit open the envelope. It was a note from Ernest Willoughby written on the hotel stationery; he was requesting that I meet with him today after luncheon at the Stones. I needn't send a reply; if today was not convenient, we could work out another time. Either way this afternoon would find him at the dig site.

"Of course it's about the Stones," I said to myself. "Why didn't I keep my mouth shut?" He wanted to question me about the uncanny experience I had undergone on my first visit there. I might as well get it over with, I thought disgustedly. Or he would very likely hound me, might even bring up the subject at dinner again. I only hoped that he would

243

not be drunk.

Emeline came in, and I folded the letter and slipped it into my pocket. There was no need for her to know anything about it; I did not wish to upset her with my weird fancies. She had never noticed anything unusual at the Stones.

After luncheon I changed into my walking shoes, put on my straw hat, and met Charlotte on my way out.

"I didn't want to ask in front of Emeline," she said, "but is Grant Schyler still at the hotel?"

"Yes, he seems to be staying for a while."

"Oh, dear. I haven't had an opportunity to speak with Drake. Did you see him last night when you dined at the hotel?"

I nodded. "We all sat at the same table. Leonora—Mrs. Curtis—seems to have taken Mr. Schyler under her wing."

She shook her head. "I was afraid of that. It's to spite Drake, of course."

"Major Curtis appears to be holding his own," I said. "Don't worry. Do you know where Emeline is?"

"In Madeline's room. She's taken the photograph albums in there. Why? Are you going out?"

"Yes, to see Mr. Willoughby at the Stones. I was hoping she'd be occupied until my return. He's—he's made some rather gruesome allegations about the Stones and I don't think it's good for Emeline to keep listening to him."

"I'm certain you're right, my dear. I won't even ask what sort of allegations; I'm not certain I wish to know. Good-bye, my dear."

It was a gray day, the sky clothed with low-hanging rippled clouds. The air smelt damp although no rain had fallen. The riders to Loon Lake would not catch a glimpse of the Old Man today.

Mr. Willoughby was kneeling where we had seen him the previous day. He was scraping at something in his hand with a small trowel.

"Have you found something of interest, Mr. Willoughby?" I asked.

"Oh, Miss Hawthorne. Good, you've come. Very good. Of

244

interest? No, no, not really. A stone arrowhead, that's all."

"But I thought you said that this place may have been taboo to the local Indians."

"It's possible, Miss Hawthorne, possible. I should think it likely in the light of what I realized yesterday. But I'm bound to come across a few Indian artifacts. However, we have something far more fascinating to discuss. Shall we sit down?" He stood up, brushing off his dusty trousers. I glanced about uneasily before taking a seat on one of the boulders. Mr. Willoughby sat across from me, taking a black notebook out of his breast pocket. He was businesslike, and did not seem the worse for drinking that day.

"Now, Miss Hawthorne, I want you to tell me everything you remember about the sensations you experienced when you first saw this place. Take your time. Are you comfortable?"

"I am never comfortable here, Mr. Willoughby. But I've come and so I'll tell you what I remember. Emeline took me up here—she's very fond of the site. I'm afraid my reaction disappointed her, to say the least. To flee down the hill as though the devil were at my heels was scarcely the reaction she was hoping for."

"Please start at the beginning, Miss Hawthorne."

"Well, sir, I came up the path and stood at the edge of the clearing. I felt uncomfortable—it was a peculiar feeling. Or only peculiar because there was no reason for me to feel uncomfortable . . . apprehensive."

"Then what?"

"Emeline started to wander about and I followed. Then she startled me by speaking from the shaft. I was standing by the slab just then."

"She frightened you?"

"Not really. I knew her voice. I was startled. But after that, I began to feel much worse." I frowned, trying to remember. "I went past those beehive chambers thinking how weird they looked, how dark the openings were, how bizarre the whole place was. I wanted to leave, but I didn't like asking Emeline to leave so soon. So I sat down just there. And then I began to feel uneasy, slightly sick." I paused, biting my lip.

"Go on, Miss Hawthorne."

"It sounds so absurd. You'll question my sanity," I said uncomfortably.

"I assure you I won't do that. Please continue."

He was scratching in his notebook.

My gaze went over the granite formations; I looked away from the gaping chamber openings. I took a deep breath. "Well, I began to hear—something. A low, murmuring sort of sound, at first, which gradually became a rushing, rumbling sound."

"Like water?"

"No, not like water. Perhaps my adjectives are not good. It was like voices, voices in a crowd, not individual ones, but the sort of noise a crowd makes."

"Ah."

"Then—then the voices began to speak together, chanting the same thing over and over. Nothing I could understand, though. Except that there was a menace in the sounds. And I was afraid, deathly afraid." I shuddered, swallowing hard.

"Chanting, you say. How very fascinating," he said, scribbling furiously.

"Yes, and then something even worse. Emeline looked at—at me and began to talk. She was talking only I could not hear her. I just saw her mouth moving, but the sounds were all swallowed up in the roar of the crowd, the clamoring chanting that was getting louder and louder. The evil was all around me—in the air, in the Stones. I—I was terrified. I knew I had to get away as quickly as I could before—before it was too late!" Chills washed over me; I gasped in sudden realization.

"Too late? What do you mean, Miss Hawthorne? Have you just remembered something?" asked Mr. Willoughby excitedly.

My voice had dropped to almost a whisper. "I—I couldn't move. Something held me in place. I was helpless; I felt I had no control over my limbs. Then I felt something pulling me, drawing me over there—to that horrible flat stone. It wasn't an arm or anything like that—just a feeling that I must go over there. The voices, I realized then, came from there as well. I had to fight an enormous impulse to move toward that slab. And then suddenly I was released. And I fled down the hill as

246

fast as I could go."

"And that is everything you can remember?"

I nodded. I was breathing raggedly; my face felt damp.

"This is most interesting, Miss Hawthorne, most interesting. And you haven't experienced these same sounds and feelings again?"

"No, thank heaven. But I never feel at ease here—I feel there's something wrong, that the evil can return at any time." Get a hold on yourself, I told myself.

"Have you experienced any other sensations attached to a location before?"

"Not that I can remember. Certainly nothing like the ones I've described to you." I gave a nervous laugh. "Well, what do you make of it, Mr. Willoughby? Am I going crazy, or do you believe in the idea of a curse? Is the Site of Stones haunted?"

Chapter Thirteen

Mr. Willoughby did not smile and shake his head reassuringly as I had hoped he would. Instead he regarded me intently, his eyes alight with the same feverish excitement he had shown over the sacrificial stone. "It depends on your definition of the word 'haunted,' Miss Hawthorne. It depends on your definition."

I tried to speak lightly. "So you do think I'm losing my mind."

"Nothing could be further from my thoughts," he said with certainty. "I only meant that if your definition of the word means a locale inhabited by headless horsemen or filmy likenesses of young ladies, then no, I don't believe the Stones are haunted in that sense. But it is very possible that certain strong emotions that have been experienced in a locale become—imprinted—on the atmosphere. Rage, hatred, fear, misery—these, some say, may linger on a particular site. They become part of that site, or house. So you see, I'm not talking about ghosts with clanking chains, not with chains, no."

"You are saying that you believe I perceived—something in the air, something . . . left over from perhaps ancient times?"

"Yes, it's very likely. Certain people can pick up feelings or signals, if you will, in the atmosphere of places. These things have been documented through the years in places such as the Tower of London. For some reason you were sensitive to certain powerful emotions here, but why it was merely for one time, I have no explanation. Perhaps the feelings or signals are

248

not always present, but just occur from time to time. Perhaps you will never have a similar experience again."

I licked my parched lips. "I sincerely hope not," I said weakly.

"You may have experienced—'relived' may be a better word—an occasion many years ago when this site was used for purposes about which I can only speculate just now. The evil you sensed—the fear—the rising excitement—the chanting. It may have been some sort of ceremony, a pagan ritual. The fear which overwhelmed you may have been the victim's fear."

I stared at him in horror. "You think that I sensed a *sacrifice*—with crowds and—and that perhaps I identified with the victim feeling compelled to go to that slab." I put my hands to my cheeks, sick terror welling inside me.

"Blood lust is most definitely a strong emotion," continued Mr. Willoughby musingly, unconscious of my shattered state. "Blood lust from the spectators, terror from the one chosen to be sacrificed . . ."

Starting up from my seat on the boulder, I put my hands over my ears. "No, no, I won't listen to any more! I'm leaving—I hate this place, I tell you!"

"What's going on here?" cried a voice behind us. Whirling around, I saw Drake approaching us, leaning slightly on his cane. He looked from me to Ernest Willoughby, his black brows drawn together. "What have you been saying to her, Willoughby?"

I took a deep breath, willing myself to be calmer. "It's—it's nothing. It's all right."

"You're white as a sheet," he said roughly. "What has he been telling you?"

"I have merely been asking Miss Hawthorne to describe certain feelings she experienced when first encountering this precise spot, Major. That is all." Mr. Willoughby spoke stiffly, but his face was flushed.

"Feelings? What sort of feelings?" asked Drake, his blue eyes narrowing. "Teresa, what is the meaning of this?"

"Mr. Willoughby seems to believe I—witnessed—an event which may have taken place here in—in prehistoric times. The first time Emeline brought me here, I—I thought I heard voices, and I was badly frightened. I thought I must have imagined it, that I was overtired from the trip and all. But mere tiredness could not explain the—evil—I felt, the sort of horrible glee and—and overwhelming fear. . . ." I shuddered, putting my arms across my chest.

"That does it, Willoughby. There's been enough of this nonsense. I have never heard that genuine archaeologists indulge in ghost-hunting. We might as well have a damn medium here, touching the Stones and chanting. I warned you that you were not to turn this—dig of yours into a circus!"

"Miss Hawthorne's rather peculiar experience just may be rooted in the history of the Site of Stones," said Mr. Willoughby with dignity. "And as such it is invaluable to my research. I must pursue any clue, any perception at all connected to the Stones."

"Frightening this young lady to death, suggesting that she's a kind of witch or something is scarcely research, Willoughby! Just look at the condition she's in!"

I could not look at either of them. I sat back down on the boulder to steady myself.

"I'm most sorry if my questions and interpretations have distressed you, Miss Hawthorne. I am very grateful to you for what you have relayed to me, very grateful. It only serves to enhance my own speculations, my own conclusions."

I looked up at that. "But, Mr. Willoughby, my feelings at that time—they are not proof of anything. Surely you will not base any conclusions on what I may have told you. Why, I might be making it all up deliberately, or—or—it may have been a delusion."

Mr. Willoughby smiled slightly, shaking his head. "I am convinced that you did not invent those perceptions, Miss Hawthorne. Not invent, no. Your psychic experience may teach me more than my own excavations. I firmly believe this was a place where certain rites were observed, certain rites to renew life—spring out of winter, fertility, that sort of thing. We know that the ancients were possessed of an overriding concern for that. The Cult of the Great Mother, for instance, was practiced by many different cultures. Rites we would consider obscene, unbearably gruesome, were commonplace, all with the same theme—the renewal of nature, the fertility of the earth. Crops were taken from the land, so to the ancient man, something had to be given back. Hence the idea of the Harvest Lord, the King Who Must Die to perpetuate the earth's cycles, the continuity. It wasn't always a male victim, though; sometimes it was a male and a female who were sent away from the settlement for a year, and then, on May Day, pursued to the death by their friends and families. There are many different versions of the Earth Mother cult, many different versions."

Drake made an impatient sound, scowling. "You think that this place was built by people who worshipped in that monstrous way?" I felt light-headed.

"It was not monstrous to them, Major Curtis, not monstrous to them. And oftentimes not to the victims themselves. They would have been brought up with those beliefs, with the rites. It would have seemed perfectly acceptable and logical to them, and even an honor to be chosen." Ernest Willoughby glanced across the site, frowning. "It's a pity that it's the time of the year it is, for stone formations in Europe have been discovered to be astronomical observatories. Do you see those standing stones placed outside the complex on every side? There are four of them, one there, one across, one there, and one up there."

We glanced to where he pointed. "So what?" said Drake curtly.

"Well, Major, they may very well be marker-stones—that is, marking an astronomical event linked to the seasons, such as the summer solstice, the longest day of the year. Ancient man watched the skies very carefully, to know when to plant and when to reap. They may also have looked to the stars, the sun, for the times to practice their rites, their ceremonies. Just now the Stones do not mark any event, but perhaps at the summer solstice—or the autumnal or vernal equinox—one stone may be in direct line with the rising of the sun."

"Don't think you're going to have the opportunity to find out, Willoughby," snarled Drake. "This is sheer lunacy, and I've had enough of it."

Mr. Willoughby, still seated, studied Drake, his gaze sharp.

"Did it ever occur to you, Major Curtis, that the unfortunate woman who died here on May 1st a year ago—the May Day of the pagans—did it ever occur to you that she did not take her own life of her own free will?"

"*What?*" cried Drake, thunderstruck.

Mr. Willoughby's expression was rapt, almost unholy. "She may well have undergone a similar psychic experience to Miss Hawthorne's. Something—some force may have compelled her to take her own life. An overwhelming compulsion . . . it would explain so much."

"It explains just one thing, and that is that you're mad, Willoughby," said Drake in a low voice, his face pale. "I never should have condoned this scheme of yours and my brother. If you dare to make public all this—this psychic mumbo jumbo, and bring Alice Schyler's death into it, so help me God I'll ruin you. I'll—"

"Just what are you afraid of, Major?" asked Mr. Willoughby in an unnatural, high-pitched voice. "You haven't wanted me here from the first. You've threatened me—you've been very upset by my presence. Are you worried that I may discover something about Mrs. Schyler's death, something that hasn't come out yet?"

"Damn you, what are you implying?" said Drake savagely. "First you claim she was—possessed—and now you're accusing me—"

"I'm not accusing anyone, Major. I'm merely curious to know why my presence here—my work—alarms you so. I could make your hotel even more famous, you know, even more famous. I could restore its flagging business; I could make it not only a New England showplace, but an international one as well, with its very own Stonehenge. My research can help you, Major, and help the hotel."

"I don't require any help from you, you bloody fanatic! Your work here—as you call it—could quite possibly ruin the Crystal Hills. But I'm not going to allow that to happen. I'm not going to permit you to remain here one more day!"

Mr. Willoughby's face had taken on an obstinate, belligerent look. He got to his feet; the mild-mannered man was gone. "I ask you to reconsider, Major Curtis. If for nothing else but the

252

sake of science."

"Science! You call poking about in the dirt and filling a young lady's head full of absurd notions science! You call searching for spirits science! No wonder you are here in New Hampshire rather than at a real dig in the Middle East! No wonder your colleagues refuse to take you seriously and you can't get backers! God knows where my brother found you—but you can go right back!"

"There is no need to be insulting, Major," said Mr. Willoughby, his face red. "You'll regret speaking to me this way."

"Don't you dare threaten me. It's you who will regret it—when I've kicked you down the steps of the hotel!" shouted Drake.

"If you do, sir, I will go straight to the press with my conclusions!"

"Conclusions! Lunatic fancies, you mean. They'll laugh you out of the newspaper offices," said Drake contemptuously.

"Perhaps," said Mr. Willoughby, "but it's still a good story all the same. You'll have to admit it's a good story. And that's precisely what papers like the New York *Journal* want. Speculation . . . sensationalism. I think they would be more than happy to resurrect the story of Alice Schyler's death, this time with a new slant. She may very well have been a victim of the so-called curse of the Stones, you know."

"The New York *Journal*," repeated Drake between clenched teeth. "Yes, I have no doubt that Hearst himself would be interested in that muck—they printed enough of it before! But your career would be finished if you went to them with your theories—and not one item of archaeological proof! You'd be a laughingstock. Your colleagues would never let you live it down!"

"That may be true. But if you refuse me permission to continue my work, if you refuse me permission, I promise that I will do just that. If, on the other hand, you allow me to remain here and proceed with the excavation, then I will keep silent for the present. Until the time, that is, when I discover something incontestable."

"This is blackmail, Willoughby." Drake was leaning on his

cane, his knuckles white.

Mr. Willoughby's gaze did not waver. "Call it what you will, Major Curtis. Both of us have needs here, needs and desires. And if we work together, they can be met with no threat to either one of us."

"Every day you—work—here is a threat to my hotel," said Drake icily.

"I regret sincerely that you feel that way, sir. I had hoped that you would come to respect my research as I respect you for managing a magnificent hotel, and for your sacrifice to your country," said Mr. Willoughby gravely.

"Spare me the flattery," said Drake, tense, hard lines about his mouth.

"It was not my intention to flatter you, Major, not to flatter you. For the present, if you will allow me to continue the dig, I will agree not to go to the newspapers. Unless, that is, I come across some tangible findings which confirm one or more of my theories."

I could see the struggle going on within Drake—his longing to send Mr. Willoughby packing, and his dread of what the consequences might be to the hotel. And yet he hated to permit the dig to continue because he just might be postponing the inevitable. For it was clear to both of us that Ernest Willoughby was a dangerous man, fanatical, obsessive. He was hell-bent on publicizing his theories at whatever cost to himself. Such a man could not be trusted to keep silent for long; eventually he would be unable to resist entering the limelight, grasping for the fame and respect that had so far eluded him in his career. When Drake had said that Mr. Willoughby was following in Heinrich Schliemann's footsteps, he had not been far wrong. Ernest Willoughby saw in the Site of Stones his own Troy. The little mild-mannered man—the man with a dream—had been transformed into a man with a cause. It had become all to him, his raison d'être. He stood a few feet from Drake, doggedly facing him, his short, stout frame as determined as that of the tall, broad-shouldered younger man. The air was permeated with the tension between them.

And then abruptly Drake turned away, saying curtly, "Let's

go, Teresa." He took my arm in a tight grip and led me across the clearing and into the woods.

"I don't want you to have anything further to do with that man. He's a lunatic. Somehow I've got to see that his work is stopped."

"But how can you, Drake? He'll go to the New York papers, just as he said. The whole story will come out again—and it could be worse this time."

"It will come out anyway if he's left to his own devices," said Drake grimly. "There must be a way to stop him." The muscle worked in his set jaw. He was leaning heavily on his cane as he walked; it thudded on the hard surface of the path. "I can't allow him to cause a sensation, not now, not with everything at stake. Not with the Hudson Lending Company waiting in the wings. The bankers in Portsmouth have dealt with us for many years. Some leniency was expected. But now that they've sold their interest, it puts a new light on matters. I've got to make those monthly payments. Do you realize that even if I agree to sell some of the land, the hotel could still be finished, even with plenty of money to run it? If Willoughby's insane delusions are given enough coverage in the press, then no one will care to stay at the Crystal Hills."

Glancing up fleetingly at his stony profile, I suddenly felt a misgiving, a feeling of dread for the future. As we emerged from the woods there came loud, raucous cries above our heads; the ravens were back, wheeling and diving, spinning and swooping, sinister splashes of black against the gray sky.

Emeline was sitting on the front porch of the hotel chatting with Miss Birche when we came up the stairs.

"There you are, Teresa," she said. "Where have you been?"

"Oh, just to the dig site." I tried to speak casually. "I felt like a walk. Your uncle did as well, I suppose." I gave a nervous laugh, stealing a glance at his dark, stormy face.

"Emeline and I were just speaking of it," said Miss Birche, clasping her hands together. "So exciting. Our very own Stonehenge, right here at the Crystal Hills Hotel. I am convinced that Mr. Willoughby will become a celebrity and his discoveries famous. Has he found anything today?"

"An arrowhead," I said.

"Really? I must tell Mr. Sloane. He will be interested to hear. None of us here have been fortunate enough to observe a proper archaeologist at work."

"If you're looking to observe a proper archaeologist, I'm afraid that you'll have to look further than Ernest Willoughby, Miss Birche," said Drake abruptly. "If you will excuse me, ladies." He moved through the door which Burrows held open for him.

"There goes Uncle Drake, cheerful as usual," said Emeline.

"He's—he's had a difference of opinion with Mr. Willoughby," I said awkwardly. "Please don't take offense, Miss Birche."

She pushed some loose strands of hair behind her ear. "Oh, no, Miss Hawthorne, I do not. Heavens no. Major Curtis is a most charming host. I daresay he has heavy responsibilities weighing on him today."

"We should return to the house, Emeline. We have another hour or so of work to do."

"Oh, very well. If I had known what a strict tutor you'd turn out to be . . ."

"Yes, I know." I smiled. "You wouldn't have allowed your uncle to hire me."

"As if anyone could prevent Uncle Drake from doing something he wanted to do," she said.

"That's just what I'm afraid of," I said, but I did not speak the words aloud.

We waved to Miss Birche, who had taken a somewhat tangled ball of yarn and piece of knitting from her bag. As we walked down a graveled drive, a trill of familiar laughter came to us from the West Rotunda. Leonora sat in a wicker settee with Grant Schyler. Her face was turned away; he was whispering something in her ear. They did not see us.

"What's Mamma doing with that awful man?" asked Emeline, craning her neck to look behind at them. "And where's Papa?"

"I think he was taking a party to Loon Lake. A pity it's not clear—they won't be able to see the Old Man," I said hastily.

Emeline shot one more look over her shoulder at her mother and Grant Schyler, her face uncertain and a little forlorn. I tried to make the lesson that afternoon as interesting as I could, but her mind was obviously not on our studies. And who could blame her? I myself had been surprised to see Leonora conducting so blatant and indiscreet a flirtation.

Some days later Emeline and I were in one of the ground-floor shops of the hotel choosing ribbons for our straw hats when Mr. Willoughby, breathless and flushed, rushed in. He requested of the shopkeeper a tape measure and a bottle of indigo ink.

"Good morning, Mr. Willoughby," said Emeline.

"Oh, my dear young ladies, forgive me. I did not see you, no, I did not see you. Such a thrilling morning! Such a find—no, a miracle!" His voice was high-pitched, his eyes glowed; again I could smell the alcohol on his breath.

"You've dug up something interesting?" asked Emeline, wide-eyed.

"Indeed I have. A most important discovery, most important. I must get back to the site to continue my work— the clearing, the examination. And then I must compare them with photographs of similar artifacts."

"Them? What are they?" persisted Emeline.

"An amazing find, Miss Curtis, amazing. Though not surprising to me, of course. I knew there must be proof of my theory if only I had patience and a little luck. Luck is important as well. And today Providence smiled on me. My work has not been in vain! Now, after some preliminary research, I should be able to convince my colleagues of the validity of my theory, of my work here. They will not be able to scoff at me any longer! From now on when they hear the name Ernest Willoughby, they will meet it with respect!"

"Do you mean that you have uncovered some artifact which seems to confirm your idea of the ancient culture that traveled here from Europe, or the Middle East?" I asked, my heart giving an uncomfortable lurch.

"I do indeed, Miss Hawthorne," he said, smiling broadly. "Yesterday I finished digging the trench, and today I sifted through some dirt I had removed from it. And I found these. . . ." He held out two dirt-encrusted reddish objects.

"Those? What are they?" asked Emeline, a rather comical

expression of disappointment on her face.

"They are pottery shards, Miss Curtis. Pieces of baked clay. Possibly from a bowl, or a jug, since they are slightly curved. And they are not, they are most definitely not, from the colonial settlers or the Woodland Indians." He took his handkerchief and wiped his heated brow.

"How can you be certain?" I asked, frowning. "Just from those small pieces, I mean."

"I am an archaeologist, Miss Hawthorne. For years I have studied very old pieces of pottery. It is my business to know these things. I cannot be sure, of course, not yet, without cross-dating, but I believe this type of pottery to be unknown in North America. I must cross-date these samples with other similar documented finds from the Eastern Mediterranean, and ancient Britain and Ireland—Bronze-Age finds which are undisputed. I must go through my books, the photographs, the diagrams, the notations. And when I have found the last proof I need, I will announced my astounding discovery to the world. Harvard will send a team of workers, of archaeologists to excavate this place, and I shall lead them. Yes, I shall lead them. Your uncle, Miss Curtis, will have reason to be grateful to me yet. Grateful, I say. Because I will make the Site of Stones one of the Wonders of the Western World! People will come from everywhere to see it. My discovery will change all present notions of the early history of this country. They won't be able to say that Christopher Columbus discovered America, or that the Vikings may have done so a few hundred years earlier. For, if I am correct, North America was discovered by Europeans, very advanced Europeans, *thousands* of years ago. Ancient man may have possessed knowledge that in all our progress we cannot even imagine. My discovery will be only the beginning of the changes in present attitudes about prehistoric man. And Major Curtis's hotel—the Crystal Hills"—he made a sweeping gesture with his arm—"will be the most famous hotel in the world, in the world, I say!"

"Mr. Willoughby," I said, gripping my bag, "you did agree not to make any announcements about your theories until you were absolutely certain, until there was no room for doubt. And even then—must you inform the newspapers immediately? Surely your colleagues at Harvard should be given time to consider your presentation."

"The people have a right to know, Miss Hawthorne," said Mr. Willoughby, jutting out his chin. "I refuse to give my colleagues the opportunity to squelch my discovery, or worse yet, to try to seize it from me. This is the discovery of the century! Why, what is Ancient Troy to this? The Site of Stones lies on our own continent! Never again can they claim that classical archaeology is the only kind worth studying, the fools! The insults I have had to endure, yes, the insults! Well, no more! No more, I tell you!"

There was no reasoning with him. He was scarcely aware to whom he was speaking. He was completely swept away by his obsession, whether true or not. It was likely that, even if he were unable to cross-date the shards successfully with Bronze-Age shards, he would still make his discovery public. And with that discovery would come his speculations on the construction and use of the Site of Stones, and his fantastic notions about the Stones having a life of their own, luring certain people to their death. Alice Schyler, for one, the beautiful socialite who, he would claim, had had no choice but to stab herself on the "Sacrificial Stone" in response to something horrible and malignant in the atmosphere. For it was clear that the fanatical Mr. Willoughby did not see the distinction between science and superstition, between facts and wild presumptions. And I, I had given him the ammunition to use. My first experience at the Site of Stones, which I had confided to him, had driven him to this frenzied state of mind, this unholy elation. There was no stopping him now, I realized with a sick despair. And I was partially responsible.

Mr. Willoughby wrapped up the shards in his handkerchief and thrust it into his pocket. Then he took his purchases from the gaping clerk, excused himself, and hurried away.

"He's crazy as a bedbug," said Emeline scornfully. "And he's been drinking—I could smell it from across the room." She shrugged. "He gets so excited over nothing—two broken pieces of a bowl. What color are you going to choose, Teresa?"

"What? Oh, I—I don't know. The sea-green, I suppose."

"Well, I'm getting the cherry-red and the rose-pink. You

259

ought to get several colors as well. And some of these silk flowers. They would look so pretty on your hat."

"Perhaps another day," I said.

We went upstairs and across the lobby. Emeline was humming to herself; she did not realize the significance of Mr. Willoughby's discovery and the severe consequences which would likely follow. Why had I been so foolish as to describe to him my initial reaction to the Stones? I had only added fuel to the fire; I should have realized that he would use my experience to inflame his own obsession.

Miss Birche and Mr. Sloane were sitting in a corner of the lobby. "Oh, Miss Hawthorne, have you heard the news?" Miss Birche asked, her voice carrying. My heart sank even lower. Drake was just coming out of the office; I cast an apprehensive glance at him. If only she would keep her voice down . . .

But she did not. She said excitedly, setting down her teacup, "Mr. Willoughby has made a momentous discovery, so he has just informed us."

"Indeed?" I said faintly.

"Yes, he passed us on his way back to the dig site. He says that he uncovered something today which should prove his theory conclusively, that the Stones were constructed four thousand years ago by travelers from across the Atlantic."

"The man is hardly in the best condition to judge any finds," said Mr. Sloane, his mouth pursed. "And just now his babbling about a kind of curse does nothing to impress me."

"I daresay he was a trifle carried away," said Miss Birche, "but if he is to be believed and he has found evidence about the Stones, I can understand his being overwrought."

"Has he—has he told you what he has uncovered?" I asked.

"No," said Mr. Sloane, adjusting his pince-nez. "He plans to make an announcement tonight, at dinner, after he has checked through a few books, he told us."

"Yes, he said that his fellow guests at the Crystal Hills should be the first to know," said Miss Birche. "Before the newspapers and his fellow scientists. I think that is very handsome of him."

"I daresay," I said. "Well, good day to you."

"If they only knew that his great discovery is a couple of

broken pieces of a dish," said Emeline in my ear. "They'll be disappointed, but I didn't want to say anything."

I scarcely heard her. I was looking at Drake; it was evident from his frowning expression and stiffened frame that he had overheard our conversation.

"Wait outside for me, Emeline. I'll be right there." I went over to the desk.

"He's found two shards of pottery. They may be nothing; they may mean nothing. He may realize that the—the Indians could have made them."

He surveyed me sardonically. "The man may be a raving lunatic, but he's no fool. If he believes those shards are from a Bronze Age culture, then it's highly likely that they are. I care nothing about that—it's his other unorthodox ideas which I find damnable. I can't allow him to publicize this find—not just now! A few weeks maybe, or better yet, sometime in October. We close at the end of that month. It may be that, without guests here, the coverage in the press will be minimal, that by next April everything will have died down, his wild notions forgotten."

"What are you going to do?"

"Speak to him. Ask him to agree to wait. What's another month or so to him? It could mean everything to us. Perhaps I can try some blackmail of my own—the knowledge of his excessive drinking would not endear him to the colleagues he'll be trying to convince."

"What if he refuses to wait?" I asked anxiously.

"He must wait." Drake's eyes were as coldly blue as a winter sky. Without another word he came round the desk and went across the lobby. In dismay I watched him leave the hotel.

"Come on, Teresa, I want to fix my hat," called Emeline from the front door.

My heart thudding, I went outside. Drake was walking across the lawn to the woods, one leg dragging slightly behind the other.

"I think I'll go up to the attic and take a flower or two from Grandmother's old bonnets," said Emeline as we walked back to the house. "I saw one with pretty pink roses just the shade of this ribbon. They hadn't faded at all. I'd like to have something

261

of hers to wear. Especially since I lost the locket. It seems like a bad dream now, that time at Miss Winslow's." She went up to Charlotte's room to show her the ribbons.

I toyed with the idea of following Drake up to the Site of Stones. At one point I began to pin on my hat again, but decided against it. What could I do? I had made matters worse between the two men when I had confided my fears about the Stones to Mr. Willoughby. My presence would not be beneficial; if I blundered in on their discussion, I might do more harm than good. I had no idea then how I would come to regret my decision.

That evening there was to be a program of musical entertainment on the back lawn of the hotel. A ragtime band had been hired to play the latest popular tunes, and I had promised Emeline that we might go. Before dinner I changed my white blouse and navy skirt for my frilled lavender cotton gown, undid the long, thick braid I had worn that day, and twisted my hair into a loose topknot. Charlotte, Emeline, and I dined alone before going over to the hotel at sunset. As we walked we looked ahead at the Crystal Hills shimmering in the early evening light. "It's always a beautiful sight, isn't it?" said Charlotte. "How I hope everything will work out for the best."

"It will, you'll see," said Emeline. "We have lots more guests now—almost as many as we used to—and soon everything will be just the way it used to be. I know it."

Charlotte smiled and patted her hand. "Dear child, I believe you love this place even more than I do. And of course you are right."

The strains of band music drifted toward us in the pine-scented night air. We went round the porch to the rear side of the hotel and found seats near the West Rotunda. The musicians were playing in one of the pagodalike gazebos; they were dressed jauntily in navy-blue uniforms with red piping and large gold buttons. The guests sat in rows of wicker chairs and settees down the length of the porch. They wore evening finery, the women in low-cut gowns, with long gloves, with jewels about their throats, the men in well-cut black suits. To see them dressed the way they were, to listen to the sort of music one might hear played in a city park on a Sunday afternoon, struck me as amusing, but their elegant attire contributed to the festive atmosphere. Mt. Washington and its neighbors, massive, purple-black, soared in the distance.

I glanced about apprehensively for either Drake or Mr. Willoughby, but I did not see either of them. Horatio Aldridge and his wife were near to us and smiled genially. Mrs. Aldridge's expression was utterly devoid of the irritability which used to be habitual to her. Her husband sat close to her, and when her shawl slipped off her shoulders, he readjusted it tenderly and whispered something in her ear. Nightshade Notch was having a good effect on some people, I reflected. Indeed, all the guests seemed relaxed and happy. Only I was restless and anxious.

Charlotte had brought her embroidery. She and Mrs. Hamilton had their heads together comparing stitches. Mrs. Hamilton was arrayed in one of her enormous bonnets, this one decorated with birds, flowers, and pieces of fruit. The man seated behind her had evidently given up trying to glimpse the musicians. He leaned back in his chair, his eyes closed.

"I hope that they play "Ta-ra-ra boom-de-ay,'" said Emeline.

Later the band took a break, and the maids passed around silver trays either filled with glasses of pink lemonade or champagne, or piled high with crisp cookies made with bits of candied ginger or lemon peel. I excused myself to go to the powder room, and walked behind the rows of seats to the back door of the hotel.

In the powder room on the first floor I met Miss Birche, sticking pins into her hair. "Such a delightful evening," she said when she saw me. "I confess I have a sneaking fondness for ragtime, though Mr. Sloane is quite contemptuous of it."

"He would be," I said. "Was—was Mr. Willoughby at dinner tonight? I wondered whether he had made his announcement."

"No, Miss Hawthorne. Mr. Sloane, Mr. and Mrs. Aldridge, and I saved a place for him at our table. Mr. Aldridge was most interested in hearing what his discovery was. He may ask Mr. Willoughby to write a book. But we were all disappointed when he never appeared. Perhaps he was working late and could not pull himself away. I had hoped he would celebrate his findings with us."

Perhaps he had been celebrating by himself and had passed out, I thought cynically. Though how could he proceed with his excavating if he were truly intoxicated I did not see.

Miss Birche left the powder room then along with most of the other ladies. Quickly I adjusted the pins in my hair. The music had begun again; it was time for me to return to my seat. When I entered the lobby, it was deserted except for Drake and Leonora, who stood in the front of the room before one of the long windows. They glared angrily at each other; neither noticed me.

"That was a very amusing little game you played the other night," Drake was saying. "Or was it Aaron's idea?"

"I don't know what you're talking about," snapped Leonora. "I have to get back outside."

He gripped her bare arm, his eyes blazing. "You know exactly what I'm referring to, Leonora. You just couldn't resist, could you? I could easily have strangled you!"

She wrenched her arm away, smiling mockingly. "It was worth it, just to see your face. You think you're king around here, telling us what to do, what not to do. Well, I have news for you, Drake. That's going to change. This place is going to fall about your ears. And I can't wait to see your face when it does. I've waited years for this—to see you beaten—!"

"Years! Because I wouldn't bed my brother's wife!"

Her eyes flashed. "Since when have you cared about morality? You were never an upholder of virtue. Grant Schyler would testify to the contrary, I'm certain."

"At least I drew the line at sleeping with Aaron's new bride! If he had known then what he had married!"

"You should know by now that he's no paragon of fidelity!"

"Yes, I daresay you suit each other very well. I suppose he's turning a blind eye to your flirtation with Schyler."

She shrugged. "If you want my opinion, I think he has his eye on Miss Hawthorne, and it's not a blind one. A pretty young virgin would be a change for him. If she *is* still a virgin. You would know more about that than I. She's certainly enthralled with you. I daresay you could get her to agree to anything you chose. Or has the apparatus failed after all? Is that the real reason behind the new leaf you have turned over? Is that why Miss Hawthorne goes about looking so forlorn? Well, I'll drop a word in Aaron's ear that the coast is clear, that there is perhaps one thing he is able to do that you are not!"

Drake struck her across the cheek. It happened so quickly that she had no time to dodge. She gasped, put a hand to her reddening cheek while he stared down at his palm, his face dark. Leonora whirled around and saw me.

"Well, if it isn't the ubiquitous Miss Hawthorne," she hissed, her eye tearing. "Perhaps she can help you, Drake. Unless, of course, Aaron gets to her first."

She swept past me and out of the room while I stood riveted in place. My face felt on fire; I was appalled by her coarseness. Why on earth had I stood there listening? What was between the two of them was none of my business—how many times did I have to be humiliated into realizing that?

Just then Mr. Sloane came through the front door. His face was pale; he was breathing rapidly, and for once was not wearing his pince-nez. I noticed abstractedly that his black shoes were streaked with mud.

"Major Curtis," he began.

"What is it, Mr. Sloane?" asked Drake.

"I've—I've just been up to the Site of Stones. Mr. Willoughby failed to appear at dinner tonight and so I decided to see whether or not he was still working. He was not in his room when I knocked."

"Working? It's nearly dark," said Drake, his black brows drawn together.

"That's precisely it, sir. He was not working. Though he is—up at the site." He glanced at me and hesitated.

"Well?" said Drake, tensing.

"Perhaps I should speak with you alone, Major. . . ."

Drake seemed to have forgotten my presence. "Out with it, man!"

Mr. Sloane swallowed hard. "He's—dead, Major Curtis."

I let out a stifled cry, putting my hand to my mouth.

"Dead," repeated Drake in an expressionless voice. "Are you certain?"

"I'm afraid there's no doubt, sir," said Mr. Sloane, swaying a little on his feet.

"Burrows, bring a brandy for Mr. Sloane. Come over here, sir, and sit down. And tell me exactly what you saw."

Scarcely aware that I did so, I followed the two of them to the grouping of chairs in the corner of the room.

"I went up to look for him, as I told you, sir, a short while ago. I called out to Willoughby. He—he did not answer. It was growing dark and I assumed that he had returned to the hotel and somehow I had missed him. But I was curious to see what he had been doing since I'd been up there the last time, and so I walked about. That—that's when I found him."

"Just what did you see?"

"Willoughby himself, lying under a pile of stones at the entrance of one of those chambers. The ones that resemble giant beehives. He must have been crouching to look inside when it caved in on him."

"Oh, no," I whimpered.

Mr. Sloane glanced at me fleetingly before looking back at Drake. "It was apparent from the prevailing odor that he had been drinking. It must have interfered with his judgment, his cautiousness. The way those stone chambers are constructed —they are not terribly secure, I should think." He took out his handkerchief and wiped his brow.

Burrows held out a glass of brandy on a silver tray to him. Drake stood up, his face inscrutable. "I'm going up there. I'll need a lantern, Burrows."

"Yes, sir."

"I ask that you do not tell anyone about this yet, Mr. Sloane," said Drake. "Not until I return."

"Very well, sir," Mr. Sloane said shakily.

"Poor Mr. Willoughby," I said, "how awful for him. He had such high hopes, he wanted so to announce his discovery. . . ." Abruptly I stopped, my gaze fixed on Drake, who was staring at the darkened window.

Burrows returned with the lantern and Drake picked up his cane.

"Do you think you should go alone, sir, in the dark?" asked Burrows. "If you were to fall—"

266

"I'm not a child, dammit," said Drake, "and I'm not a cripple!" He flung down his cane.

"I beg your pardon, sir," said Burrows, but Drake had already left.

From the opened back door came the lively tune "Ta-ra-ra boom-de-ay," complete with cymbals. Emeline had got her wish.

The concert was ending; there was applause and then a buzz of conversation. People began to drift into the lobby and up and down the stairs.

Charlotte and Emeline made their way to me. "You never came back, Teresa. Do you have a headache? They played 'Ta-ra-ra boom-de-ay," said Emeline.

I forced a smile. "Yes, I know. I listened from in here. Shall we go back to the house now? I—I'm tired."

When we reached the house, Emeline went on up to her room, but I detained Charlotte. "Could we have a cup of tea before going upstairs?"

She saw my face. "Of course, my dear. Let's go in. Now what is it?" she asked when we had sat down. "You look most distressed."

"It's about Mr. Willoughby. I didn't want to say in front of Emeline, not just before bed. But he—he's dead." I shuddered, my teeth beginning to chatter.

"Oh, no, you don't mean it! How—how—?"

"Mr. Sloane found him. He was buried underneath a pile of stones at the entrance to one of those chambers. He came and found Drake and Drake went to see for himself, just as the concert was ending."

"Have the police been notified?" she asked.

"Perhaps by now. I—I don't know."

"It was an accident, of course," she said, but she was looking very pale.

"Of—of course. Mr. Sloane said he had been drinking and must have gotten careless. I was always afraid of those chambers—they look so sinister. . . ."

The maid brought the tea then and Charlotte handed me a cup. "Drink this and you'll stop trembling."

"He had uncovered two items today which had greatly

excited him," I said, taking a sip of tea. "Two pottery shards. He thought they were from a bowl or jug, made in 2000 B.C. or thereabouts. If he had been able to prove that they were, by comparing them to others found from that time, he would have astounded the academic world, he said."

"The Site of Stones would have become famous," said Charlotte, gazing into her teacup.

"Drake was afraid it would become notorious. He—he was going to talk to Mr. Willoughby, to ask him not to make any formal announcement about his findings, not yet."

"Was he?" asked Charlotte faintly.

We said nothing more, but the fear in our eyes spoke for itself.

Chapter Fourteen

The next morning at breakfast I broke the news to Emeline. I was heavy-eyed and listless, having gotten little sleep the night before. I wasn't hungry, but forced myself to eat a piece of toast with blackberry jam and drink a cup of tea.

"Gosh, Teresa, that's why you looked the way you did last night," said Emeline. "I thought you were coming down with something. How awful. And just yesterday he was so happy. Grandmother always told me to stay away from the chambers, that they might be dangerous and collapse, but I didn't believe her."

A little before noon we walked over to the Crystal Hills. The lobby was more crowded than usual and people were standing or sitting and conversing in hushed tones. Drake was at the desk talking to two men, one of them in uniform. Before I could stop her, Emeline walked up to them. I had no choice but to follow.

"This is my niece, Lieutenant Striker. Miss Hawthorne, Lieutenant Striker, Sergeant Scully."

"I'd like to talk with you ladies," said the lieutenant, a thin, gray-haired man of medium height with an angular face.

"Why?" asked Emeline, round-eyed. "We don't know anything."

"Just routine, Miss Curtis. We'd like to ask you about the last time you saw Ernest Willoughby."

"It was yesterday afternoon, sir," I said. "About one or one-thirty. We were in the shop downstairs when he happened to come in." Briefly I told them about his excitement over the two pieces of pottery, and his intention to cross-date them with others documented in his books.

The lieutenant's eyes bored into mine; the sergeant was busy taking notes. "He had the shards with him at the time?"

"Yes. After he showed them to us, he wrapped them in his handkerchief and put them in his pocket."

"Now why would he show them to you when he didn't show them to any of the other guests?"

"I suppose because I'd been at the site earlier in the week and he had discussed his theory with me," I said awkwardly.

"And just what theory was that, Miss Hawthorne?"

"Well, that the Site of Stones was built four thousand years ago by a group of people not indigenous to North America," I said.

"Yes, we've heard about that. Do you know where he was going after he left the shop?"

I glanced uneasily at Drake. "Back to the site, I believe. Miss Birche and Mr. Sloane saw him headed in that direction. He wanted to compare the shards with photographs of others that he had. I gathered his books and documents were at the excavation."

"Yes, we found his books and materials. But this is the first we have heard of the existence of any shards. We did understand, though, from a few of the other guests that he believed that he was on the verge of a momentous discovery."

"He was referring to finding the shards, I suppose," I said. "He hoped that they were at least part of the evidence he was looking for."

"I see. When you saw him, Miss Hawthorne, had he been drinking?"

"Well, I'm afraid . . ."

"He was drunk," said Emeline flatly. "You know he was, Teresa."

"And that was the last time you saw him? Early yesterday afternoon?"

I nodded.

"And you, Miss Curtis?"

"Yes."

"And you spoke to him soon after that, up at the site, Major Curtis?"

"I did," said Drake shortly. "I was there about one half hour before returning to the hotel for a meeting with my staff at two-thirty. And he was very much alive when I left, I assure you."

"What was the nature of your business with him?"

"We were discussing the dig."

"So it was just a friendly visit, Major?"

Drake's voice was curt. "He was working on my land, Lieutenant Striker. I considered it my business to see what he was up to from time to time."

"And was he drinking while you were there?"

"Yes, from the flask found near his body."

"Very well, sir, ladies. That is all for now. If something occurs to you that you have not mentioned, do not hesitate to come to us."

"Gosh," said Emeline when both men had moved away, "I've never been questioned by policemen before. I wouldn't have even thought that man was a policeman."

"Certain detectives wear ordinary clothes, Emeline. Let me assure you that he is very much an officer of the law."

I looked up at him. "You know him, then?"

Drake's face hardened. "Very well."

"There's Miss Birche. I'm going to find out what the police asked her," said Emeline, and she went off.

"How do you know him?"

"He was sent here from Concord to investigate Alice Schyler's death," he said grimly. "I believe I mentioned him to you."

I caught my breath. "He was the one who believed that she had not committed suicide? The one who suspected you?"

"The very same."

"Oh, no. They—they aren't thinking that it was something other than an accident now, are they?"

His black brows drew together. "Why should they? That's all it was. The man had too much to drink and somehow jostled the stones above the entrance to the chamber. The stones are piled and fitted together by weight, a very primitive method. It's a wonder there haven't been more accidents to curious people."

"Yes, of course, that's how it must have happened," I said weakly.

"They've assured me that Willoughby's death will be kept out of the papers, except for a brief mention in the obituary columns. Unless some newer evidence turns up, that is."

"Wh—what should turn up?"

He surveyed me ironically. "I think the mention of the shards has given them pause."

"You—you hadn't told them?"

"I never saw the things, did I?" he asked curtly.

"What happened yesterday at the site, when you spoke with him?"

His eyes narrowed. "You ask too many questions, Miss Hawthorne. If you must know, there was no reasoning with him. Now if you will excuse me, I have work to do. The police have taken enough of my time today."

Flushing, I bit my lip. He went into the office. Unhappy, I wandered out onto the porch, where I found Emeline sitting with Miss Birche, Mrs. Hamilton, Mr. Sloane, and the Aldridges.

"I just feel so terrible," Miss Birche was saying, a crumpled handkerchief in her hand. "Poor Mr. Willoughby. To think that it was just yesterday afternoon when we saw him and he was so excited. And now, to think he will never finish his excavations, never realize his dream. It's tragic."

"What is so tragic is that he found it necessary to imbibe while he worked," said Mrs. Hamilton sternly, her large hooked nose pointed at Miss Birche. "And now I daresay people will begin to say that it's that foolish curse again."

"The curse? What curse?" asked Mrs. Aldridge.

"Oh, there's some sort of silly legend attached to the place where he was working. The maid who's been attending me here told me about it this morning."

"What is the legend?" asked Mr. Aldridge.

"I suppose legend is the wrong word. It's just a feeling the local people have that the Stones up there—not that I've seen them myself—are not to be disturbed, that sort of foolish nonsense."

272

"How—how odd," said Miss Birche, putting a hand to her throat. "I had not heard about that. And now Mr. Willoughby . . ."

"Yes, his death will no doubt have some bizarre interpretation placed on it," said Mr. Sloane. "It's all mere superstition, of course."

"I understand from the maid that years ago the families who attempted to build homesteads nearby were driven away by tragic events they somehow linked to the Stones," said Mrs. Hamilton.

"Nonsense. They just chose to blame the place for their trouble. All early settlers had some tragedy attached to their lives."

"It's true. I mean, that local people do believe there's a curse on the Site of Stones," said Emeline. "Some believe the Indians put it there, in revenge for being driven away. Others say that the Indians were afraid of the place too. My family, though, has never paid any attention to such tales," she said loftily.

"No, I can't see the major being the superstitious type," said Horatio Aldridge, grinning.

"You must admit, all of you, that it is strange that last year that woman was found dead, and now the archaeologist," said Mrs. Aldridge.

There was a palpable silence. "I'm certain there—there's no comparison whatsoever," said Miss Birche faintly.

"Well, I must say I wouldn't choose to be in the major's shoes just now," said Mr. Sloane.

"Don't flatter yourself," said Mrs. Hamilton.

"Excuse me, ladies, gentlemen. But I'd like to have a few more words with you." My heart gave a thud; it was Lieutenant Striker. I wondered how much he had heard of what had been said. "Do any of you, aside from Miss Hawthorne and Miss Curtis, know anything about the two pieces of pottery Mr. Willoughby uncovered yesterday?"

The company looked blankly at him. "That's news to me," said Mr. Aldridge, frowning.

"The only thing I heard he had uncovered was an Indian arrowhead," said Mrs. Hamilton scornfully.

"Perhaps he planned to show them to us last night at dinner

when he hoped to make his announcement about a discovery. Could they have been the discovery?" asked Miss Birche.

"Even if he had shown them to us, how would we have known that they were the real thing and not something he fashioned himself?" asked Mrs. Aldridge.

"I don't believe that Mr. Willoughby's integrity is at question here, my dear. There are ways to uncover hoaxes, you know."

"Well, the man did strike me as someone determined to discover something at all costs," said Mrs. Hamilton.

"Where are the artifacts now?" asked Mr. Sloane. "Perhaps another archaeologist could examine them and present an opinion."

Miss Birche clasped her hands together. "Oh, yes! How wonderful that would be. His work would not have been in vain!"

"I'm afraid there's little likelihood of that," said Lieutenant Striker. "The shards are missing."

"Missing!" repeated Miss Birche.

"He probably dropped them somewhere," said Mrs. Aldridge. "If he could get himself killed, then I should think he'd be just as capable of losing the artifacts."

"He drank, Lieutenant. Quite a lot," said Mrs. Hamilton bluntly.

"Yes, madam, so I understand. But I'm curious to know whether you think the deceased could have been murdered for the sake of the shards."

"Murdered!" I whispered.

"Oh, no, you must be mistaken, Lieutenant," exclaimed Miss Birche. "Who would want to murder that poor man? Why, it doesn't bear thinking of!"

"Unless there was another archaeologist who got wind of the idea that his excavating here might not be a wild-goose chase after all," Mr. Aldridge put in. "However, I consider that highly unlikely."

"Are you saying that someone would care that much about two pieces of clay that they would kill for them?" asked Mrs. Aldridge.

"But there was never anyone up there with him when we

visited," I said. "He always worked alone."

"The artifacts will doubtless turn up," said Mr. Aldridge. "I assume you've made a thorough search of his belongings?"

The lieutenant's gaze was ironic. "You assume correctly, sir." He turned to the sergeant. "We'll make a visit to each house in the Notch to learn whether anyone has been putting up a stranger. Perhaps some of the local people know something. But first I must speak with Mrs. Curtis. Is she expected here soon, Miss Curtis?"

"My mother doesn't care anything about archaeology," said Emeline. "I don't know why you'd want to talk to her."

"Her interest is irrelevant," said the lieutenant brusquely. "We are questioning everyone here at the hotel."

"Well, she ought to be here soon if she's not already. She usually takes luncheon here," said Emeline.

"Speaking of lunch," said Mrs. Hamilton, getting ponderously to her feet, "I want mine."

"Yes, I daresay we may as well go in," said Miss Birche.

As a group we moved indoors, just as Leonora, in a midnight-blue skirt and jacket, came riding up. A boy took her horse after she had dismounted, and I heard Lieutenant Striker say, "Mrs. Curtis, I presume?"

"Yes?" she said, striding up the porch steps. "Oh, I believe we've met before." Her eyes narrowed. "You're the detective."

"Yes, madam." His voice was curt. "Lieutenant Striker. I presume you've been informed of Ernest Willoughby's death?"

They were in the lobby now. Picking up a brochure from a table near the door, I pretended to read it.

"I assure you I have heard the ghastly details. Not that I'm surprised. The man was a drunkard as well as a fanatic. I knew my husband shouldn't have agreed to let him come here."

"You did not like him," said Lieutenant Striker.

"No, I did not, Lieutenant, but what is that to the point, pray?"

"Why did your husband invite him here?" asked the detective.

"Oh, Aaron had some absurd notion that the publicity would be good for the hotel, that that foolish little man's digging would draw more guests. That's just like Aaron. As if anyone would care whether the site was built by cavemen or not. Instead, the man's dead and now you policemen are back. Surely you don't think the two cases are related?" Her voice was amused.

"What other case are you referring to, Mrs. Curtis?"

"Why, Alice Schyler's death, of course."

I held my breath.

"We are here looking into the death of Ernest Willoughby, Mrs. Curtis. That other matter was closed over a year ago."

"But not to your satisfaction, as I recall. I must tell you, Lieutenant, that while my husband invited Mr. Willoughby to come here, my brother-in-law was adamantly opposed to the idea."

There was a slight pause. "And why was that, Mrs. Curtis?"

"Why don't you ask him, Lieutenant? Or are you going to hold his hand through all this because he went on to be 'New Hampshire's Own Rough Rider'? How amusing. I wouldn't have thought it of you, Lieutenant. Once a murder suspect, always a murder suspect, I should think."

Thank heaven for her malicious tones, her mocking glances. For she had set Lieutenant Striker against her. "You don't like your brother-in-law very much, do you, Mrs. Curtis?" he asked evenly.

"Why, how clever of you, Lieutenant. You will have this case solved in no time. Now if you will excuse me, I'm late for luncheon."

I thought he would detain her, but he did not. Instead he went over to the desk and spoke to Drake. After a moment the two of them went into the office.

Emeline and I took a walk later that afternoon as neither of us were in the mood to do lessons. On the way back we passed through the hotel. Leonora, Aaron, and Grant Schyler were sitting in front of the large stone fireplace.

"Hello, Mamma, hello, Papa," said Emeline.

Leonora waved at her carelessly while Aaron said, "How's my girl? And Miss Hawthorne as well." His gaze moved slowly over me. "I suppose you've both heard about Willoughby. Shame, damn shame. He might have brought in more business

276

to the hotel, if he had managed to make a discovery. Nothing more than a mess now. And with the police questioning all the guests, and marking off the site . . ." He stopped, glancing at Grant Schyler. "Well, it's not good for business."

"Are the police still here, Papa?"

"No, they've cleared off for the day. They left after talking to your Uncle Drake a while earlier."

"I told them that Drake was strongly opposed to Mr. Willoughby's work," said Leonora.

"You always did have a poisonous tongue, Nora," said Aaron, grinning.

"I wonder what Major Curtis had to say to that," said Grant Schyler, smoothing out a wrinkle on the sleeve of his jacket. He stood up and leaned against the mantel, taking out a large gold pocket watch. "Five-thirty. Time for the papers to arrive, isn't it? I believe they are sent on the morning train from Boston and New York?"

"Are they?" said Leonora carelessly. "I daresay. I never read them. So dreary."

"Not always," said Grant Schyler coolly, his gold tooth flashing.

"Let's go, Emeline," I said to her.

"Yes, I must change for dinner," said Leonora. "Will I see you later, Grant?"

"You can count on it, my dear," he said.

"Will you join me downstairs for a drink, Schyler?" asked Aaron.

"All right. And I believe I owe you a chance to even matters." The two men went downstairs; Emeline walked away with her mother. I followed them, but on my way I nearly collided with a young man who carried a stack of newspapers.

"Excuse me, miss," he said, taking off his hat. "I wasn't lookin' where I was goin'. But I never expected to read about the hotel in the paper. I hear someone else is dead at the Stones."

"You say you read about it—in the newspaper?"

"Yes, miss. Would you like one?" He untied the string and handed me a copy of the New York *Journal.*

"Oh, no!" I gasped.

277

"Took me by surprise too, miss." He went inside while I stared down at the headline: "Ancient Curse Claims Another Life." How in the world had they found out so quickly?

Swiftly I went after the young man. He was depositing the stack of newspapers on the front desk. "I'll take those," I said breathlessly. "You can go now."

"All right, miss. Have a good night."

The lobby was empty; at this time in the evening the guests were bathing and dressing for dinner. I had to hide the papers before anyone saw them, but where? Anywhere—only outside the hotel. Picking up the stack, I turned to go. Fortunately Burrows was not at his usual post at the front door.

"Miss Hawthorne." It was Drake's voice behind me.

"Yes? I'm just on my way back to the house," I said, not looking around. "I have to catch up with Emeline."

"What are you doing with those newspapers?"

Stupidly I had hoped that he hadn't noticed. I turned around slowly. "I didn't want anyone to see them," I said miserably.

He took them from me, frowning. With dread I watched his face blacken as his eyes scanned the tabloid. "Come into the office," he said grimly. When he had closed the door behind us, he flung the stack on his desk. "They promised me no publicity! Not while it appeared to be an accident."

"The police, you mean? I don't think they sent the story, Drake."

"No, you're right. This is a morning paper. The story would have had to be telegraphed to New York last night. And this—muck—is certainly not from a police report. There are no real facts, other than Willoughby is dead. Just insinuations and sensationalistic statements."

"So it—it had to be someone from the hotel who wired the *Journal* last night. I can't imagine that Mr. Sloane would do such a thing. Do you think—Leonora? Or there may be a guest here who has a peculiar sense of humor, who got a thrill from sending such a story. It could have been anyone. Wouldn't the telegraph office know?"

"I doubt whether the person who wired the story was foolish enough to do it from the hotel," Drake said dryly. "Whoever it was must have gone down to the train station last night.

There's a telegraph office there."

"Did some of the guests find out about Mr. Willoughby last night?" I asked.

"I suppose so. News like that can't be kept quiet for long. When I returned from the site and wired the police, there were a number of guests still up. And the employees, of course, would have spread the word."

There was a discreet knock on the door. "What the devil is it now?" he ground out. "Well, Burrows?"

The burly doorman stood outside, looking uncomfortable. "Well, I'm sorry to disturb you, sir, but there's a—a person to see you."

"Just sign him in, will you?" said Drake wearily.

"He's not interested in a room, sir. Indeed, I'm certain he could not afford one," said Burrows frankly, his glance distasteful as he looked back to the lobby.

"Well, what does he want?"

"It's a reporter, sir. From the Boston *Globe*. He wants to ask you some questions. I assume they pertain to Mr. Willoughby's death."

"The devil he does!" cried Drake harshly. "Get him out of here!"

"If I might offer a suggestion, Mr. Drake, it might be advisable if you spoke with him. To send him away with nothing would only antagonize him, and it might make matters worse."

"How the hell could they be any worse, I'd like to know!"

"Burrows is right, Drake. You don't want to set him against you. Perhaps, if you are tactful, and seem to cooperate, he will see that there's nothing to the *Journal*'s story and go away. It's important how you handle it."

He raked his hair back with his fingers and seemed to get a grip on himself. We went into the lobby. There was a heavyset man waiting there. He was flashily, rather cheaply dressed, his hair oiled.

"What can I do for you, Mr. —?" Drake asked coolly.

"Robinson. Jack Robinson's the name. Here's my card. Boston *Globe*."

Drake glanced at the card and handed it back to him. "Yes?"

279

"I've come to look into the mysterious death of one Ernest Willoughby, archaeologist. He was a guest here, I understand, conducting an excavation somewhere near this hotel?"

"That is true."

"You are the owner of the Crystal Hills, sir? What can you tell me about Willoughby's death?"

"Who set you on to this?" Drake asked bluntly.

"Oh, I got a hot tip. Can't squeal on my sources, y'know. Gotta make my living."

"Well, if you're hoping to make a good deal out of this, I'm afraid you'll be disappointed. Mr. Willoughby was killed accidentally when a pile of stones he was examining fell on him. That is all."

"Any witnesses?"

"No."

"Then we can't be sure it was accidental, can we?" asked Jack Robinson insolently.

Drake was struggling not to lose his temper. "The police seem to think that it was. They will be back tomorrow morning. You can speak with them then."

"Oh, I will, sir. There was another death in the same location last year, wasn't there? One of my colleagues handled the story at the time. I was reading the old articles on my way up here. You are Mr. Drake Curtis, I presume?"

"I am."

"And the woman who was found dead was your mistress, wasn't she? A society lady. Married."

Drake said nothing, a muscle working in his jaw.

"And now, just a little more than a year later, another body turns up at these Stones of yours. Is there a connection, Mr. Curtis?"

"Coincidence."

"Really? I've heard there's supposed to be a curse on the place. Two deaths in sixteen months in such an isolated location seems more than coincidence—both guests of your hotel."

"Surely you don't believe in the existence of a curse," said Drake with scorn.

"Me? No, I don't. But people like to read about such

280

things—and wonder. They get delicious thrills from stories like that."

"I should think your readers would be interested in solid facts, Mr. Robinson. Perhaps you reporters ought to give them those for a change. Ernest Willoughby's death was an unfortunate accident. And that is all I have to say on the matter. This is not a public place. Either you take a room or you must do your—work outside these walls."

"Oh, your prices are too steep for me, Mr. Curtis," said Mr. Robinson, grinning, "but I'll be back. You can count on that."

The ball was to be held in three days' time. For weeks Emeline had insisted that I should have a new gown; all my clothes were several years old and none elegant enough for such an occasion. She herself was planning to purchase a new dress from those ready-made and sold in the hotel shop, and she urged me to do the same. Leonora had agreed that Emeline could stay up for part of the evening. I was tempted; I had not spent any of my salary of the past two months. Buying a gown would deplete the amount considerably, though, and so I was doubtful. But I did agree to accompany her to the shop and assist her in making the selection. After the stress of the past few days, I sorely needed to indulge in a few enjoyable and frivolous hours.

In the early afternoon the two of us walked over to the hotel. I was excited at the prospect of a shopping expedition, and longed to try on something at variance with my usual attire. As we came up the porch steps, we saw Mrs. Hamilton and Mrs. Aldridge seated in the wicker chairs conversing with a man whose back was to us. When I realized it was the reporter, Jack Robinson, my heart sank. So he was busy at work pumping the guests for their speculations concerning Mr. Willoughby's death. . . .

But one glance at his broad face reassured me. He looked disappointed, even faintly exasperated, the smug, zestful look of the previous night gone from his face.

"There's no question," Mrs. Hamilton was saying briskly. "It was an accident."

"Most definitely. The man was usually intoxicated, and he certainly was on the afternoon in question. Anyone will tell you so. I understand that when they found him he positively *reeked* of whiskey, and the flask was empty," declared Mrs. Aldridge.

"Ask anyone you like—you'll get the same story," said Mrs. Hamilton. "And in my opinion it's not much of a story."

"No, indeed," agreed Mrs. Aldridge. "Why, the man might have died in any number of accidents. I knew a man once who, while intoxicated, fell down the stairs and broke his neck. Though naturally his family did not like to admit the cause."

"Naturally not, Mrs. Aldridge. One time my sister was at a dinner party in Cambridge where one of the guests was so much the worse for drink that he put an enormous bite of steak in his mouth and choked to death," said Mrs. Hamilton.

The ladies exchanged nods. "He might have died any number of ways—and all of them in accidents caused by imbibing too heavily. So let that be a lesson to you, my man," said Mrs. Aldridge, pointing her fan at the reporter.

Mr. Robinson scowled. "Have you ladies considered the idea of the curse that is supposedly haunting these Stones?"

Both ladies regarded him scornfully. "Certainly not," said Mrs. Hamilton, bristling. "Do you take us for fools, Mr. Robinson? A certain class of your readers may be interested in that sort of thing, but let me assure you that we have spent a most enjoyable summer here and quite reject the notion of any curse. The man was drunk and got careless, and that's all there is to it. I should think you newspapermen should be on the trail of some real news, and not this tomfoolery!"

"But you have heard, I take it, that a woman was found dead at the same place just a year ago?" he persisted, his face reddening.

"So what if she was?" Mrs. Aldridge startled me by answering. "That case bears no resemblance whatsoever to Mr. Willoughby's death. The police, I believe, agree on that. So you had best take your pen and paper elsewhere, rather than bothering people who are trying to relax and enjoy themselves. If you persist in speaking to us, I will have to call my husband."

"Did I hear my name mentioned?" Horatio Aldridge, obviously amused, came up to his wife and took her hand. He wore his Panama hat and was dressed for riding, his small whip

282

in hand. "Is he pestering you, my dear?"

"I was just asking the ladies one or two questions," said Mr. Robinson peevishly.

"One or two questions! Why, the man hasn't left our side for close on half an hour! He's refused to leave us in peace, hasn't he, Mrs. Hamilton?"

"He has, with no thought or consideration to your bad headache, Mrs. Aldridge," said Mrs. Hamilton, clinching the matter.

"All right, I'm going," mumbled Mr. Robinson, glowering. He turned and stomped heavily down the steps.

"Brilliantine," said Mrs. Hamilton. "On his hair."

"Well, he's not going to spoil the rest of my stay. You saw what the New York *Journal* printed. 'Doomed hotel,' indeed!"

Bravo, ladies, I wanted to say.

"Would you care to go in and lie down, my dear?" asked Mr. Aldridge.

"Whatever for?" asked his wife. "It's quite delightful out here, now that that man has gone."

"But I thought your head was aching."

"Oh, there's nothing wrong with me. You go and have a ride if you like, Horatio. I'm quite comfortable here." Her eyes twinkled.

"I'm happy to hear it, my dear," he said, grinning, and bent and kissed her cheek. "Miss Hawthorne, Miss Curtis," he said, lifting his hat.

"We're going to get something to wear for the ball," said Emeline.

"Oh, yes, the ball," said Mrs. Aldridge. "I confess I'm much looking forward to it. Though in New York I was unused to going out a great deal."

"I know what you mean," said Mrs. Hamilton. "The air in cities can be so stifling, and all the hustle and bustle, people dithering this way and that. I suffer greatly from allergies. That's why my doctor recommended this place to me. And not one sneeze I've had since I've been here!"

"I have been a martyr to suffering as well, Mrs. Hamilton. And the doctors did nothing but tell me to drink this tonic and that one which did nothing but put me to sleep. I never had the slightest energy. My husband threw them out one day and brought me to a new doctor. And *he* suggested we go away to the mountains. I didn't think much of the idea at first, I must confess."

"Doctors do know what they are about once in a while, but not very often," said Mrs. Hamilton.

Emeline and I went downstairs to the shop. I was delighted with the way the two ladies had dealt with Mr. Robinson, and the sudden shift in my spirits left me feeling giddy and exhilarated. That is the only way I can explain my decision to buy what was really a most expensive and unsuitable gown for a teacher, but as soon as I saw it I knew I must try it on, and once I had tried it on, I needed no inducement in purchasing it.

The gown was of shell-pink moiré, with only the feeblest excuses for sleeves in the shapes of narrow little bows which fastened on the shoulders. The neckline was cut daringly low, and the waist tightly fitted. The trailing hem was flounced in a ruched fabric of the same delectable shade. As I looked in the mirror, I thought I looked totally unlike myself.

"I'll take it," I said, and counted out the money in my purse with bravado.

"I can't wait until I can wear one like that," said Emeline wistfully, and I did wonder for a moment whether perhaps another gown . . . But no. I might never have another occasion to wear such a gown and I was not going to be prudent.

Emeline tried on five or six dresses before eventually deciding on one of eyelet lace with full sleeves to the elbow and a demure embroidered neckline. She bought a new, wide ribbon to wear in her hair and a new pair of lace gloves. Recklessly I purchased a pair of gloves as well, white calfskin ones which came halfway up my arms.

In the course of the next couple of days we spent little time at the hotel. I knew the police were still about; a surgeon had performed an autopsy on Mr. Willoughby's body and found a high level of alcohol in his blood. Mr. Robinson wrote an article for the Boston *Globe* in a vein similar to the one in the New York *Journal*, but in Robinson's article the convincing note was gone and it was evident he had come up with nothing new. "Beating a dead horse," said Mrs. Hamilton.

On the evening of the ball, the clouds began to swell and roll across the dusky blue sky. None of the guests, to my knowledge, had departed before schedule. Charlotte told me that Drake had received a couple of cancellations for the end of September, but not enough to count. Circumstances could have been far worse.

I poured a few drops of lily-of-the-valley scent into my bath water before bathing and dressing in my new gown. I had to ring for one of the maids to help me fasten the satin buttons in the back, something which made me slightly uncomfortable as I was used to waiting on myself. But the look on the woman's face when she saw me set me at ease.

"Oh, Miss Hawthorne, how beautiful you look! I was just helping Miss Emeline to dress, and she told me about your new gown. The gentlemen will be turning their heads to look at you tonight, there's not a doubt of it. Now don't color up. You must know what you look like in that gown. Won't Mrs. Curtis be cast in the shade! Always actin' as though she don't have a grown daughter!"

A little later Emeline, Charlotte, and I walked through the trees and across the sweeping lawn, damp with dew, to the hotel. The clouds were massive and dark, tumbling across the mountains. From far off in the distance came the faint rumbling of thunder. High up the tree branches rustled and swayed.

But from the opalescent Crystal Hills Hotel, a thousand lights glimmered in the deepening dusk. The French doors of the ballroom were opened onto the long porch, and the strains of a lilting Strauss waltz floated on the night air. I was suddenly both unbearably excited and unbearably nervous. What on earth had come over me that I had chosen so daring, so unsuitable a gown? It left very little to the imagination. And if Drake did not take notice I did not know what I would do.

The ball had already begun. Dancers spun in graceful turns; jewels glittered around white throats; chandeliers flickered in the slight breeze from the opened French doors. At one end of the room a long table was set with food and drink—strawberries floating in glasses of champagne, finger sandwiches and cookies pressed into shapes of hearts and stars, a lacy coconut cake in three tiers.

Charlotte moved away to join several of the older ladies while Emeline and I stood drinking in the sight of the festive room, the twirling dancers in their beautiful attire.

"This is just the way it used to be," said Emeline softly, "when I used to creep out of the house and watch."

I smiled at her and was about to reply when Aaron Curtis came up to us. "So it *is* you, Miss Hawthorne."

"Of course it's she," said Emeline. "Didn't you recognize her in her new gown, Papa?"

"I should recognize Miss Hawthorne anywhere, Emmie." His bold gaze rested on my bare skin and he took my hand in his. Highly uncomfortable, I pretended to be interested in the conversation of the people next to us.

"You must waltz with me, Miss Hawthorne," continued Aaron. "Privilege of the proprietor, you know." His starched collar was tight about his neck, giving him a rather pink puffed look.

"Perhaps . . . your daughter," I began, and he answered heartily, "Yes, Emeline must promise me a waltz as well. But just now I'm going to dance with you. You're not here as the child's tutor tonight, you know. You're here to enjoy yourself."

But not with you, I wanted to say. Instead he pulled me into the throng of dancers and was twirling me about on the floor. His large hand was tight about my waist, his fingers pressing into the thin fabric of my gown. His eyes lingered on my shoulders and throat greedily.

"You have been working too hard, Miss Hawthorne," he said.

"Not at all, sir," I said stiffly. "I enjoy tutoring Emeline. You have a wonderful daughter, Mr. Curtis." Which you'd know if you bothered to spend the slightest bit of time with her.

"Now, not that formal 'Mr. Curtis.' We're all one family here, you know. My name is Aaron."

I said nothing, staring over his shoulder, praying the waltz would soon come to an end. I caught sight of Leonora dancing with Grant Schyler. Our eyes met; she looked at me in her husband's arms, arched her brows, and smiled. The nature of the smile made the color rise in my face; I wanted to slap her.

Aaron was holding me closer, pressing my body to his. His head leaned over to mine. "You look very beautiful tonight, Teresa. I am a sincere admirer of yours, you know. And I could make your position here very pleasant, if you'd let me." His breath was hot on my neck.

There was no mistaking his meaning. Wildly I glanced about, turning my head away from his, and I felt his fingers moving above my waist. I felt hot and cold all at once; my corset stays were unbearably tight.

"You're trembling, Teresa," he said.

"I—I think I should sit down," I said feebly.

"Nonsense—the evening's barely begun, my dear," he said, and then he added in a different tone, "unless you mean you'd like to go somewhere where—"

Suddenly he was stopped in mid-turn, a hand on his shoulder. In relief I realized that the room had ceased to whirl and Aaron's clasp had loosened.

"Sorry, old man," said Drake ironically, "but Miss Hawthorne is promised to me."

"You—you can't waltz!" said Aaron belligerently.

"No, but I can procure the lady a glass of champagne and something to eat. She looks rather in need of, er, restoration. You do have a curious effect on women, Aaron."

He took me from Aaron's grasp and ushered me through the crowd of dancers. I stole a glance at him. He was very handsome in black, the white points of his collar setting off his dark good looks. When we reached the end of the room he said, still holding my hand, "As much as I'd like to, I can scarcely blame Aaron. You are the most beautiful woman in the room, you know. And all of the men are aware of that. But I can't let you dance with any of them. Do you mind, Tessa?"

Flushing, I smiled and shook my head. The evening had begun again, wonderfully, and I was so happy I had chosen a new gown. Drake brought over two filled plates and glasses of champagne. I have no idea what I ate or what the food tasted like; I could think of nothing but the man beside me. He was not the grim stranger I had met in Portsmouth, but a carefree, teasing host with blue eyes whose warm, lingering gaze reminded me not at all of Aaron's. The glorious music swirled about us; we could not have enjoyed it more had we been dancing.

"The police have concluded their investigation," he said. "They have decided it was accidental death."

"Oh, Drake, I'm so relieved. What about Mr. Robinson?"

"He took off as well," he said, grinning, "with his tail between his legs. I don't suppose we'll hear any more from the *Globe*."

"You should have been there the other day to see Mrs. Hamilton and Mrs. Aldridge put him in his place," I said. "You'd have kissed them."

"You're the only one I want to kiss, Tessa," he said softly. "Come on, let's get out of here. I want you all to myself."

He took my arm and guided me out of the crowded room. A sudden clap of thunder sounded above the orchestra. In the lobby Leonora was drinking champagne with Grant Schyler. Drake ignored them, leading me across the carpet to the front door.

"I see you've spoiled Aaron's evening, Drake," said Leonora's mocking voice. "It was clear he had other ideas for Miss Hawthorne. I never would have guessed that our little schoolmarm could look the way she does tonight. Shouldn't she be chaperoning Emeline? That is her purpose here, isn't it?"

"One of them," said Drake silkily.

"Not that I blame you, Miss Hawthorne," said Leonora. "Drake is a better specimen than Aaron—at least he used to be."

"You can't provoke me tonight, Leonora, so you may as well save your breath."

"How disappointing. I was so hoping for another of our comfortable little chats."

"Is that why you notified the papers of Willoughby's death?" asked Drake, but there was no malice in his voice.

There was another clap of thunder, followed by the roaring and whistling of the wind.

"Oh, I didn't do that, Drake. Although it's flattering of you to think so," said Leonora.

Drake shrugged. "Say what you like. Robinson has given up and gone back to Boston. Your little plan failed, Leonora. Though why on earth you'd put the hotel at risk just to get back at me—it's your bread and butter as well."

Lightning flashed outside; the night sky was lit eerily before subsiding into blackness again. "Let's go, Drake," I said, "before the storm breaks."

As we were on our way out the door we heard Grant Schyler's crisp voice. "*I* sent the wire, Curtis. Two, in fact. One to the *Globe*, one to the *Journal*."

Drake dropped my arm and turned around. "You," he said, his black brows drawn together.

Outside the rain began to pour, lashing at the windows, striking the porch like hundreds of tiny hammers.

"You see, I'm going to ruin you, Curtis," said Grant Schyler, his gold tooth flashing.

The two men gazed across the room at each other. Then Drake said very softly, "Get out. Get out of my hotel."

"I wouldn't talk to Grant like that if I were you, Drake," said Leonora, her lips curved.

"You heard me, Schyler," said Drake. "I've put up with your presence for long enough. But tonight is the end."

"How well you put that," said Leonora.

Schyler made no move to leave. He continued to regard Drake with bland amusement.

"Do I have to send for Burrows?" asked Drake.

"He'd find himself without a job if he did that," said Leonora.

"What are you talking about, Leonora?" Drake asked savagely.

"Haven't you figured it out yet, brother-in-law? Isn't it clear to you yet? God, this is better than I thought it would be!"

"We may as well tell him, my dear," said Grant Schyler, taking a gold cigar case out of his breast pocket. "You see, Curtis, I am the Hudson Lending Company. So you see, throwing me out would not be in your best interests. I own this hotel, in a manner of speaking. I bought the mortgage your brother so fortuitously took out at the Portsmouth bank. And I promise you, my boy, that if the payments are not made

289

precisely on the first day of the month, I will take immediate possession. Forgive the melodrama, Curtis, but I am going to ruin you, and take immense pleasure in doing so."

"What a scene!" cried Leonora, choking with laughter. "I couldn't have written it better myself."

The rain battered at the long windows; the wind moaned and gusted. Drake stood rooted to the spot, his face sickly white, his eyes blazing.

"So that's why you've come," he said hoarsely.

"That is why I've come," said Grant Schyler.

Chapter Fifteen

The moment seemed frozen in time, the four of us caught and held together while outside the storm howled and raged. Grant Schyler, his mask of nonchalance gone to reveal his malignant hatred; Leonora, jeeringly triumphant; myself, helpless, stricken; Drake, carved into stone, incredulous. Then suddenly the moment was broken; Drake spun about and stumbled toward the door. He was outside before I could react. Without a backward glance at the other two, I rushed out into the storm, hurrying down the steps of the porch, nearly falling as I did so for they were slippery with wet. I was drenched in a matter of seconds, my gown clinging to my wet skin, the hem dragging along the soaked ground. At first I did not see Drake, and then the lightning came again and the black sky flashed pearly-gray to reveal the brooding heights of Nightshade Notch, and the man I loved.

Catching up to him, I gripped his arm but did not know what to say.

"Go back to the hotel," he said, but there was no force in his voice, just a bleak emptiness which chilled me to the bone.

He was limping noticeably; I held onto his arm as we penetrated the thin stretch of woods. The narrow trees bobbed back and forth like buoys, the torn leaves spinning wildly before the downpour pelted them to the ground. We came round the side of the house and through the front door. The house was silent; the servants had finished their duties and retired; the rest of the household was still at the ball. *Emeline,* I thought. I had left her there; she should be in bed by now.

Drake had closed the heavy front door; water dripped from our sodden clothes onto the flagged stone floor. He limped toward the stairway.

"Where are you going?"

"To get out of these damn wet clothes. You had better do the same."

When we had reached the gallery, I said desperately, "He hasn't won yet, Drake."

He turned on me, snarling, "Oh, yes, he has. It's all been for nothing, can't you see that? Everything . . . and for nothing. It's finished. I can't go on fighting, holding it all together with sheer willpower for an interminable time. And he can. All the while he has been there . . . waiting. And doing more than that, if I know him. He'll find ways to squeeze us so that I won't be able to make the payments. Or he'll try again to see that business falls off."

"You'll think of something, Drake, you must. You've already overcome so much—"

"And I can't go on, Teresa. Willoughby was disposed of— poor bastard—and for nothing. Schyler means to destroy me. And all because he was publicly humiliated when it came out that his wife had been my mistress. This is not some sort of revenge for her death—he cared little enough for her. And so, God help me, did I. She's the center of this thing, yet it's not really about her. It's the devil's own jest! No, it's because the proud name of Schyler was dragged through the mud."

"Oh, Drake—"

"You must leave here tomorrow, Teresa," he said, his face granitelike, implacable.

"No!"

"You're leaving if I have to carry you out and put you on a train myself! I'll give you some money. And to think that earlier tonight I was going to . . ." He broke off, his face hardening, tinged with color. "But that scarcely matters now. You'll leave tomorrow."

"I won't, you know," I said stubbornly. "There's Emeline to think of."

"I won't have you here when he takes possession!"

"That may not happen, Drake. You must not give up! We—we all depend on you; we all have faith in you!"

"Am I a sort of Providence then? If so, God help me!"

"You can fight him, Drake. It's still your hotel," I said. I was shivering, my teeth beginning to chatter.

"You'll make yourself ill," he said more calmly. "Go and take off those wet things. I won't have you sick with pneumonia on top of everything else."

I hesitated, hating to leave him. I had never seen him so low in spirits, so *beaten*. I was helpless against his wall of despair. There was no telling what he might do, driven to desperation as he was.

"Well, what are you waiting for?" he asked, scowling.

"I—I love you, Drake," I said.

He had been frowning, his face unapproachable, his frame unyielding. But at that he slackened, groaning, and seized me, pulling me against him. His mouth came down hard on mine, searching, demanding, as though he desperately sought something to ease his pain, his misfortune, in me. Through my drenched gown I was conscious of every part of his taut, hard body, his heart pounding, shuddering into my damp skin. His fingers raked through my tumbled hair, tilting back my head, his lips scorching a trail across my jaw to my earlobes and down to where a pulse beat wildly in my throat. I clung to him, trembling, my bare flesh on fire, my legs giving way beneath me. Swiftly he scooped me up and carried me into my bedroom, closing the door behind us.

I was beyond stopping him, beyond embarrassment or shame. Every pulse in my body throbbed for him; every pore in my flesh longed to be heated by his tongue. He carried me across to the bed, stumbling slightly, his cheek against my hair, his hands gripping where he held me.

He set me on the bed and I reached up, drawing him to me, my mouth eager, my body aching. He stretched out on top of me and I found a delicious warmth in the pressure of his body. His arms were about me, his lips devoured mine. I caressed the back of his neck with my fingers, straining against him, wanting to cry out my love over and over had his mouth not stifled any sounds mine could make.

His hands were unfastening the buttons of my gown until he was able to slip it off my shoulders and wrench it downwards. I began to shiver again as the cool air washed over my nakedness, but then his mouth had resumed its burning onslaught on my flesh and my shivers became those of another kind.

"Tessa," he said hoarsely, his breathing ragged, his hand stroking my breast, his rough fingers kneading its smooth roundness. "I've wanted so long to do this—to have you like this. Every night I've dreamed of it, every day I've been tormented—I've wanted you so desperately. That time at the Flume—I thought you hated me—I cursed myself for once again losing control with you. . . ."

"I've wanted you too," I whispered, "even though I knew that I shouldn't, that it was wrong."

"There's nothing wrong between us, Tessa," he said seriously. "Whatever else comes, this was meant to happen."

I gasped as he took a nipple in his mouth. My nails clawed at the bedclothes, my need for him now overwhelming. When he removed his shirt and trousers and covered my body with his own, there was no longer anything between his steely hardness and my own pliant, trembling body. And there was no more cold or damp, only a rising, throbbing heat, a craving which I did not attempt to understand.

Caressing his broad shoulders, I lifted my head from the pillow to kiss his chest, to rub my cheeks against his matted black hair.

He groaned, gathering me tightly in his arms. "Do you know what you are doing to me, Tessa? I—I can't hold back any longer. I must—have you."

"Then take me," I said, aware of nothing else but our need for each other. "Don't hold back."

His raw nakedness pushed between my legs, parting my thighs, and then I felt the desperate urgency of his manhood entering me, filling me . . . I cried out in pain and confusion, but there was no stopping him now. His mouth came down on mine, stifling my moans, distracting me from the rough, searing hurt inside me. Still I pushed at his shoulders, trying to break away, to separate from him. But there was no dividing us, for I could not tell where he ended and I began, nor could I identify what was a part of him or a part of myself. We had become one another, and my body was as much his as my own, as his was mine.

And then he spoke one word, "Tessa," before suddenly he powerfully stiffened in a series of spasms, his weight bearing me down into the bedclothes, his arms crushing me to him until I was gasping for breath. He cried out again and again before collapsing against me, his cheek pressed to mine, his breathing slowing and deepening.

My eyes were closed; my cheek felt chafed from the roughness of his.

"Teresa?" came his voice, uncertain, barely above a whisper.

I opened my eyes.

"I'm sorry I hurt you. I should have warned you—it generally does the first time." He kissed my brow and eyelids, nuzzling against me. "Forgive me?"

"I think the storm has stopped," I said.

"Has it? I confess I'd forgotten the storm."

"I—I think you'd better go, Drake. Anyone could knock on the door—Charlotte—Emeline. They'll be back anytime. Even now they may be returning, suspecting. . . ." I covered my face with my hands.

He took my hands in his. "It's all right, Tessa. We've done nothing wrong."

I turned my face away. "And I suppose you think you did nothing wrong with all those other women," I blurted out, a break in my voice.

"Don't say that," he said harshly. "This was nothing like that. Don't compare yourself to them!"

"Why not?"

"Because they were—nothing like you. There was no love, no wonder. . . . But I'm not going to spoil this by talking about the past. Kiss me. . . ."

"No, Drake. You—you must go. Before anyone hears or suspects . . ." My voice was hard. I drew the sheet over me. "Go, please!"

He sighed heavily. "All right, I'll go. But you're not going to turn away from me now, Teresa. I won't let you. We'll talk in the morning."

From below came the sound of a door opening. "For God's sake, Drake, get out!" I whispered frantically. "Just get out!"

He hesitated, frowning, before reaching for his trousers and pulling them on. Then he grabbed his other clothes and padded softly across the room in his bare feet. Before letting himself out the door, he threw me a meaningful glance, but I ignored him, steeling myself for the sound of voices or footsteps. When I heard Drake's door shut down the hall and realized our secret was miraculously safe, I curled up in a ball, hugging my arms across my breast. My relief was short-lived, though. Overcome with a sudden wave of shame, I began to cry. The only response was the melancholy voice of the wind.

I awoke at dawn, the forlorn gray light filtering into the room. For an instant in half-sleep, I sighed and stretched in remembered pleasure before the oppressive feeling of remorse came over me and I recalled with red-faced clarity the events of the previous night.

I had given myself to Drake out of love and as a means of solace. Perhaps he had been right when he had claimed such an act on our part to be inevitable, even destined, but I could not remain here to repeat it again and again. I would not live here as his mistress in the house of his family. My own life had become increasingly entangled with the people and events at Nightshade Notch. It was time that I broke free. The previous night had made that now inevitable.

I had no idea what I would say to Emeline; she would think I was deserting her. But she was no longer at Miss Winslow's Academy. She was at home and happy.

My fingers shook as I buttoned my most prim blouse. Glancing into the mirror, I noticed my cheeks were flushed, my lips rosy, my eyes that bayberry shade they sometimes took on. With a shock I saw a red mark near my throat, and recalled the pressure of Drake's mouth, of his teeth and tongue. Hastily I fastened the collar of my blouse, shielding it from sight. When I turned away from the mirror, I saw the shell-pink taffeta gown lying in a pale, shimmering heap on the floor. Quickly I stuffed it into the wardrobe, thinking I would leave it for Emeline. I never wanted to wear it again. Swiftly I packed my things in my bags, cast a tear-blurred glance about the room, and slipped out softly into the corridor.

I crept downstairs, realizing that I would have to walk to the station. Perhaps it would be better if I left without speaking to Emeline. I needed no entreaties to stay. I could write her a note, craven though that was. Setting down my bag, I stepped across the hallway and into the library.

And then I caught my breath because Drake was there before me, seated at the desk. He was frowning slightly, staring off into space, but he looked over and saw me in the doorway. In spite of myself my heart fluttered at the sight of him.

"I was just going to come in search of you," he said with a smile, rising. "Although I was afraid that you had locked your door and might refuse to let me in." There was a warm glint in his eyes.

Flushing, I said, "Drake, I—I'm leaving. Today. Now. I was going to leave Emeline a note."

His black brows drew together as he came round the desk. "Leaving? What are you talking about?"

"I have to. It's—it's for the best. Last night . . ." I looked away from him, hot color flooding my face.

"So you want to leave me, just when I need you the most."

My eyes lifted to his narrowed ones. "You don't need me, except perhaps as a—"

"Damn you, Teresa, I won't let you leave."

"You were determined to send me away last night."

"I was a fool. And that was before . . ."

"Yes, it was, wasn't it?" I said bitterly.

He reached out and drew me to him. "Oh, darling, you're being foolish. I won't lose you." Without another word he kissed me, first with tenderness, then with a rising passion and fervor.

"Well, so this is what the two of you get up to alone," said a voice behind us.

Drake released me and I whirled around. Leonora stood in the doorway wearing a pink ruffled dressing gown. "Isn't it a bit early in the morning for this sort of thing—or are you only continuing what happened last night?"

Her question was so to the mark that I flushed to the roots of my hair.

"Emeline came to me last night, wondering where you were, Miss Hawthorne. She was quite concerned. You were to see that she stayed for part of the evening and then that she went to bed. But then it's apparent that you think little of her and even less of your responsibilities. Drake brought you here for his own purposes, that's certain."

"That's the pot calling the kettle black, isn't it, Leonora?" asked Drake silkily. "After all, whose desires have you been satisfying lately? Not Aaron's, I'll warrant. You set a fine example for your daughter to follow."

Her eyes flashed angrily. "That's none of your business. But Little Miss Tutor here is going to go. I won't have Emeline under her supervision any longer. She leaves today."

My gaze met hers without flinching. "I *am* leaving today, Mrs. Curtis, but of my own accord. Not because you are sending me away. And after I've collected my wages."

"Wages for what—tutoring Emeline, or something else entirely? This whole thing has been a charade from the first. The sweet and pure Miss Hawthorne. Well, if I'm not mistaken, she's a little bit sullied this morning. Oh, I do believe I've struck a nerve. And it wasn't much more than a shot in the dark, you know."

"Shut your filthy mouth, Leonora," said Drake. "Teresa is not leaving. Because she is going to marry me."

"*What?*" she cried while I gazed at him, bemused.

"That's right. We were just discussing it when you so rudely interrupted."

"Drake, you can't be serious! You—marry—this little nobody! I recall the days when you vowed never to be married at all!"

His face tightened. "I recall those days as well, God help me. But I didn't exactly have good examples to follow, not in this house."

"Have you lost your senses? Whatever you've done, you don't need to offer her marriage! Just give her some money and let her go!"

"Do you know, Leonora, you revolt me? I think I am just coming to my senses. But I'm certainly not going to discuss the matter with you, dear sister-in-law."

Her eyes narrowed. "You were never a fool, Drake, no matter what you did. And I would think that if you felt inclined to marry anyone, it would be an heiress—someone who could do something for that doomed hotel. You've had enough of them thrown in your way these last months." She turned to me. "Well, Miss Hawthorne, you may think you've done very well for yourself. But if the hotel goes, he will have nothing. You'll be penniless and married to a failed man. And you, Drake, will have a dead weight round your neck. Grant Schyler is a very determined man, you know. I wouldn't underestimate him." Turning on her heel she walked away, her high heels clicking across the stone floor.

"She's right, you know," said Drake. "If the Crystal Hills goes, we'll have to start from scratch. Are you willing to risk a future with me?"

"If we do start from scratch, I won't be going anywhere I've not been before," I said. "Oh, yes, Drake, yes!" I threw myself into his arms.

"Together we'll fight for the hotel," he said, holding me tightly to him. "Grant Schyler won't get his hands on it, not if I can prevent it. But I can't do it alone, Tessa. I can't do it without you."

"You won't have to, Drake," I assured him.

Still, in my glowing happiness, I could not suppress a vague feeling of misgiving. His proposal had been so sudden, so unexpected. Was he motivated to marry me more out of an obligation than out of love? Did he feel it was the honorable thing to do because of last night? But I could not ask him—I was afraid of the answer. It was true that I could bring nothing to the marriage, no dowry, no funds to put into the hotel. Yet he still wanted to marry me. He *must* love me, I told myself. But he had never spoken of marriage until today. . . .

Later that afternoon I had discarded my blouse and skirt for my gown of ivory muslin, allowed my hair to fall in streams of tight curls, and was standing beside Drake in one of the parlors on the first floor of the Crystal Hills. Charlotte and Emeline were there to see us married; we had wanted no one else. I could see the local minister considered it a hasty affair, but I put aside my doubts for the time being and joyfully clutched a bouquet of lavender Michaelmas daisies and white roses that Emeline had picked for me. When Drake slipped a gold ring on my finger, Madeline Curtis's ring, I thought of her portrait in the lobby, and hoped that she would have approved.

After the ceremony we drank champagne and had some of a cake that the chef had prepared that day. Charlotte kissed me with tears in her eyes. "It's the best thing that could have happened," she said, "to both of you."

And Emeline said, grinning, "I had a feeling about you and Uncle Drake. Now you'll never go away, Teresa, and everything will be wonderful."

"Can you foretell the future?" I asked, laughing. "Like Bridget and her tea leaves?" Suddenly I frowned. I had not thought of that scene in the kitchen at Miss Winslow's in months. The tea leaves . . . what on earth was it that Bridget had babbled out that night? A cave, and rushing water, and— danger.

"Oh, Teresa, your glove," said Emeline. "It's got blood on it."

Looking down, I saw that I had pricked my finger on a thorn.

In the lobby we came across Horatio Aldridge, reading a newspaper. Drake told him our news and he grinned, clasping Drake's hand and clapping him on the back. "Capital news! May I be permitted to wish you the very best life has to offer, Mrs. Curtis? I confess I envy you both living here year-round. I'm sorry to say that my wife and I will have to return to New York before long, and I'm not looking forward to leaving this splendid country."

"You must return to Nightshade Notch next summer," I said, smiling.

"Indeed we must. This place has done wonders for Mrs. Aldridge's health. She is dreading our departure as well. She will be delighted with your news. We must get in at least one more day of hard riding and climbing, Major, before I leave."

"I look forward to it," said Drake.

"Now, if you'll excuse me, I must go dress for dinner. Again, best wishes to you, Mrs. Curtis, and congratulations to you, sir."

"Are many of the guests leaving now that it's September?" I asked Drake when Mr. Aldridge had gone.

"A number of them. But we have a good sum of reservations for the next couple of months. With this fashionable new pastime of vacationing in the fall to see the leaves turning, we are bound to do well. That is, if . . ." He broke off, his face hardening.

"Don't worry, Drake. I feel confident that everything will work out."

But my mood of cheerful bravado was slightly pierced when we went into the dining room and I saw Grant Schyler taking his seat at a nearby table. When my eyes met his, he bowed with marked urbanity, flashing his gold tooth in a sudden ironic smile. I turned away.

Aaron slapped Drake on the back. "Drake, you sly devil! You've kept this pretty quiet! What is this about you marrying Miss Hawthorne? And you didn't ask me to stand up for you! Well, I won't take offense. You're a lucky devil, you know. And so am I, with such a pretty sister-in-law!" He bent and kissed my cheek, squeezing my hand in his.

Leonora said scathingly, "You're probably the last person Drake would have for best man, Aaron, especially if he were aware of your latest financial debacle." We had sat down at the table. I wanted nothing less than to be seated with Aaron and Leonora, but they had followed us to a table. Drake shot Leonora a swift, keen look.

Aaron reddened angrily, glancing at Drake. "Just shut up, Leonora. You don't know what you're talking about. No one but me and—"

"Oh, yes, I do. Grant told me himself. And it's a rather fitting wedding present for Drake, I must say." Leonora looked from one man to another, her lips curved derisively.

"What does she mean, Aaron?" asked Drake quietly.

"Let's talk about whatever it is later, shall we?" said Charlotte nervously. "This is supposed to be a wedding dinner, you know, hardly the time to discuss financial affairs."

"If I were you, Teresa, I would consider myself very ill-used," said Leonora. "No honeymoon, and a paltry dinner. A poor way to begin married life!"

"I couldn't be happier, Leonora," I said deliberately.

"Isn't that sweet? Well, I hate to burst your bubble, both of you, but I think, Drake, you should insist Aaron inform you of his losses."

"Damn you, Nora!" cried Aaron.

Drake's black brows drew together. "What losses?"

"Nothing—forget it," mumbled Aaron.

"What losses?"

"Oh, if you must know, I've been playing poker with Schyler—that's all. And I haven't won every time." He laughed forcibly.

"Have you won at all?"

"Well, you know how it is. I daresay I've won a bit here and there, but . . ."

"Well, I hope you can come up with the money, Aaron," said Drake coolly. "Somehow I doubt whether Schyler will wait."

"You—you can't say you won't agree to meet my losses, Drake," Aaron blustered. "Affair of honor, you know. Must pay one's debts."

"I had your word of honor that you wouldn't gamble anymore, Aaron. As you seem to take honor so lightly, I hardly see why you trouble yourself about the necessity of paying Schyler."

"I must pay him, Drake," said Aaron, red-faced. "And you must advance me the money. I swear it'll be for the last time."

"I have no intention of doing any such thing, Aaron. Have you conveniently forgotten that your unfortunate habit has placed us in the position of owing Schyler a large sum of money—a share in the hotel, in fact? If I find you make any attempt whatsoever to take money from the hotel, I will bring a suit against you for forging my name. I trust I make myself clear."

Aaron turned to his wife furiously. "Damn you, Nora! You had to tell him tonight, didn't you? You've a damn poisonous tongue."

"What better day than his wedding day? I assume he'd be in

a more mellow, more receptive mood than usual. Don't blame me if he's not—I'd say it's Teresa who's at fault. Perhaps he's already regretting marrying her." She gave a light laugh. "You know what they say. Marry at haste, repent at leisure."

"Really, Leonora, this is most uncalled for!" cried Charlotte.

"Are you speaking from experience, Leonora? The only thing I do *not* regret is my marriage to Teresa. But I do regret not sending the two of you packing when I returned from Portsmouth after learning Aaron had forged my name on a mortgage contract. I should have kicked you both out then."

Leonora's fork clattered to the plate. She rose from the table, her eyes sparkling with malice. "You make me sick, Drake Curtis!" she said, not bothering to lower her voice. "That *you* of all people should criticize us, with your past, your—"

"Leonora, for God's sake, be quiet!" pleaded Charlotte in anguish, her hand trembling at her throat. "Don't—don't say any more!"

Leonora ignored her. "You always talk so self-righteously about our conduct, Drake, our habits. Well, I'd like to remind you of your particular habit. No, I don't mean his former weakness for married women, Teresa. You know all about that—and you've decided it doesn't matter. How touching. But I'm willing to give very good odds that she doesn't know about your other dark little secret, Drake. You've taken care to conceal that from her, haven't you, brother-in-law?"

Drake stood up, his hands gripping the table, his knuckles white. "So help me, Leonora, one more word and I'll kill you!"

I looked from one of them to the other in horror.

She went on jeeringly, "'The Pride of New Hampshire,' they called you! 'Our Very Own Rough Rider.' If they had only known then what a tremendous joke it was! What their very own Rough Rider had been reduced to! A low, common drug-fiend. Yes, Teresa, that's what I said. The man you adore came home last December a trembling wreck, a slave to morphine! The 'Army disease,' I believe they call it. You would scarcely have recognized him. He was discharged from the Army hospital with a supply of the stuff. He may have disposed of it all, but I should think the craving never goes away. So, you see, Mrs. Curtis, it's only right that you should know that the years ahead may not be what you've imagined, what you've dreamed in your starlit dreams."

Drake lunged across the table, his features transformed by raging hatred, and seized Leonora, a hand going about her white throat. She gave a strangled cry, her eyes bulging in terror.

Charlotte cried, horrified, "Drake, stop! Let her go! Think about what you're doing, where you are!"

Gradually the mad light dimmed from his eyes; he flung Leonora away so that she fell against the table. His square jaw was clenched, a muscle jerking in his cheek. With dismay I realized that many in the room had witnessed the ugly scene and were gazing in our direction, appalled.

Drake did not look at me. He limped from the room.

"Leonora, how could you!" cried Charlotte, tears running down her face. "I never thought that even you could be so . . . so pitiless, so sadistic." She wiped her cheeks with her handkerchief. "You've gone too far this time, Leonora. Most people, I'm sure you'll agree, have skeletons in their closet, things they wish to conceal from others. We all have them, don't we?"

"Oh, what do I care for that?" said Leonora carelessly. "It does not matter a jot now, I tell you, if it ever did. You can't hold it over my head any longer. Not that you've ever had any proof."

"Proof of what?" asked Aaron, puzzled.

"I—I must find Drake," I whispered to Emeline. "Stay with Charlotte." And I fled from the room.

He was not in the lobby, and when I rushed out the front door, it was just in time to see him fling himself on a black horse and bolt off furiously, horse and rider fast becoming a dark speck in the distance as I watched.

"I had merely exchanged one nightmare for another," he had said. I remembered coming across his uniform and discharge papers in the trunk in the attic. I had been wrong when I had thought that his suit of clothes had not been through a battle. They had been through the worst, and with no weapons but his own courage and pride to sustain him. He had emerged the victor, but by no means was he unscathed, unscarred.

"Teresa, dear child, let's return to the house," Charlotte said, coming from behind and taking my arm. "I've left Emeline with Miss Birche—they're going to listen to a poetry reading tonight. She'll be all right. And don't worry about Drake. He'll be back. He just—it was terrible you finding out that way. Leonora is the most evil creature. . . .

"When Drake was let out of the hospital, his leg was still causing him a lot of pain. The doctors had relieved it with morphine injections in the field hospital, when he hadn't the strength or the will to stop them. And very soon . . . well, his body became used to the drug. Soon after he was home, he refused to continue using it, and he suffered through a most horrible ordeal. I don't believe you or I could imagine the agonies he suffered. But he recovered through tremendous willpower and determination. And during that time, Aaron was off mortgaging the hotel, forging Drake's signature! Truly, I do not see how we can go on like this. There is so much hatred, so much vindictiveness. I'm afraid."

With concern I noticed that her slight body was shaking, her face was unhealthily pale. "Come, Charlotte, we'll go back to the house. And then you're going to go to bed. I'll see that the maid brings up some hot milk. You must rest. And don't worry about Drake. I will make him see that it doesn't matter."

I saw her tucked into bed and then went to my room to wait for Drake's return. All evening I strained my ears for the sounds of an arrival, for the crunching of a horse's hooves on the graveled drive, for Drake's heavy footsteps on the stone floor below, or on the stairs.

Emeline came in later and I sat with her for a while before she went to sleep. She was both subdued and confused by the scene at the dinner table, and I took care to reassure her as best I could. But I was feeling wretched, wondering where Drake could be and when he might return.

About midnight I took a hot bath, hoping it would soothe my

305

shattered spirits, but I felt much the same afterwards. Slipping on my nightgown, I crawled beneath the covers. It was some time later when I sat up with a jerk, realizing I was still alone. I had fallen asleep without meaning to. Getting out of bed, I took a candle and slipped out into the corridor, moving quietly down to Drake's room at the end of the hall.

I did not knock; I turned the knob and went in. My gaze flickered over the dark heavy furniture, the old sea chest, the enormous Eastlake bed with its elaborately carved headboard. It was empty.

Drawing a blanket from the bed, I sat down in a chair and wrapped it around me. A fire had been lit hours ago in the hearth, but it was nearly out, and the black night poured in from the abyss outside. I remembered then that this was our wedding night.

When I awoke again, I was not alone. Drake was lighting the gas lamps, his hair wind-blown, his evening clothes disheveled.

"Where have you been, Drake?"

"Nowhere in particular. Why?" There was a peculiar look on his face, and his eyes did not meet mine.

"I've been worried about you. You've been gone so long. And tonight is our wedding night, don't you remember?"

"Our wedding night," he repeated, a flat tone in his voice. "It seems a long time ago since this afternoon." He raked his fingers through his hair. "Go back to bed, Teresa. You look exhausted."

"No, you can't push me away so easily. I love you, Drake, and I don't care anything about your—about what happened at the hospital. And I won't let you care."

"The hospital?"

"You don't have to talk about it if you don't wish to. But I wish you'd give me more credit for understanding. Did you really think, Drake, that my knowing you were once addicted to morphine would have made any difference in the way I feel about you?"

The fierce anger had evidently burned itself out. He was calm, but there was a strange quality to his calmness which puzzled me and filled me with misgiving.

He shrugged. "Perhaps not. But I do know that I would have moved heaven and earth to keep you from finding out, Teresa. I—I was like an animal. It was the lowest form of hell, of degradation. And there were many like me in the field hospital, and later in New York. Men who screamed because of their wounds, and then who later screamed more for the morphine, caring little for those wounds."

He sat down on the bed, pulling off his boots. "They gave me the Medal of Honor, for conspicuous gallantry above and beyond the call of duty, because I had demonstrated a complete disregard for my own safety, as they said. It wasn't gallantry— it was just that reckless, uncaring state I was in. They pinned on the medal and told me I was lucky to be alive. Lucky." His voice was bitter. "Do you know what it's like to have so little control over your own body? To feel so deadly sick that your body craves the very poison that caused the sickness in the first place? To lie awake at night in terror, knowing there is no reason for that terror. And to know that all of it—the pain, the terror, the anxiety—can be swiftly allayed by one small injection that takes only a few seconds. But knowing you must fight all alone, fight the fear and pain and the ferocious longing, fight your way back to being human, although it's nearly impossible to recall what being human is like, and how it feels."

"But you did fight your way back, Drake! You're free of it!"

He said nothing, shrugging off his creased dinner jacket and loosening his shirt collar. "I still have the dreams," he said quietly, staring off into space, "not as often, but once in a while."

"The dreams? What do you mean?"

There was a pause. Then he said, "They're always the same, the dreams of a narcotic user. Faces, so many you cannot take them in, faces by the thousands, a vast sea of them, pursuing me, and I flee from them in terror, hiding for what seems like years, alone as no man is ever alone. And then, inevitably, they are all about me, imprisoning me for some dreadful deed, some heinous crime. I endure what seems, in my dreaming state, to be centuries of incarceration, time and space swelled to an

307

indescribable infinity. And I cannot wake up because, you see, I'm not truly asleep, not in the true sense. Opium—morphine—they put one in a twilight sleep, where one part of the mind is wide awake and functioning. Even though I'm free of the drug and have been for months, it crops up again, the same ghastly effect."

"But what is this crime you believe you have committed—why do they seem to pursue you?"

"That part eventually comes. It is she who leads the sea of faces, you see."

"She?"

"Alice. Alice Schyler. Only she resembles a fiend:

> "'Her lips were red, her looks were free,
>   Her locks were yellow as gold:
>   Her skin was as white as leprosy,
>   The Night-mare Life-in-Death was she,
>   Who thicks man's blood with cold.'"

"'The Rime of the Ancient Mariner,'" I said. "I—I don't understand."

"Coleridge was addicted to opium, you see. He knew firsthand the nightmares that a narcotic user suffers. The poem describes it exactly—the evil deed committed by the sailor, the helpless flight, the inescapable persecution, the fiend come to punish, the sense of solitude and desolation on an enormous scale. Nothing in my waking hours could equal that sense of abject misery, of indescribable horror. I knew—I knew I must stop using the drug, just as the one doctor had said, if only to be free of those dreams."

"Oh, Drake, I'm so sorry, so terribly sorry. To know how you've suffered, I almost can't bear it. But everything will be better now, because there are no more secrets, and gradually the dreams will go away. Leonora tried her best to destroy us, to tear us apart. But we cannot let her succeed, Drake. We can't let her win."

"She hasn't won," he said quietly.

"No, because you've talked to me, you haven't turned away, or pushed me away. She tried so hard to—"

"She's dead, Teresa."

"What?" I whispered, appalled. And then, when he did not answer, I managed to say, "Are—are you certain?"

"Quite certain," he said, his voice once again curiously flat. "She was found lying at the foot of the stairs at the Crystal Hills. Her neck is broken."

Chapter Sixteen

For a long while I could not say anything else. My mind played over the scene in the dining room: Leonora's triumphant malevolence as she blurted out Drake's former affliction, his violent response when his hands closed round her bare throat, the scorching hatred in his face. Had she goaded him too far this time? Had he been riding all night and happened to come upon her body at the hotel? Or had he plotted to kill her while riding? Had he himself sent Leonora tumbling down the stairway to lie in a broken, battered heap on the lobby floor? I sat in the chair very calmly, gazing at the intricate pattern of the Oriental carpet by the bed. There was a particular shade of blue which appeared again and again in a crescent. . . .

"What was she doing . . . so late at the hotel?" I finally asked, my voice sounding unnatural.

"I imagine she'd been in Schyler's room," he said shortly. "I scarcely expect him to confide in me, but when the police come I daresay it will all come out."

"The—the police? But why should they come again? It was an accident, wasn't it?"

His black brows drew together. "What else? She always would wear those ridiculous high-heeled shoes. I assume she lost her footing and then could not stop herself from falling."

"It's horrible—horrible," I said, shuddering.

"I think we can count on another police investigation, especially since her death has followed so soon after Ernest Willoughby's."

I had forgotten the little archaeologist. "Mr. Willoughby's death? Why, what does that have to do with—with this? You're not implying there was any connection?"

"Certainly not. But two fatal accidents in less than two weeks will no doubt look odd to the detectives. It won't look well to many of the guests either."

"Do some of them know already?"

"Leonora fell down a flight of stairs, Teresa," he said crisply. "When that happens, there is a great deal of noise. Naturally a few people whose rooms are just off the second-story landing were roused. I came in the front door and walked across the lobby. Upstairs I could hear doors opening, and voices. It was then that I saw her lying at the foot of the stairs."

"Is she—still there?"

"No. I couldn't leave her there. It'll be hours before the police come, and by morning the news will be all over the hotel. I can't help that, but I couldn't leave her there for anyone to see. She—she was not a pretty sight."

"But, Drake," I said sharply, "should you have moved the—the body? Won't the police think that . . . I mean, I always thought one wasn't supposed to touch anything, to disturb the—evidence."

"What are you saying, Teresa?" he asked, his voice suddenly harsh. "Are you implying that by moving her into my office I was attempting to conceal or destroy evidence?"

"N-no. Of course not, Drake. It's just that your doing so may—may look suspicious to Lieutenant Striker, if it is he who comes again."

"I think there is no doubt that it will be he who comes," he said grimly. "But when I picked up Leonora's body and carried it into the office, I wasn't thinking about the police—or whether my actions might look suspicious!"

"No, you were thinking about the hotel—about the guests."

"Damn it, she was lying in the middle of the lobby!"

I bit my lip. "Perhaps they'll understand after all. They'll realize you just had the interests of your guests at heart. Perhaps they won't think anything of it."

"You know they will. And I know it. Damnation!" He

covered his face with his hands.

"At least a few people saw her lying there. At least you didn't carry her away before they realized she was dead, and how she must have died. Then it would only be your word that you had come in and found her there."

He lifted his head. "It is only my word that I entered the hotel by the front door, that I came across her body just prior to a few of the men coming downstairs."

The large knot tightened inside me. "What do you mean, Drake? They didn't see you walking toward the stairs?"

"I mean precisely that they found me kneeling by the body. And then a short while later they watched me carry her across the floor and into the office. At the time I'm certain they were relieved. They wouldn't have wanted their wives or children to stumble across her on their way to breakfast, not with her head twisted halfway round her neck—"

"Don't, Drake! For God's sake!"

"But they will describe what they saw. And I can imagine what our friendly detective is going to make of it."

"What should he make of it? There's nothing to make of it!" But my voice sounded uncertain.

Drake sighed heavily. "I realize now that it's only my word that I had just come in and found her, Teresa. And it's certainly been clear to many people that there was never any love lost between us, to say the least. And Teresa, there's something I haven't told you. One of the men who came downstairs was Grant Schyler."

"Oh, no! He'll say anything! He said he would ruin you, one way or another." I gazed at him with shock and alarm.

Drake ran his fingers through his hair. "Lieutenant Striker's not a fool. Surely he can't imagine that I would have murdered Leonora, no matter how much I disliked her."

"Does Aaron know?"

"No. I tried to rouse him just now. He's in a drunken stupor."

"You don't think that he—"

"No, I do not."

"But it was no secret that she was unfaithful to him, Drake. And she did divulge the truth about his gambling debts to

Grant Schyler."

"That doesn't make him a murderer. Besides, he would have been seen by those who were roused from their beds."

"He may have been hiding somewhere until the hue and cry died down. In a linen closet or—anywhere. And then he could have stolen away, and come back to the house with no one the wiser."

"Nonsense. I tell you he is drunk. I couldn't wake him," he said impatiently.

"He might have gotten drunk just after returning to the house, and passed out quickly. Especially if he'd been drinking all evening. Or he might only have been pretending to be drunk, to be asleep."

"This is ridiculous," Drake said curtly. "Aaron couldn't have done it. He doesn't have what it takes to kill someone."

Do you have what it takes? I wanted to ask. But of course he did; he'd probably killed many men as a Rough Rider.

"He couldn't plan something like that and carry it out. Not only is he a coward, but he would make some mistake and slip up."

"Perhaps he didn't plan it. Perhaps he only meant to confront her with Grant Schyler—perhaps Aaron saw her leaving Schyler's room—"

"And in a fit of rage knocked her down the stairs? I don't think so."

"Well, maybe he didn't mean to kill her. He might have struck her, especially if she said something to anger him—and she lost her balance and fell."

"Why are you so determined to view this as murder, Teresa?" Drake asked coldly, his eyes narrowed.

"I—I'm not," I said, regarding him with dismay.

"Well, you seem most eager to blame someone."

"It's just that you did say—about the police—about Mr. Willoughby's death . . ."

"Willoughby. Yes. And now Leonora," he said, his jaw hard, the cleft marked in his chin.

"Police are naturally suspicious," I said.

It was nearly dawn. Drake's face was pale and haggard in the dim light, as mine likely was. There was nothing more to say. I returned to my room to bathe and dress for the day; Drake was going to do the same before returning to the hotel to await the police. He had sent them a wire after putting Leonora's body in his office.

I would be questioned, of course. All of us who had witnessed the scene between Drake and Leonora the previous night at dinner would be rigorously interrogated. Aaron, Charlotte, myself, Emeline.

Emeline! I had forgotten her. Dear God, her mother was dead and I had to be the one to tell her. And Charlotte would have to be told. And Aaron. As yet, none of them knew. Drake had said he would break the news to Aaron, but it was up to me to tell the other two. Drake had enough on his mind. But whether there was more on his mind than attempting to run a hotel while a second investigation was going on, I could only wonder.

I decided that I would tell Charlotte first, and together we could go to Emeline. Leonora had been a poor mother, but even so, her death could only be a great shock to the child.

Knocking on Charlotte's door, I heard her soft voice telling me to come in. She was sitting up in bed in a lavender ruffled dressing gown, looking frail and tired.

"Good morning, my dear," she said. "I'm afraid I've had breakfast brought up to me this morning. I'm not feeling quite myself."

"I'm sorry, Charlotte. I wish I didn't have to—that is, I'm afraid I have some bad news. Very bad."

"Emeline?" she asked, a hand to her throat.

"No, no, Emeline is asleep. It's Leonora. She fell down the stairs at the Crystal Hills last night."

"She's not—?"

I nodded painfully.

"Oh, merciful heavens, no!" Her eyes were wide with horror, the violet shadows under them deepening. "What—what was she doing at the hotel?"

"Drake thinks she must have been with Grant Schyler."

Charlotte let out a long breath. "Of course. Who found her?"

"Drake did. He—he'd been out riding."

"So we've come to this," she said levelly. "I've felt such dread . . . all these weeks." She was staring into her teacup. "I felt something building . . . something evil."

"I—I wondered whether you'd help me break the news to Emeline, Charlotte. But if you'd rather not . . . I can see you're not at all well. . . ."

"Of course. We must both be there. Not that Leonora was an affectionate mother . . . but to die—violently—like that. Has Aaron been told?"

"I assume Drake has roused him by now and they've gone to the hotel. He couldn't wake him earlier."

"The police will come, of course."

"Yes, Drake wired them hours ago."

She rubbed her brow. "We must tell Emeline now, before she learns it from one of the maids. You can be sure the news is all over the hotel by now, and our servants have doubtless heard of it as well."

She pushed aside her tray and slowly climbed out of bed, wincing slightly. Then the two of us went down the corridor to Emeline's room.

Emeline was sitting up in bed, one of Charlotte's old photograph albums across her lap. "Good morning," she said sleepily.

"I'm afraid we have some bad news for you, darling," said Charlotte.

"Bad news? What is it? You're—you're not going to send me away again, are you? Now that Teresa's married? Because she can't be my tutor any longer?"

"No, Emeline," I answered. "It's nothing like that. It's your mother. I'm afraid that she—that she has had a bad accident."

"An accident?" she repeated, pushing back her spectacles.

"Yes, she fell down the staircase at the hotel last night," I said painfully.

"Is she very badly hurt?"

Charlotte and I exchanged glances. "She's dead, dearest," I said.

"D-dead?" She sounded dazed, lost.

We sat beside her on the bed, each taking one of her hands in ours. "We're so terribly sorry, Emeline," said Charlotte.

315

"She can't be dead. If she's dead, she won't ever see me grown up. When I'm older and prettier. She wants me to be pretty and graceful like she is. She hates my spectacles, and my big hands and feet."

"Oh, Emeline," I said, tears pricking my eyes.

She said nothing for a while, her lip quivering, her hands clenched. "It's just that I wanted her to see me when I'm pretty . . . someday."

"You *are* pretty, Emeline. You have beautiful eyes, and your hair—"

"I know you think I'm pretty, Teresa. Or you always say you do. I just wish she does—did. I was waiting to grow up, hoping she'd like me better. Poor Mamma." She began to cry, burying her face in my shoulder.

It was much later, when the three of us were downstairs in the sitting room drinking cups of tea, when the police came.

"We meet again, ladies," said Lieutenant Striker.

"Would you care for some tea or coffee, Lieutenant?" asked Charlotte.

"No, thank you, Miss Conway. If you and Miss Curtis will excuse us, we'd like to talk to Miss Hawthorne."

The sergeant cleared his throat.

"That's right," said Lieutenant Striker. "It's not Miss Hawthorne any longer, is it? It's Mrs. Curtis."

I said nothing. Charlotte and Emeline left the room. The two detectives sat down in the wing chairs.

"Things happen fairly quickly here, don't they? You and Major Curtis marrying suddenly, two deaths within two weeks," mused Lieutenant Striker.

"How do you know my marriage to Major Curtis was sudden, Lieutenant?"

"Wasn't it?"

I looked away. "I've loved him for a long time."

"That's not precisely the same thing, is it?" He paused. "I want to know when you last saw the deceased."

"It was yesterday evening at dinner."

"You were just married yesterday afternoon, isn't that correct?"

"Yes."

"And so the dinner was a sort of family celebration?"

I said nothing.

"And was it a celebration?"

I looked hard at him. "Lieutenant Striker, you have obviously been talking to others before coming here. So you know very well that there was some—some unpleasantness at the dinner table last night between Leonora and my husband. I see no reason to beat about the bush."

"Tell me about the unpleasantness."

"Don't you know? Hasn't Drake—?"

"I'd like to hear it in your own words, Mrs. Curtis."

"Leonora said some ugly things to me about Drake last night. She didn't exactly approve of our marriage and she wanted to humiliate him."

"What did she say, Mrs. Curtis?"

"She—she brought up old wounds."

"About Alice Schyler?"

"N-no. About the war. That—that he'd become addicted to the morphine the doctors gave him."

"And this was news to you?"

"Yes."

"Your husband had deliberately kept this from you."

"Would you have wanted your wife to know, Lieutenant, if you hoped you could keep it from her?"

"What happened after Mrs. Curtis told you this?"

"Drake left the room, and Leonora went to another table."

"Is that all? Mrs. Curtis, isn't it true that Major Curtis bolted from his chair and seized his sister-in-law by the throat?" His eyes bored into mine.

"He was angry, Lieutenant. He hadn't wanted me to find out, and she'd announced it like that, for all to hear," I said desperately. "He released her almost instantly and left the room."

"Isn't it true, Mrs. Curtis, that your husband threatened to kill Leonora Curtis?"

"He didn't mean it, he was just warning her—trying to shut her up!"

"When did you see your husband again?"

"Sometime in the night, about four or later, I think. I'd

been asleep. . . ."

"You did not see him before then? He did not return before? On his wedding night with his bride waiting for him?"

I colored. "I've told you. He was out all night." Then I realized what I had said. Should I have lied, told them Drake was with me? But he hadn't asked me to. "But that doesn't mean anything. He was upset—he was out riding. He had nothing at all to do with—with Leonora's death."

"But you did not see him until after he found the body, is that correct?"

"Yes," I whispered.

"Let's assume he was riding. Why do you think that afterwards he went back to the hotel, at three in the morning, instead of returning to the house where his new bride waited for him?"

"I—I don't know."

"What did he tell you when he returned to the house?"

"That Leonora was dead. That she'd fallen down the stairs and broken her neck, and that the—the noise had roused a few of the guests. He'd just come in and found her."

"Do you have any idea as to why she was at the Crystal Hills so late?"

"She . . . I believe she was . . . with Grant Schyler. You know who he is, of course."

"Did your husband tell you that Grant Schyler was one of the men who came downstairs last night and saw him kneeling over the body?"

"Y-yes. But I wouldn't believe anything Schyler says, Lieutenant! He hates my husband! He'll say anything to destroy him! He's already promised to do everything he can to hurt business. It was he who sent the story to the newspapers about Ernest Willoughby's death, trying to make it look as though it was something it wasn't."

"Schyler admits she had just left his room a short while before. He claims he heard Mrs. Curtis's voice outside in the hall just after she'd gone out. She was talking to someone— he'd assumed it was one of the servants and so he thought nothing of it. Now he says it may have been your husband she was talking to."

"Of course he'd say that!" I cried furiously.

"Mr. Schyler says your husband was leaning over the body soon after the fall. There may have been another person on the stairs with her, who followed her fall and then made certain she was dead."

"That's ridiculous. Drake had just come in. She had already fallen."

"But no one saw him come in. He stabled the horse himself, and the doorman, Burrows, was off duty. So we just have his word that he came in and discovered Mrs. Curtis lying there."

"You also have just Mr. Schyler's word that he heard Leonora speaking to someone in the hall. And if she did, it still may have been an accident. That person may come forward."

"Perhaps he—or she—will. I understand that Mr. Schyler and a few others saw Major Curtis remove Mrs. Curtis's body and take it into his office."

"Yes. He—he didn't want anyone to be upset seeing her there in the morning. He wasn't certain when you would arrive. . . ."

"Yes, that is what he told us. Do you think that is the real reason, Mrs. Curtis?"

"What other reason could there be?" I asked, my blood running slow and thick.

"Perhaps there were signs on her person that she had been pushed. Signs he had to carefully remove before we came."

"What signs? I know what you are trying to do, Lieutenant Striker. You're trying to find out if I think my husband killed Leonora."

"Would you say that, aside from the scene last night, the relations between your husband and his sister-in-law were friendly?"

"You know, I'm certain, that they were not." I glared at him mutinously.

"Scenes . . . arguments were, in fact, common between them, were they not?"

I said nothing. The sergeant was scratching furiously in his notebook.

"How has Mr. Aaron Curtis acted lately? He must have known or at least suspected that his wife was involved with

319

Grant Schyler."

"I know nothing about what Aaron suspected or knew. But he became very incensed with Leonora last night as well."

"Why was that, Mrs. Curtis?"

"Leonora had taunted him with losing money to Grant Schyler. I don't know how much. Drake had warned him the gambling had to stop, that there was no money to support that type of activity. Leonora knew Drake would be furious and so she made certain that he found out. She was—like that. Mr. Schyler had apparently been her informant."

"And her own husband?"

"I don't think she cared about Aaron's reaction. She said it only to anger Drake. She often did things like that." The two policemen exchanged glances. I could have bitten off my tongue.

"She often taunted your husband with his problems, didn't she? With his troubled past?"

"Yes," I said, twisting my hands in my lap.

"So last night at dinner Aaron Curtis and Major Curtis were both very angry with her." Lieutenant Striker nodded to his sergeant and then rose. "Thank you, Mrs. Curtis. That's all for now. Would you please ask one of the servants to fetch Miss Curtis?"

"Must you talk to Emeline now?" I asked in dismay. "She's just lost her mother. And she is just a child. Surely you don't need to question her."

"This is an investigation into possible murder, Mrs. Curtis. I appreciate your feelings, but we need to speak to everyone."

"Have you—have you perhaps considered that if Leonora was murdered, then it was Grant Schyler who pushed her down the stairs?" I asked desperately.

"And why do you think he would have done that, Mrs. Curtis?"

"To—to frame Drake, to ruin the hotel. He holds a mortgage on it. If Drake were to be arrested—if he couldn't make the payments, Mr. Schyler would foreclose. He hates Drake because of . . ."

"Because of your husband's involvement with his late wife. Yes, we know all about that. I was in charge of the case myself,

320

and it's been a thorn in my side ever since. I was never convinced that Mrs. Schyler's death was suicide, you see, despite the inquest's decision. Your husband, Mrs. Curtis, had grown tired of Alice Schyler, and when she threatened to make a public scandal of their affair, he may have killed her. Such a scandal would not have looked well for the hotel. But there was a scandal anyway, wasn't there? Perhaps he couldn't foresee one at the time or the proportions it would take. And then a year later, Mrs. Curtis dies. Someone else who, by all accounts, had been giving your husband a great deal of trouble. Just as Ernest Willoughby had been doing. Major Curtis was strongly opposed to his excavating at the Site of Stones. We know that."

"But you were satisfied that his death was an accident, Lieutenant. You declared the investigation over."

"Not exactly satisfied, Mrs. Curtis. But again, there was no hard evidence to arrest anyone. It's just that I find it curious that several people who were of great trouble to your husband are now dead."

"What about Grant Schyler? The same could apply to him. His wife was unfaithful."

"True. But are you saying that you suspect him of contriving Ernest Willoughby's death?"

"Mr. Willoughby's death has nothing whatsoever to do with Leonora's, except that they were both accidents," I said.

"That is what I will determine, Mrs. Curtis. But I think that a suicide and two accidental deaths such as these in just over a year in one isolated location are quite possibly more than coincidental."

"Perhaps it's the curse," I said with an attempt at lightness.

"I don't believe in such a thing, Mrs. Curtis. And, I would hazard, neither do you."

After he dismissed me, I had to get away from the house. But I had no wish to go to the hotel. I could imagine the atmosphere there—all the guests discussing Leonora's fall, speculating on the cause, their faces lively with excitement, their voices speaking in breathless whispers. Other people's tragedies were always fascinating topics of conversation, and such a tragedy had occurred under their very noses—or in this case, beds.

This was far more interesting than the obscure little archaeologist's death. The beautiful Mrs. Curtis was known to everyone; she numbered friends among the guests. It was well known that she had not got along well with her brother-in-law, Major Curtis, who had in the recent past been involved in another unsavory scandal, and that she had treated her husband, Aaron Curtis, with indulgent contempt. Wouldn't this enliven tea parties throughout the fall in Boston, Philadelphia, and New York? I wondered whether any of the guests would pay their reckoning and depart today. Likely very few, if any. Not, at least, while all the macabre excitement was going on, not until the matter was resolved one way or another. After all, it wasn't a scandal. Not yet. They might stay and observe with perfect propriety.

I went out the front door and across to the woods on the opposite side of the house from the hotel. The trees closed about me comfortably. No one could scrutinize me there to discover what I was thinking. The long amber pine needles cushioned the rugged path. The forest was hushed and gloomy, the light barely filtering through. The slim, mottled birches grew thickly amidst the dark, sturdy spruces and pines. Splashes of color heralded the approach of autumn, scarlet staining the veins of a maple leaf, yellow rimming the green oak leaves. It was September, and in a few weeks the trees of the Notch would be ablaze, shimmering and vibrant in the mellow sunlight. But what would have happened by then? Would Leonora's death have been resolved one way or another? Would Drake and I be permitted to begin our married life in peace, without turmoil?

The interview with Lieutenant Striker had shaken me considerably. I had to be alone to think. Perhaps I should have gone to Drake at the hotel, in a show of support, but I could not just yet. I felt strangely reluctant to see him. Lieutenant Striker had unnerved me by his mention of Ernest Willoughby's death, by his implication that the two deaths might be linked in some way. Drake had been strongly opposed to the archaeologist's work; he had hoped that his digging would be in vain, and he had threatened him with eviction should a hue and cry arise, drawing attention to the Site of Stones, the kind

322

of attention he feared would hurt business. If the Site of Stones had been turned into a place which might lure a questionable group of people, the sort of people who would not mix well with the guests of the hotel, then the usual hotel guests would likely have stayed away in great numbers. And the archaeologist, with his frenetic babble about evil forces in the atmosphere, might very well have attracted an odd jumble of people. If the shards he had found had been proven to have come from a Mediterranean or European culture which had existed nearly four thousand years ago, there would have been no stopping Mr. Willoughby. He had been a fanatic, his zeal uncontrolled and often bizarre, and thus his presence was a very great danger to the hotel. I myself had witnessed an ugly argument between my new husband and Ernest Willoughby, an argument wherein each had threatened the other. And shortly afterward Mr. Willoughby had been found dead.

Drake had hated Leonora with far more vigor than that which he had displayed to the archaeologist. Time and again she had enraged him. And it was she who had placed the syringe on the table that night, just to get a reaction out of him. I understood that now. She had derived a sadistic pleasure out of taunting him about his weaknesses, and he had hated her for it. Just as he had hated her for seeming to join forces with Grant Schyler against him and against the hotel. And then had come the final humiliation—her brutal denunciation of him as a former drug user. She had not bothered to lower her voice, so it was likely that a number of other people had heard her besides those of us seated at the table. And hours later she had fallen to her death.

No, it could not have been Drake. If Leonora's death were not accidental, it was far more likely that it had been Aaron who had given Leonora the push to send her sprawling down the staircase. He had to have known that she was having an affair with Grant Schyler. Had he positioned himself outside Schyler's room very early this morning and waited for her to come out? Drake had claimed that Aaron was a coward, so naturally he would not have confronted Schyler with his wife's infidelity. But he could have confronted Leonora herself. Had he threatened her, and eventually, when they reached the landing, knocked her down the stairs to fall under Madeline Curtis's portrait? Grant Schyler had said that he'd heard Leonora speaking to someone. If he were speaking the truth, had it been Aaron that Leonora was speaking to? He had been very angry with her for telling Drake that he had lost a large sum of money playing poker with Grant Schyler. Had that, coupled with her flagrant infidelity, driven him to kill her? It was also possible that he had *accidentally* sent Leonora crashing to her death, that they had argued and she had lost her balance and fallen. Had he then rushed down the back stairs, overcome with horror? With all the noise of Leonora's fall, it was likely that he had not been heard hurrying along the carpeted corridor. Had he then, on reaching home, drunk himself into a stupor? If that were the case, I did not think that Aaron would come forward and admit it. Not only would he not wish to implicate himself, but he might consider by his silence that he was implicating Drake, and thus, if Drake were arrested, the hotel, and financial control, would go to him. I could imagine Aaron killing Leonora, whether with intent or not, but try as I could, I could not implicate him in Ernest Willoughby's death.

Grant Schyler's role in this I questioned as well. He had come to the hotel, determined to see Drake ruined and the Crystal Hills fall into his hands. He had informed the newspapers of the archaeologist's death, hoping that the ensuing publicity would result in cancellations. But I couldn't seriously believe that Grant Schyler had killed Ernest Willoughby just to create a possible scandal. And what on earth would his motive have been if it had been he who had killed Leonora? To make it look as though Drake had done it so that he would be arrested and convicted as he had not been for the death of Schyler's own wife, Alice? But would he actually have killed Leonora in his consuming obsession to bring Drake down? Or was he now merely taking advantage of her death by implicating Drake?

If the police were convinced that Drake killed Leonora, he would be arrested, held, tried, and if found guilty, then he would be hanged. The thought clawed at me from within; I felt weak and sick with a sharp, corroding fear. That could not happen. Drake could not be arrested, he could not be found guilty. Whether he were tried and condemned, or tried and acquitted, he would be away for months. Aaron would be left to manage the Crystal Hills. I could imagine how few guests would come to stay if one of the owners was arrested and tried for the murder of a member of his own family. It would be the end of the Crystal Hills Hotel. And Aaron would, through his poor business judgment, run the hotel into the ground. Either way, who wanted that end? Grant Schyler.

Drake had threatened to press charges against Aaron for forging his name on the mortgage if he tried to take any sum of money from the hotel to pay his gambling debts to Grant Schyler. Perhaps he had hoped to find a way to embezzle the necessary funds, paying off Schyler before Drake became aware that the money was missing. Leonora may have spoiled his plan when she informed Drake of Aaron's losses to Grant Schyler. If Aaron had hoped to keep it a secret, the secret was out. I would not have been surprised to learn that Grant Schyler had told Leonora, hoping for just that result, or that the two of them were plotting together against the hotel and to drive yet another wedge between the two brothers to undermine their strength as partners. Perhaps Leonora had been planning to go away with Schyler; she had not seemed at all concerned that the hotel was her own means of support. Perhaps she had other plans for her future.

Now that I seriously thought about it, there seemed to be motives everywhere. Had Aaron turned a blind eye to her infidelity, but then learned that she was meaning to leave him for Grant Schyler? Had that been too much for him; had he been determined to stop her from doing so? Or had they argued about it, and subsequently she had fallen?

Yet how did Ernest Willoughby's death figure into any of this, if at all? Had they both been nothing more than tragic accidents, caused by clumsiness, fatigue, or alcohol?

Eventually I returned to the house, more overwrought than ever. Guiltily I realized that I was sadly neglecting Emeline; I should have remained at the house to be with her after her interview with the police.

But when I returned to the house, I found only Charlotte in

the sitting room, knitting. "There you are, my dear," she said, smiling weakly. "I was concerned about you."

"I went for a walk," I said wearily, unpinning my straw hat and sitting down. "Have you seen Emeline?"

"She went out a little while ago. When the police had finished with me, she was gone."

"I wonder where she is. I shouldn't have gone out like that."

"She may have gone in search of her father. Naturally Aaron didn't bother to come and comfort her earlier. I assume he is at the hotel. Heaven only knows what is happening over there now."

"I'm afraid, Charlotte, terribly afraid."

"There's no reason for you to be afraid, Teresa. I'm convinced that Leonora's death was a tragic accident, nothing more. The police swiftly resolved Mr. Willoughby's death, didn't they? And soon they will Leonora's."

"Do you really think so? That both deaths were accidents?" I asked hopefully.

Something flickered in her eyes for an instant and then disappeared. "I'm certain of it, my dear. This has been a very bad year for those of us at Nightshade Notch, but no one here could have committed murder."

"But you spoke of an evil."

"I did not mean the so-called curse, or anything supernatural. Just that events have been pushing us toward an end. But perhaps we have reached that end and now we can begin to—to improve things."

"I hope you are right, Charlotte," I said heavily. "But I'm afraid that there may be worse to come. If Drake is arrested—"

"Don't think it, child. He will not be. Leonora's death was an accident. The landing was dark; she lost her footing and fell."

"I wondered—about Aaron. I think Leonora may have been planning to run off with Grant Schyler sooner or later. Perhaps she asked Aaron for a divorce—perhaps they argued about it. He may not have cared about her—flirtation—with Schyler until he realized it might have resulted in her leaving him. And you remember that he was already furious with her for telling Drake that he owed money to Grant Schyler."

Charlotte's eyes had grown wide with horror. "No! No, I

326

can't believe it," she whispered. She set down her knitting, her hands trembling.

"I'm sorry to upset you, Charlotte. I'm just grasping at straws. I—I'm so afraid they'll think it was Drake—because he nearly choked her at dinner, in front of everyone. Lieutenant Striker knows about that—he knows why—and I seriously believe he may try to pin Leonora's death on Drake as he was unable to do Alice Schyler's and Mr. Willoughby's."

Chapter Seventeen

Shortly afterwards I left the sitting room and went upstairs. The afternoon was far advanced, the gray veil of the sky a murky gloom. Standing at the window, I watched the ravens swooping and reeling, their black wings swiftly sinister against the backdrop of the mountains.

I was sapped of energy, overwhelmed by fear and dread. Desperately I wondered what the police were doing now, whom they were questioning, what conclusions Lieutenant Striker was beginning to draw. But I could not hide away in my room away from it all. It was important that I find Emeline and help her to cope with the realization of her mother's death.

She was not in her room. I went down the corridor, calling her name, and discovered her in her grandmother's room. She was sitting on the medallion-backed tapestry chair, her face pinched and solemn, her hands folded in her lap.

"Is this where you've been, Emeline? Charlotte thought you had gone out."

"I did go out for a while. Then when I came back, I wanted to sit in here. I like to sometimes."

"Yes, it's a beautiful room." But I did not want to talk about Madeline Curtis, but about how she was taking Leonora's death. Yet somehow I could not bring up the subject; she was withdrawn, closed off in her pain. I could sense some anger in her, mixed with shock and loss, and I thought I understood the cause. Leonora had never attempted to be a real mother to Emeline, had never given the child what she craved or

328

deserved. And now she was gone. No, I did not find it surprising that Emeline was silent and remote. They had not been a usual mother and daughter. I would not press her to talk. I would be there for her, and in time she might come to me.

"Have you been at the hotel?" she asked after a pause.

"No, I went for a walk."

"Why was the lieutenant asking all those questions, Teresa? Like he did about Mr. Willoughby. Does—does he think that Mamma didn't fall by accident? Does he think she may have been . . . murdered?" She spoke the last word in a whisper, and I looked across to see that she had begun to tremble, her face pale, her eyes horror-stricken behind the spectacles.

"Oh, Emeline," I said, putting my arms around her. "I know how ghastly all this is for you. Charlotte and I—we believe that your mother fell by accident. But the police always investigate when a person has died . . . violently." I shuddered, wishing I had not chosen that word.

"Who do they think did it, Teresa? Not—not Papa?"

"They are questioning everyone, Emeline. They must do a thorough job. Hopefully it will all be over very soon. Today has been the worst—for all of us."

"I wish Papa would come and see me. I haven't seen him since you told me about—about it."

I felt a wave of fierce anger welling up inside me toward Aaron Curtis. He had not bothered to learn how his own daughter was taking her mother's death, to offer her any modicum of solace. He had left her all day to cope alone.

As I had left Drake to do the same. I had been too much of a coward, too self-absorbed in my own doubts and fears, to go to the Crystal Hills to stand by his side. By my absence I had revealed my own suspicions, my own apprehensions concerning my new husband. I had stayed away out of fear and confusion. I had not wanted to see what was happening, to listen to the wagging tongues and meet the staring eyes. I had not been there when he needed me, affirming my love and support.

"Emeline, I—I must go to the hotel to see Drake. Charlotte is below stairs in the sitting room. Why don't you go down to her?"

"All right, Teresa. I keep forgetting that you're married to Uncle Drake now."

I had acted as though I had forgotten it myself.

But Drake was coming up the stairs when I had reached the landing. There were shadows under his eyes and the lines were tight about his mouth. His limp was more pronounced, I noted with concern.

"Drake, I was just coming to find you," I said lamely.

"Were you?" He had reached the top of the stairs, leaning on the bannister. His voice was cool, distant.

"I thought you would still be at the hotel," I said. "I was just on my way there."

"Well, you can spare yourself the exertion. I'm home for the night," he said curtly.

I regarded him with dismay. "How—how did it go?"

"For the second time in my life I seem to be the chief suspect in a murder investigation, so how do you think it went?" His eyes were cold.

I gasped. "Murder? Do they truly believe that?"

He shrugged. "How should I know what Striker truly believes?"

"Well, how—how are things at the Crystal Hills—the guests?"

"How do you think they are, Teresa?"

I bit my lip. "I—I suppose the police were questioning everyone."

"How astute of you. Quite frankly, the place is in an uproar. The cancellations haven't begun just yet—the news is too fresh, too exciting. But they will. The newspapers have already got wind of it. I suppose I have Grant Schyler to thank for that. Quite an enterprising gentleman, Mr. Schyler."

"I think he may have killed Leonora," I said wildly. "If anyone did."

He regarded me with disdain. "For what possible reason? They were on very friendly terms, as many have attested to today. It was I who, it was well known, was not on—friendly terms with her."

"Then Aaron . . ."

330

"Teresa, I have been all over this ground time after time with Striker. Forgive me if I am not disposed to traversing it with you."

"I'm sorry, Drake, sorry that I stayed away from the hotel, from—from everything that was going on," I said desperately.

"You would have doubtless been in the way."

I winced. "Where is Aaron? He never came to see Emeline today."

"I haven't the slightest idea. Drunk somewhere, I suppose." He limped down the corridor while I looked after him miserably. He resented me; he was hurt and angry because I had not seen fit to outwardly support him, to close ranks with him at the hotel. He must have felt very alone, very vulnerable with all the eyes of the guests on him, with the police questioning his every word, his every move of late. The fact that it had all happened before only made it worse. He had needed me and I had not been there for him. He had faced and battled so much in the last year and a half, and he had done it entirely alone. Today had been an opportunity for me to prove my love and trust, and I had not found the courage to do that. He would not soon forgive me.

I dined alone with Charlotte and Emeline, neither Drake nor Aaron joining us. I had no appetite, none of us did, but Charlotte made an effort to reminisce about former, happier days at the hotel, coaxing a smile or two from Emeline. But I do not believe that any of our attention was truly diverted from the most recent, less happy events.

After dinner Charlotte suggested we go to the sitting room and asked if I would read to them. Although I longed to speak with Drake, I agreed because it wasn't fair for Charlotte, who was so frail, to be solely in charge of Emeline's care at this time. The girl needed me as much as Drake did.

So I read while Charlotte sat in the chair beside the fire, her eyes closed, and Emeline curled up on the sofa, hugging one of the tapestry pillows to herself, listening to Mr. James's *The Turn of the Screw*. After a time Charlotte suggested that Emeline go to bed and said she would be along to tuck her in. Emeline kissed me and went on upstairs. Then Charlotte said, "I'm sorry to have kept you from your new husband, my dear, but I know you'll agree with me when I say that Emeline needs very special care just now."

"Of course, Charlotte."

"Good night, my dear. Do not give up. Do not give in. The situation is far from hopeless. The police cannot arrest Drake merely because he and Leonora argued frequently, you know."

I gave a tremulous smile. "I hope you are right."

"Leonora's death was an accident, my dear. I keep telling myself that, and you must too."

When she had gone, I got up and went across to the arched, mullioned window to gaze out at the night sky. There was the faintest glimmer of light coming from behind the mountain crests, though the sky was too overcast to show the pricking of stars. There was a strong wind blowing which rustled the tree branches and crooned about the house. The Notch truly looked its name tonight.

I had to make Drake forgive me; I had to show him that I believed in him and would stand at his side come what may.

There was the sound of heavy footsteps in the hall and I turned, hoping to see Drake. But it was Aaron who entered the room. His gait was lumbering, his face slack, portly, his eyes bloodshot, slightly glazed. But they sharpened as they rested on me.

"What have we here? If it isn't the lovely new bride. But why alone, Mrs. Curtis? Not that I'm complaining. Not at all. But Drake should have a care in leaving you alone. Where is my little brother?"

"Upstairs, I think," I said.

"You think? Haven't seen him then? Poor Miss Hawthorne, pretty Miss Hawthorne. Until my brother married you. I always suspected Drake was more interested in you than he let on. Still, Nora and I were surprised that he married you. We'd given up on him long ago. And you weren't exactly Drake's type. Don't misunderstand me, Teresa. You're a lovely girl, you know. But then Drake always had all the luck." He scowled.

"I think he has the devil's own luck, and not his own," I said coldly. I was looking past him at the door, thinking that I must get by him and out of the room. He was drunk and I mistrusted him. And we were alone on the first floor of the house.

"Yes, the boy's had his share of trouble, I'll admit. But now he has you. And whom do I have? No one. It doesn't seem fair, does it? Not fair at all." He took several steps closer to me. His fine clothing was rumpled; I could smell the alcohol on his breath.

"You have Emeline. She needs you," I said deliberately.

"Emmie. Yes, well, I have her. But that's not precisely what I meant, Teresa. I meant a companion, an adult companion. Drake has taken that away from me."

"What do you mean?" I asked sharply.

His slack smile vanished. "I mean that Drake has taken Nora from me. He said he would. He said he'd kill her. You were there . . . last night at dinner." His mouth twisted. "I told the policemen what he said."

"You know he did not mean it; you can't really believe that Drake killed Leonora."

"Why not? He always hated her. Just as I've hated him, for getting what he wants, for doing what he wants, thinking he can take over everything, treat me like one of the employees."

"Drake would never have killed Leonora," I said. "He—he couldn't kill anyone."

"You don't know everything, Little Miss Hawthorne. You don't know why he hated her. She told me once. He'd started in on her. She's beautiful, you know. But she set him straight—she told him she wasn't interested. I could have killed him when she told me, but she said to let it go. That he'd just deny it anyway."

"Leonora told you that Drake tried to seduce her? And you believed her?"

"Course I believed her. Beautiful Nora. What man wouldn't want her? But she was mine. She was always mine. She never would've left me—not really. If Drake hadn't killed her. And now she's gone. No more Nora. No more pretty Nora. But there's still pretty Teresa. Drake will understand. After all, he took Nora away. I have to have someone."

I had to get out of the room. Desperately I looked on both sides of him, calculating the distance around him to the hallway. Once out of the room I would be free. I could rush up the stairs much faster than he in his present inebriated condition. I was not frightened, just uneasy and disgusted. But I had to get away from him.

He was close to me, reaching out his arms, when abruptly I swerved to the side and took a few steps toward the door. I heard him swear and jerk around. But the dragging hem of my skirt caught on the leg of the heavy sofa and I stumbled, nearly falling on my face. Hastily I regained balance, not caring that the hem had torn, but then I felt two large hands on my shoulders which grabbed me to him, turning me around.

"Don't run away, Teresa," he pleaded, and the look on his face, the tone of his voice, made me sick with terror and revulsion.

"Let me go, Aaron," I said, trying to speak forcefully. But before I could scream, his hand had clamped down on my mouth like a vise and, despite my furious struggles, he pushed me down on the sofa. His clumsy, heavy body came across mine so that I could barely breathe. My heart was pounding wildly; I felt as though I might suffocate. His other hand was cruelly pressing into my breast. Flailing my legs, I tried my hardest to kick him, but with his legs on mine I did not have the force that I needed. I did manage to bite the palm of his hand very hard and he gave a tremendous oath, jerking his hand away, but then bringing it against my face with a resounding slap. I cried out at the sharp pain, tears pricking my eyes, but then his wet mouth was on mine and I was drowning, drowning in horror and nausea. His hands were pushing up my gown and petticoat while I still struggled and tried to kick up my legs beneath him. I was shocked at the brute strength he was displaying, drunk as he was, and cursed myself for not fleeing from the room as soon as he had entered it. The smell of him, the taste and feel of him revolted me so much that I wanted to kill him, but he had my arms pinned at my sides to prevent my reaching out to claw him or strike at him. With an extreme effort I wrenched my mouth from his to scream, but I had little breath and so was unable to make much of a cry before he viciously struck me again. I began sobbing in earnest, feeling helpless as an animal in a trap, thinking that if any of those upstairs knew what was happening down here, what a monster

Aaron Curtis was, they would not believe it.

But just as I had ceased to struggle, realizing that there was nothing I could do to prevent him from realizing his intentions, just as I was escaping into a dark, faraway part of my mind where I began to plan some horrible death or torture for him, there came a terrific noise in the room, a sound of fury, of outrage. Aaron's shoulders were wrenched up, his clumsy, heavy body was flung off mine and onto the floor.

I took in great gulps of air for a few seconds, scarcely conscious of the two others in the room. But then my head cleared enough to realize that it was Drake who had come in, thrown Aaron to the floor, and was now above him, his hands around his throat. Drake's face was scarcely recognizable, livid, the blood pounding at his temples, at the veins in his neck, his eyes blazing with rage. Aaron was making whimpering sounds, his eyes bulging with terror, his hands trying ineffectually to loosen his brother's grip.

"Drake!" I cried out. "Drake, stop, for God's sake!" I jumped up from the sofa and came down beside him, grasping his arms. If I did not stop him, there would be a real charge of murder to face.

He turned to regard me, some of the inhuman look leaving his face, some of the fire in his eyes dwindling.

"Let him go, Drake," I said more calmly.

Slowly he loosened his hands, taking them from his brother's neck, his breathing coming rapidly.

Aaron continued to lie there. He began to cry, making horrible sounds which filled me with disgust and pity. "Nora," he blubbered, "Nora."

"Get out of here, Aaron," said Drake, but his voice was his own once again, as were his impulses. With a slight shock I realized it had been he who had emitted that roar of outrage.

Aaron sat up shakily, wiping his face on his sleeve, still emitting those pitiable sobs and gulps. He reached out an arm to the chair to pull himself to his feet, steadying himself, before lurching clumsily from the room. He did not look at us. We heard him stumble up the stairs.

Then I began to cry myself, great, heaving sobs which wracked my body. I could not stop myself. Too much had happened in the past twenty-four hours. I had never felt more battered, more bewildered. Drake took me in his arms, stroking my hair, holding me tightly against him.

"It's all right, Tessa. It's all right now," he said soothingly, over and over. And I shuddered in his embrace, my face wet against his broad chest that was partially covered by his dressing gown.

"What made you come downstairs?" I finally managed to ask.

"I was looking for you. I had gone to your room. I realized you must still be downstairs even though I had heard Charlotte and Emeline go to bed. But I had no notion of what I'd find. When I entered and saw the two of you—saw what he—my God, Teresa, your face!" He touched my sore cheek gingerly. "Did he—?"

"He was drunk, Drake. I don't think he knew what he was doing."

"Naturally," said Drake bitterly. "That damn bastard."

"He said that you had taken Leonora from him. He believes you killed her."

"And this is the way he mourns her, by trying to rape you. I was going to kill him, you know."

"I know. And then there would have been a real charge of murder against you. I wanted to kill him myself."

"If he had"—he clenched his teeth—"nothing could have kept me from wringing his bloody neck. When this whole mess is cleared up—Leonora's death, the police, everything—I'm going to send him away for good. He owns property and a house in Rockport—he can go there. I never want to see him again. Tonight was—the end."

"What about Emeline? It will break her heart to leave here."

"Oh, she can stay. He's no fit father anyway. He'll just continue to drink and gamble until he's lost everything or is dead—or both. She may live here with us. But tonight was the last straw. He goes."

"Oh, Drake, I'm so frightened. What about the police? Are you really their chief suspect?"

His eyes looked directly into mine. "I'm *your* chief suspect, isn't that so?"

I bit my lip. "Of course not." But my voice lacked conviction.

"You see? If my own wife wonders whether I might be guilty, how can the police think any differently?"

"Oh, Drake, I'm sorry. Sorry for not being at the hotel with you today, sorry for doubting you. It was just the way things happened . . . the argument at the dinner table . . . and then her dying a few hours later. I've been so confused, but it hasn't affected my love for you." I almost wouldn't have blamed him if he *had* killed her, just so he was not arrested. Just so we were not separated, not torn apart by these dreadful events.

He raked his fingers through his hair. "I'm sorry I was a boor to you earlier," he said. "How could I expect you to act any differently after all that's happened? It was bad enough my bringing you into all this hideous mess. But I really was a damn fool to—to force matters so that you had to marry me. Because now you're in the thick of it as well. You're no longer just on the fringes, looking in."

"That is just where I want to be, Drake. Please understand that. I love you, I've always loved you. My life only truly began when I met you and came to Nightshade Notch. I want to be here for you, to help you. Together we can fight the police, and Grant Schyler, and the newspapers, and all of them."

"I just hope you are right, Teresa. For we must find a way— a way to pay off Schyler and keep the hotel afloat until we close at the end of October. After that—I don't care. But I won't—I can't live with Schyler at my back. If the hotel goes, well, then it goes. But not while I owe Schyler all that money. I can let it go, but not to him. I must find a way to pay him off."

"Not now, Drake. Don't think of it any longer. Forget the police and Grant Schyler and all of it. Forget everything except that I love you, and we were married yesterday."

"It hasn't been much of a marriage so far, has it? I'm sorry, Tessa. You didn't bargain for all of this. Someday I'll try to make it up to you."

"Let's go to bed," I said.

My arms went round his neck and I kissed his rough cheek. His arms tightened about me, his face pressed into my curls.

We went upstairs and down the hall to his bedroom.

"From now on you're sleeping nowhere but in my bed," he said huskily.

He slid my gown over my shoulders and sat beside me on the bed, cradling me in his arms. But I sensed he was holding back, restraining himself, though he caressed my cheek and dropped light kisses on my brow and hair.

"Shall I turn down the lamp?" he asked. "You need to get some sleep. It's been a long day—and it's likely it will be another one tomorrow."

"But I'm not sleepy, Drake," I murmured.

He lay down next to me, supporting his head on one arm. I smoothed his brow, running my fingers along his cheek and jaw, touching the cleft in his square chin.

"Aren't you going to kiss me?" I asked, wondering why he hesitated.

As though unwillingly, his gaze raked over my throat and lower.

His eyes were on the tops of my breasts where they peeped out from beneath my camisole. He gave a slight tremor, a muscle jerking in his cheek. "Are you certain, Tessa. After— what happened with Aaron?" The words seemed to be dragged from him; his face hardened as he spoke his brother's name. "I confess I've been afraid you might—shrink from me." He ran his fingers through his black hair.

"Hush," I said, putting my fingers over his mouth.

He kissed my fingers, looking into my eyes a moment longer before lowering his head to mine. His lips touched mine tentatively, gently, as though fearing a sudden instinctive withdrawal. But I wound my arms about his neck and opened my mouth beneath his. I felt his restraint slacken as his kisses became hungry. His fingers pulled at the lacing of my camisole, loosening it until it came apart. Gathering me close to him, he buried his face in my breasts, kissing, nibbling until I was shivering with a feverish delight. His cheeks were rough against my skin, but his mouth was soft and warm. I clasped his head to me, my fingers in his hair while my breathing quickened, while the fire in me stirred and swelled in intensity.

"Drake," I moaned softly.

He slid my pantalets down my legs and then paused, shrugging off his dressing gown. His gaze moved over me. "I want you so, Tessa," he said hoarsely before covering my unclad body with his own hard, naked one.

His lips once again took possession of mine, one hand dragging through my curls, the other cupping my breast. The urgency was surging to a fever pitch in both of us when he nudged my thighs apart. I moaned in his ear, feeling his heart thunder in his chest, my own body quivering and straining against his. When he entered me I gasped involuntarily, and he, quick to notice, became motionless, his face poised above mine, his eyes unsure. But I whispered to him, encouraging, laying bare my longing, my hunger which only he could satisfy. And then he was giving free rein to his fierce impulses while I trembled in delicious surrender to his masterful embrace, to the driving force in his powerful, hard body which could evoke such responses in me as I had never imagined. There was a wild urgency inside us which soared to a white-hot state, suspending us in a desperate sort of ecstasy, where we were consumed wholly in what each of us demanded and seized from the other, and lavished freely in return.

"Drake," I said much later. "I'd like to begin helping out at the hotel. There must be work I can do, details to take care of. If I assume some of the duties, you'll have more time and energy to devote to possible solutions in dealing with Grant Schyler. And Emeline doesn't take all my time."

"Well, if you're certain you wish to, there's plenty you could do," he conceded. "Aaron's useless now, so I may be conducting excursions in the coming weeks. If we still have a fall season, that is."

"Don't say that, Drake. Don't talk like that. We can't let ourselves be beaten before we've even fought. Tomorrow you can show me what to do. And we'll take it one day at a time, just one day at a time."

"The September mortgage payment has been made. But if business falls off this month, it will be difficult to meet the October payment. And the ones after that, when the hotel is closed, may be impossible. I was counting on the profits from the fall season getting us through the winter. So it's vital that I find a means to pay off Schyler."

"If there is a way, you will find it," I said confidently. "We won't let the hotel go without both of us doing all we can to save it."

The following day saw me behind the desk in the office at the Crystal Hills. I wanted to learn as much as I could about running a grand hotel. Drake had done it on his own, for Aaron and Leonora had never been much help, but now I wanted to share it with him, to take some of the burden from him. It was my home and livelihood now, as well as his, and together we would work to keep it afloat. And so I answered letters requesting information or reservations for the month of October. It cheered me to be useful and to have evidence in my hand that there was hope for the success of the hotel. However, as Drake pointed out, none of those who were writing to ask for rooms knew about Leonora's death and the possible consequences of the investigation. But I did not allow that to daunt me. It was later, when I spent some time at the desk in the lobby, that my optimism was fractured and my spirits disheartened.

A man approached the desk, asking to speak with Major Curtis.

"He is not available just now," I said. "May I help you? I am Mrs. Curtis."

The man hesitated, glancing about as if he hoped Drake would suddenly materialize. Then he frowned. "Well, ma'am, I have decided to cut short my family's stay here."

My heart sank, but I tried not to show how I felt. "I'm sorry to hear that, sir."

"Yes, well, I must get back to Boston—affairs to look into, business affairs," he muttered.

"When do you wish to leave?"

"Tomorrow morning."

I made the necessary arrangements and he walked away, a look of relief on his face.

It happened several times that first day, and more often on the days that followed. Guests were cutting their stays short, and some did not bother to give "pressing business affairs" as a reason. "It's no longer the place for my family," said one man bluntly. "What with a woman getting killed and the police everywhere. We're moving to another hotel." And he was not the only one. Gradually the cancellations began to come in by mail, first a trickle, then more and more. The big-city newspapers were having a field day, as Drake had dreaded. Jack Robinson, the oily reporter, had returned, along with several others this time. There were more foolish and speculative stories about the Site of Stones being cursed, about it claiming three lives (in spite of the fact that Leonora had not actually died there). Drake stopped the delivery of the newspapers, but such an action was more a futile gesture than anything else.

Lieutenant Striker and his sergeant continued to work at the hotel, going over the same ground as before, taking those of us chiefly concerned aside and asking the same questions over and over, but in slightly different ways to compare each answer. An autopsy was done on Leonora's body, but no new evidence came to light as a result. A bleak funeral was held at a church in Littleton, and then she was buried in the family plot in the woods near the hotel beside Madeline and Theodore Curtis.

Emeline was subdued, and I was too concerned about Drake and the hotel to devote much individual time to her. We had suspended lessons for the time being. She assisted me a few times in the office, which seemed to please her, and she told me that she hoped that the more I learned about the hotel, the more I would teach her. I promised that I would.

Charlotte seemed even more frail and worried, but she kept Emeline company when I could not. We were all facing a good deal of strain and unease, which increased as the number of guests and reservations dwindled. As for Aaron Curtis, I rarely saw him, and ignored him when I did so.

Drake was remote from me, even as we worked together. He would return grim, tight-lipped, from speaking with the police, and he would closet himself in the office while I remained at the desk or took care of matters in different areas of the hotel. He led a few excursions, and I encouraged him to do this as it got him away from the hotel and out in the Notch which he loved. I was deeply concerned about him, and it did not help any to have Grant Schyler sitting in the lobby, watching all the proceedings with the look of a fox who had trapped a rabbit in its lair. But I tried desperately to not allow him to see how he affected me; there was plenty of work for me to do, seeing to details in the ordering of food and arranging various entertainments for the guests who remained.

Among those were the Aldridges, and Miss Birche and Mr. Sloane. Mrs. Hamilton had declared it was getting too chilly for her, and as she had only booked through the first week in September, I was certain that that was the actual reason. Miss Birche, bless her, seemed wholly unaffected by the police and the reporters. Her normal ebullience had not dimmed. She went off merrily every day on her bird-watching ventures, later reporting to me which varieties she had seen. Mr. and Mrs. Aldridge had planned to leave at the same time as Mrs. Hamilton, but one morning he declared his intention of extending their stay. At his suggestion he and Drake went riding a few times, and I was grateful to him for once in a while providing Drake with a much-needed diversion. Mrs. Aldridge was greatly altered from the peevish, unwell woman she had been earlier; she sat on the porch with a number of the other matrons, drinking tea or mulled cider, or played croquet or took walks about the grounds. There were other guests who did remain as well, and a number of new ones did arrive, but it was painfully obvious that Leonora's death had hurt business severely. In less than two weeks we had gone from nearly full to about one third of capacity, and if business continued to fall off before we closed for the winter, I did not see how we might meet the mortgage payments. Drake did not confide in me; again he had withdrawn into himself; he was short-tempered and silent much of the time. And with all the duties I had assumed, I was too busy to press him to talk, too busy to force him to seek comfort in me. His passion had not faded, but even then he was silent, grim, taking me almost out of desperate anger than a shared need for solace. We were battling against the odds now; when matters were resolved one way or another, there would be time to devote to one another. At least now we were pooling our efforts to save the hotel rather than Drake carrying the load alone as he had done for so long. At least we were single-mindedly working toward that goal.

One morning I was sitting in the office with Drake, drinking a cup of coffee as we sometimes did together, when he said, "I've decided to close the lower-level shops. We can't afford to keep them stocked with merchandise. They're not necessary to the hotel, and so we must do without them for the rest of the season."

"Do you think that closing them will help?" I asked.

He scowled. "Barely at all. But they are luxuries I just cannot afford right now. I have to start cutting expenses somewhere."

Before I could reply, there was a knock at the door. "Come in," called Drake irritably.

The door opened and Grant Schyler stood there, immaculately clad in gray.

"Good morning, Mrs. Curtis," he said, flashing his gold tooth in a swift smile. "Quite a beautiful morning, isn't it? The leaves will be turning quite soon now. Unfortunately not many seem to be here to enjoy the sight."

"What do you want, Schyler?" said Drake, rising to his feet.

"To do you a favor, my boy, what else? By my calculations the October payment will have to be mailed to my office in New York in a day or two so that it reaches there by the first of October. I thought I would save you the trouble of mailing it and collect it now. Or had you forgotten—what with one thing and another?"

"I had not forgotten," said Drake, his jaw set hard. "I have it already written out." He took it from a ledger and handed it to the older man.

"And I trust the funds are there to back it with?" he asked, smiling. Drake said nothing, his eyes narrowed. "How gratifying. So you've managed to make this payment. But what of the next and the next and all those that will follow? You may even be able to make those, but I seriously doubt that you'll have the capital to reopen the hotel in the spring. A pity, isn't it? Perhaps I'll have better luck at running the Crystal Hills."

"I have no intention of discussing my hotel with you. I've given you the check. Now get out of my office," said Drake.

"Certainly, my boy, certainly, while it *is* still your office."

He saw Drake's fists clench into balls and smiled again. "Why do you fight? You can't win, you know."

A few days later I had my usual breakfast of tea, toast, and blackberry jam taken with Charlotte and Emeline, before going across to the Crystal Hills. Charlotte was still looking pale, but she assured me she was as well as could be expected for someone of her age. I knew there was more to it than that, but I had worries of my own.

"Are the police still about, Teresa?" asked Emeline, her brow knit.

"I haven't seen them in a couple of days," I said, the possible implications of that striking me for the first time. "Perhaps they've concluded their investigation. What a relief that would be!"

"If only they would go away and leave us in peace," sighed Charlotte. "I hope to God they have."

"A barbershop quartet is going to perform tonight," I said. "Why don't the two of you have dinner with us at the hotel and stay for the music?"

"That sounds very pleasant, my dear," said Charlotte.

A short while later I went over to the hotel. I drank the coffee Drake had ordered for us in his office, but he scarcely spoke to me except to request that I sort through a new pile of mail on his desk. He then went in search of Mrs. Burrows, the housekeeper.

Wearily I set down my empty coffee cup and went across to the desk. It was becoming increasingly more difficult to summon that air of cheerful bravado I had felt earlier in the month when I believed that together we were dauntless. Now it seemed that nothing short of a miracle could save the Crystal Hills from falling into Grant Schyler's hands, and I knew that Drake felt the same way.

There were a few people writing to request rooms, but nearly as many canceling earlier reservations, so the general situation was unaltered. I replied to each letter, and when I had finished, opened the top drawer of the desk to look for some stamps. As I shuffled through a few papers inside, my eye was caught by one of them because it had my name typewritten on it. Picking up the paper, I saw that it was a letter from an insurance company in Littleton, and that it was dated two days ago.

Dear Major Curtis,

This is to inform you that the life insurance policy you requested be taken out on your wife, Teresa Hawthorne Curtis, is now in effect as of today to the amount of $25,000. Should you have any further requests or questions, we will be pleased to address them.

The words swam before my eyes, the black, typed letters merging, blurring on the glaring white paper. Slowly I put down the letter, smoothed out the pile of papers, and pushed closed the top drawer. I sat there staring at the envelopes on the desk, ready to be mailed out, except that something was missing, something . . . stamps. That was it. I had been searching for stamps and instead I had found the letter from the insurance company.

Drake had taken out a $25,000 policy on my life. He had not mentioned to me his intention of doing such a thing, and of the reason behind it. $25,000. It was a great deal of money. It was the exact amount of the mortgage Aaron Curtis had taken out on the Crystal Hills Hotel, the amount that Drake owed Grant Schyler.

With that realization my blood ran slow and thick. If I were to die by some means, and Drake were to receive that sum of money, he would be able to free the hotel of Grant Schyler's clutches and set it back on its feet for good.

Had the desperate state of affairs of the last weeks somehow led Drake to this conclusion—killing me so that he might collect $25,000? I had watched him grow more and more grim as we lost guests and reservations, as he worried about paying Schyler in the months to come. Had he hit on the only solution, somehow staging my accidental death so that his financial troubles would be over once and for all? If he were able to buy Grant Schyler's interest in the hotel, he could keep it closed indefinitely until the scandal of three accidental deaths was long forgotten. Or he could open again in the spring and it would not make much difference if the hotel was half-full, not as it mattered now. He would have the opportunity to gradually build back business, without owing a mortgage, without Willoughby stirring up dubious interest in the Site of Stones, without Leonora flouting him at every turn. Without me.

Was he capable of pretending to love me while instead plotting my death? Had this scheme, in fact, occurred to him even before we were married? Our marriage had been so sudden, so unexpected. I had had doubts at the time, I recalled. He had made me believe that because he had seduced me and taken my virtue, the two of us had no choice but to get married. I also believed that he loved me. Had it all been pretense, what we had shared together? Or had he gradually felt impelled to take this step, convinced that only by killing me would he be able to save his family's hotel? Did the Crystal Hills mean that much to him, that he would willingly kill me to save it?

Why not? answered a part of my mind. He could have killed three people for it already. First, Alice Schyler, who had threatened to cause a scandal if he refused to run away with her. Second, Ernest Willoughby, who had planned to announce his discovery of the pottery shards had they been proven to be as old as he believed, along with his theory that the site had been used for grisly pagan rituals, and might even now be inhabited by unseen forces. And lastly, Leonora, who had derived enormous satisfaction in taunting him with all his weaknesses.

But had he also loathed her for another reason? Aaron had told me that it was Drake who had been rebuffed by Leonora, that he had sought her attentions and been refused them. At the time I had dismissed such a notion out of hand, but could it have been the truth after all? If indeed I were wondering whether Drake had actually murdered three people in cold blood, then why should I believe him about Leonora and her attempts to seduce him as a very young man? Had he gotten a twisted sense of elation, a perverse pleasure, out of killing the one woman who had refused him? Could what I had assumed to be hatred on his part have been something entirely different? Thwarted lust, desire, masked as contempt? That's what Aaron apparently believed. But no, that was ridiculous. How could I

346

listen to a man like Aaron Curtis, a man who had embezzled funds from his family's business, forged his brother's name on an official document, and then tried with all his might to rape his brother's wife? I could not believe anything he told me. But even so, Drake could still have knocked Leonora down the stairs. He had hated her enough that night in the dining room to kill her.

And now I had just discovered that he had taken out a policy on my life. I stood up unsteadily. Gripping the back of the chair, I passed my hand over my face. My skin felt hot and dry all of a sudden, and I was light-headed. I went across the lobby and outside, hoping the fresh air would soothe me. I had to think. But as I went down the steps of the porch, the ground lurched before me so that I nearly lost my balance. I began to stumble in the direction of the house, terrified by the sudden physical sensations, shielding my eyes from the blinding sunlight. My heart was pounding and racing; my mouth felt unbearably parched. Reeling through the trees, I made my way round the house to the front door, opened it, and stumbled inside. But I fell against the stairs, watching the room spin crazily before my eyes, and I cried out in terror before the world went dark.

Later I came to. I was stretched out and the light was very dim. I believed I was in my coffin. "No! No!" I began to shriek, waving my arms wildly, clawing out. And then my arms were pinned to my sides in a vise, and Drake's face was above me, swimming before my feverish gaze in a sickening, frightening way. And I was calling out again, screaming, "No! I'm not dead! I'm not dead! You killed them all—but not me! Not me!"

Then I was violently ill, heaving, choking, shivering, and there were other voices, other faces. I was so thirsty, my throat raw with thirst, but they would not give me anything to drink. They were all trying to kill me.

I saw Drake take a woman into his embrace, a woman I knew to be Alice Schyler, before raising his arm and stabbing her. I saw him come up behind Ernest Willoughby kneeling at the entrance to the chamber and send the stones tumbling on his head. I saw him concealed in the shadows of the landing at the hotel before stepping out to send Leonora sprawling down the stairs. And then I saw him as he had been this morning, his face grim, inscrutable.

"It was poisoned!" I cried. "It was the coffee!" His face once again swam before me and I shouted, "No! No—don't let him near me!" until he was gone and I was alone in the deepening darkness with no more energy to speak or struggle. I must be dying, I thought, and by then I did not care.

Chapter Eighteen

But I was not dead. When I came to myself, it was like coming back from a very distant, very dark place. Opening my eyes, I stared up at the ceiling of my room, uncertain of where I was. But then my eyes traveled over the familiar objects of the room—the little table beside the bed covered with the lace cloth, the Gothic window with casement just ajar, the garden print on the wall. I felt incredibly tired; I wanted to return to that far, dark world. Then I realized that someone was sitting in a chair by the fire.

"Charlotte?" I asked, and my voice sounded faint and weak.

She looked up, smiled, and put aside the knitting she had been working on. "So you finally decided to wake up. How do you feel, my dear?"

I thought about it. "All right, I suppose. Weak. Why? Have I been ill?" I frowned. "I have been, haven't I?"

"Have you been ill! Child, you gave us all a terrible fright! You've been sick for more than a day and a half—and not yourself at all."

"I remember going to the hotel, answering some letters. . . ."

"And soon after you came back, delirious with fever, dizzy, very sick indeed. And you were shouting all sorts of things. Thank heaven you are much better. Your fever is gone and at least now you are making sense."

"Why? What was I saying?"

She laughed uneasily, smoothing the bedclothes. "You were not yourself at all, Teresa, dear. You seemed . . . quite frightened—of Drake—you did not want him near you. We sent for the doctor in Littleton and he came as quickly as he could. Drake was beside himself with worry."

Drake. I was married to him. He was my husband. What was it about hearing his name that sent an icy wave through me? I concentrated, trying to brush away the filmy coils of sleep and illness. Charlotte had said that I had been answering letters at the hotel. Letters requesting reservations, letters stating cancellations, letters . . .

And then I knew. There had been a letter, but not one I had answered. It was one from a life insurance company, and it concerned a policy Drake had taken out on my life. My life for $25,000. $25,000 to save the Crystal Hills Hotel—a driving compulsion that obsessed my husband.

After reading the letter, I had begun to feel ill. I recalled leaving the hotel and stumbling across the lawn to the house.

"The doctor said it was one of the most virulent cases of stomach flu that he had ever treated. Most flu patients have no energy, but you were . . . well, almost violent. Last night, when the worst was over, the doctor returned and gave you a sedative which made you sleep all night and all this morning, until now."

"What time of day is it?"

"After three in the afternoon."

"And I've slept all that time?"

Charlotte nodded.

"And you've sat with me all that time?"

"Well, not all of it, my dear. I stayed with you yesterday afternoon, but once you were asleep from the sedative, Drake was with you all night. I insisted he return to the hotel this morning, and I promised him that I wouldn't leave you."

"Thank you, Charlotte, for taking such good care of me," I said, a catch in my voice.

"You had us all very worried, my dear. Emeline as well. She couldn't go to sleep last night before she was certain that you would be all right. I suppose that after losing her mother, she was terrified she would lose you as well. The doctor reassured her that it was just a virus and you would recover soon, but I think he was more worried than he let on. He said you might have some broth when you awakened, and some toast, if you felt like it. He will be here again later to check on you."

"He is convinced that—that it was just a virus?"

"Why, of course, child. What else could it have been? You seemed to think at the time that . . . well, I've said you were delirious. But you seem to think you had drunk something that had disagreed with you. You kept saying, 'It was the coffee!' Drake was frantic with anxiety—as were Emeline and I."

Drake had ordered coffee as he usually did in the morning, and the two of us had sat in his office drinking it. Or rather I had sat drinking it. I had poured him a cup and one for myself. Shortly after, he had rather abruptly left the room. Had he slipped something into my cup, and then deliberately left? I remembered his silent, morose manner, which naturally I had put down to worry over the hotel finances. Was, in fact, that manner the result of a decision he had made concerning me, a decision to trade my life for plenty of money to solve his financial problems? I closed my eyes, my head throbbing.

"I'm going to tell the cook to prepare a tray for you, my dear. I think you need some nourishment. We must start to rebuild your strength."

I did not attempt to protest. I appeared to be lying there peacefully. In reality my mind was a torturous whirl of fear and shock.

I marveled at Drake's audacity to attempt to do away with me under the very noses of the police when Leonora's death had not been resolved one way or another, but I was beginning to realize that he must not be a rational person. He was obsessed with making the hotel an undeniable success once again, and it was obvious to me now that he would stop at nothing to attain that goal. Even though he was suspected of causing at least one person's death, Leonora's, he was still determined to see me dead in order to collect the money.

Then why had he married me? Had this diabolical plan been in his mind all along? Or was it only a last resort now that things looked blacker for the future of the hotel than they ever had? What about the alternative of selling some of the Notch? He had said that he would only do that as a last resort, because he wanted the wilderness preserved. Was he actually more willing to *murder* me than to sell off a portion of the land? Had he hit on that idea as a way to avoid dividing up the Notch between the Crystal Hills Hotel and perhaps another hotel?

No, he loved me! I was certain of it. Or rather, I *had* been certain of it. But had he felt only great desire, even affection for me, and now that matters are so desperate was he willing to sacrifice me because of the money? Why not? That was obviously how things had been with Alice Schyler. He had begun an affair with her, and then, when she had wearied him and posed a threat to the success of the Crystal Hills, he had killed her.

I could understand Drake being frantic with anxiety at my bedside, but not out of fear for me. Out of fear that I would *not* die, that the doctor might listen to my ravings about being poisoned. No wonder he had been beside himself. Yet he had stayed with me alone most of the night; why hadn't he finished me off while I slept from the effects of the sedative? It would have been a simple matter to press a pillow over my face. I shuddered. But last night the doctor had been certain that I would recover. Perhaps Drake feared the police would demand another autopsy if I died when the doctor had predicted that I would get well.

If I had died, it would have been the result of a violent, uncontrollable illness. Unlikely perhaps, but not unheard of. It was possible that Lieutenant Striker would have thought little of it since the local doctor himself was convinced I had suffered from a particularly bad case of flu. But poisoning . . . the notion had obviously not entered anyone's mind. But they did not know about the insurance policy. And if I had not seen that letter, the possibility that I had been poisoned would not have occurred to me either. I had been lucky this time; I had been granted a reprieve. I might not be so lucky the next time. Drake had tried poison, but for some reason it had not proved fatal.

Now he would try something else.

Just now he must be cursing himself because he had not used enough of the poison, because I was still alive. And there was no solution in sight to the financial burdens which plagued him. No solution, except another attempt on my life.

I wondered whether I should go to Lieutenant Striker when I was fully recovered and tell him what I suspected. Surely I had to; surely I should not hesitate. Yet part of me shunned the idea of going to him and saying, "My husband (who I thought loved me) has tried to kill me." Because, when I said it aloud, it would become real, undeniably, horribly real. No longer just a suspicion.

Besides, there was nothing I could prove. I had no evidence, just a wild fear. I could tell Lieutenant Striker about the life insurance policy, but then Drake would undoubtedly have a plausible reason for obtaining it if he were questioned. To approach Lieutenant Striker with the statement that Drake had somehow put something into my coffee cup might make me look very foolish. For there was no way to examine that coffee; I had finished the cup and it would have been carefully washed by now. And the coffee was the only real evidence that had existed. If I went to the police and they subsequently questioned Drake about the coffee and the life insurance policy, he would naturally have a story which would satisfy them. Worse yet, he would know that I suspected him. And I might have very little time to live after that.

So for the time being, I had to keep my own counsel. I had to be very wary, avoiding all opportunities of being alone with my new husband.

Charlotte returned, followed by the cook, who was carrying a tray. "After some of this good hot broth, you'll begin to feel stronger," said Charlotte. She arranged some pillows at my back and the cook set the tray across my lap. "Now eat up. Try to swallow a few bites of toast as well."

I did not argue with her; I began to eat. Because she was right—I did need my strength, but for far more than she supposed. I needed to be strong and alert, not helpless and vulnerable. I needed to be in control.

When the tray was removed, all of the broth was gone and most of the toast. I was feeling stronger already, and no longer so tired. When Emeline came in to sit with me, I was able to listen to her observations of some of the guests with apparent interest and amusement.

All the while, though, I was dreading the night. Drake had

spent last night with me and would likely want to do so again, playing the concerned, loving husband. Last night I had been safe with him, but only because we were known to be alone together and Lieutenant Striker's suspicions might be aroused if I had indeed died. It was likely that since the poisoning had not worked, he would bide his time until a better, more certain method presented itself. But he could not wait forever; he had to devise a means of paying off Grant Schyler before that man claimed the hotel for his own.

I could not be alone with Drake. He would sense the terror in me and that would be my undoing. If he suspected that I blamed him for my illness, he might not wait for the perfect opportunity. He would have to find a way to silence me before I had a chance to voice my suspicions.

"Has the detective been at the Crystal Hills today?" I asked Emeline. I had a sudden fear that Lieutenant Striker might have left for good, having completed his investigation. Just yesterday morning I had prayed for such a thing.

"Yes, he was asking me more questions this morning, about Uncle Drake and Mamma. And he was in the office speaking with Papa, and then with Uncle Drake again. I wish he would leave for good—he can't help Mamma, can he? And he just makes everything awful. It's his fault that lots of the guests have left. He makes everyone nervous, even Charlotte. Tomorrow Uncle Drake is taking a party up the cog railway."

So Drake would be away from the hotel tomorrow. The group would be gone for hours, and I would not have to be afraid that he was lurking about somewhere. Tomorrow I would feel stronger; I would consider wisely what course of action I should take. My thoughts would be clearer, and without his presence to threaten me, I could think and act constructively. But I still had to get through tonight.

Emeline went away to change for dinner and Charlotte returned with the news that the doctor had returned. "See, Dr. Hollis, how well our patient does this evening."

"How do you do, Mrs. Curtis?" said the doctor, a soft-spoken man with thick white hair and eyebrows like tufts of fur. "There's certainly a big change in you today, though you need some color in those cheeks." He took my wrist, a finger on my pulse, while Charlotte left us alone.

"You're coming along fine, Mrs. Curtis, just fine. Miss Conway tells me you took a bowl of broth and some toast. Excellent. By tomorrow you should be able to get out of bed, perhaps even out of doors. But don't try too much. You were very ill."

"Dr. Hollis, I would like to ask you something. I wonder if you might request that I—that no one . . ." I colored, biting my lip. "I'm still not myself, you see, and I'd prefer to be alone tonight. I feel very foolish about my husband seeing me so ill yesterday, and I'd rather he not see me again until I'm fully recovered. I'm not exactly used to—being married. I know it sounds silly, but . . ."

The doctor smiled and patted my hand. "I understand, Mrs. Curtis. You're just a bride, new to the married state and all that it entails. And it embarrassed you for your husband to see you not at your best. I'm not surprised to hear it—you cried out every time he came near you," he said, chuckling. "Don't like a man in your sickroom, is that it? Or at least not a brand-new husband. All right, my dear, don't fret. I'll give strict instructions you're to be left alone tonight. But in return you'll have to promise me that you'll get a good night's sleep."

"I will."

Releasing my hand, he stood up. "If you begin to feel poorly again, send me word. But if not, tomorrow you should be able to handle mild solid foods. I'll tell Miss Conway. Good evening, Mrs. Curtis."

"Good evening, Dr. Hollis, and thank you," I said gratefully.

Thank heaven for his gullibility in believing that it was maidenly modesty which kept me from wanting to see my husband while I was indisposed. That he could believe. Had I told him the real reason, he would have thought me still sick and confused, and doubtless would have given me another sedative. And that I could not risk.

It was twilight outside. One of the maids had lit the gas lamps, which cast a soft warm glow about the room. There came a knock at the door, and before I could answer, Charlotte entered the room, Drake behind her. I felt myself tense, but managed to give a feeble smile.

Drake was leaning heavily on his cane; his leg must be paining him, I thought with quick concern. And then it struck me how foolish I was to care about a man who had attempted to kill me.

"How are you, Teresa?" he asked. He was frowning slightly, and there were dark smudges under his eyes. He looked curiously vulnerable and I had to steel myself from any feelings of solicitude.

"All right," I said unsteadily. "I don't remember much about being ill."

Did he look relieved or was it just my feverish imagination?

"The doctor said that you must get to sleep and we are not to disturb you. Is there anything you'd like, anything we can do for you before we say good night?" asked Charlotte.

I shook my head. "No. I just feel very sleepy, as though I could sleep for a long while."

"It's probably still the effects of the sedative," said Drake.

"Dr. Hollis says you will be back on your feet tomorrow if you sleep well tonight. I'll say good night now."

"Good night, Charlotte," I said, and she closed the door behind her, leaving Drake and me together.

"I have a good mind to ignore the doctor's orders and stay with you all night," he said, his smile lopsided.

I tried to keep the alarm from creeping into my face. "It's just that I'm so tired, Drake," I said and yawned.

"Are you sure you are feeling better?" he asked, a pucker in his brow. Was he wondering again why the poison had not done the trick?

"Yes, much better. I'll see you tomorrow, all right?"

He came close to the bed, looking down at me. Under the bedclothes my body was rigid. "Just tell me that everything is all right, that you're not truly frightened of me."

"Frightened—of you?" I repeated faintly.

He nodded, his black brows drawn together. "You seemed— I can only say—terrified—of me yesterday. It was—disconcerting, to say the least."

I brushed back my hair nervously. "Terrified? I don't remember." I gave a little laugh. "Charlotte said I was delirious. Perhaps I was dreaming."

It was imperative that he be convinced that I harbored no suspicions against him. "How are you, Drake? How are things at—at the hotel?"

He made an impatient sound. "Damn the hotel. I love you, Tessa. I'm sorry I've been such a brute lately. If anything had happened to you, well, that would have been the end of everything," he said huskily. He took my hand and brought it to his lips. Then he said, "Sleep well," and turning, went from the room, one leg dragging slightly behind the other.

When he had gone I dissolved miserably into tears, hating him for deceiving me, for putting just the right touch of anguish, of despair in his voice. I wanted so desperately to believe that he did indeed love me, that I had imagined all of this, that the insurance policy held no ulterior motive. But I was engulfed in fear, and that fear now held sway over my every thought, my every movement.

Getting out of bed, I walked unsteadily across the room and locked my door. Then I went back to bed and shortly fell asleep.

The next morning when I awoke I felt refreshed and stronger. I ate all of the breakfast the maid brought and drank two cups of tea. It would be a long time before I could drink coffee again.

The maid drew my bath, and by the time I was dressed, I was feeling myself once again. It was noon by then, and Charlotte told me that Emeline was outdoors somewhere.

"Poor child, I think she minds her mother's death more than we would think, considering the fact that Leonora rarely gave her any attention. As for her father, he has done nothing to help her through this painful time. He spends his hours in the parlor on the ground floor—drunk, I understand." She sighed. "Well, at least Emeline has you and me."

But I had not paid her any attention myself these last weeks. I had devoted my time and energy to the hotel, to Drake. I saw now how unbelievably foolish that had been.

"I'll go and look for her. Perhaps she's at the Stones." There would be no danger of my encountering Drake as he would be well on his way to Mt. Washington by now.

"Do you think you should go out? You've not been on your feet at all for two days," she pointed out.

"I won't go far, I promise. And I'll come home if I start to feel poorly. But Dr. Hollis said I might go out if I felt well enough. And it's such a beautiful day."

The casement windows were open and the fall air was like chilled champagne. Against the vibrant blue sky the mountains surged, granite-pocked, the blue-green slopes glinting with color. On the lower ridges, the maples were turning crimson and apricot, other trees a deep cranberry, or a delicate silvery raspberry.

On my way downstairs to look for Emeline, I had a sudden impulse. If I were able to find some proof, any proof that Drake had actually tried to poison me, then I could go to the police with my suspicions. That would be far better than waiting with bated breath for the next murder attempt he might make. It was highly unlikely that Drake had left any evidence lying about, but it would not hurt to look. Perhaps he had a bottle of something, or perhaps he had taken something from the kitchen used to kill mice. I could not go to the cook, but I could search his room.

I believed that arsenic caused stomach upset and that it was a way of poisoning someone over a period of time, in small doses. I felt impelled, driven, to see whether I could find anything. So I went back upstairs and down the corridor to Drake's room.

The maid had already been in to tidy it. I stood on the threshold, wondering where to begin. There was a large dark chest of drawers on one wall. I went across to it and began opening the drawers, lifting out the neatly stacked piles of linens. I was conscious of no embarrassment, no guilt, so determined was I to search his belongings. But nothing turned up in the chest of drawers, and so I moved on to the nightstands and the wardrobe. I even slipped my hand beneath the mattress, but again I found nothing. I was beginning to feel foolish. I opened the rolltop desk, but it was fairly empty; Drake kept most of his important papers in the library or at the hotel. As I had learned.

Going into the bathroom, I looked in the medicine chest. But there was nothing suspicious in there, just straight razors and toilet water and shaving creams and brushes.

Desultorily I walked out of the bedroom. I should have known that I would not find anything. I went along the corridor and down the stairs. Perhaps whatever he had used was at the hotel, in the office. After all, that was where I had drunk the coffee. I could go and search that room without incurring suspicion.

And then I remembered the library. I might as well look there, I thought, while Drake was out. I might not have an opportunity later. Although it was very likely that I would find nothing there. I realized that I was searching for a needle in a haystack, that if there had been poison Drake would surely have got rid of it by now. Unless he meant to use it again, slowly weakening me by apparently natural means.

Entering the library, I went over to the desk and began pulling open the drawers. I didn't really know what I was looking for, a bottle, a packet of powder. . . . But I could not find anything like that.

Instead, I came across a book bound in red. Impatiently I lifted it, feeling underneath with my fingers, shifting through the blank sheets of writing paper and envelopes. No, I realized with disgust, there was nothing here either.

But just as I was setting down the red book, I happened to glance at the title. *Wildflowers of New Hampshire.* A book like Mr. Sloane would have, I thought wryly. And he would read from it aloud to anyone who would listen, and even to those who would not. I recalled the excursion we had gone on when he had read from his book on the geological development of Nightshade Notch. And then the conversation had shifted to the Notch's curious name. Mrs. Cooper had taken exception to spending her honeymoon in a location named for various possibly morbid reasons, and had said she hoped it was not bad luck for their marriage. And Mr. Sloane had held forth on the different sort of nightshade plants which were all poisonous to one degree or the other.

The nightshade plants.

One of the family grew here, in the White Mountains. What was it called? What had he said about it? I stared at the book in

359

my hand, mesmerized, my heart thudding so that I could almost hear it. And then I began to skim the pages with my thumb. I was not even surprised when I reached the page where a corner was slightly turned down. I looked down at the page.

There was a drawing of a coarse weed with thin, pointed, hairy leaves and a white trumpet-shaped flower. Next to the illustration was printed: "*Datura stramonium,* better known as jimsonweed. The plant contains scopolamine, which can be extremely poisonous in high doses. Highest concentration to be found in the seeds and lowest in the roots. Causes delirium, dizziness, vivid hallucinations, fearful dreams, disorientation, the subject losing all contact with normal reality. Some amnesia resulting. Effects can last from twelve to twenty-four hours: skin hot and dry, feverish, parched mouth, burning thirst, eyes sensitive to bright light and unable to focus at close distances, rapid heart rate. Roots, seeds, leaves can be ground, eaten, brewed into teas. In some cases fatal. A member of the nightshade family."

The clock was ticking on the wall, its strokes resounding in my ears, in my head. Abruptly it struck the half hour in a hollow vibration, shattering my bemused state.

This, then, *Datura stramonium,* was what he had used to poison me. There was no doubt in my mind. The symptoms I had suffered matched those in the book exactly. If jimsonweed could be ground and brewed into teas, it could certainly be ground and added to coffee. If it could be eaten, it could be consumed in a cup of coffee.

Drake had studied this book, taken note of the look of the plant, dug some up somewhere, ground it, and added it to my coffee when my attention was elsewhere. But somehow he had not got the proportions quite right, because the dosage had not proved fatal. It would never have occurred to the good country doctor Dr. Hollis that I was suffering from a dose of jimsonweed. But I was certain of it.

Should I now go to the police, book in hand? But still, what proof was there? Would Lieutenant Striker recognize and admit the sinister significance in the dog-eared page as I did? If only Drake had written something on the page. A marked page of a book on wildflowers which just happened to discuss various nightshade poisons—was it really enough for the police to go on? Such a book could be in any house, and the fact that I had found it in Drake's desk was not real evidence, not the kind the police would need to arrest him. It might alert them so that, if something were to happen to me, they would suspect Drake. But by then it would be too late for me.

Carefully I put the book back where it had been, making certain that the contents of the drawer looked untouched.

Nightshade Notch. A flashing image came to me of Drake, Emeline, and myself at the train station in Portsmouth when he had ordered, "Three tickets to Nightshade Notch . . . one-way." Then I had been conscious of a sudden sense of misgiving, of dread, as though I must not go with them.

I felt I must confide in someone. I could take the book upstairs to Charlotte, telling her my fears. But I hesitated. She had known Drake most of his life, since he was a small boy. It was likely she would not believe me; she might suspect that it was I who was not well, that the recent events had unhinged my mind. She knew little about me, after all. It was probable that she would dismiss anything I might say as being grossly farfetched, and then discuss it with Drake, questioning my sanity. "Poor Teresa, she is not herself at all these days. So depressed, so on edge." And Drake would know that I was on to him and that he had to act swiftly to put me away. If not an accident, then why not suicide? People who were depressed and on edge, succumbing to wild fears and fancies, did occasionally decide that life was too much for them. . . .

But there was Emeline. She was not particularly close to Drake, by her own admission and my observations. She knew me better than she did him, even though they were uncle and niece. There was six years' difference between us in age, but she had always been my friend. She would not automatically assume that I was losing my reason.

Leaving the house, I hurried across the sweeping lawn in front of the Crystal Hills and into the crowding columns of trees in the far woods, not looking toward the hotel. When I was among the trees, I paused for breath, feeling my heart pounding in my breast, before continuing on. I passed the enormous boulder spanned by the huge tree roots, moving deeper into the shrouding forest until the path began to climb up the hill to the clearing of the Site of Stones. As the trees were thinning out before me, I heard a rustling sound and gave a start, freezing. But it was only a squirrel scampering through the fallen leaves in search of acorns.

Ahead loomed the Stones, and I felt the familiar uneasiness creeping over me as I approached them. "Emeline!" I called out. "Emeline! Are you here? It's Teresa—I have to talk to you! Emeline?" My voice rose sharply in disappointment and frustration. She was not here after all.

I stood there listening to the droning of insects, the flurry of the wind in the trees. The narrow trench that Ernest Willoughby had so painstakingly dug had been filled in, and there were no longer any signs that a police investigation had taken place here. There was just the forlorn, dirt-filled rectangle, and the beehive chamber, the front of which was still in a state of collapse, the stones tumbled across the black, gaping opening. No one had bothered to try to arrange them over the entrance. I shuddered, feeling a stab of sympathy for Mr. Willoughby. He had been a victim of Drake and the hotel as much as I had nearly been—and might still be if I were not very careful.

Had these granite monoliths, chambers, and tables actually been constructed for mysterious purposes by a race of people four thousand years ago? A race of people that had worshipped pagan gods, understood navigation and mathematics to the extent that they were able to cross the sea and travel inland over one hundred miles to these mountains where they had erected this . . . temple? A temple where they could practice weird and hideous rites, rites which had impregnated the very air, the very stones, the very ground with traces of long-ago emotions. Mr. Willoughby had theorized that the place would have been a sort of astronomical observatory as well, where the ancient ones had plotted the course of the stars, but for what purposes? What forces had they called to in the sky, what powers had they evoked in their rituals, and had they received any answers? And did these forces, once summoned, return again and again to terrify and threaten the unwary?

With an unholy, morbid fascination I moved across to the Sacrificial Stone. It was then that I became aware of other sounds, not the timid rustlings of a small animal, or the harsh cries of a raven, but those which unmistakably heralded the approach of another human being. Someone was coming up the path in the woods; I could hear twigs snapping and shoes scudding on rocks. It must be Emeline, I thought in relief. I was just about to call out when a voice reached my ears.

A voice that did not belong to Emeline. A voice that I knew well, better than any other voice. Its every inflection, its every timbre was known to me.

It was the voice of my husband, my lover, my enemy.

Drake was not on the excursion as I had been led to believe. He was very close by, and in a few moments he would be out of the woods and looking across at me.

My heart lurching in my breast, I looked about wildly for a place to hide. Should I dash across the site to the forest on the opposite side? But he would hear me in the woods and, despite his bad leg, might catch up with me. Besides, I did not know those woods and could get lost even if I managed to evade him. In a few hours it would be night, and I had no wish to be wandering aimlessly in the dark. Especially not near the Site of Stones.

"Teresa, Teresa? Are you here?" came his voice, closer now.

Oh, God, I thought, agonized, what should I do?

And then it came to me. The stone passage which went underneath the Sacrificial Stone—it was large enough for me to hide in. Quickly I went down the few steps and round to the entrance of the passage which contained the speaking tube, the oraclelike device. Just as I crouched low to enter, I caught sight of Drake coming toward me from the woods. I crawled as fast and quietly as I could into the dark chamber, moving out of the light of the entrance, far back against the stone wall so I could not be seen. My heartbeat throbbed in my ears; I pressed my hand against the smooth wall of the cave, scarcely breathing.

"Teresa!" His voice was closer now, but muffled, as I was underground. Faintly I heard his boots scuffing the stone surface, his voice calling again, "Tessa, are you here?" His use of the endearment form of my name cut me to the heart. I sat there, biting my lip, hating him, the tears running down my cheeks, praying that he would not find me. Why had he not taken that group up Mt. Washington? Why had I left the house, left Charlotte's side? Was I to be crushed like Ernest Willoughby beneath another pile of dislodged stones? Or stabbed like Alice Schyler, my body splayed across the Sacrificial Stone?

When the sounds of his footsteps sounded directly above, I had to clap a hand over my mouth to prevent a scream. I bit my finger, listening to him move about, terrified that he would come to the entrance and find me. And then he moved away and I let out a deep breath, my heart leaving my mouth.

But then to my horror I heard him coming down the same steps as I had, the steps which led to the entrance of the cave where I crouched.

The cave. My eyes widened; I nearly gasped in shock. In these last few minutes, I had sensed something vaguely familiar, something I could not identify, so paralyzed was I by terror and dread. But now I knew. This was Bridget's prophecy—this was what she had read in the tea leaves. She had seen me hiding in a small dark cave. And then I myself had dreamed the same image on the night of the carriage-house fire. I had been crouching in blackness, my hand touching stone, my skin crawling with fear. Yet even then I had known that it was not the *place* that I feared, but a person who was searching for me, calling my name. A voice I had not known then, but one I knew now. Bridget had seen and warned me. And I had been given a warning of my own and had dismissed it, never identifying the small dark cave of my dream with the stone chambers here at Nightshade Notch.

He was standing at the entrance now, only a few feet away. I did not dare to breathe; I did not dare to move. And then his footsteps were on the stairs, growing fainter, and I realized that I was safe.

Soon there was no longer anything to be heard but the drone of insects, the chirping of birds. I waited a while longer before crawling out, grateful to stretch my cramped muscles but unwilling to leave the seclusion of the passage. There was no sign of him. He must have gone to seek me somewhere else. He may have gone through the woods. It was probable that he or someone else had seen me heading in the direction of the Site in the first place, and he had followed me.

It was imperative that I leave here and return to the house in case he were to pass this way again. I had to go to the library and take the book on wildflowers to show to Lieutenant Striker. Now I did not care who thought me foolish or insane. This afternoon had convinced me that Drake would stop at nothing to kill me. Desperately I hoped the police were at the hotel; I had to see them as soon as possible.

As I passed the Sacrificial Stone, to my ears came that peculiar sort of noise I had heard before, a rushing sound, the sound of voices in a faraway crowd. But then, gradually, the rushing grew to a rumbling as though the crowd was drawing closer and closer. Glancing around wildly, I could see nothing but the maples gently swaying, the tall sentinels of pines standing sturdily, and the Stones themselves. But there was no drone of insects; there was no rustle of wind in the tree branches, no scurrying of animals nor chirping of birds.

I realized that the same phrase was being repeated over and over in a kind of chant. And still the sound grew in intensity until I clapped my hands over my ears to blot it out. And I sensed a terrible glee, a horrible excitement which permeated the atmosphere, and I was its focus. The inhuman forces were unseen, but there was no doubt that they existed. That they existed for the very reason to reach out, grip, and suck me into their own abominable, monstrous world which, like them, was unseen, but very close and undeniable.

"No!" I cried in a strangled voice, wrenching myself away, turning about with a great effort. I began to put one foot in front of the other, unable to do anything more than take one step at a time. I felt as though I were walking through water, and still I heard that baleful chanting. It took all my concentrated energy and determination to continue to move away, to shut my ears to the loathsome, but compelling, sounds. I had an almost irresistible urge to turn around, to gaze back at the Sacrificial Stone. My chest was heaving, the perspiration beading on my brow, my heart a stone in my breast, but still I went on.

When I reached the path to the woods, I lunged forward and began to run, taking great, sobbing breaths, tearing through the trees like a wild animal, stumbling over rocks and roots, slipping on patches of moss, until I was clear of the woods and on the lawn in front of the Crystal Hills. This time as it rose before me, sugar-white against the violet-blue highlands, I felt no fondness or glow of admiration. For the hotel was as much my enemy as Drake was; I was to be sacrificed so that it might endure.

I hurried on to the house.

I knew that I must get away as quickly as I could from the bizarre and accursed forces before Nightshade Notch claimed another victim. Taking the red-bound book from the desk drawer, I hurried out of the library and into the hall, only to see Charlotte coming down the stairs.

"Teresa! Good heavens, child, what has happened to you?"

"I—I was walking through the woods," I stammered, dismayed. My gown and hands were streaked with grime, probably my face as well. My hat had come off and my hair had tumbled out of its pins. I knew I looked a sight, but that scarcely mattered now.

"You're very pale, my dear. You had better go lie down. You shouldn't have gone out today."

"No, I—I've got to go over to the hotel."

"In that state? Why? At least change your gown."

"No, I must go now. It doesn't matter at all what I look like."

"Won't you tell me what has upset you, Teresa? Don't forget, you've been very ill. What do you have there, a book?"

"Yes, it—it's a book on poisons, I mean, wildflowers. I was just looking at it."

"One of the books from the library, isn't it? Drake's father was very interested in wildlife."

"Well, someone else is apparently very interested in it as well. One of the pages in here is marked, turned down, and it's one of the pages where a kind of nightshade plant is mentioned. And Charlotte, the symptoms of that poison match the symptoms of my illness exactly!"

I watched the color drain from her face. "What . . . what are you saying, Teresa?"

"That I believe that Dr. Hollis was not correct in assuming I had contracted some sort of flu. I believe I was poisoned, with jimsonweed. I—I'm sorry to blurt it out like this. I hadn't meant to, Charlotte, but I'm very frightened, and I'm going to find the detective."

"Teresa, please," she said, grasping my arm. "Hasn't there been enough mistrust, enough suspicion lately? I never thought that you . . . And the police have caused so much harm already." Her slight frame was trembling, the violet stains under her eyes giving her a ravaged, wraithlike look.

"Harm to what? The hotel?" I cried angrily. "That is all you people think about, isn't it? Well, there is a great deal more at stake here than the future of the Crystal Hills. I like to think that people's lives mean more than a building!"

Loosening myself from her grasp, I was soon out the door. When I reached the hotel, I hurried up the steps, ignoring the curious glances thrown at me by a few guests sitting on the front porch. I hoped the police were inside, but if not, I could send them a wire from the telegraph office. I no longer cared whether Drake was there or not; he certainly could not harm me in the lobby with people coming and going, and I would not make the mistake of being alone with him again.

Burrows held the door open for me. "Have you seen Lieutenant Striker?" I asked him breathlessly.

His face was very grave. "The police are inside, Mrs. Curtis. The major was looking for you."

Inside the lobby I nearly collided with Grant Schyler. "Oh, the lovely Mrs. Curtis," he said. "But scarcely her incomparable self today. Can it be you've already heard the news?"

"What news?" I snapped. "I'm not interested in any news you have to tell me."

"Tut, tut, so new a bride and already acting just like a Curtis. That may not serve you well in the future. I'm referring to the news of the moment, my dear. The news I've been waiting for for weeks. I confess I had almost lost patience with the good

367

detectives." He flashed his gold tooth, the cologne he wore giving off a heavy sweet smell which sickened me.

"Get out of my way," I said, sweeping past him and heading toward the two detectives who were standing by the staircase, just underneath the portrait Sargent had painted of Madeline Curtis.

The sergeant had noticed me and nudged Lieutenant Striker. They began coming toward me.

"Teresa!" Drake was beside me; he gripped my arm.

"Don't touch me!" I said viciously, jerking away.

His face darkened. "So they've told you. Striker, you assured me that I would be the one to . . ." He broke off, his fists clenching.

"We haven't said a word to Mrs. Curtis, Major," said Lieutenant Striker.

"Said a word? About what? I was just coming to talk to you, Lieutenant."

"I'm afraid I can't talk now, ma'am. You've had plenty of time to tell me your story. What's done is done."

"But—but it's part of the investigation!" I blurted out. "You must listen!"

"The investigation is over, Mrs. Curtis. Naturally you'll have a chance to speak at the trial."

"The trial! But—I don't—what?"

Lieutenant Striker looked from my bewildered face to Drake's stony one. "I mean that we are apprehending your husband, Mrs. Curtis."

"You're—what?"

"They're arresting me, Teresa," Drake said, his voice curiously devoid of expression. "I was looking for you earlier, to tell you."

"Arresting . . . you?" I repeated blankly.

"For Leonora's murder. I didn't want you to find out like this. I wanted to tell you myself, in private," he said quietly.

"We have to go now, Mrs. Curtis," said Lieutenant Striker. "You can walk out on your own, Major."

"What does it matter? Everyone will know soon enough," Drake said, giving me a long, penetrating look. He made no move.

The sergeant coughed. "It's time, Major," said Lieutenant Striker.

Then Drake gave a slight nod and, turning away, walked out of the hotel followed by the two detectives.

Stunned, I gaped after them while there came the fiendish sound of Grant Schyler's laughter booming from all sides of the room.

Chapter Nineteen

"That is the news to which I was referring, Mrs. Curtis," said Grant Schyler. "That is the news for which I have been waiting. Drake Curtis has been brought down at last. And now there's no way he can pay off that mortgage—not where he's going." His gold tooth flashed in an ugly smile. "I don't imagine many guests will want to stay at a hotel where the proprietor was hanged for murder."

I winced.

"And then I'll take this place over and bring it down until it's nothing but a heap of rubble. And I'll live to see it destroyed and the name Curtis dragged through the slime the way my name was in New York after Alice died."

Gazing across the lobby, my eyes happened to fix on Sargent's portrait of Madeline Curtis, the former chatelaine of the Crystal Hills Hotel. She was a memory now, to some a legend, and it seemed as though the hotel would become a legend as well. And I was conscious of a great sadness welling inside me, a feeling of almost unbearable desolation. I had been determined to go to the police about my husband to insure my own survival; I should now be feeling relief and peace of mind. But I felt neither of those things.

"I think I'll go inform the hapless brother of the turn of events," Schyler went on. "Not that he'll be sober enough to comprehend it."

Outside on the porch steps I was just in time to see the black police carriage moving down the graveled drive.

"Weren't those the two detectives who were asking so many questions?" said a woman. "They took Major Curtis with them. You don't think that—"

"I don't think anything at all, madam," said Horatio Aldridge briskly. And then he was beside me. "Mrs. Curtis, are you all right? Let me take you back to the house."

"N-no. I'm fine. I can go by myself."

"You must not let this distress you unduly. I'm confident that everything will be all right. It's all circumstantial evidence, you know. They really haven't a leg to stand on. A good lawyer will tear their case to shreds."

He thought that I was devastated by my husband being arrested; he couldn't know that the truth was far more complex than that.

"Mrs. Curtis, I want to speak with you on a business matter. To assure you. Major Curtis and I have been discussing—"

"I really can't talk about business or anything else now, Mr. Aldridge. You'll—you'll have to excuse me." Without another word, I hurried down the steps and across the lawn to the house, tears blurring my vision.

Charlotte was coming round the house and I nearly collided with her. "I was just coming after you," she said. "You—you haven't already shown the book to the police?"

I had forgotten the book. "No." I noticed she was white and trembling. Taking her arm, I said, "Let's go back to the house. I have something to tell you."

"Something to tell me? You mean you—what is it?"

"Drake has been arrested."

She covered her face with her hands. "No, no!" she cried, her frail body going rigid. "That's . . . that's impossible! They've made a terrible mistake! Oh, God!"

"It was bound to happen, Charlotte," I said softly. "Drake tried to kill me as well."

She stared at me, aghast. "You can't believe that! Tell me you really don't believe that! Oh, God, if only I knew what to do—what to say . . ."

She was weeping, and so caught up in the throes of her shock and grief that she seemed scarcely aware of me. I did not blame her; I myself had been stunned by Drake's arrest when earlier I had longed for just such an occurrence. I led her upstairs and into her room, my arm round her drooping shoulders.

Speaking soothingly to her, helping her into bed, I decided to send for Dr. Hollis. He could give her a sedative. She must have been dreading this exact outcome, for she had not been herself in weeks. She might even have known that Drake had killed Leonora and perhaps the others, and yet she could say nothing, do nothing against him. For years she had attempted to hold the family together out of loyalty to Madeline Curtis, and now she knew as well as I did that this was the end. God only knew what would happen to each of us, but I knew that I had to stay and look after Charlotte and Emeline. I could not flee Nightshade Notch and the memory of the past few months there as I would have liked to have done.

Charlotte lay in bed, her face ravaged, tears streaming down her cheeks. She seemed not to hear me when I spoke to her, and I was very worried. I rang the bell and, when the maid appeared, I asked her to send one of the men for Dr. Hollis. "Please tell him to hurry. It's an emergency. I'm afraid for Miss Conway."

Dr. Hollis came over an hour later. All that while I had sat on the bed beside her and held her hand. I had thought the doctor would never come. Charlotte had calmed down, but she was staring off into space in a dazed way, which greatly alarmed me.

"Shock," said Dr. Hollis. "I've heard about Major Curtis—it's all over the Notch. I would have come to see how she did even if you hadn't sent for me. Her heart's not strong, you know. I'll give her a sedative and she'll sleep through the night. It'll be the best thing for her now. Once she's awakened tomorrow she'll be better able to cope with the news."

"I hope so."

"I'm terribly sorry, Mrs. Curtis. No one around here believes that Major Curtis had anything to do with Mrs. Curtis's death. If you ask me, the police are tired of not making any arrests. They think it makes them look bad, incompetent, and so they've felt compelled to arrest Major Curtis. There's no real evidence from what I understand. He'll be home again soon, I'm certain."

I smiled weakly, not able to answer him. When he had given

Charlotte the sedative and we both were assured that she slept deeply, I escorted Dr. Hollis down the stairs to the front door.

"I'll call in sometime tomorrow," he promised. "How are you feeling, Mrs. Curtis?"

"I? Oh—well enough."

"No more nausea or dizziness or weakness?"

"Oh, that. No. No, I'm all right."

"Good. Well, good night, my dear."

"Good night, Dr. Hollis."

Closing the door, I went across the hall and into the sitting room, collapsing into a chair. Some minutes later I heard the front door open and stiffened, brushing aside my tears. If Aaron Curtis came into this room I would hurl the crystal decanter at him.

But it was only Emeline. She stood on the threshold, her face full of concern and a degree of awkward embarrassment. But then she was in my arms and we were both crying and consoling one another.

"Oh, Teresa, I'm so sorry about Uncle Drake—about the police taking him away. I can't believe it. I've been with the Aldridges. Mr. Aldridge told me what happened. They wanted me to stay with them, so I sat at their table at dinner but I couldn't eat anything. Uncle Drake didn't kill my mother! I know he didn't. He just has to come back. The police will let him go, that's what Mr. Aldridge says."

How could I tell her what I suspected—that Drake had killed Ernest Willoughby and Leonora, and perhaps Alice Schyler as well, in cold blood, that he had plotted their deaths even as he had plotted mine?

Smoothing her hair, I said, "The doctor has been here. Charlotte took the news of your uncle's arrest very hard. He's given her something to help her sleep."

"Oh, poor Charlotte. I hope she's all right. She loves Drake, you know."

"I know. It's been quite a shock to her."

We sat there for a while longer in silence. I felt very tired, all energy, all capacity for thought and decisions drained away. Finally I said, "I'm going to bed, Emeline. And you must too. Charlotte will need our support tomorrow, and we'll need strength. There's nothing more we can do tonight."

"All right, Teresa. I suppose Charlotte will sleep for a long while, like you did."

"I hope so. While she's asleep she's not suffering."

We went upstairs and, saying good night, each went to our own rooms. I took off my dirty, torn gown and washed the grime and salt residue from my face. I had wondered if I would be able to get any sleep at all, but when I lay down, I could barely keep my eyes open. I had locked my door, not trusting Aaron Curtis's presence in the house.

When I awoke the next morning I was surprised to find that I had overslept, that the morning was already advanced. A bleak light filtered through the leaded panes of the Gothic windows, casting its dull, grayish tint over the room. I bathed and dressed quickly. The muscles in my legs and shoulders were cramped and sore from the stooping and crouching I had done yesterday underneath the Sacrificial Stone. Thank God for Bridget's prophecy, or I might not be here today. But I was here, and safe, and Drake had been taken away. But with that realization came no comfort. I felt instead only an enormous dejection from which I could barely rouse myself to meet the day.

I hoped that Charlotte was still sleeping; I did not know how I was going to look after her today when I wanted nothing more than to be put under sedation myself. Moving to the door, I caught sight of a white paper which had been folded and apparently slipped under my door. I remembered that last night before retiring I had locked it. Stooping to pick the paper up, I opened it and saw Emeline's handwriting.

Dear Teresa,

I must talk to you. I think you are in danger. Teresa, I know who killed my mother. And it wasn't Drake. But I'm frightened—we can't talk at the house or at the hotel. Please come to the footbridge at the Flume. I'll be waiting there for you. Don't say anything to anyone. Be very careful.

Emeline

I wondered at what time this morning Emeline had written this note and slipped it under my door. The poor child, she sounded so frightened. Had she been carrying around a terrible secret, afraid to confide in anyone? I had been so preoccupied with my own concerns these last weeks that I had paid her little mind. She needed me now. I had to go to the Flume without delay.

Taking a shawl from the drawer, I wrapped it around me and went out into the hallway. Softly opening Charlotte's door, I saw with surprise that her bed was empty, and the room as well. Where on earth could she be? I went downstairs, but could not find her.

If Drake had not killed Leonora, then who had done it? What exactly did Emeline know? "I know who killed my mother."

And then it struck me. Aaron. Emeline's father. Leonora had been repeatedly unfaithful to him, flaunting her latest affair with Grant Schyler in his face. Perhaps she had threatened to leave him. I recalled that I myself had suspected Aaron before I became convinced that Drake had murdered Leonora. Emeline might have suspected, even known for certain, for days or longer, but she had been too frightened and confused to confide in any of us. I had been ill; Charlotte had been looking after me. Neither of us had had time for her. The realization that her own father could have caused her mother's death, whether accidentally or deliberately, must be more than she could bear.

She had told me to be careful, that I might be in danger. And not from Drake. Drake was now in the hands of the police. Could it actually have been Aaron who had poisoned my coffee with jimsonweed? Could he have been in the kitchen when the coffee had been prepared, and sprinkled some of the ground seeds in the coffee grounds while it brewed? That seemed rather farfetched. And Drake would have been taken ill as well.

But Drake had not drunk any of the coffee as he usually did. He had asked me to go through the letters and abruptly left. Not once could I remember him taking a sip of the coffee. I had thought that that was because he had poisoned the pot himself, but could it be that the coffee had been meant for him and not for me at all? Could Aaron have tried to kill Drake, and I had instead been the victim?

There was certainly no love lost between the two brothers. Drake had refused to pay Aaron's gambling debts to Grant Schyler, and he had threatened to press charges over the forgery on the mortgage contract. Then Drake had nearly killed Aaron himself that night he had come upon us in the sitting room. Had Aaron attempted to get even with Drake by poisoning the coffee?

But why then had Aaron claimed that Drake had killed Leonora, if in fact he had done it himself? In some twisted way did he interpret his actions on the night of her death as Drake's fault?

One thing was certain. I could not go to the Crystal Hills in search of Charlotte and risk coming across Aaron. Emeline had warned me to be very careful. Leaving the house by a side door near the kitchen, I glanced about furtively before heading toward the back meadow.

The air was damp and chilly, the sky gray with loss. I was sure of nothing any longer. I had suspected Drake of murdering Alice Schyler, Ernest Willoughby, and Leonora. I had believed him to have poisoned me. Was it possible that I had made a very great mistake? Why, then, had he taken out the insurance policy on my life? Why had he come looking for me at the Site of Stones yesterday? Had he come to tell me that he was going to be arrested? Was that the reason for his search—not because he wished to harm me? He had accused Lieutenant Striker of telling me when he had wanted to break the news to me himself. Did he love me after all? Had all my doubts, my fears of the past few days been hideously misguided? Had I been terrified all along of the wrong person?

The blood was coursing through my veins. I felt an elation rising within me, wiping out all listlessness and misery. Perhaps Drake did love me; perhaps there was an innocent reason for the insurance policy. But he was in custody; he would be forced to face a trial. Would I learn something from Emeline which might spare him that?

Hastening across the meadow, I was so caught up in my own thoughts that I did not notice a rider on horseback until he was almost on top of me.

"Mrs. Curtis!" It was Horatio Aldridge. He swept off his Panama hat, his face full of concern. "I'm glad to have the opportunity to speak with you. I want you to know that I wired my lawyer in New York earlier this morning. He's the best, and he'll defend your husband. I told him to be on the first train he could."

"That's very good of you, Mr. Aldridge," I said, tears pricking my eyes.

"You must not worry, my dear. I'm going to do everything I can. The notion that your husband was responsible for his sister-in-law's death is sheer lunacy. Why don't you come with me to the hotel now? You shouldn't be alone. My wife and I would be happy to keep you company."

"Thank you, Mr. Aldridge. I do appreciate your kindness, but I—I can't just now. Perhaps later."

He frowned. "Very well, Mrs. Curtis. But if there is anything that Mrs. Aldridge or I can do, please do not hesitate to call on us. Will you come to the hotel later?"

I nodded, forcing a smile. Then I turned away as he rode off toward the hotel. Once I had reached the woods, I found I was looking over my shoulder even more than I had while out in the open. Every rustling, every stealthy sound took on a sinister significance.

The woods were dark and cheerless. I walked rapidly, hoping that Emeline would still be at the footbridge and had not given up on me. Or had not come to some harm herself. The sudden possibility shot through me, the sharp fear splintering painfully. But that was unreasonable, I told myself. No one could have known that she had written the note. I had it safely in my pocket.

There was a harsh, unhealthy smell in the woods; I realized it was the fallen leaves beginning to decay. The birches shimmered in the gloom like pale wraiths in golden garb; the spruces and fir trees loomed black and brooding, piercing the gray mantle of the sky.

The path was climbing now. Soon I would be at the Flume and I would learn what Emeline knew. And then the two of us could face it together and save Drake. That thought spurred me on; I was consumed with a potent surge of energy and hope

As in the past, I heard the Flume before I drew close enough to see it. The rushing sound of the floodlike waters intensified as the trees thinned, making way for the lush bright-green ferns which grew on the cliffs above the Flume.

"Emeline!" I called over the mighty torrents. "It's Teresa!"

"Here I am!" She stood up from a rock she had been sitting on. She was on the opposite side.

I went across the slightly swinging footbridge, my hand clenched to the side rails of rope. The sight of her in her sweet middy dress steadied me. Dear Emeline, she had always been the one person I could depend on.

But she was pale with two bright spots of color in her cheek and her eyes were frightened. "Oh, Teresa, I'm so glad you've come. I waited and waited. I was afraid for you."

"I'm sorry it's so late, Emeline. I overslept. But I came as soon as I found your note." I patted my pocket. "What is it you have to tell me? You must tell me everything you know. Don't be alarmed. I'm here to help you. And perhaps we can even save Drake, Emeline. You said he didn't kill your mother."

"No, of course he didn't."

"Then who? You must tell me, Emeline!"

She looked down at her high-buttoned black boots. "Papa," she said faintly over the tumult of water.

I felt a great relief; the constriction in my chest was gone. "Oh, Emeline, are you certain? How—how do you know?"

"I've known it since the morning after she died. When the police were questioning me, I thought of something—but didn't tell them. The detective had asked me when I had last seen Uncle Drake and my father. I told him at dinner the night before."

"Yes, go on," I said, tensing.

"Well, that wasn't true. About the last time I saw my father, I mean. I couldn't sleep that night—I knew you were so upset when you should have been happy on your wedding day— Mamma had said all those awful things to Uncle Drake, about that drug he used to take. I lay awake very late, and I heard someone walk up the drive. My window was open. I got out of bed and looked out the window. It was pretty dark, but I could

378

see it was Papa coming home. I know he told the police he'd been in bed, but that wasn't true. Because I had seen him come in myself."

"Did you happen to notice the time? You have that pretty clock in your room."

"I did, because I was sick of lying in bed not being able to fall asleep. I wondered how many hours it would be before it got light. It was twenty minutes past three."

Breathlessly I said, "Your uncle and the other men found Leonora's body at a quarter past three."

She bit her lip. "I know."

"Your father must have hurried back to the house just after . . ." I broke off, seeing her face.

"Why do you think he did it?" she asked tremulously.

"I don't really know, Emeline. He knew she was—becoming fond of Grant Schyler. Perhaps she threatened to leave him. In some ways he loved your mother. Emeline, why didn't you come to me with this before?"

"I just couldn't, Teresa. I didn't think anyone would be arrested; I thought they'd think it was an accident. I didn't really want Papa to be arrested. And I never thought they would take away Uncle Drake."

The Flume churned below in its turbulent cascade, but we were scarcely aware of it.

"Do you know where your father is now?" I asked her.

"I suppose at the hotel," she said unhappily. "Will—will the police take him away now?"

"I think they will when you tell them what you know, Emeline. And Drake will be released."

"Uncle Drake must be let out of jail. He didn't kill Mamma. That's why I decided to tell the truth."

"You must tell Lieutenant Striker that. We'll wire him from the hotel. Don't be afraid—I'll be with you. I think they took Drake to the Littleton jail, because it's the closest one." Something else had occurred to me. "You said that I might be in danger, Emeline. What gave you that idea?"

"You were so ill the other day, Teresa. I began to wonder why. I was so worried about you. Uncle Drake was very frightened that day . . . and Charlotte."

379

"I admit I've questioned the nature of that illness myself."

Emeline shivered. I put my arm around her. "You must be brave for a little longer, sweetheart. We must tell the police what you saw. It may be enough for them to release Drake today. And then when everything is over, perhaps we can all go away for a while. After the hotel closes for the season . . ."

Beside us the footbridge swayed slightly in the breeze; the mist rising from the swirling torrents moistened our faces and hair. I smoothed the hair at the back of her head. "You must see that to tell the police is the only thing to do, Emeline. We can't let Drake be tried and punished for a crime he did not commit."

Absentmindedly I touched the skin under her hair and felt the clasp of a chain between my fingers. "What's this?" I asked, distracted. "A new locket?"

"No, not a new one," she said, pulling out the chain from under her dress. On it hung a heart-shaped pendant, a pendant I recognized.

"Emeline, your grandmother's locket! How did you get it? Did Elizabeth or Mary find it and send it to you? Why didn't you tell me?"

An expression unlike any I had ever seen crossed her face. It was a combination of smugness and contempt. "You're not very clever, are you, Teresa? For all that you are a teacher. But you're not really clever—not about things that matter."

"What . . . what do you mean, Emeline?"

"See? Even now you don't guess the truth. On the other hand, I am very clever."

A cold sluggishness crept through my limbs. "You've had that locket all along, haven't you?" I said slowly.

She grinned, delighted with herself. "Yes, I have. The whole time."

"You didn't lose it in Portsmouth, on the picnic. But the carriage house—the fire . . ."

"I had never started a fire before, you see, but it was a lot easier than I had supposed," she said ingenuously.

"You started the fire . . . deliberately?"

"Of course. I knew I had to do something terrible so that Miss Winslow would expel me. I decided that I had stayed in that horrible school long enough. It took me a while to think of a good plan, but I finally did. And it worked."

"But why, Emeline?" I asked faintly, my heart a stone in my breast.

"Because I couldn't bear to stay in Portsmouth any longer, why do you think?" Her eyes and tone were scornful. "It was my fault I'd been sent there in the first place, though I never imagined at the time that I'd be sent away. I never forgave my mother for that, for bringing me to Portsmouth. I knew then that I'd kill her someday. I used to fall asleep at the Academy thinking of all the different methods I could use. I had a lot of time to think about doing it. She was as stupid as you. She hadn't wanted me to find out about the dead woman at the Stones, so she took me away to school."

"Do you mean Alice Schyler?"

"Yes, her. They—my mother, Charlotte, my father—were all determined to send me away before the police came, before it all came out. Charlotte said they wanted to protect me. But there was just one thing they didn't realize. One little thing. I had killed that woman myself!"

"What?" I said in a strangled voice. "*You* killed her?"

"That's what I said. I used to play at the Stones often, you know. I'd go underneath the stone slab, the one Mr. Willoughby called the Sacrificial Stone. I was under there the day they had the picnic, the day she died. I couldn't hear what they were saying, but later I heard Uncle Drake leave, and she was crying. I went outside and went close to her, picking up the knife they'd used for the picnic. She was sitting on the slab, her hands over her face. I touched her shoulder and she looked up at me. It was then that I stabbed her, before she could speak or move."

"My God, Emeline, why? Why did you want to kill poor Mrs. Schyler? What had she ever done to you?"

"She might have married Drake. I had heard my father and mother talking. They wondered if he finally might get married if Mr. Schyler gave her a divorce. They liked him not being married, you see, because it meant there was more for them. If Drake got married and had children, we would have to share everything with them, wouldn't we? I couldn't allow that to happen, even though my mother told my father she didn't think Drake would get married. You see, someday the hotel must be all mine."

"You killed that poor woman—and then you were bustled off to school before the police could even talk to you!"

"Oh, I wouldn't have minded talking to them. What would I have known about it? Just as I didn't know anything about Mr. Willoughby's death."

"Mr. Willoughby?" I repeated, catching my breath. "Emeline—you—"

"I couldn't allow him to keep on excavating at the Stones, Teresa. If he had truly discovered something, then all sorts of people would have come to see the Stones. Uncle Drake said it wouldn't have been good for the hotel—you heard him. But it wasn't just that. I didn't want crowds of people coming there all the time. They are *my* Stones. I wasn't about to share them with other people who would hang about, making a mess, digging around them. *They* wouldn't have liked that."

"So you killed poor Mr. Willoughby." I could not believe any of this was happening.

She nodded. "That was harder, but I managed it. You and Charlotte thought I was up in the attic that afternoon. That's what I wanted you to think. You remember he had found those pieces of pottery. I wouldn't have had to kill him if he hadn't found them, if he'd given up and left Nightshade Notch. I hadn't planned to kill him, not at the beginning. But he wouldn't give up; he had to keep on digging. He had to prove his silly theory. I slipped out and went up to the Site of Stones. He liked to have me there, you know. He liked it when people were interested. He wanted to impress people. I let him think I was very interested. He was talking to me while he was just underneath the entrance of the chamber."

Below us thundered the water, the clamorous sound echoing off the glossy red-brown walls of the cliffs. I was gazing at her in horrified fascination. She was no longer the young girl I had known, if ever that young girl had existed. There was something in her eyes which repelled and frightened me— something inhuman.

"He was down on his knees, holding his lantern so that he

could see. He was talking to me; he had not noticed anything. I had a stout stick I had found in the woods. With all my might I brought down the stick on his head—twice. I don't think he was dead then. And I had to make it look like an accident. So I took the stick and stuck it between some of the stones above the entrance to the chamber. I pushed on the stick hard, but nothing happened. So I tried again. And again. And suddenly one of the stones shifted and the rest just toppled down on top of Mr. Willoughby. Then I took his flask and shook out some of the whiskey on his clothes so everyone would think he was drunk and hadn't noticed that the roof was unsteady and likely to give way. Which was exactly what they did think."

"You forget that they suspected Drake of killing him," I said, my voice harsh.

She frowned slightly. "I hadn't thought of that. I was afraid for him. I didn't want him to be arrested. But I would have thought of something, just as I'm going to tell the police that I saw my father enter the house very soon after my mother's death."

"You're going to lie and possibly send your father to the gallows—for something he did not do?"

"Why not? He's not important. He'll just make a mess of everything. Uncle Drake must come back. The hotel needs him now."

"What happened to Leonora, Emeline?"

"I knew you'd ask me that. After you and Drake left the dining room, and Charlotte too, I stayed for a while. Mamma drew me aside and told me that she was leaving here, that she was going off with Mr. Schyler and that I'd have to come too. She said that Mr. Schyler was a very rich man and soon he would own the hotel. But he wasn't going to keep it running—she said we would never come back here again. I said I wouldn't go, that I'd never leave the Notch. 'The hotel will be mine someday!' I said. 'Grandmother wanted it to be mine!' She laughed then and said it could never be mine. 'Because Madeline Curtis was not your grandmother,' she said. 'Aaron Curtis is not your real father.' She said there had been another man, a guest at the hotel a long time ago. Before that she had thought she couldn't have any children. She was certain I was not Papa's child. By the time she found out she was going to have a baby, the other man had gone. 'So you're not one of these damn Curtises at all, my dear! Quite a surprise for you, isn't it?' She laughed and I hated her, more than I had ever hated her. She was going to tell my father about the other man, that I was not his child, so that he would give her a divorce and she could marry Mr. Schyler. She said the three of us would go to New York, and that I'd lead a normal life and go to parties and all that. 'We won't be stuck in this god-awful Notch any longer,' she said.

"After she left me I ran in the bathroom at the hotel and threw up all my dinner. I knew I couldn't let her tell my father her lies—I had to stop her. Later I came back to the house and pretended to go to bed. I knew she would be in Mr. Schyler's room until very late. About one o'clock I left the house by the back stairs and went across to the hotel. Everything was very quiet. I went up the side stairs to the corridor where Mr. Schyler's room was. I waited in the shadows by the landing for a long time. I got tired waiting, but I knew I had to be patient. If she were to go to my father with her story, I knew the hotel would never be mine. When she did finally come out, she saw me and asked me what I was doing there. She thought she was always so clever, but she wasn't clever enough. She never suspected that I would shove her as hard as I could down the stairs. But I did."

"Oh, my God," I said, pressing my hands to my hot cheeks. "I—I can't believe any of this."

"Then I hurried down the hall to the side staircase before anyone was roused and opened their doors. I heard voices and doors opening when I was on the stairs, and then I was out in the night and on my way back to the house.

"She landed just under Grandmother's portrait, you know. I'm certain Grandmother would have approved. She didn't want me to be like my mother; she wanted me to be like *her*, to run the hotel just as she had done. She used to tell me that someday I'd have to take her place at the hotel. I promised I would. And in just a few years I'll be helping to run the Crystal Hills. That's why Uncle Drake must be released—he's the only one who can run the hotel successfully—he's the only one who

384

can keep Mr. Schyler from taking over. I thought about killing Mr. Schyler, but I didn't see how I could manage that. He *is* clever, not like the others. I've worked it all out. Papa will go to jail for killing Mamma. The police will believe me—people always believe me. Uncle Drake will come back to the hotel and teach me everything I need to know. Grandmother told me that Uncle Drake was the one to depend on. We used to sit together at the Site of Stones. She couldn't hear the voices, though."

"The . . . voices?" I asked hoarsely.

"Yes. I've heard them all my life—not that they are always there. Or perhaps they *are* always there, watching, but they don't want you to know it." Her eyes glinted, an unnatural light in their depths.

"What have you heard, Emeline?"

"Why ask me? You know. You've heard them yourself. That first time, remember? I was so afraid they wouldn't speak that day, because I'd been away for so long. I'd heard them the day I killed Alice Schyler—she was the sacrifice, you see. For them, for the hotel. They *wanted* me to kill her. Then Mr. Willoughby called it a Sacrificial Stone. I wanted to laugh out loud."

"Good God—Emeline—"

"I saw your face that first day. I knew you'd heard them too. I thought that meant they were pleased you had come. I was fond of you; I was happy when Uncle Drake asked you to come home with us. I didn't know then that he would fall in love with you and you would be like Alice Schyler. I saw the two of you here at the Flume once. You thought I was in bed, taking a nap. But I hadn't wanted to stay indoors, and I love to come here. I knew when I saw him kissing you that day that I'd have to get rid of you."

"You hid your mother's bracelet in my pocket!" I whispered.

"Yes, I did. I came back to the house and did it before you got back. I knew she'd want to search your room. She didn't like you and wanted you sent away. But when she found her bracelet, no one believed that you had really stolen it. No one but my mother. Charlotte and Uncle Drake thought she had put it there herself. I didn't want to kill you then, just have you sent away. But it didn't work—Drake wouldn't dismiss you. I knew that I'd have to get rid of you once and for all, but then Mr. Willoughby came and he was more of a danger to the hotel than you were. I didn't think Uncle Drake would marry you, or not anytime soon. He was too busy. There was no hurry to kill you, not until you married my uncle."

"But why, Emeline? Why should you feel threatened by your uncle loving me? You could have remained at the Notch always—you could have worked with us at the hotel like you had always planned."

"But I'm not about to share it with you, Teresa, or any children you might have," she said, her eyes narrowing. "I've hated to see you working there day after day—as if you've any right to it at all!" Behind the spectacles her eyes had darkened to a charcoal with little trace of blue. "It will be my hotel as it was my grandmother's. After you're dead, I'm sure Uncle Drake will never want to marry again. So someday it will all be mine. Uncle Drake will be able to save the hotel from Mr. Schyler and the scandal. Next summer, or the one after, everyone will have forgotten about what all has happened."

"But Emeline, you don't know that for certain. Mr. Schyler may get the hotel after all. Your uncle hasn't the money to buy him off."

She smiled. "I said you don't know everything. I know a lot more. I know that Mr. Aldridge has offered to buy some of the land for enough to pay Mr. Schyler. Uncle Drake will get out of jail and Papa will be arrested. Mr. Aldridge will pay Uncle Drake a lot of money and then Mr. Schyler will go away."

"You have it all figured out, do you," I asked grimly. "Somehow you poisoned my coffee. I don't know how, but somehow you did it."

"The coffee? What coffee? No, Teresa, I poisoned the blackberry jam. The jam that you like so much and that Charlotte and I never eat. I ground up some seeds and a part of a leaf of a nightshade plant and stirred it into the pot of jam before you and Charlotte came down to breakfast that morning. Nightshade, you see. I think that was very clever. Remember the day Mr. Sloane was describing nightshade plants? I did, and I knew there was a book in the library on all sorts of wildflowers. But I didn't do it right. You got sick but didn't die. I pretended to be so concerned about you."

"I found that book, in the desk in the library. Why did you leave it there?"

"Oh, I'd forgotten about that. I was reading it, checking to see if the plant I had found matched the description, and Charlotte came looking for me. I stuffed the book under some papers before she saw it."

I had to get away from her while I still had a chance. She was dangerously unbalanced; she had killed three people and had attempted once to kill me. Now she was doubtless planning to knock me off balance so that I fell into the gorge below. But she had had to confide in me first; she must have desperately wanted someone to see how clever she was, how much power she had. I still could not believe it. A girl of fourteen, my friend Emeline. My pupil. How in the world had she evolved into a pathological murderess?

Charlotte knew. Or at least she suspected that Emeline might be responsible for one or more of the deaths. And last night— her collapse—then she must have been certain beyond a shadow of a doubt, and the shock had been more than she could withstand. She must have noticed things about Emeline all along. . . .

But there was no time to speculate. Emeline's face had taken on a watchful, determined look, the look of a cat about to pounce on a bird. She was smiling slightly, reaching toward me. Her eyes behind the spectacles were glazed . . . mad.

Swiftly I stepped back, turned, and stepped onto the footbridge. In my haste I stumbled and the bridge gave a sudden lurch. Gasping, I took the rope sides in both hands and began moving across the bridge. I was anticipating her following me, so, when I was about halfway across and had not felt her weight, I turned and looked over my shoulder. To my surprise she was still standing on the edge of the ravine. It took me a few moments to realize what she was doing.

"Emeline! No!" I shrieked, and then felt both sides of the bridge go limp in my grasp. *She had unfastened the side supports.* Now I had nothing to guide my unsteady progress across the rest of the bridge. I let out a strangled scream, for she was bending down and reaching for the slats of the bridge floor. If

387

she jostled them only slightly, I would topple over and fall to the turbulent water and boulders below.

I had only one chance to get across the bridge before I lost my balance. In two leaps I might make it. A shout came from nearby, but I took no notice. Lunging forward to the far side, I landed too hard on the slats just as they were jolted. I fell forward. In mind-shattering panic I collapsed on the bridge while it shook and writhed underneath me. Clinging to one of the slats with both hands, I tried to wrap my legs underneath the floor to further hang on. But my long skirts impeded me, and my legs, instead of clutching the floor boards, flapped helplessly on either side. My fingers gripped the slat, but its edge was sharp and splintery, cutting into my fingers. I knew I would not be able to hold on for long. Dizzy with the movement of the bridge, I gazed, mesmerized, into the tremendous surge below.

"Teresa! Teresa!" Someone was shouting my name, but I could not withdraw my mind from the sight and sound of the Flume gorge.

"Teresa, let go one hand. You're almost at the edge. Emeline, for God's sake, stop!" It was Drake's voice, but I was too paralyzed with terror to look up at him from where I lay.

"No, no," I whimpered.

"Tess, you can do it. Just let go one hand and reach up—and I've got you. You must try. It's the only way. Tessa, please, *look at me.*"

Lifting my head a little, I saw Drake, white-faced, on the cliff with Horatio Aldridge. "That's it, Tessa. Now just let go one hand and I've got you."

Let go! If I let go I would tumble off for sure. I wanted to scream at the very idea, but I was too terrified to even do that.

"Come on, Tess. The police are going up the other side for Emeline but they may not make it in time! *You must let go one hand!*"

By releasing the slat with one hand, I would be losing control, the control I was now seizing to stay alive. But if I did not, I would remain prostrate on this jostling bridge and eventually I would lose my balance and fall. I could not hold on forever.

My face was wet from the spray below. My ears pounded with the thundering noise.

"Tessa, please, you must do this! I promise we will catch you, but we cannot do that unless you reach out to us."

Closing my eyes tightly, I slowly unclenched one fist. The bridge flapped and shook underneath me. I was biting my lower lip as hard as I could but I could feel nothing.

"That's it. Now extend your arm. Reach out to me."

"I—I can't!" I sobbed.

"Yes, you can. Give me your hand. *Give me your hand, Tessa!*"

Very slowly I began to stretch out my arm across the remaining slats. Just as I did so, the bridge gave a tremendous lurch and I screamed, opening my eyes to see the violent progress of the water far below. But then I felt a viselike grip on my wrist, and I knew that there was hope.

"I've got you!" shouted Drake above the clamor of the raging tumult. "Now the other arm!"

Unclenching the other fist, I reached out, feeling him draw me forward. My legs came together on the bridge, and I was nearly to safety when abruptly something held me back.

"My boot—my boot's caught between the slats!" I cried. I was going to fall after all.

"Twist it! Lay your foot on one side. Then it will be out. Hurry, Tessa."

Gasping with terror, I managed to do as he ordered, feeling the tip of the boot free itself. Twisting the other to the side as well, I was dragged the last few feet across the rocking footbridge.

Drake crushed me to him while I took great, heaving breaths, sobbing in wild relief and remembered horror. There was something wet and warm on my chin, and my lip now throbbed painfully. Drake pressed his handkerchief to my mouth to stop the bleeding, kissing my brow and hair and murmuring endearments and soothing phrases.

"They're almost to her," I heard Horatio Aldridge say close by. "She can't get away."

But then there came a ghastly high-pitched scream, and Drake said, "Oh, my God," holding my head fast so that I could not see. And then there was no sound but the roar of the water charging through the gorge.

"It's over. It's all over," said Drake in my ear, and then he took my face in his hands. "Do you understand, Tessa? It's over. Everything will be all right now."

"I'll ride back and tell my wife and Miss Conway that she is fine," said Horatio Aldridge tactfully. He reached out his hand and Drake gripped it hard, his cheeks tinged with color. Horatio clapped him on the back before mounting his horse and riding off through the woods.

"If Aldridge hadn't seen you walking in this direction we'd never have reached you in time," said Drake.

"I don't understand. How did you get out of jail?" I asked weakly.

"Charlotte sent Lieutenant Striker a wire this morning. She had proof that Emeline was responsible for the tragedies we've had here."

"How did she know for certain? She was so ill last night—"

"Yes. Last night she realized Emeline had killed Leonora and tried to poison you. Apparently she's had her suspicions for some time but she would not allow herself to believe it. This morning she went to Emeline's room and found a man's handkerchief among her things. In that handkerchief were two pieces of pottery."

"Mr. Willoughby's shards! She—she had them?"

"Yes. Emeline was out and you were still asleep. Charlotte went over to the hotel and wired the police in Littleton. She did not realize that you were in immediate danger. When the police brought me back, we rushed to the house to find you. But you weren't there and neither was Emeline. We went to the hotel, just as Aldridge was coming in from his ride. He said he'd seen you on the back meadow heading toward the woods. We rode as fast as we could. . . ." His arms tightened about me.

"She had written me a note, asking me to meet her at the Flume. She said she knew who had killed her mother. I—I thought she meant Aaron."

"Charlotte knew you would never suspect Emeline, just as Willoughby and Leonora didn't. I can't tell you how—terrified we all were."

Alice Schyler hadn't suspected her either, I thought to myself. But I would tell him about her later. "No, I suspected you had killed them," I said softly.

His face was grim. "I'd figured that out for myself. When you were ill . . . and acted so frightened of me. And then when I'd gone after you to the Site of Stones and you wouldn't answer me. I knew you had to be close by."

"I was hiding. I thought you were the one trying to kill me."

He was astounded. "My God, Teresa, how did you come up with such an idea? How could you *think* that?" His hands gripped my shoulders, holding me away from him; his blue eyes blazed into mine.

"I saw the letter about the life insurance policy. Twenty-five thousand dollars. I knew you needed money to pay off Schyler, to save the hotel."

"And you thought—you thought the hotel meant more to me than you!" He broke off, controlling himself with a visible effort. "I took out two life insurance policies after we were married, Teresa, one on myself and one on you. It seemed a practical step, that if something happened to one or both of us, the hotel could still remain in the family. That money or lack of it would not be a concern if something happened to both of us. Ironically, in the light of future events, I was thinking of Emeline, and my mother's wish that the Crystal Hills never be sold outside the family." He shook his head, his jaw set hard.

"All that she did, she did for the hotel, so that it would someday be hers, and be a success," I told him.

"I still can't believe you actually thought I'd want to . . . I love you, Tessa. I've always loved you, since the night at the Rockingham Hotel when you came in to see if I was all right after I'd fallen."

"I thought you hated me for that, for being concerned about you."

"I did. But only because I felt like a damn cripple and hated that you should see me that way. You stood there in the doorway in your nightgown looking so lovely, so concerned, that I wanted nothing more than to take you in my arms. But there I was on the floor, feeling humiliated, overwhelmed by sudden desire for you—and hating you for it."

391

"I wasn't certain if I ought to go with you to Nightshade Notch after that. I knew that somehow I had made you angry."

"And you had no idea why," he said, touching my tender lip with the tip of his finger. He frowned. "I knew you'd eventually find out about me—about Alice Schyler and everything. I hated for you to know what kind of man I'd been. I'd lived through enough remorse for the past year that I hated the idea of it beginning all over again once I saw in your eyes that you knew the truth. I was falling more and more in love with you and dreaded your reaction to my past. I told myself over and over again that you had no effect on me, but then my instincts would get the better of my judgment and I couldn't resist taking you in my arms. I hated that you pitied me, that my bad leg was the way it was."

"I never pitied you, Drake. I was fascinated by you—and concerned because I loved you too, almost from the first."

He ran his lips along my cheek to my earlobe. "I'd finally realized that I couldn't deny my need for you any longer, that having you for my own had become a necessity. But things at the hotel were so uncertain, and I didn't know if I'd have anything left after this season to offer you."

"You had yourself, Drake," I said.

"Well, I wanted there to be more. I knew you'd had very little all your life and I wanted to be able to give you all I could. And then when Willoughby was killed and the police suspected me, I couldn't ask you to marry me. But on the night of the ball, after the investigation was over, I'd planned to propose. The hotel was practically full; there was a promising fall season lined up. I knew I couldn't wait any longer. But then I learned that Grant Schyler held the mortgage. I thought everything was over then. But you told me to fight, to hold on. And I was so consumed with love for you that I couldn't stop myself from taking you. I did a terrible thing that night. The next morning I was appalled at what I had done. And I was more determined than ever to marry you, no matter what the future held."

"I was afraid you were marrying me out of guilt, out of obligation," I said. "Or to somehow atone for the other women—and Alice Schyler—and the night we had spent together. I even wondered if part of you did it to spite

Leonora—she was so determined to send me away."

"I married you because I was certain that I could not live without you," he said. "And yet you thought I wanted to see you dead. You obviously suspected that I had killed Willoughby, and later Leonora. Because she had told you that I used to be a morphine addict."

"You became so distant, so cool, Drake. I was unable to reach you. I knew you were worried sick about the Crystal Hills."

"I know," he said heavily. "It's my fault you didn't trust me. I hated to keep confiding my fears to you, leaning on you. I felt it was my fight. After all, I had become involved with Alice Schyler, and then the whole hellish thing had begun. But after you were so ill, I realized that the hotel meant a lot less to me, that I didn't care whether Schyler got it. I just wanted you to be all right."

"Emeline said that Horatio Aldridge had made you an offer for some of the land. Was she right—or was she just . . . ?"

"She was right. We no longer have to worry about the mortgage payments. Mrs. Aldridge wants to spend her summers here. I wouldn't sell to a hotel developer, but I will sell to Aldridge. He feels the same way about the Notch as I do. And with the money from the sale I can pay off Schyler. I'm going to give Aaron some money as well—to pay his gambling debt, and because he's leaving and never coming back. He won't be staying here, not after everything he's done."

"Will he go?"

"It was his idea, not that I wouldn't have put it to him very soon. After Horatio proposed the deal to me yesterday, I discussed it with Aaron. Before the police came to arrest me, that is. He's going to Rockport to live."

"What about Emeline's death—will it all come out?"

He shook his head. "The police have assured me that they are going to keep it very quiet because a minor was involved. The last reporter left yesterday after I was arrested. There'll doubtless be some sort of follow-up story, but I think we can weather it—now that I don't have to worry about finances."

"Oh, Drake, I'm so glad!"

He nodded. "Perhaps now we can get the Crystal Hills off to

a fresh start. But I cannot do it without you. Will you help me?"

I held his hands tightly. "You know I will. It's what I've wanted for months now, and what I was afraid was lost to me, a life with you, here at Nightshade Notch."

He took me in his arms, pressing his rough cheek to mine. "After we close for the season, I'm taking you on a long honeymoon trip. We could go to Europe, if you like." And then, before I could answer him, his lips came down on mine.

We rode back to the house a little while later to be met by a relieved, but still overwrought, Charlotte. After the detectives had taken our statements, the three of us sat in the sitting room by a crackling fire. I was close to Drake, wrapped in a blanket, sipping brandy because of the chills of delayed shock which ran through me, but content and happy just the same.

Charlotte had always suspected that Emeline might not be Aaron Curtis's child, she told us, though she had never confided this to Madeline Curtis, who considered Emeline her own grandchild. Two summers after Leonora and Aaron were married, a handsome widower had come to stay at the hotel. He had recently lost his wife in a transatlantic crossing; it was suspected that she had either jumped or fallen into the cold, rough waters. Charlotte had glimpsed him and Leonora together once, and was in no doubt about the intimacy of their relationship. By the fall the man had left the Crystal Hills, and soon after Leonora had announced that she was with child. Charlotte had said nothing to Leonora at that point. But later a report of the capture of a man who had committed multiple murders had run in the Boston newspaper, and Charlotte had recognized the man in the photographs as the widower who had stayed at the hotel months before. A cabin boy on an ocean liner had finally come forward and told what he had seen—that the man had pushed his wife overboard one night sometime before. Charlotte had shown Leonora the article, but she had laughed it off, saying she guessed she had gotten off safely.

But Charlotte had always wondered. Was Leonora's child Aaron's or the seed of that homicidal maniac? "When Emeline was born, and was such a good, sweet baby, I tried to put the matter out of my mind," Charlotte told us. "Although it was something I felt I could hold over Leonora. If I had told Madeline what I suspected, she would have sent them all packing—Aaron too. I watched Emeline grow; I saw the way she adored Madeline, how quiet and well-behaved she was in those early years, and I was relieved. If she were indeed that horrible man's child, she had not been tainted with his mania. But homicidal maniacs are often very charming people, you know, people you would never suspect in a thousand years. When Madeline died, I knew Emeline was deeply affected, but I thought it natural that she should be heartbroken. Her parents paid little attention to her—Madeline had been her world."

"It was Madeline who filled her head with the idea of running the Crystal Hills, of following in her footsteps," I said. "To another child perhaps it would have had little effect, nothing out of the ordinary, but with Emeline it became a dangerous obsession. And anyone who seemed to threaten that dream was disposed of."

"I don't excuse Madeline's part in this. The hotel was her whole life as well, and that was not healthy. But her marriage wasn't the happiest, despite what I always told Emeline. Madeline could not share the hotel with Theodore," said Charlotte.

"I still find it difficult to accept," said Drake. "She was little more than a child."

"And she was even younger than that when she killed Alice Schyler," I said. I had told them that part of it too.

"She would play with her grandmother's things, dress up in her clothes, pore over the old photograph albums, but by then I had stopped worrying," admitted Charlotte. "She seemed so normal, so—balanced. Then, when Leonora was killed, I began to wonder, to dread. You told me, Teresa, that Leonora might have been planning to go off with Grant Schyler. It struck me then that Emeline, and not Aaron, would have considered that idea intolerable. When I learned that you believed you had been poisoned, I was terrified—because I knew that I couldn't discount my fears any longer. What I'd dreaded all of Emeline's life—what I'd kept to myself out of loyalty to the family and out of a desire to keep the peace, that she had the potential to be a deranged killer, I knew I could no longer refuse to admit."

She had awakened that morning, calm, certain of what she must do. She had gotten out of bed and gone to Emeline's room. The girl was not there, and so she decided to search her room. She had to send for the police as quickly as she could and she needed some sort of evidence which would compromise Emeline and make them release Drake. She had not known what she was looking for. But she had found Ernest Willoughby's handkerchief, and his pottery shards. And then she knew that not only had Emeline killed Leonora and tried to poison me as well, but that she had killed the archaeologist.

At that time I did not tell them about Emeline's unholy impressions of the Site of Stones, nor of my own bizarre experiences which had twice sent me fleeing from the clearing and through the woods to the hotel. Drake knew about the first time because he had come upon Ernest Willoughby and me discussing it, and later I told him about the second occasion after I had been hiding from him beneath the Sacrificial Stone. Together we decided not to send the shards Mr. Willoughby had uncovered to other archaeologists. Whatever the Site of Stones was, or had been, it had witnessed two recent tragedies, two lives lost. We were determined to see that it was not disturbed again.

To this day I have no idea whose voices I heard on those two occasions, nor whose voices Emeline had also claimed to hear. Whether remnants of a long-lost civilization lingered to infest the atmosphere, or unearthly forces were summoned down from the sky by the precise placement of the Stones themselves, we will never know.

In the tea leaves Bridget had seen me crouching in terror in a cave, and then poised above rushing water. I had misinterpreted the first foretelling and ignored the second.

I never heard the voices again. Perhaps Emeline herself had awakened them; perhaps they had come in response to the demoniacal impulses within her. Perhaps it was she, and not I, who was the real sensitive—perhaps I'd been sensitive only because of my relationship with her. For when Drake and I walked up the hill and stood gazing across the site, I felt no unease and no fear. The place was nothing more than an arrangement of stones on a blustery autumn afternoon. And I have never sensed, even remotely, a strange stirring since.

Yet there are nights when the wind howls about the house and the trees are bent low and I wonder if whatever forces were there have truly departed, or are only waiting for another to rouse them from their slumber. The mountains may know for certain, for they have gazed across Nightshade Notch for countless centuries. But they remain silent in their knowledge, their massive bulks somberly brooding. And on those nights I snuggle against Drake's chest, and try to forget.

The Stones continue to sit peacefully on the hilltop in the woods, and we too are at peace with ourselves. For we have known great bliss together, and great contentment, as well as the fear and doubts and sorrow which came before. And we are grateful for the richness of our life together, the life we have lived for the past thirty years, the life that began on the day that Drake brought me to Nightshade Notch.

THE BEST OF REGENCY ROMANCES